REVENGE
OF AN AMERICAN WIZARD

Joe Hawk, the old Seneca warrior, knew.

Crouched beside the corpse of the unknown Indian, he lifted the blanket, sliced apart the frozen vest with his hunting knife and exposed the painted chest and stomach. His eyes widened in horror as he read the pictographs.

"I have enemies—They have killed my sons—I hate them—I will kill them—" Symbols in black, yellow, and red revealed the names of ancient Iroquois and Algonquian gods of revenge and war.

As Joe stared at the ancient face, his heart began to recall with dread what his old eyes had forgotten. This was Malsum! With a cry of anguish Joe turned his face to the sky and shook his fists.

Malsum had returned . . . lusting for vengeance.

MalsuM

GERALD JOHN O'HARA

AVON
PUBLISHERS OF BARD, CAMELOT AND DISCUS BOOKS

MALSUM is an original publication of Avon Books.
This work has never before appeared in book form.

AVON BOOKS
A division of
The Hearst Corporation
959 Eighth Avenue
New York, New York 10019

Copyright © 1981 by Gerald John O'Hara
Published by arrangement with the author
Library of Congress Catalog Card Number: 80-68421
ISBN: 0-380-77289-2

First Avon Printing, February, 1981

AVON TRADEMARK REG. U.S. PAT. OFF. AND IN
OTHER COUNTRIES, MARCA REGISTRADA, HECHO EN
U.S.A.

Printed in the U.S.A.

To my wife, Carole, who was patient enough and loving enough to see me through this first novel.

The author wishes to mention that this story is fictional, and that any similarity to persons living or dead is entirely coincidental. He would further like to express that he holds nothing but the highest esteem and admiration for all American Indian cultures and peoples, and the fact that the villain chosen in this case is a Delaware Indian in no way reflects unfavorably on that noble nation.

THE OAK TREES

A legend among the first Americans of many centuries ago tells of a boy who looked upon the plight of his fathers with sorrow and set off on an odyssey to the "place of shadows" to challenge the plaguing demons of misfortune.

Once there, he chose to do battle with the most cunning demon of all, the great demon who was known as "Malsum."

Because the boy knew no fear and his heart was pure, he won out over the demon and defeated him, where great warrior chieftains had failed before.

Yet his was not a tale of conquest, but of misery and grief.

For, when the boy demanded long life and great strength for his fathers and himself as reward, the demon changed them all into oak trees.

PART I

Fear

Chapter I

Shaman tested the wind, his muzzle wet against the driving snow. The stench of gun oil and man's sweat filled the buck's nostrils. He recognized the scent of the hunter as belonging to a skilled adversary who had already put three bullets into his hide in as many years. Irritably pawing the deep snow, and rumbling low in his swollen throat, he put the wind at his back and headed into the five-mile stretch of pine and spruce that bordered the greater Seneca Woods.

Shaman knew that the man who hunted him was an expert tracker, so he devised a ruse to conceal his trail. Ten feet away from a thicket of chokecherry brush, the deer tensed his muscles and sprang sideways into it. The brush crumpled beneath his four hundred-plus pounds but, being green and pliable, with the food reserves of autumn still stored inside, it recovered easily. The deer crawled on his belly through the dense bramble, and came out a considerable distance away from his last set of tracks in the snow.

From the other side of the wall of brush he leapt onto a fallen tree, hoofs breaking off pieces of the decaying bark, traversed its rough stem fifty feet, and stepped down into the snow. He then clambered back onto the trunk, ran again to the front end and made a magnificent leap of thirty feet. Bellied out in the snow, he arose and bounded away regally, like the king he was.

Zeb Simpson surveyed the mysterious end of Shaman's trail. He knelt down and noticed that the hind leg spur impressions in the powdery snow were wider. For a moment he was puzzled; then his experienced green eyes discovered a broken tip in the nearby thicket. He laughed wryly and shook his head. Shaman sure was a smart old bastard. Zeb had tried to keep downwind of the animal, but the changing November winds were as unpredictable as the old one-eared buck himself. (Zeb had shot the other ear clean off two years earlier.) He studied the brambles for a while longer, wondering if he should circle and pick up the trail, but he knew better. Shaman would lead him a merry chase, and in the end Zeb would have little more than a cold ass and two frozen feet for his trouble.

"Hell," he said aloud, taking a pint bottle of vodka from his hip pocket and unscrewing the cap. "Nobody gets that frigger when he knows he's being tailed."

He warmed the chill in his aching stomach with a drink and headed off for the Seneca Woods, where the deer were plentiful (even if they didn't have $500 bounties on them), and the game wardens of old Joe Hawk managed to look the other way whenever he trespassed the barbed wire to poach his illegal venison.

"Watch your step, old timer," the bus driver said, as the hydraulic door opened and Malsum hobbled slowly down the rubber-matted steps to the cinder shoulder of the road.

Once down, the ancient man walked off toward the woods, sinking to his knees in the snow and struggling with the beaten brown leather satchel clutched heavily in his tan, liver-spotted hands. He presented a pathetic picture.

"Now where do you suppose he's off to?" the passenger in the front seat asked.

"Beats me," the Greyhound driver replied. "A minute ago he pointed to a tall scraggly oak, and he said he wanted to get off a mile farther on. That's right here."

They watched the old man wade through the snow.

"But there's nothing out here but woods," the passenger protested. "He'll freeze to death, crazy old addle-brained Gypsy."

"Ain't no Gypsy," the grey-capped driver said, as he pulled the lever and the door sighed shut. "Only one breed of men carries a nose that big." He flashed a left blinker, checked in the side-view mirror for traffic, and drove out onto the freshly ploughed highway.

"He's an Indian?"

"Sure. He's probably a Seneca. They own most of the land around these parts . . . Cattaraugus Reservation."

The passenger weighed this information and turned in his seat to catch a last glimpse of the old man trudging painfully toward the woods. He shook his head with sympathy. "Must be over a hundred years old," he said. "A regular living history book."

"Yeah," the driver agreed, "and I don't think he cares much for his white *benefactors*—couldn't get a word of conversation out of him in two hundred miles."

"Can't blame him," the passenger said. "We sure gave his people a rough time. I, for one, say God bless him."

The brush and trees had closed in around the Delaware shaman's cabin. What had once been cleared land, fifty-five years before, was now almost totally reclaimed by nature. Malsum stood, resting quietly, his ragged breath steaming before his face as it froze and crystallized in the winter air. His grey cloudy eyes feasted on the sight of the weather-worn shelter. The windows had long since shed their glass panes, and were now nothing more than gaping apertures for the snow and wind to howl through. The roof was still intact, but sagged stressfully. The stone chimney was chipped and eroded by time, the elements, and target practicing hunters. The somber grey log walls were defaced with carved initials, names, hearts with arrows through them and strange sayings of the white men, such as "Kilroy was here." It appalled the Indian. The whites had robbed the venerable structure of its dignity—as they had robbed him during his long years of imprisonment. Hunters, campers, and teen-aged boys with their girl-friends had trespassed here. His old home had survived, though, as Malsum himself had, and it linked the Indian to his past, giving him strength of purpose. The Seneca lap dogs of the whites had not destroyed it, and that had been a major worry on the tedious journey home.

The door creaked and rusted hinges protested as the Indian opened it wide enough to take himself and his belongings inside. Someone had left a good supply of firewood stacked haphazardly by the hearth. A crude wooden table with a tree stump base still stood against the back wall. Malsum went to this, touching it, reflecting back over the years and remembering it as a table his sons had made while in their boyhood. His old eyes filled with hatred. They had died at the hands of the whites.

Wenegawa: They had slaughtered him—slit his throat.
Tegagiche: They had butchered him—disemboweled

5

him—and now they would pay! Even though fifty-five years had gone by, and they were all rotting in their graves, they would still pay. They had killed his sons.

Knowing that night was fast approaching, the Indian went into the woods and hacked off small pine branches with a knife he had purchased in a pawnshop in Schenectady while waiting to board the bus home. He stuffed the branches into the window openings, as a makeshift barrier against the frigid wind, and swept the floor and fireplace of the cabin free of snow with a broom of short-needled spruce branches. He started a fire for warmth, and the cabin retained heat. By nightfall he was comfortable, seated on a blanket before the flames, opening a can of yellow peaches with his knife. He drank the nectar greedily, mashed the fruit to a pulp between his gums, and swallowed it for nourishment. Better, he thought, to eat soft foods than to use the cursed set of false teeth supplied by the white prison doctor. The Danemorra prison board had released him when he was diagnosed as being tubercular, with only a short while to live. The forbidding questions "Where will you go?" and "Who will take care of you?" were soon forgotten when he bribed a parole officer with $500 to champion his quest for freedom. The money had been hidden in his cell, won at gambling and saved from his minuscule prison wages. One thing Malsum did not want was to die in the white man's prison unavenged. Now he was finally free. They had let him go to die, to save the expense of his burial. And he would die—but only when he chose to. He had outlived them all. He had been fifty-five when he went to prison in 1897, and now he was one hundred ten.

The fire blazed inside and the wind howled outside, trying to get at the centenarian, to dislodge the woven pine branches from the windows and fill the cabin with its icy breath. The old man ignored the sounds of the angry elements and undressed. He stood naked by the fire and began to chant in a singsong fashion, once more becoming the wizard Malsum as he felt a surge of power enter his old bones. Many curses, intrigues, feats of magic, prayers, and demonic spells had been cast and offered to the spirits in the Place Of Shadows from this dark abode in the forest. The spirits returned as Malsum called and commanded them, invisibly seeping in through the walls, under the

6

door, down the chimney—he sensed their glorious presence all about him.

"I am Malsum—it is I. I will destroy all things . . ." He chanted, danced, made shuffling gestures as he tossed his white man's clothing into the fire. The woolen suit burned, he cried: *"Hoo-oo-oo! Tawiskaron!"* The plastic buttons melted, dropping sizzling gobs of brown tar into the hungry orange flames, turning them yellow. He cried: *"Yowige, yowige, yowige-Tawisk-aron,"* calling on the Evil Twin; the sea-father of the twins; the Four Brothers who control the winds; the Whirlwind Spirit, and He Whose Body Is Riven In Twain.

His penis burned from a full bladder. He slid the foreskin back and urinated on his stomach, on his feet, in the fire. He cried: *"Hoo-oo-oo! Shagodyoweh! Hai ge hai-Shagodyoweh,"* calling on the Great World Rim Dweller, the servant of Tawiskaron whom the Iroquois knew as the giant, Bent Nose.

The wind howled louder as if in answer, the walls shook and the door rattled, strange shadows danced ominously on the sagging ceiling.

"Hoo-oo-oo!" Malsum wailed, calling the spirits and demons.

"Hoo-oo-oo!" the forest winds answered the wizard.

Suddenly the banshee voices of the Four Brothers were all around him! Their icy breaths dislodged the branches in the windows, hurling them into the cabin. Frigid wind buffeted the witch's frame and made him shiver in his urine-soaked skin. He trembled, picked up the branches, dreading to approach the north opening. *Had he offended? Were they now waiting for him just beyond the dark holes, where they could grab him with beak and talon, tooth and claw?*

It attacked his face as he reached a window, and he dropped the green branches and screamed, *"Yai-i-ie-ee,"* thinking the Good Spirit had sent a messenger of punishment and death to carry him high and drop him on the rocks below. "My face! My face!" he cried.

He grabbed at the demon and it clung to his hand moistly. His panic died as he saw that it was merely a piece of paper. With a shudder he replaced the branches, wedging them tight against a powdery flurry of snow that bombarded his chest and shoulders. His old heart accelerated and set his temples throbbing; the stiffened pain

7

of warm oxygen turned frigid caused his lungs to ache; he coughed violently, spitting up blood-flecked gobs of mucus. Moaning *"Hai . . . hai . . . hai . . ."* he went barefoot to stand before the fire and shake, with his arms wrapped over his flaccid flesh. As the warmth of the flames, blazing with the added fuel of shoes and garments, forced the chill from him, he noticed the paper that had flown into his face through the window. It stuck wetly to a bulbous-veined foot, impaled on long, thick, curled toenails.

It was a poster with the image of a one-eared stag. The wet thing read: WANTED! Renegade deer of the Cattaraugus Creek Woodlands. $500.00 Reward."

The Lenni Lenape wizard could not read, even if his eyesight had not been clouded with cataracts. He could not read "This animal has gored hunters on occasion, and is dangerous when cornered. It has been known to lead bands of deer into crops, causing massive destruction—" and other paragraphs in small print, but Malsum could read "$500.00"—it was the amount paid for his freedom from the hated whites.

He stared at the illustrated face of the deer, who sported a huge ear, the likes of which he had never seen before. It was a mule deer, and a rarity among a forest full of whitetail deer. Malsum had passed many such posters stapled to trees in the woods on his way to the cabin earlier, but he had paid them no attention. Now he did.

"Hoo-oo-oo! Tawiskaron has sent a sign—the whites offer five hundred dollars—the price I paid for freedom!

"Hai ge hai! It might happen, it might happen. From the mighty *Shagodyoweh!* A wolf? A dog? A bear? An eagle? But a wrathful stag of the woods! *Yowige, yowige, yowige!* A long voice, a long voice . . ."

With a look of satisfaction on his ancient, cunning face, Malsum took jars of black, blue, and vermilion paint from his satchel. He painted his emaciated body with elaborate magical signs and symbols. This was to be his funeral adornment, and it would never be removed while he remained alive. He then dressed in fringed deer-hide leggings and a furred vest of wolfskin, thick wool socks, and knee-length moccasins; all purchased from a roadside store near Albany and handmade by Algonquin women, the merchant had said. Even a blanket, his favorite form of dress for winter, he had purchased, and now draped over his shoulders.

Newly appareled, the Lenape prayed all night with a loud wailing song. As the steel grey of dawn approached, he surrounded himself with a throng of burning branches, in front of the hearth, and picked up the dried poster of the wanted deer, *Shaman*.

The spirits Malsum, Tawiskaron, Shagodyoweh, Gaoh, and many others were beseeched and commanded to make their presence felt. In answer, the wind lessened and ceased to howl. The atmosphere in the cabin thickened with heat. The flames in the fireplace lengthened and lashed out— orange, red, yellow, blue, tongues of fiery fury threatened to devour the sorcerer as he sat cross-legged before the hearth.

Yes, the stag was certainly to be used! The Evil Ones had brought it to the woods from the west to serve him. It had waited, was waiting, for him to use. A king of deer! A shaman stag! Malsum grew convinced that the animal was to be his means of facing his enemies in the time ahead.

"Hoo-oo-oo!"

The sorcerer plunged his hand and arm into the fire. The flames licked at his flesh and curled around his arm, but there was no smell of burning skin. He laughed confidently and tossed the poster into the fire, watching it turn to ash.

"We shall see now . . ." he said bitterly, his hatred ignited.

White Throat stood amid the pines. The submissive doe at his side was in heat. The forest was thick with the musky smell of their mating, and White Throat knew that the tyrannical mule deer who watched him from a distance, hungrily sniffing the doe's scent in the wind, was intent on fighting for her. The buck knew that even though he was large and strong himself, in his prime, endowed with a bowl-shaped rack of sharp spiny tines and razored hoofs that could slash a marauding bear's face to ribbons, he would be hard put to defeat this rogue king of the woods. Still, it was not in his nature to run from a fight, so it was that when Shaman brayed out his hoarse challenge to the winds White Throat answered him bravely.

For tense minutes each animal stood his ground, kicking

at the snow, building his temper to a fever pitch. They slashed bark from pines, sharpening their antlers. They set up a nerve-shattering din that drove small forest creatures high into the trees, or deep into the safety of burrows. Shaman was the first to charge. The defending buck lowered his immense rack and ran forward to meet the attack. With a resounding impact that rent the air like an explosion, the two great stags collided. Tremendous beasts, they rammed, kicked, and fought with terrible strength.

After several rushes, they grew wary and began circling. Experience warned that, should they lock their antlers, they would remain entrapped to die a hopeless death from starvation. The spring-thawed forests of New York had often revealed the bleached bones of such unfortunate combatants. Twisting their racks low to the ground, each made the effort to snag the soft stomach skin of his opponent. A contest to the death was not generally the rule, but Shaman was an exception to all rules. Unlike other victors, at battle's end he pursued his foe and destroyed him, leaving himself with less competition during rutting season. Whitetails mate singularly until a hind passes from heat; mule deer gather as many shes as they can find or win, herd them into a harem and stud for all, voraciously.

The young doe stood by, shaking visibly with fear as the bucks fought. Her feelings lay with White Throat, who was suffering, outmatched by Shaman's greater ability. The buck had been a considerate mate, often playing and romping through the woods with her before and after their unions. She did not want Shaman for a mate.

Malsum labored with pain as he climbed the hill, resting at each tree along the way, coughing blood and feeling the sharp needles in his chest and shortness of breath of consumption. He huddled inside his grey blanket, aware that his feet would freeze if he did not keep moving. The white man's clothing and shoes—he should have kept them. They would have been better than the souvenir garments he now wore. The moccasins had been cheap, and had practically disintegrated in the two days spent searching for the shaman deer. He cursed the maker of the apparel with a plague of boils.

As he topped the hill he lifted his brown leathery face toward the noonday sun and shielded his eyes. His snow-white hair gleamed fluorescently on his neck, grown long over his ears. Angrily, the sorcerer shook a rattle made from a dried gourd painted black and red, and plastered on two sides with decals of the great Ottawa chieftain Pontiac.

"Guide me to the stag!" Malsum called, shaking the rattle vigorously at the sky, both hands grasping the long, round, varnished handle. Suddenly the ball-like object broke away at the base, where it had been poorly glued, and sailed off toward the horizon. The Indian looked at the weightless stick in his hands with astonishment. A sign? No! More bad workmanship by the cheating scoundrels who had sold him the worthless garments in Albany. Souvenir shop Indians! Liars! Thieves! Boils were not enough to repay such treachery. The Indian flung the stick away and trudged on, grumbling beneath his breath.

The doe was small and her ears perked straight up as she stood in the pine grove, listening to the distant sounds and noises of two fighting bucks. She was of a mind to seek out the males, as she was just now entering into her first heat. As she turned to run off, a terrible frightful noise burst upon her, and she felt her insides exploding. Her spindly legs collapsed and she floundered in the snow. She tried to rise, unable to comprehend the sudden weak numbness spreading through her. Then a second frightful explosion, which she did not hear, ripped through the side of her narrow, brown-eyed face, and scattered her brains over the surrounding whiteness.

Zeb Simpson walked over to the doe, rifle in hand, and stared soberly down at her. She twitched and jerked, her pink tongue thick and lolling from the side of her mouth. The hunter took his knife and straddled the animal, gloved hand clamped to muzzle, and slit her throat. He knotted one end of a nylon rope around her hind legs, threw the other end over a pine limb, and hoisted her hundred seventy-five pounds off the ground, so she could swing and drain freely. The blood gushed from the gaping incision in her neck. Two crimson rivulets, melting twin holes in the snow, sent up wispy columns of tenuous steam to disperse in the wind.

"Well, young lady," Zeb said listlessly, "I guess you're one cow old Shaman won't screw this winter."

*   *   *

11

White Throat was dead, lying at the bottom of a small cliff, where Shaman had butted him. Malsum stood silently in the woods and watched the giant stag mating with the doe. Unable to support his massive weight, the doe was kneeling in the snow, bleating painfully while the tyrant expended his fury and energy into her. Unwilling to mate with him, she trembled noticeably, after having been pounded into submission. At first she had tried to outrun him, but found this impossible; he was faster and more agile than she. Shaman merely ran at her side and punished her with his antlers until she gave in and let him claim her. The stag assaulted her torturously.

Malsum stepped out of his hiding place among the trees and walked toward the two deer. At his sight the doe burst away into the woods, but Shaman stood his ground, eying the intruder meanly. His eyes were yellow with fear and hatred as he lowered his sweeping antlers and pawed the snow, ready to charge.

Chanting loudly, the Indian walked up to the beast. He could see the ear which had been chewed or shot off, and knew this to be the stag on the poster. He had sought him for two days, and now that he had found him he was not disappointed. Even with his poor eyesight he could see that the deer was a magnificent brute, worthy of his magical spells. The deer grew more and more docile as the Indian chanted and danced around him. Finally he permitted Malsum to extend his hand and touch the wounds on his haunches, newly inflicted by White Throat.

As if entranced, the quivering beast stood by and watched as the old Indian cut open the dead whitetail buck and wrenched out his liver. The sorcerer sawed off several long strips of the steaming red meat and chewed them with great relish.

"It is good," Malsum sighed contentedly, "it is good that I should have such a tasty meal on the day I have chosen to die."

For nearly an hour Zeb had let the doe bleed while he sat down on a log and drank himself into a peaceful bliss. Now he took his knife and slit the carcass open. With his coat and shirtsleeves hiked up around his elbows, he emptied her out in great bloody handfuls. He scraped her rib cage clean, not wanting to stain his clothing with gore when he carried her home on his shoulders. Then he wiped her out with snow until she shone pink and prime, and his hands felt as though they were going to freeze. He was ready to take her down and head off for home when something—a soft noise, a sixth sense, something intangible—made him whirl around.

Shaman stood as bold as life fifty feet away, staring calmly at the hunter. Zeb blinked with disbelief. It was incredible, he thought. The big bastard was committing suicide! Instinct told him there was something wrong as he snatched up his rifle and fired a shot, but he refused to hesitate. He levered another shell, as the deer remained standing, but the magazine was empty. He cursed, expecting to see the cash on the hoof run off any instant, while he reloaded. But Shaman didn't run. His form became wavy and unstable. It blurred, as if Zeb was peering through unfocused binoculars. A mirage? Wonder of wonders, the animal suddenly dropped to the snow. The shot hadn't missed, after all!

With a whoop, Zeb ran for his prize. Old One-Ear had bit the dust. The five hundred dollars bounty was going to come in handy. Pearl could use some new clothes, and Charlie had hinted that he wanted a Red Flyer sled for Christmas, like the one that pisspot Mark Banner owned. He could pay Pete the money he borrowed for . . .

The bubble of elation burst as the veteran hunter was confronted with the real horror of the situation. There in the snow, with blood frothing on his lips, was an old white-haired Indian wrapped in a grey blanket and clutching the severed head of a one-eared buck in his bony hands. He coughed and wheezed, the bullet lodged in his chest.

"Christ!" Zeb exclaimed. "I thought you were a deer." His mounting panic changed to fleeting anger as the white-tail head riveted his attention. "What the hell are you doing, walking around with that thing?"

"Who are you, white man?" the sorcerer gasped.

"Are you one of Joe Hawk's people? I'll try and get you home, or go for help, whichever you want. Jesus, I'm sorry I shot you, old man." Zeb rubbed his forehead and winced.

"My name is Malsum," the Lenni Lenape offered proudly. "Tell me who you are, before I die."

"You're not going to die, old timer," Zeb replied,

13

unbuttoning his heavy plaid coat and placing it under the old Indian's hoary head.

Malsum accepted the gesture with a slight display of gratitude on his leathery face, which soon changed into an expression of irony and cackling laughter as the white man said, "My name's Zeb Simpson."

"Yes, you spring from his loins," the shaman said with fiery eyes, "I see the resemblance . . ."

He spat in Zeb's face, fell back, and died, his eyes wide, his face contorted and consumed with hatred.

"You crazy old bastard!" Zeb yelled, wiping the spittle away. "It's your fault, not mine!"

But his anguished words fell on the ears of a dead man. He liberated his coat as he realized the Indian had died and put it on quickly. He broke a pine branch from a tree and wiped out his tracks as he made his way back to the doe. His green eyes darted nervously about the woods, fearing witnesses. In his worried mind there was an Iroquois behind every tree, waiting to step out and exact revenge. He slung the doe over his shoulders and dragged his feet through every boot print he had made in the vicinity, being as sure as he could be that he was leaving no traces in the snow to identify him. Guilt and fear hung over his head like a dark cloud as he went, taking a circuitous route through the woods and fields instead of his usual direct path home. During the war he had killed a number of men. He and others had left Japanese soldiers lying on the ground by the hundreds after a battle. But the dozens of lives he had taken in combat had never produced as terrible a conscience as the death of this one innocent man did now. The guilt and fear intensified as Zeb's liquor ran out.

After he threw the useless flask away he cursed himself and went back, wasting valuable time, until he found it. It would have been a meager piece of evidence at best, but if there were fingerprints on the glass . . . ? He cursed the doe's hindering weight, and wished he could discard it, but he had left his calling card on her. Men had different ways of gutting. Zeb ripped from the bottom to the breastbone in order to remove the bowels without rupturing them and spoiling the meat. It was the Indian way, but leaving the liver and heart to rot on the ground was not. A combination of both found near the site of Malsum's body would be damnable evidence. Many farmers and

14

townsmen poached venison on Seneca land and left the worthless intestines behind, true, and, alone, the guts he had left in the snow would prove nothing. Still, he hoped the body wouldn't be found immediately, and definitely not by Joe Hawk. The rugged chieftain had no equal when it came to reading sign. Zeb felt unclean, wanting to cleanse himself of his guilt. He toyed with the idea of calling Sam Parker once he arrived home. It had been an accident, surely the law would . . .

Then a vision of prison doors clanging shut rocked him to his senses. They hadn't shown Pete any mercy. They'd lock him up, too, and call it murder. This wasn't deer season. He had been poaching illegally. And while he had committed one crime, he had then compounded it with a greater crime. That is what they would say—just before they sent him to the penitentiary. Zeb couldn't bear the thought of being separated from his wife and son. If they wanted him, they would have to prove his guilt. For damn sure, he wasn't going to confess.

The overwhelming fear of it all struck him so hard his legs buckled, and he sank to the snow on his knees with a loud groan. He had left a 30-06 slug in the man's chest. The police would match it to his rifle. He sat down in the snow and worried over it, the inside of his mouth feeling as though it were packed with cotton. For a long time he searched for a solution short of returning to the scene and prying the bullet free. He reasoned optimistically: the bullet might have passed through, or smashed into bone and become useless for identification. Rifles weren't registered, with expired cartridges on file, as pistols were. As an added safeguard, Zeb decided to purchase another 30-06 Springfield from the army surplus store in Buffalo, and change the barrels. Perhaps a dousing of salt water would make the new barrel seem to match the old hand-tooled stock, worked by his grandfather and namesake Zebediah. Displaying the beautiful rifle upon request, even with a counterfeit barrel, would be less cause for suspicion than saying it was lost or stolen.

The wind picked up, hurling stinging snow in Zeb's face as he crouched on the ground with the doe over his shoulders. He arose on cramped legs and walked on, his mind still filled with fear and apprehension at being discovered. His liver ached and painful indigestion stuck in his chest. Even so, he wished he had a drink.

* * *

Chucky Simpson was dark-haired like his father. A band of freckles that were fading as he grew older speckled his nose and cheeks. For going on ten years old he was runty and lean, but he made up for any physical shortcomings with a quick temper and a perseverance that pulled him through scrapes with bigger and older boys at school. His mother Pearl accused him of being ninety-nine and forty-four hundredths percent pure Simpson, like the soap commercial on TV, whenever he dismayed her—as he did now.

"Charles Simpson!" she scolded, seeing the legs of the yellow marbled vinyl chair gouging holes in the kitchen linoleum, "You stop that right now!"

"I'm not going to fall, Ma," the boy replied from the heavy tubular chrome chair balanced on its rear legs. The rubber caps had broken through and slid up ages ago. Like all the furniture in this two-story farm house, the chair was worn and in need of replacement or repair. Only Pearl's diligent housework made the home presentable.

"It's not your falling I'm talking about, you little snip. Look what you've done to the floor!"

Pearl shoved the chair down flat and cuffed the boy lightly on the back of his head. "Your pa and me's not made of money," the fair-complected woman said, "and that floor has got to last us a good long time yet."

"I didn't know I was doing it. I'm sorry, all right?"

"Why don't you go watch television until your father and uncle get home? You're a pest, Charles. Let me make dinner in peace."

"There's nothing good on TV," retorted the boy, resolutely bored.

"Isn't Howdy Doody and Flubbadub on now?"

"It's not called—It's *Buffalo Bob and Howdy*—"

"I don't care what it's called. Go watch it."

"It's already over. Stupid *Kukla, Fran, and Ollie*'s on. Who wants to watch that dumb show?"

Pearl shook her head, and, with a sigh of resignation, went to the stove. She turned the fried potatoes in the pan, salting and peppering them as she did so. Dinner was ahead of schedule tonight. Pete had called earlier from the bank and apologetically told her that he would be at least a half hour late. Zeb was still out traipsing around in the woods, poaching deer. Heaven only knew where they would get the money to pay the fine if he was caught. Pearl didn't appreciate it when her menfolk failed to show

16

her consideration. It was turning dark and she was secretly worried for her husband. Zeb didn't normally stay out so late. Also, it had begun snowing a short while ago, and that would mean that the highway from Gowanda, twelve miles south, would be slippery. Pete still hadn't put snow tires on his car. He would this weekend, even if she had to take her Christmas money from the bureau drawer and force him! She turned the burners down under the potatoes and corn and checked the pot roast in the oven.

As the auburn-haired woman bent over she felt a trickle of sweat roll through the cleavage between her breasts. She took a dish towel, unbuttoning the top of her dress part way, and daubed at the bothersome perspiration.

"Can't a girl have any privacy?" she squeaked, as she saw the boy's eyes prying interestedly at her bustline. The brassiere she wore had shrunk during repeated washings, and didn't offer much in the way of respectability.

Chucky grinned sheepishly and stuck his nose up to the kitchen window, sneakily watching by the reflection from the overhead light. Pearl turned her back when she discovered his game. Little snip, she thought with a smile; her son was going to be a connoisseur of big-busted women when he grew up, exactly like his father. He was going to be a real heart-stealer some day, with his cute dimples and that slanted sideways grin. Mothers guard your daughters, another Simpson's on the way!

"Hey, Ma," Chucky squealed. "Look, my nose is stuck to the window!"

"Good. I hope it rips off on you. It'll teach you not to put it where it doesn't belong." The mother bubbled with laughter as her son's situation brought a look of fright to his face. "Just hold still a second, and the ice'll melt," she promised.

Chucky stretched his face, as if with a nosebleed, as he gained his release. His forehead and nose were numb from the cold.

"Stupid window!" he complained, testing his face to see that the skin hadn't pulled off after all.

"Stupid boy!" Pearl said, and attacked him with playful fingers. "Chee-chee-chee-chee." She made little squirrel-like chirpings as she tickled his stomach, finally stopping when her son's helpless laughter became unbearable and reached the point of tears and anger.

"You made my stomach hurt!"

"Aww . . . Mama's so sorry . . ."

The boy's shrill laughter filled the kitchen as his mother hugged him tightly from behind and nudged her chin into his collarbone. He dropped to the floor, seeking an escape from the sensitive shudders, but there was none. The woman continued to force his laughter. She prodded tapered fingertips into his ribs and armpits; her beautiful hair, faintly sweet with the odors of soap or shampoo, draped over his face and threatened to smother him.

"*Kukla, Fran and Ollie* is a good program, isn't it?"

"No—n-no! I hate it!"

"It's a good program and you're going to go watch it and let me cook supper!"

"Y-yes! Yes!"

Chucky screwed up his face madly and leered at his mother as he left the room. "Stupid!"

"Monkey says what monkey does," Pearl beamed. "You wash your hands and face and clean your fingernails before you come to the supper table."

A few minutes later daylight began to fade. The kitchen window rattled from the gusty wind as Pearl wiped it clean, feeling the small space of cold air on her face near the pane. Zeb never stayed out so late, and she was worried. Seeking, her eyes found him.

Zeb was off in the cow pasture, trudging home through the deep snow. He seemed to be barely placing one foot in front of the other, hunched against the stinging wind, with a deer's carcass draped over his shoulders. It looked like Old Man Winter was getting the best of him. At times the freezing wind obscured him from view entirely with a violent flurry of snow.

"Chucky," Pearl said in a pained, hurried voice, "your father's stuck out in the meadow with a deer on his back; slip into your coat and boots and go help him."

The boy turned away from his program in the living room and looked at his mother rudely, as she stood in the kitchen doorway separating the two rooms.

"Why should I?" he said disdainfully. "He killed it, let him bring it in."

"You little snot," Pearl said, "I'll find the time to see to you later, just you wait!" She eyed him angrily as she took her coat from a wall peg and quickly went outdoors.

Zeb saw his wife coming from the house to meet him. The wind was at her back, pushing her along, making her flimsy housedress fly up around her thighs. Her coat was too short to cover her, and after fighting a losing battle she forgot her modesty and let the garment blow. There was only her husband present anyway. She wore neither hat nor scarf, and her shoulder-length curls blew over the back of her head and into her face. They blinded her and made her stop and wedge them down inside her coat collar.

Zeb should have been angry with her for pulling such a foolish stunt, running out of the house dressed like that, but seeing her brought an elation to him. It made him forget the bitter cold and his exhaustion as his windstung eyes blinked and filled with the sight of her.

> "Of treasures rare and bountiful,
> brimmed coin and ingot gleaming,
> Sol's shiny rainbows in your hair,
> by far surpass with streaming.
>
> Of precious jewels and lust'rous gems,
> steeped high in princely fashion,
> your sighing smiles of em'rald eyes,
> by far surpass with passion.
>
> Of men who seek for riches fine,
> to ransom off the world,
> I hunger not for what they'll buy,
> for I've purchased one sweet Pearl."

Zeb had written the sentimental poem during the first year of their marriage, while he was overseas. At the time Pearl had recently presented him with an infant son, and Zeb composed the verse from his hospital bed in Australia where he was recovering from wounds in his groin from mortar shrapnel. He sent it with a letter telling his wife how much he loved and missed her. He had never forgotten the foolish thing (not that Pearl would ever let him), and recalling it now brought back all the miserable loneliness of that time, making him ache for her. Away from home for merely hours, the horror of killing another human being again made it seem like years.

"Are you okay, honey?" Pearl asked as she reached him.

Zeb shoved the doe from his shoulders and let it fall to the field. He sat on the carcass in the snow and pulled his wife down onto his lap, embracing her tightly. He surprised the woman with his sudden rush of feelings.

"Zeb, what's wrong with you?" Pearl leaned away and looked into his sad eyes. "You look like you're sick."

"I'm just tired . . . let me rest a spell," Zeb said forlornly.

"Have you been drinking?" Green eyes scolded green eyes.

"Hell, you know me, Red . . ." It was the same teary-eyed smile that Pearl had picked from a crowd and fallen in love with almost eleven years before.

The war was four months old when they first met. Pearl was nineteen at the time, and Zeb was twenty-three.

Pearl watched him as he stood in line, waiting to purchase a ticket. He was a handsome man, wearing a Marine Corps uniform. Her brother Charles had died at Pearl Harbor on the morning of December 7, 1941, when the Japanese attacked, having been two months out of boot camp and just seventeen years old. Socializing with the opposite gender, especially men in uniform, who ran the risk of getting killed in the war, hadn't interested her. At least, that was what she told herself until Zeb Simpson appeared that day at the Elmira, New York, theater where she worked. All men in uniform were handsome to an extent, but it was the Marine's eyes that got to her. They made him stand out among all the other sailors and soldiers around him. They were green eyes, just like hers. And they were glassy and heartbroken, just like hers. It was like looking into a mirror and seeing herself. When Zeb gazed at her, the green eyes said, "Hi; I'm an ophan too."

Pearl didn't know it at the time, but Zeb had taken leave, before shipping out, to visit his eighteen-year-old brother at the penitentiary on the outskirts of the city. Their reunion had lasted but two hours; just long enough to bring out Zeb's hidden emotions. When the guard came to take Pete from the visiting room, Zeb had tried to bribe him. He pleaded for a few more minutes, explaining that he was stationed in Florida and might not get another chance to see Pete for a long while. The guard denied the request. Zeb had hit him, and ended up being thrown out, his name stricken from the visitors' roster. He was in low spirits when he showed up at the theater where Pearl worked, friendless and alone.

"Hello, sad eyes," Pearl said in her mind, as her future

husband stepped up to the booth. She could see he was troubled and heartbroken.

Zeb looked at her softly for a moment, taking in her hair and face, her full bust beneath a brown V-neck sweater. She was as pretty as the lobby posters of Vivien Leigh kissing Clark Gable.

"Do you want a ticket?" Pearl asked as he stared trance-like.

"No . . . I don't like love stories."

"Then why are you in line?" Pearl wanted to laugh. He had such a colorlessly blunt way of speaking.

"Because I saw you from the sidewalk. What time do you get off?"

"I'm sorry, but you're holding up paying customers."

He was no different than all the rest, Pearl thought, merely out to have a good time before shipping out.

A sailor behind Zeb tapped him politely on the shoulder, and Zeb moved off to the side of the booth to stare at Pearl's profile through the glass. At times, while the red-haired girl attended to the shortening line of moviegoers, she would glance at the Marine, and little sparks would ignite in her mind. He was waiting for the line to end, evidently so he could make another pass at her. Strangely enough, she found herself looking forward to the moment.

The Marine surprised her, though, and began to walk off as they were left alone.

"You know," Pearl called out to him, "you might like the picture. It's not just a love story; it's also very exciting."

Zeb turned and approached her, making love to her with his sad eyes. "So are you," he said in that flat, serious tone of voice.

"What? Exciting?" Pearl smiled, displaying a dimple in each rosy cheek. "Thanks, I guess," she laughed.

Zeb took a dollar from his wallet and placed it on the marble shelf before her hands. "One, please," he said, his voice rich now.

"You've decided to go in, after all?"

Zeb's eyes sparkled as she took the bill. The left corner of his mouth tugged boyishly upward into a mischievous grin. He took the ticket and his change and said, "There isn't anything in there that can beat you. Do you mind if I just stand out here and look at you all night? I did buy a ticket."

"I won't be here all night," Pearl said. "My shift ends in another hour."

Three days later they were married.

"Want me to help you carry her in?" Pearl asked, feeling the wind cutting through her coat. Her legs were bare and freezing to purple.

"I can manage."

Zeb hoisted the frozen carcass to his shoulders with a groan and stood up. His eyes were still glassy and haunted.

"Get behind me," he ordered, as he saw her shivering against the wind, tucking her chin down. He had to raise his voice to be heard above the tempest. "You must have a screw loose somewhere—coming out here dressed the way you are!"

"Hell, you know me, Zeb!" Pearl mocked his favorite expression in a deep voice. "Hurry up, slowpoke!" She pounded on his back playfully as he laughed and felt better. "I've got a roast in the oven."

"Shit . . . I'm a little tired, do you mind?"

Chapter II

Shaman left his warm bedding with the does in the Seneca Woods and walked off through the night forest. A haunting command urged him toward an unknown place. He sniffed at the cold wind and tested his way warily as he went. At first he was confused, and then the faint scent of the wizard who had bewitched him earlier that day came to his moist nostrils. He bolted forward, excited, the thick hairs on his neck bristling.

Malsum's frozen corpse lay half-buried in the blowing snow, sightless cloudy eyes opened wide. Shaman approached the sorcerer hesitantly. The gale wailed *Hoo-oo-oo!* through the shapeless trees and caused the deer to grumble and paw, shaking his antlers violently. A mystery as old as the world revealed itself to the beast and subdued him until he gentled and became docile. He went back to the Delaware's stiffening cadaver and settled down beside it, his wide barbed antlers hovering over the Indian's still form. All that night he stayed on, a guard, a sentinel for a murdered witch.

The Indian boy awoke with dawn's light, bundled warm beneath a covering of white sheets and patchwork quilts, his shaggy head of black hair nestled into a goose feather pillow. This morning he did not arise with the burst of quick energy that normally sent him hurrying from his bed to greet a new day. But with a troubled look on his ten-year-old face, he remained beneath the blankets and stared at the painted ceiling over his head and tried to remember the dream before it slipped away completely. A Seneca woman—no—a Seneca angel had visited him while he slept and stroked his face, kissed his cheek. Tommy tried to recall her words, her features, but the contents of the dream proved too elusive. All he could recall was a bright gold radiance that filled the cabin bedroom and that the woman had been Seneca and very beautiful in white doe-skin. His mother? He didn't know. He thought of asking Joe to interpret the mystifying experience, but then decided against it. Any mention of Tommy's mother or father always left the old chieftain sad.

The Seneca boy looked at his grandfather asleep in his bed. Joe Hawk snored loudly when tired, but the rasping noise had ceased a short while before, telling the boy that his guardian had slept long enough to dispel his weariness.

Tommy stoked the fireplace in the main room with fresh wood and turned the propane up on the brown roof-vented furnace in his and Joe's bedroom. Although Joe hardly ever complained, he suffered from a touch of arthritis in his joints, and morning coldness made him ache.

The Indian boy was excited this morning. While Tommy was listening to the large wood cabinet radio by the fire-place, the announcer had said that there would be no school for the Cattaraugus area residents due to heavy snowfall throughout the night; that meant that his grand-father would take him hunting for Shaman! If they got him, Joe had promised he would purchase one of the new giant seventeen-inch screen television sets that had just come on the market with the reward money. Since their twelve-inch model had broken, and was too old and expensive to repair, the only programs Tommy had gotten to watch were at his Uncle James' house, or at Chucky Simpson's, whose Uncle Pete had just bought them one of the giant screen models two weeks before—lucky Chucky!

Anxious to get started, Tommy shook his grandfather roughly. The man's lips crept into a slight smile, but he pretended to be fast asleep.

"Get up, old man!" the boy hollered. "Get up, or I'll give your breakfast to the village dogs!" Tommy mimicked the words of Hiawatha to Atotaharo, a favorite story with him.

In answer, Joe Hawk began snoring loudly.

The young Seneca crossed to his bed and picked up his heavy linen-cased pillow. With a blood-curdling whoop the small savage attacked the slumbering man mercilessly, and slammed the cushiony weapon into his face. "Ha! I got you, Joe! Come on, lazy Grandpa, get up!"

Joe Hawk reached out suddenly with a bear paw of a hand and caught the spry youngster as he meant to deliver still another blow. He held his grandson tight and pinned him to the bed.

"Who has who now?" Joe laughed. Tommy struggled to break the hold, flailing out and punching the man's thick frame with small fists. "Who has who, Thomas?"

The boy's laughter mingled with the man's deeper voice. "I give up, Joe. I surrender to you."

"So I am an old man, am I? You cannot break my hold?"

"No, you're too strong for me."

"One day you will break my hold. My father was strong. Your father was strong. You will be strong, too."

Joe threw his covers off, sat up, and rubbed the arthritic pain from his thick neck. Tommy quickly handed him his trousers and shirt.

"I have breakfast warming on the stove. Let's hurry and eat so we can get out after Shaman. There's no school for me today."

As they nourished themselves on a thick stew of meat, potatoes, corn, and flour, a troubled expression gradually came over the grey-haired man's rugged features. He sat motionless at the table as if trying to hear something outside that disturbed him.

"What is it?" the olive-eyed youngster asked.

Joe waved him off, motioning for silence. After a moment he shook his head and admitted defeat.

"I don't know," he said finally. "I sense wrongness . . . Do not the woods seem too quiet to you?"

Tommy listened attentively, as Joe had taught him. He shrugged. "The *pukwudjinnies* whisper nothing to my ears," he said apologetically.

The dream—what was the dream about? Did I have a dream?

"Perhaps there are white hunters poaching deer on our land?"

The ten-year-old's black eyes sparkled, his face glowed, as he rushed through his breakfast, anxious to be done and on the way.

"If we catch them, you gonna beat them up?"

"Maybe they'll beat me up," the grandfather quipped.

"Are you kidding? Nobody can beat up a Seneca chief—and especially not a *Hawk!*"

Joe Hawk laughed, the creases on his wise old face deepening.

"At least they haven't yet," he nodded, "but the world is big, and there are many who could beat an aged man with sore bones."

"Ha! Maybe when you reach eighty . . ." The grandson shook his fist and made a muscle stand on his husky arm. "But they'll have me to fight then!"

"Yes," Joe laughed, squeezing the small bicep, "you will protect me when I am old and toothless."

They finished eating and dressed warmly for out-of-doors. Joe donned his hat with the gold medallion sewn into the black band. The hat had once been white, but the years had turned it a yellowish tan. The medallion was Joe's only symbol of leadership that denoted his position among the Cattaraugus Seneca. It had been in his family for almost two centuries, originally belonging to Sagoyewatha, the Seneca whom the whites revered as a great spokesman and orator, Red Jacket.

An Enfield .308 rifle, a memento of Joe's fighting days in the World War I trenches of France, hung on the wall. Joe took the weapon down, along with a few cartridges which he shoved into his coat pocket. High-powered rifles were illegal for hunting large game such as deer in New York State, and only shotguns were allowed in the forests. But on Indian land the Seneca did what they pleased. A shotgun slug was no good for a shot of any distance, and distant was the only kind of target that Shaman presented.

The big Seneca hoisted his grandson to his broad shoulders and opened the cabin door. Tommy reached up over the jamb and grabbed his .22 from where it rested on two wooden pegs.

"You leave the rifle home, boy."

Tommy's face filled with disappointment. He knew there was no need to take a .22 when they were going hunting for Shaman, but it was the only weapon he owned. He used it for hunting squirrels.

Still he protested, "Then you leave your rifle home!"

"Mind your manners," Joe said, and Tommy placed the rifle back on the pegs. "And button your ear flaps down on your hat. Your ears are thin and can freeze easily."

"Shit!" the boy said, trying to lace the ragged chin strap through a flap buckle. He hated the baby cap and wanted a cowboy hat like Joe's.

"*Shit* you say?" Joe's lips pressed into a frown. "So now you swear like the white boys you go to school with?"

"It's only a word, Joe . . ."

Joe grunted and walked through the doorway without stooping low enough while the boy attended, unaware, to his cap. Tommy's forehead clipped the top of the frame, and he would have fallen from his guardian's shoulders had not Joe tightened his grip on the boy's thighs. Outside, the boy righted his posture and rubbed his brow. A soft chuckle escaped the Seneca man's mouth as he closed the cabin door.

"You did that on purpose!"

Joe patted his grandson's legs, squeezed a nerve softly above the knee, evincing a startled yelp from the boy.

"I did not strike you," the smiling man said, "but our home does not like idle cursing."

A short way into the woods Joe stooped to inspect some deer droppings. "Look, Tommy," he said chidingly, "there is *shit!*" and then joined the boy in laughter.

"Does the word sound honorable on my tongue?" he asked.

"No, Grandfather . . ." Tommy replied sheepishly. The boy had never heard the aged man use a cursing expression in English before.

"It does not sound good on yours either," Joe admonished, and the matter was forgotten.

Once on the ground the grandson walked in the Seneca's tracks, slipping quietly through the pines. Both had ceased talking long before, as the deer sign was now plentiful and they were in the midst of Shaman's stamping grounds. Joe took a pair of hardwood sticks from a pocket and began clacking them. A moment later came back an answering clacking sound. Distant on the wind was heard an odd-sounding challenge, deep and bellowing, the voice of an excited buck in rut and looking for a battle. The Seneca giant cupped his hands to his mouth and bawled loud in his throat, imitating the challenge perfectly. Then he and his grandson stepped into a thicket and crouched down to wait. The boy had visions of a seventeen-inch television set seated in the bed of his grandfather's pickup truck. He

27

hoped that it would be Shaman whom Joe lured into the trap.

It was not Shaman, but rather a tough old whitetail with handsome antlers and a bristling collar of grey winter fur. The creature was tremendous, a superb specimen. He stood nobly, rack held high, and stared at the thicket impatiently, snorting steamy breath through flared nose slits, and beating the ground with strong forelegs.

As Joe rustled the bushes the deer opened his mouth and hurled a loud defiant protest at him.

The Seneca stepped forth. He spoke in Seneca. "Joe Hawk has fooled you, deer," he said. "Yet today, old father, I have no fight with you. Run away and remember this lesson so that your life may be long."

The deer's eyes widened with surprise. At first he began to bolt, but as he saw the Seneca hold out empty arms in homage his startled flight became a dignified gallop through the trees.

"Why did you let him go?" Tommy complained.

"Do we hunt for meat?" Joe asked. "Do we or any of our people need venison?" His dark eyes sparkled. "Old deer is many times a grandfather. Are not grandfathers treasures worthy of kindness and special considerations?"

Shaman's tracks were around the corpse in the snow. Joe was puzzled. That the signs were made by the king of deer was evident. The tyrant's hoofs had a wider split than the resident whitetail population and were easily identified. Also, the animal's hind leg spurs were longer and made deeper drag marks. That the buck had actually bedded by the corpse during the night was shown by the impression of his body in the packed snow. Such a thing was strange and troubling. He recalled the past night's fitful sleep—feelings of unrest when he awoke. Past times of trouble had often been seen beforehand by him: Thomas's and Virginia's deaths, his wife's deserting him for a white man. He had inherited the gift—or was it a curse?—of precognition from his mother.

"Who is he?" Tommy asked, as Joe brushed the body clean of snow. "Is he an Iroquois?"

"No, he is an Algonquin, Delaware or Abnaki . . . I do not know who he is . . ."

The Seneca chieftain surveyed the shoddy moccasins, cheap uncured leather, rawhide lacing broken at the

28

seams, and thick wool socks bulging through the bottoms, white yarn turned green and worn thin over the balls of the Indian's feet. He pried back the grey blanket, stiff as cardboard, and eyed the pathetic souvenir shop clothing. The man must have been out of his mind to wear such foolish apparel in the dead of winter!

"Did he freeze to death?" Tommy asked.

"No," Joe answered, seeing the small hole through the blanket and feeling through the dyed German Shepherd vest. "He was shot."

He rewrapped the body respectfully and gently propped it against the base of a nearby tree. Overhead he noticed a freshly white branch stub, where Zeb Simpson had broken it off to wipe out his tracks. A moment later Tommy found White Throat's head buried in the snow where Shaman had kicked it during the night. It had been almost entirely hidden from sight in the drifting snow, only the tip of an antler poking out.

The boy noticed the severed ear. "Is this Shaman's head?"

Joe's face was now intense with the need to solve the riddle. "If you look closely, you will see that the ear has been removed recently with a knife," he said. But he was still stumped for an answer.

Was it a clue to the murderer? The dead man obviously belonged to the wolf clan, as denoted by the fake wolf-skin vest he wore. Had the murderer been a member of the deer clan, as the Hawk family also was? Could the severed head have an unknown meaning? If so, Joe was sure he would figure it out.

Joe walked across the open space to the tree where Zeb had gutted the doe. He found the female's guts frozen in a heap, and spotted where Zeb's rope had scraped the bark off the pine limb overhead when he hauled the carcass up for bleeding. A few tufts of white nylon were stuck on the branch, and they sent a sinking sensation through the Indian's heart. Only one hunter that he knew used such a rope. He pulled his gloves off and began searching around with his fingers in the snow. In a minute he found a 30-06 caliber casing and held it before his troubled eyes. The firing pin had left an uneven groove in the percussion cap where the pin had been worn away and blunted. It was a negligible piece of evidence, but

29

enough for Joe to identify the murderer. He had learned to recognize Zeb's shell casings years ago, out of the need to identify trespassing hunters and ignore those who were welcome. Troubled with the discovery, Joe Hawk led his grandson back to Malsum's body, determined to investigate further, regardless of protocol.

Beneath the dead wizard's fingernails Joe found blood and deer hair, telling the shrewd woodsman that this unknown Indian had severed White Throat's head. Zebediah had killed a doe. Joe knew it was a doe from the size of the intestines. The Lenape might have thought to try and pass the deer head off as Shaman in order to collect the reward from the local authorities. A foolish ruse. But the Indian was obviously senile, or he would not have worn such worthless clothing. It was too simple a conclusion, though, thought the Seneca.

Might the man have severed the ear and carried the head for another reason—witchcraft? If true, that made him responsible, in part, for his own death.

Again Joe lifted the blanket, this time slicing the frozen vest laces apart with his hunting knife and exposing Malsum's painted chest and stomach. His eyes went wide as he deciphered the pictographs.

"I have enemies—they have killed my sons—I hate them —I will kill them—" Symbols in black, yellow, and red revealed the names of Iroquois and Algonquin gods of revenge and war.

Joe stared at the ancient face, the bulbous nose, and his heart began to recall with dread what his old eyes had forgotten. He took snow and rubbed at the funeral paint until some of it was erased.

There, over the heart of this wizard, was an ugly scar. As though it were yesterday, the years slipped away and Joe Hawk once again was a boy daring a witch to wage a contest. "Look, Seneca boy!" Malsum had said, showing the scar. "I did not die! I possess strong magic. Powerful gods and spirits protect me and obey my every command!"

This was Malsum! With a cry of anguish, Joe turned his face to the sky and shook his fists. The arteries on his bull neck bulged with the hot coursing of his blood as he swore an oath, his face livid with rage. Tommy stood frozen, horrified, as Joe grabbed the shaman by his long white hair and dragged him off effortlessly like a rag doll to a nearby tree stump. He placed Malsum's bony right hand on the flat surface.

"Grandfather!" Tommy cried, as the Seneca took his short-handled axe out and cleaved off three fingers. "Why—"

"He is a demon!" Joe yelled, "a worker of curses and witchcraft!"

Still seething, Joe took his knife and dug down into the wizard's chest for Zeb's bullet.

"Turn away, Thomas!" he said, seeing the frightened boy's gaze. "This is not for your eyes."

The words were in Seneca, as was his grandfather's way when he meant to assert unquestioned authority. Biting down on his lip, the boy obeyed and looked off into the woods, his keen young mind reeling with dawning suspicions.

By the time Joe found the bullet Malsum's chest had become a gaping bloodless hole. He flung the conical lead into the forest, then picked up White Throat's head and poised the wicked antlers above Malsum's chest and slammed them down to disguise and disfigure the wound he had made in search of the bullet. The sharp curled tines of bone pierced the frozen flesh and crushed the sorcerer's emaciated breastbone like an egg shell. The noise of punctured lungs and cracking vertebrae brought the grandson's eyes back around involuntarily to stare with fascinated horror.

The antlers lodged tightly as Joe finally stopped. He pressed a heavy-booted foot on the mangled remains and pulled the punishing rack free, hurling the head off through the forests. His eyes went sick like the eyes of a man with fever as he saw his gruesome handiwork. He blanched with reproach as he saw his ward's startled face staring at him.

"They do not send deer to prison for murder . . . Do you understand my words, Grandson?"

"Yes . . ." Tommy replied, thinking of seldom used Seneca words with which to answer. "You would have it appear that he was not killed by a bullet . . . The fingers—"

"They were a debt long owed and never paid!"

"He is the witch who caused the murder of Wise Thomas? He is the devil, Malsum?"

"You remember the story?"

"Yes, Grandpa." The boy's eyes widened more and he swallowed through a lump in his throat at sight of the legendary wizard. "Is this a deed of honor?"

Joe's face filled with unaccustomed shame and he bowed his head. "No," he said sadly, "it is a deed of blind hatred and revenge . . . and to prevent more injustice because of this evil scum."

Malsum! A long-ago nightmare back to plague him—and for what terrible reasons? The chieftain's mind returned to his boyhood and to the last day of his father's life.

Young Joe fired as the quail burst from the brush. Wise Thomas chuckled as his twelve-year-old son tried not to show pain, tears smarting in his eyes. He had not held the shotgun tight to his shoulder, as the father had instructed.

Wise Thomas was a tall man, muscular of build and rugged in appearance, with clear black, piercing eyes that often smiled, as they did now. Yet those eyes were also capable of seeing through another man's defenses to his very soul. His name was Tall Tree also but he was better known as Thomas Hawk—"Wise Thomas," so named by the white community after he resolved an argument between townsmen and Seneca men before it erupted into bloodshed. To them he was like Solomon of the Old Testament, endowed with charm and wisdom.

The Seneca chieftain rubbed his son's shoulder, easing the soreness. "Does your shoulder hurt, Joseph?"

"I feel as if I have been struck with a large stone," young Joe Hawk said.

"You are a terrible shot," Wise Thomas laughed. "The quail have flown away. With what will we make soup?"

"I would have gotten him if you'd let me use my bow."

"That may be so, but a man must become skilled with the weapons of his own age and not only those of his grandfather's age," Wise Thomas admonished.

The smiling man loaded a fresh shell in the chamber and handed the shotgun to his son. "Is your shoulder too sore to try again?" Joe looked at the weapon with painful remembrance and winced, reluctantly taking the gun. His father grunted an approval and they went off.

As they walked the snow-covered field, hoping to flush other game birds from the brush, Wise Thomas heard a noise behind him and turned to see three white men coming out of the woods. They were friends and no cause for alarm. The solemnity of their faces, their lack of greeting, told Wise Thomas that the white girl, Melissa Banner, had been found, and was dead as feared, even before the men spoke.

"Your men found her, Tom," County Sheriff Matt Parker said. "She was almost shot in half." The lawman's eyes were a sad grey, the smell of liquor was on his breath, as on the breaths of his companions. "She was stuck high up in a pine tree. She could have been murdered last week when she disappeared—there's no way of telling. We haven't had a thaw, and her corpse was frozen."

"Nathan Banner has been told?"

"I've seen to it," said Zebediah Simpson, a farmer and Wise Thomas's close friend.

"Old Nate grieves terrible," said Keever, also a farmer. The stench of drink was strongest on Will's breath. "We all grieve, Thomas . . . She was such a pretty, sweet little gal . . . always laughin' and playin' with the young'uns . . ." He took a crumpled handkerchief from his coat pocket and blew his nose ceremoniously.

Wise Thomas's face reflected their sadness. Young Joe seemed especially grieved. Melissa had been a joy to him, always trying to convert his teasing denial of Christian tenets into faith. She had arranged for him and other Seneca children to attend school and learn to read and write. She had conducted classes on the Bible, the Old Testament, whose people, she taught, were very much like the Indian tribes of North America, farmers and warriors. The daughter of Parson Nathan Banner, a strict hellfire and damnation preacher and leader of a lesser Christian sect in the community, Melissa had complemented the man's harshness with her own gentle ways, while trying to draw converts to the Light. Young Joe had loved her and, although stoic while he listened to the group, he could not prevent the tears in his eyes. She was dead.

With Joe's mother and other Seneca women, Melissa had worked in the fields at their side, assuring them of her good intentions toward all, taking the opportunity, but never abusing it, to read from the Bible during noon-day rest. Blonde, fair of skin, precocious, with a tendency for sudden laughter, the girl had been accepted by all. They had adopted her as a Seneca.

"My heart tells me the Lenape devil-worshipper and his

33

sons are guilty," Wise Thomas said. "But as always, my eyes seek and find no proof. What would you have me do, my friends?"

"Turn your back while I go give 'em what they give Lissy!" Will Keever exploded, gripping his shotgun.

"You know I can't allow that myself, Will," Parker said. He turned to Wise Thomas. "It's not your way either, Tom."

Malsum, Tegagiche, and Wenegawa walked through the Seneca settlement of cabins and clapboard houses with their heads held arrogantly high, as if there were not angry white men with guns at their backs. The Seneca at work or play around their homes cast hateful looks at the Delawares.

Joe Hawk was in the field near his home with other boys, Ezekiel Simpson, Samuel Parker, and Will Keever, Jr., sons of the three white men escorting Malsum and his sons. All of the boys became excited over the arrests.

"My pa's got the murderin' vipers," Sammy said, tight-lipped. "I hope he hangs 'em good!"

Wise Thomas appeared in the doorway of the long-house, where the council of Seneca elders and sachems had come to a decision regarding the Lenape. He joined the party of prisoners and guards and led them to his home.

Thomas's wife, Beautiful Mary, was busy canning preserves in the kitchen with Nettie Parker, Matt's wife, and another Seneca woman, when the men stepped in. She wrinkled her pretty face and spat on the floor in front of Malsum as she saw him. Her black eyes danced with fire. Melissa had been dear to her.

"I would ask you and your friends to leave our home while I attend to business," Wise Thomas said politely in the Seneca language.

"I understand, my husband," Mary answered. "We will go to our neighbors."

The women dressed for outside without wasting any time.

As Mary buttoned her coat, her eyes smiling at Matt, she said, "I have shown Nettie how I make my apple-sauce, and she has taught me the secret of her apple butter."

"That's fine, Mary," Matt said. "My children are sure fond of your recipes."

34

"They should be," Nettie said, laughingly. "They've eaten as much of Mary's cooking as they have my own!"

The women were trying to be casual and at ease while they dressed, but their tension could be felt. They cast furtive looks towards Malsum from time to time.

As they left the cabin, Mary stood for a moment before Malsum. "You are a foul and vile man," she said boldly. "You are soulless and have raised your vermin sons without souls—which demon did you sell them to at birth? In a vision I saw you kill Melissa Banner. You are going to pay for that!" And then the Seneca woman said in English, "You are the serpent in the garden of Evan and Ada that my white daughter taught me of!"

Malsum's tawny eyes narrowed into two slits of hatred, but the lovely Seneca woman's own smoldering gaze was more than a match for him and he turned away.

"What'd she say to him?" Will whispered to Zeb, not understanding the language at the beginning of Mary's eruption.

"I said I believe he is guilty and I hope your courts hang them," Mary answered Keever.

The toughness left her face and she smiled at the white men politely, a gracious hostess now.

"You men be sure to take some preserves home for your families when you leave," she said cheerfully. "We always have more than enough."

She took her husband's hand for a moment, squeezed it, her eyes saying "show them no mercy," and then joined her friends outside.

Keever, Simpson, and Parker thanked her warmly and bid good-bye as Wise Thomas closed the door and walked to the large oak table in the center of the kitchen.

"Sit down, wizard," he said, directing a stiff look toward Malsum. "We will talk now."

Outside the cabin, Mary's face filled with foreboding.

"What's wrong? You look as if you've seen a ghost," Nettie said.

"I have a feeling," Mary answered. "A terrible dread fills my heart."

"It is a sign of coming grief," the Seneca neighbor echoed. "Your feelings are always true."

"Oh, nonsense!" Nettie said, taking Mary's hand and pulling her away. "Somebody just walked over your grave."

She laughed as she saw the two Indian women become puzzled.

"I am not dead. I have no grave," Mary said.

"Of course not, honey." Nettie led them off. "It's just an expression."

Joe Hawk, Sam Parker, and Will, Jr. were on the side of the cabin, peering in at their fathers through an open window.

"Joseph," Mary called as she saw him, "why do you spy on your father? Is his business your concern?"

"We want to see what happens," Joe said. "We'll be quiet, Mother." A slow smile crept onto the boy's face. "Wouldn't you like to know also?" He was being charmingly impertinent, knowing well that Mary was a curious sort.

"See that you behave yourself," Mary said, duplicating the impish look in his eyes with a secret smile of her own.

"You children button those coats to the collars," Nettie Parker admonished, "and come get us if there's trouble brewing."

Mary told the boys where they would be if they decided to go indoors with the coming of night or sharp appetites and went off with her friends.

Nathan Banner, dressed in a frock coat and wide-brimmed hat, reined his horse and buckboard in front of the Hawk cabin. His gaunt, whisker-stubbled face was grieving over the loss of his daughter. Young Luke Banner, his son, a boy close in age to those in the yard at the open window, was dressed in imitation of his sire. His ice-blue eyes were red-rimmed and puffy from weeping.

"Is your pa inside, Joseph?" Nathan asked.

His lanky legs creaked as he stepped down from the wagon. His voice was thick and crackly, rumbling in his throat before it reached his tongue.

"Yes, Brother Banner," Joe said respectfully, knowing the man appreciated this address.

The black-suited parson nodded and told his son to put a bag of oats on the horse's muzzle and to wait outside with the other boys. Nathan rapped on the door and went inside as Matt Parker opened it for him.

"Nate?" Matt said worriedly. "You shouldn't be here."

"I've come to see justice done," the parson said.

"You're not carrying a sidearm, are you?"

"I am not. A man of God does not commit murder," Banner announced.

Matt was satisfied with this and admitted him to the table. Again the door was shut.

"Luke, we sure are sorry about your sister Lissy . . ." Ezekiel Simpson said, helping to carry the bag of oats from the buckboard floor and hitching it over the horse's muzzle.

"My mama and papa lost the love of their lives with her departing," Luke said, his face tight, eyes hateful and accusing to Joe. "The Lord Jehovah will lay his wrath on the red savages for her murder."

Joe wished to offer consoling words, but Luke's hard look left him speechless. It was apparent that they were no longer friends. Wise Thomas had warned that there would be bitter feelings reaching even to the Seneca over Melissa's death, but until this moment Joe had seen nothing of the sort. With a heavy heart he turned back to peer through the window, praying that somehow Malsum and his two sons would be found out and made to pay for their terrible crime. In his mind they were already guilty.

Luke Banner stood by his pa's horse, refusing to go near Joe. Each time a Seneca hunter entered the village with his game, or a woman passed by on some errand, his burning eyes glowered at them. Melissa had helped and loved the Indians; they had raped and killed her. He would never forgive them—never!

Inside the cabin Sheriff Matt Parker locked up all firearms in a closet, except for his own Schofield .45 in its holster on his hip. Knives were allowed to the men seated at the table when the Lenapes refused to part with their own. Matt could have pushed the matter and completely disarmed everyone, but Will and Zeb only grinned when he asked for theirs. Rather than force an issue, Matt had let it lie.

Will obviously hoped for a form of provocation that would justify bloodletting, but Matt trusted that he could control the resentful farmer, counting on their friendship. Zeb and Tom were peaceful enough if not riled. And Nathan—well, he hadn't said anything since he'd entered the cabin. He just sat, staring at Malsum and his sons coldly. When Wise Thomas offered his condolences, the preacher nodded a brief thank-you and remained quiet.

Nathan was going to be mighty disappointed by the time he left. Matt knew that he couldn't hold the Delawares unless he arrested them. And he couldn't arrest them because he didn't have any proof. This conference was merely an exorcism, ridding the community of its three demons.

"Nathan's girl was raped and then shotgunned to death," Matt said, scanning Malsum's calm face.

"I am sorry to hear that, Brother Banner," Malsum said sadly.

"Don't call me 'brother,' " Nathan said tightly. "I may have no proof of your guilt yet, but nor am I convinced of your innocence."

"We are innocent!" Malsum pounded the table. "By your Christ I swear this!"

"Goddamn heathen witchman!" Keever spat. "You're less of a Christian than the Devil himself. You own a shotgun, and you killed that girl with it!"

"Many men own shotguns," Malsum said, matching eyes with the tough farmer. "You, and other white men own shotguns also."

"Yeah, but the evidence points to Injuns killing her," Zebediah Simpson said. "White men don't hide bodies in the tops of pine trees. They bury 'em, or throw 'em in holes."

"There are many 'Injuns' living here!" Malsum said angrily, knowing that Parker was purposely allowing his rough friends to conduct the interrogation, relying on their gruff natures to intimidate the suspects, anticipating that they would slip with their alibis or display guilt under pressure.

"Not the likes of you three, there ain't," Keever said. "Only three devil-worshippers around here near as I can tell."

"We do not worship devils! We believe in many gods, both good and evil," Wenegawa countered.

"Same pie no matter how you slice it," Zeb said. "Forgettin' religion, I know for a fact you bucks have been troubling the ladies for some time now. Where were you two Sunday mornings past, when Lissy disappeared?"

"We were hunting deer in the hills," Tegagiche answered. "We know nothing of the white girl's death!"

"You have no proof that we did anything wrong. Tell them to leave us alone, lawman!" Wenegawa clenched his jaws, the muscles in his whiskerless cheeks throbbing visibly. "The white pigs are not man enough to protect their sows. So they accuse us of crimes out of hatred and prejudice!"

Malsum grunted appreciatively and nodded, understanding the bastard mix of Delaware and Seneca that Wenegawa used. He searched Wise Thomas's face for any sign of emotion. The stalwart leader glared at him intensely.

"I caught one part of that little spiel, sonny," Will Keever grimaced. "You wouldn't be calling this old boy a pig now? Man insults me personally, I normally kick the shit out of him . . ."

"Settle down, Will." Matt finally spoke up, seeing hands on knives. "A little name-calling can't hurt anyone."

"Do you have any evidence or proof, Sheriff Parker?" Nathan Banner asked. His face showed worry over the lack of any evidence. Retribution was a way of life with the man, but not lynching.

Malsum grinned defiantly as he saw the lawman secretly wince at the question—Nathan had unknowingly foiled the gambit.

"There's some evidence point—"

"You are a liar! There is no evidence!" Again Malsum made a fist and slammed the table top.

Matt's tight look cooled the sorcerer's bravado. "There's some evidence pointing to them, but I'm afraid it's all circumstantial."

"Then you must make them confess before man and God!"

"You leave ol' Zebediah here and me alone with 'em for a few hollers, and you can have confessions or bodies, Parson—you say which," Keever said, bushy eyebrows arched.

"I don't hold with murder or violence, Brother Keever," Nathan said sadly. "Fire against fire only broadens the flames of Hell."

"An eye for an eye!" Keever spat back. "Ain't worried about my redemption—man can't have a try at proddin' a hot poker up the Devil's ass if he don't go to Hell . . . That right, Zeb?"

"That's right, Will," Simpson said, eyes tough on Tegagiche, making him tense, like a cat in a windblown tree. "My guts still ache from seeing that poor child with her . . ."

Matt grabbed Zeb's hand as it slipped toward his knife. The bearded farmer's eyes glistened with emotion as his mind recalled the girl's corpse.

"You two settle down right now or I'll send you packing!" Matt warned.

Zebediah nodded and placed empty hands on the table. Will sighed disgustedly and sat back in his chair.

Matt's eyes turned to Wise Thomas, finding him attentive but patient. The lawman nodded, and the Seneca chieftain resigned himself to a prepared course of action. Parker was an honorable man, unable to establish guilt. The cursed devil-worshippers would have to go free. But they would not stay on Seneca land.

Wise Thomas placed a small bag of gold double eagles on the table before Malsum. "This is many times what you paid for your land from my father," he said. "It is the price you will sell it back for."

Malsum feigned disbelief. "You would side with these whites against your own people?"

"Neither the color of your skin nor the blood of your veins makes you my people," Tall Tree spoke in Seneca. "These men and the murdered girl are more my people than any of you."

Malsum ranted. "I will not sell my land! It is good land and our home for many years now. My wife lies buried there. My cabin is there."

"You will sell the land and leave here quickly."

"I refuse! You cannot force me to sell."

"I would have no need to force a dead man to sell land." Wise Thomas's eyes hardened. "I, too, know how to hide bodies in trees."

Like a whipped dog, Malsum wavered under the chieftain's gaze.

"Let us go, Father," Wenegawa said suddenly, his fear evident. "Let us take the gold and leave this house of dishonor now."

Tegagiche, inflamed by the discussion, perhaps still under the influence of an earlier drinking bout, rose up with reckless abandon, reaching for his belt knife. Matt's pistol was out and aimed in a flash. "Yank it out and I put a bullet through your hand." he said.

"Through his hand?" Will roared. "Put it through his goddamn belly button if you've a mind to spend a cartridge, Matt!"

The Indian sat down and order resumed at the table. The indignation on Malsum's face smoothed over, to be replaced with a look of glassy tearfulness. He opened his dry calloused palms in a gesture of supplication before Wise Thomas.

"Brother!" he said. "Why do you turn your face from me and side with these strangers?" His dark eyes blinked rapidly as if he had been stunned by a blow. The Seneca chief's eyes wizened with quiet derision, and the sorcerer took note.

"That I call you brother, is this so distasteful?" Malsum asked. "Which of these white men bears even the slightest kinship to you? Which of these white men share your beliefs, your troubles, your hopes for your people—as I myself do?"

Wise Thomas smiled softly. Malsum had asked a question, but any answer before the man had finished speaking would be improper, and an interruption contrary to custom. The Lenape wizard closed his eyes, an even more solemn expression carrying his message.

"Many ages ago," he recited in the Seneca language, "after our mother descended from the upper world and came into the lower realm where she bore twins on the back of a great turtle; many ages after the sons grew up and fought, one becoming the Good Spirit and the other becoming the Evil Spirit; many ages later, when our nations were both strong and lived as true men with true faiths, courageous hearts, and minds filled with wisdom, the lying, cheating, murdering fathers of these white men came to our council fires. We welcomed them, gave them land and sustenance. We taught them how to grow corn, gave them 'our life' and graciously shared the 'three sisters,' maize, beans, and squash with them.

"They swore undying gratitude, and we, our peoples, having never known a lie, and always found truthful, believed them and gave them still more.

"As they grew stronger in numbers they became more treacherous, and soon my people, the Lenni Lenape, found themselves fighting for their lives. We were weakened and our numbers decimated by their evil sicknesses and scheming ways." Malsum now eyed the whites with anger, turned a more softened look on the Seneca chief.

"The Delaware sent out runners to the great nation of the Iroquois in the west. We went bearing gifts and arm-

41

loads of the precious wampum that the Hodenosaunee had treasured so highly. 'Brothers!' we cried then. 'We are no longer of a disposition to make war with you. The white demons are going to rob and kill us, as they intend to rob and kill all Indians. If we do not unite, our peoples will surely be taken from the face of the land."

Wenegawa and Tegagiche nodded their heads bitterly.

"What's he saying?" Will Keever asked, but Zeb, whose father's mother had been a Seneca, and had taught him her language, made no reply.

"Do you know the treachery of your fathers, Wise Thomas?" Malsum asked.

Still the Seneca made no reply, although his cheeks tightened and began to twitch.

"I would tell you without malice, for it has been a long time, and happened even before the birth of my grandmother, and I hold no grudge, but wish only peace and brotherhood with my chosen uncles, the Seneca . . .

"After the nations of the Seneca, the Mohawk, the Oneida, the Onondaga, and the Cayuga received our gifts, and knowing only false pride in their hearts because of their might and prowess, they laughed at the Delaware and called us cowards. 'Do not worry,' they said, 'we will protect you from the whites, so you will not disappear from the face of the land. But then your men must live like women and children, for we of the Iroquois allow no warriors but our own within our domain.' "

Malsum pounded the oak table with his fist. "Slavery or death! That is the choice your fathers gave mine. We asked for help, and instead the League gave us protection at the cost of our freedom and dignity!"

"Then why didn't they refuse?" Zeb suddenly asked.

Malsum looked at him with surprise, but ignored him. "Wise Thomas," he beseeched, "I bear your people no wrong. Yet, this day is like that day long ago. I have lived on your land many moons—and now you tell me I am outcast. You tell me I must sell my home and leave— you warn that I must obey you, but how can you ask such a thing. Has your heart turned to stone?"

The white men watched Malsum as his eyes filled with tears and his leathery face reddened to a rich earthy brown. He beat his chest miserably, a skilled actor giving his best performance. He continued.

"Am I now a Delaware slave to an Iroquois master?

Are you my master that I must do your bidding, Wise Thomas?" The tears rolled down Malsum's cheeks. "Do you deny me fair justice and side with these treacherous white men over an unproven crime of which I and my sons are innocent? Is there still no justice for a Lenape brother this day, Wise Thomas?"

"What kind of shit is he up to?" Will groaned, turning to Zeb again. But Zeb waved him off, knowing the art that went into eloquent speechmaking. Indians looked upon the craft with honor and respect. If Malsum could best Wise Thomas, whose skin was said to be 'seven thumbs thick,' he would be shamed into letting him stay. The Seneca's reply would be interesting, for he was related to Red Jacket, one of the greatest of all Indian orators. A gold medallion, given to Red Jacket in gratitude by the British for his aid against the rebelling colonists, hung about Thomas's neck on a gold chain.

"What you say is truth mixed with lies of your own making," Wise Thomas began. "The Iroquois and the Delaware were sworn enemies when your fathers came to us for help. Many times before they were asked to join us and be our brothers, but always they refused and showed us only contempt and disfavor. We warned them not to trust to their own alliances, for those alliances were as water is to ice when compared to the alliance of the Iroquois; but they always spoke loud and long, caught up in their own pride, and never once stopped long enough until it was near too late, to take notice that they were like the foolish crows of the woods who were always talking, but never making any sound reason . . ."

Malsum's eyes narrowed into two dark slits. His sons became quietly belligerent, their faces smoldering.

". . . The Iroquois fought for your fathers and shed much blood in protection of your homes and peoples. How often and when did the Delaware fight for the homes and peoples of my fathers? How often in later years and generations did the Lenape, the 'true men' of the land, turn against us and attack us with the sons of their white enemies? Tell me now of one instance where the Seneca turned against their allies with treachery or dishonor, and I will let you stay on the land for eternity. If we must dwell on the wrongs of history I could mention many perpetrated by your people against mine. Who did the Tuscarora turn to for solace when they were driven from their homes? Were they powerful and warlike when you refused them land in your midst? Did we make slaves of them or kill them without mercy when we found them poor and wretched by our sides, or did we give them solace and raise them up to become a great nation? Do not try to shame me into thinking I have been born into a nation that knows no fairness or justice! Had the tables been turned, the Lenape would have left the Hodenosaunee to their fate, or perhaps even joined in and helped to kill us. You speak of yourself as a Delaware, but you are nothing! For your own people drove you away and disowned you as a young man.

"Once you pleaded for adoption among the Seneca, renouncing your birthright, but my people found only shame in your request, and wondered—not knowing then your foul nature and evil identity. They knew not of your own crimes of witchcraft against the Lenape, but believed you on a holy pilgrimage of despair, as many homeless Indians were in those days.

"This moment you stare at me with hate-filled eyes, choking on your own tongue to keep from losing your dignity, but only moments earlier you were weeping and whimpering like a whipped dog. You know that the Seneca are a fair people. A people of compassion and goodness, for you have often successfully defended yourself in the past by throwing yourself on our mercy. That time is over, witch!"

"You speak lies, and none of what—"

"Shut up, Malsum!" Zeb Simpson said. "I don't think Tom's done with you yet."

"You would have yourself cleansed of suspicion over the child's death, because we cannot prove your guilt," Wise Thomas said, "but one does not welcome the wolf at the door, but drives him away; for all wolves are the same and will eventually devour the hand that feeds them. I am not a fool to be tricked by you, demon-lover. I did not give you the land you live on, and as such I owe you no personal bond. My father gave you the land, later regretting the bargain until the hour he passed from this world. He gave you the land for a measly sum, which you insisted to pay for, demanding a signed paper in his hand. That paper is worthless, as you, and your wicked sons are worthless."

Will Keever grinned at Matt as they both saw the fury

appear on the Lenape's faces. Neither understood much of anything being said, but they mentally kept score by the changing expressions.

"The Lenni Lenape had cast you out for sorcery and the invocation of foul gods to do your bidding. This day you defiantly bear the name Malsum, the epitome of wickedness, placed on you by your own tribe after the great Algonquin demon who bears the name before you. Do you think we are stupid and without knowledge of the customs and beliefs of the Lenape?

"Your people hate and fear you. My people also hate you, and have for years. But we have never feared you!" Wise Thomas's eyes mocked the three enraged Delaware. "We have tolerated your presence among us too long. As to justice. Justice is for men, and not for sorcerers and demon-worshippers. Do not ask me for justice—for if you truly desire it, I will gladly face all three of you in combat and kill you like the curs you are!"

Malsum's eyes narrowed into slits, knowing the Seneca had defeated him. Standing, his sons beside, shaking with terrible wrath and hissing like the serpent in the garden Mary described earlier, he said, "Once the Seneca were greatest among all the Iroquois. The first and last to fight. The Keepers Of The Western Door whence all enemies attacked. The Seneca are now wagging-tailed dogs in the white men's laps! The noble Seneca chiefs and sachems are no more! They are gone! And a dog stands in their place! A dog who is the stupidest of men with the lying legend of 'wise' before a name that is foreign and meaningless to our peoples! Thomas Hawk! The Tall Tree! If we are curs we lift our legs and urinate on you!"

While Malsum was ranting, Wise Thomas kept his composure. A murderous grin curled the corners of his mouth and his eyes shone with secret humor. "You will be the first man I have killed in my life," the Seneca chieftain said matter-of-factly. "But there will be no honor or test of courage involved, for you are a coward. Your corpse will rot in the tree where I hide it. The birds will not eat it. Your tongue I will pull from the roots and display in a jar. Men will look upon it and say, 'See Malsum? There he lives, all that was, all that is, and all that there ever would be.'"

Matt Parker recognized the killing look on Wise Thomas's face as the Seneca grinned broadly and stood up.

Malsum backed away from the table with fear, his sons nervous but ready to defend him. "Please, Tom," Matt said, "if you go for him I have to stop you . . . I don't know what the bastard said, but this isn't the time or place."

The Seneca chieftain appeared troubled, the look of a man being robbed. "There will be time another day," he conceded. "My patience is at an end. I cannot forever let dogs yap at my heels without kicking."

"Thank you, Tom," the lawman said, as the giant chieftain resumed his chair. "Put the knives away," he said to Zeb and Will, both men holding their weapons hidden beneath the table. He then turned on the Lenni Lenapes and disgustedly instructed them to leave the cabin, and the county, if they valued their lives. It was disheartening, but there was no proof that they had killed Melissa Banner.

Nathan Banner clamped a tight lid on his disappointment, saying nothing as Zeb and Will argued with Matt about the principle of it all. Wise Thomas sat silent also, his heart and mind respecting the stoic sense of honor to which the parson clung. Lesser men, such as Simpson and Keever, did not know how to accept defeat with such grace. The Indian learned from the man of God. What were mere insults compared to his tragic loss? Soon, when he sought the Delawares for an accounting, he would rise above their taunts and not kill because of injured vanity; he would kill them for the girl's father, for the girl. The last words Malsum would ever hear, "Brother Banner wishes you a pleasant journey to Hell," would ring from his lips, as they rang now through his mind.

As the room quieted, Malsum smirked at Wise Thomas, and with a dexterity that defied his fifty-five years he scooped the bag of gold from the table and deposited it in his clothing beneath the shabby grey blanket he always wore.

The boys' eyes were at the window of the cabin.

"They gonna let 'em go, Joe?" Sammy Parker asked with disbelief as they watched Malsum and his sons starting to leave.

"Maybe my pa's gonna catch them in the woods when they're alone, and shoot them, like they done Lissy?" Will, Jr. offered.

46

Luke Banner stepped up to the window and looked in. He glared accusingly at Joe Hawk.

"Your father's letting them go!" he said. "You're all nothing but filthy savages!"

Tears streamed down the boy's cheeks. He pounced on Joe and hit him hard in the face. Joe backed away, his nose bleeding.

"Hey!" Ezekiel Simpson blocked Luke's way, as he meant to continue after the Seneca boy. Joe was a good fighter; why was he backing down? "Leave him alone, Lucas!" Ezekiel warned.

Joe had no heart for hitting the grief-stricken boy. He was ashamed to think that his father would allow the Delawares to escape justice and go free. He wanted to run away and hide from his friends.

Luke's eyes blinked rapidly with tears as Ezekiel held him, twisting his black coat at the neck. As Ezekiel released him, Luke covered his face with a sleeve and returned to his father's buggy.

"You should have hit him back!" Will Jr. whispered, as Joe bent over, dripping blood into the snow.

Sammy Parker took a kerchief from his pocket and handed it to the Seneca. "He's kind of small and runty for hitting," he said to Joe, and the Indian youngster knew that his friend was telling him that he understood.

Malsum grinned at Wise Thomas seated at the table. "You have no honor," he charged.

"That's enough talk," Matt said, knowing they were astride a bomb, with a lighted match held to the fuse. "Get your asses out of here before I boot 'em out!"

Malsum ignored him, ignored his cowering sons. With a reckless courage born of hatred, and the knowledge that the honorable lawman would protect him, he took a leather fetish bag from the thong around his neck and emptied its contents onto the table.

"There is honor," he said. "Men who would wager more than just words with me! Men of honor and bravery, as I am!"

"Jesus, Mary, and Joseph!" Zeb exclaimed. He was staring at the remains of five well-preserved human fingers, ghastly, brown, and shriveled.

"Filthy heathen spawn of the devil!" Nathan Banner exploded. "If but one of those be the finger of a girl, you'll not escape the hangman's noose—by God I swear this!"

Will Keever picked up each digit in turn, examining them with disgust. "They're all too big to belong to a woman," he said. "Besides, Lissy weren't missin' none, anyways . . ."

Malsum grinned again and returned the grisly trophies to his bag, tying the thong around his neck. "Redeem your honor, Iroquois man," he demanded. "Wager with me a finger, the way our fathers, men of courage and dignity, wagered before us!"

Young Joe and the other boys stared in through the window at the broad knife heating in a lid hole on Mary's wood stove. Will Keever withdrew the steel blade, displaying its fiery red blaze of readiness. He nodded.

"I'm not one for standing by while the law is being broken," Matt Parker said. "I wish you wouldn't go through with this . . ."

"In this house, my friend, I am the law," Wise Thomas replied.

From outside the window, the boys watched as Malsum placed a worn deck of playing cards in the middle of the table. The two kerosene lamps inside were burning brightly. The wind and snow were blowing fiercely in the settling blackness of night, but the boys held their vigil. Even young Luke, prompted by the cold, had left the buckboard and stood at the window with the others. The settlement itself was lonely. The only signs of life were the light behind the curtained windows and the smell of food cooking as Seneca housewives fed their husbands and children.

"Boy! I wouldn't want to miss this for nothing!" Will, Jr. said.

"Miss what?" Luke Banner asked.

"Wise Thomas is going to cut that old fart's finger off!"

The Seneca chieftain drew a card from the deck. Malsum sat with his eyes clenched, chanting in a low voice. Simpson grinned and Keever broke out laughing as Wise Thomas turned over the king of hearts. Malsum opened his eyes and stared at the card with disbelief and fear.

"What's the matter, witch-man?" Will goaded. "Losing your nerve?"

Malsum's hand shook visibly over the deck. Finally he

drew a card. There were loud groans and curses from several of the white men. It was the ace of spades.

The door opened and the boy, Joe Hawk, walked into the room. Matt Parker and the other white friends were arguing with Wise Thomas's quiet resolve to forfeit the finger he had lost. The Seneca would listen to none of their excuses, knowing such a cheating would brand him forever as a coward and a dishonorable man.

"You go on outta here, Joey," Zeb Simpson said. "This ain't no time for young'uns to be underfoot."

"Father . . . I want to stay," the boy said.

Wise Thomas considered the request for a moment and then nodded his consent. Young Joe walked over and took his father's left hand, squeezing it tightly. The other hand Wise Thomas placed on the table. Matt, Zeb, and Will had argued for the taking of the smallest member on the left hand, but the wizard had claimed his choice, knowing that Wise Thomas was right-handed. Malsum chose to cripple. The Seneca chief would have to learn to shoot a rifle and draw a bowstring anew. Malsum claimed his index finger.

The wizard toyed with the idea of offering mercy. He even acted as if he was reluctant to take the finger. He looked at Matt Parker. "If I do not take my prize, will you let me stay on my land?"

"I will," Matt said quickly.

"Yes—but you have not the authority!" Malsum said. He then turned to the Seneca. "Will you allow me to keep my home?"

He held the knife edge to Wise Thomas's finger, drawing a trickle of rich blood. Young Joe winced.

"I will allow you the finger you won!" came the reply.

"Watch," Malsum said to the boy. "He will wail like a woman!"

"Oh Christ. . ." Matt Parker groaned as Malsum began sawing.

"Heathen swine!" Nathan Banner cried. "Filthy Godless swine!"

Wise Thomas closed his eyes, but he made no protest or outcry. And Malsum claimed his prize. Will Keever applied tight pressure to the artery in Wise Thomas's wrist and Zeb Simpson cauterized the wound with the hot knife. A smoky stench of burnt flesh filled the room and Wise Thomas sagged back into his seat, his eyes closed.

Young Joe stifled a sob and quickly masked his emotions. Malsum and his offspring cast triumphant looks at the party. Without a word, the magician rose and nodded for his sons to follow.

Wise Thomas's eyes burned brightly. He held up his blood-soaked hand with the remaining four fingers and the inflamed stump.

"There are four more, wizard," he said, "and five more on the other hand. Sit down. You are not leaving yet!"

A sudden flash of cowardice united the Lenapes. Malsum merely shook his head in refusal and continued to exit the cabin with his sons. Wise Thomas arose from his chair like a wounded bear set for the kill.

"Let him go, Tom," Matt Parker said. He took his friend by the shoulders, blocking his path. "I can't allow any more."

Seeing his escape secured, Malsum allowed a faint sneer to curl his lips. His eyes gleamed with a bold scornful triumph at his defeated foe. The look yanked Will Keever out of his seat with rage.

"I'd reserve a seat in Hell could I have but two minutes at your throat, devil-man!" he ranted.

"Come morning I'm going to be hunting deer around your cabin," Zebediah said. "They say you can change into a Johnny buck at will. That's going to be my excuse if I find any of you around! You savvy?"

As Malsum's hand reached for the door latch, young Joe suddenly stepped in front of it, barring his way. With the pure hatred of a boy setting fire to his heart, the Seneca youngster held up a finger that wasn't even a good bite for a grown man.

"I would gamble for this," Joe said between his teeth. "Take my finger also, Toad Face! If you dare try!"

With a look of scorn, Malsum pushed him aside. "I do not want your finger, boy!" the Delaware snapped, opening the door.

Joe threw his back against it, slamming the door shut. Their eyes met, and the hatred became thick in the room.

"But I want yours!" the boy said.

Malsum found himself incapable of brazening his way past. Gathering his dignity and manner, he turned to face Wise Thomas and said, "You would allow this child to wager with me?"

Silently, the father and son looked at each other. At first

the concern and love of a father for a small son could be seen, but this look changed. Wise Thomas grasped that this was no longer a twelve-year-old boy playing at a game. This was a Seneca warrior! Perhaps the spirit of a returning chieftain from the legendary ages past? Young Joe's unwavering courage demanded that the Tall Tree allow the contest.

As the chieftain struggled with indecision, the voices of the friendly *pukwudjinnies* inaudibly filled the cabin. "Yes! Yes, Wise Thomas," they said.

With a look to Matt Parker and the other friends that warned them not to interfere, Wise Thomas nodded his head affirmatively in answer to Malsum's waiting question.

"Waughh! The boy cannot beat me! It is over, let me leave now! Accept your defeat!"

But Wise Thomas's confidence did not falter.

"Let us draw cards now, wizard," Joe Hawk said, and moved toward the table.

"Look, boy," Malsum demanded, throwing the grey blanket open and parting his garments beneath. Directly over the man's heart was an ugly patch of thick scar tissue. "Years ago a white man did this to me. The pieces of metal went into my heart, but I did not die! I possess strong magic—powerful gods protect me and obey my every command."

"Then why are you afraid?" Joe Hawk asked.

Without further excuse, Malsum returned to the table and sat down. His sons, worried looks on their savage faces, stood on either side of him.

"Tell me, lawman," Malsum said, "if the boy loses, will you allow me to chop his finger off?"

A look of revulsion came over Matt. He hesitated for what seemed too long, and then with a look of meaningful respect toward Wise Thomas, he apologized. "I'm sorry, Tom," he said, "but I just can't."

Again triumphant, the Lenape shaman rose to take his leave. Zeb Simpson's chair, sounding like wet chalk on a blackboard, scooted across the plank floor. He reared up like a wild animal.

"Sit down!" he said. "Joey loses, you get mine, you bastard!" Turning quickly on Parker, he fumed, "You keep out of this—I'm a grown man and used to having my own way!" Palms flat on the table, he surveyed Malsum, impatient for his reply.

"I agree," Malsum said stiffly, knowing he had no other choice. He pushed the cards to Zeb. "You go first, brave white man."

"Joey will do my gambling," Zebediah said, placing the deck in front of the boy.

A moment later Joe turned a card face up. The allies lost heart at sight of it. The bearded farmer swore loudly and slapped the table. The card was the four of hearts.

Malsum's sons laughed nervously, and Malsum, gloating with victory, reached for the deck.

"Wait your turn, witch-man!" Will Keever scolded, snapping up the deck. "I'm comin' in on this thing myself!"

Wise Thomas stirred in his chair, his pain-filled face softening, stoic features melting, betraying the sense of gratitude and proud fellowship that coursed through him. Eyes truly the windows of his soul shone out on his friends, thanking them for their kinship. White or not, these men had proved themselves as brothers.

Keever drew the five of diamonds and slammed it down, skidding it off the edge of the table. He folded his arms over his chest and mumbled something under his breath.

"And you, 'Jesus Man'?" Malsum confronted Nathan Banner. "Will you wager also?"

"A man does not follow in the light of the Lord by bargaining for the wages of sin," Nathan said. "Satan's hand lies heavy on this house. I will not affront my Creator by taking that hand in shake."

Taking this as cowardice, Malsum nodded, chuckling low in his throat. "What is your excuse, Lawman Parker?"

"I don't have one," Matt said tightly, drawing a card. "You may end up with three more fingers for that goddamn bag of yours."

Matt's card was the seven of spades.

"What shall I draw, young magician?" the sorcerer asked Joe.

"A deuce," Joe said confidently. "It waits for you."

Malsum's eyes narrowed in wonder and locked with the boy's. He shrugged and spread the cards elaborately before him. Each time his fingers chose a card he watched the boy for a reaction, moving on to another selection, seeing only young confidence. Finally, as his thumb touched a card near the end of the stack, a nervous flicker went across Joe's face. With a grin, Malsum plucked the card free and cupped it in his palm.

"Show it!" Keever ordered. Malsum's mouth opened in horror. Joe snatched it from the wizard's hands and tossed it to the table.

He had drawn the two of spades!

"One of you boys better go heat the knife up for your daddy," Will Keever taunted the sorcerer's two sons. They remained stone still, emotions masked.

"How you want it done, Lenape?" Zebediah asked. "One at a time? Or all three at once?"

"The boy called in evil spirits to help you win! I was cheated!"

"You don't have the notion this old boy wants to welch on our friendly wager, Will?"

"Hell, I hope not, Zeb," Will smirked. "Hate to kill a man over a few goddamn fingers!"

"Wise Thomas," Malsum begged, taking the chieftain's severed finger from his fetish bag. "Accept your loss in place of my wager? We will depart this very night as you have decreed . . ."

Wise Thomas sneered with disgust. He spat into the Indian's face and turned away.

Malsum held the grisly trophy out to the white men.

"What the hell are we supposed to do with that?" Zeb said. "Sew it back on Tom's hand?"

"Please . . ." Malsum said to Nathan Banner, "does not your god tell you to forgive, to show mercy? Plead my cause and I will allow you to submerge me and my sons in the river."

"Get ye away from me, Satan!" the parson roared. "The wrath of God has found thee guilty, and no man escapes the Day of Judgment! Nay, even the demons of Hades tremble at the mention!"

"You can keep your friggin' money!" Keever cursed as Malsum offered the men the bag of gold coins given to him for his land. "No man does a friend of mine like you done Tom and gets away with it—I wish it were your balls you lost!"

"If this is against the law," Simpson said to the sheriff, his steel blade gleaming in his clenched fist, "I'd take it kindly, Matt, if you removed yourself to the out-of-doors . . ."

"Authorities just might believe this to be a personal matter." Matt pursed his lips and rubbed his chin thoughtfully. "I'll have no part in the cutting," he said, "but I'll be damned if I'll give up my share of the watching."

Zeb accepted this with a nod. He took the cauterizing knife back to the stove and buried it deeply within the hot coals. He stood by, waiting for the metal to heat up. The way Malsum had sawed off Toms finger, Zeb was going to relish seeing the wizard lose three of his own. Small payment, indeed, for young Melissa's life. And Zeb was sure the Delawares had murdered her. The thought of letting the sorcerer bleed to death crossed his mind, but he knew Matt would never stand for it. He also knew that he could not murder a man in cold blood. Once he had killed a rough man in a tavern in a violent argument, but it was either the other fellow or him. It had been self-defense.

Bowing his head in resignation, Malsum waited quietly, as if he were accepting his fate. Tegagiche and Wenegawa fidgeted, eyeing the revolver in Matt's hand, as he made sure there was no trouble.

"You boys just keep your hands in plain sight and sit down," the lawman said quietly.

"Come on, Zeb!" Will shouted. "What's taking so long?"

Malsum opened the bag of coins and spilled the shiny double eagles onto the table. He knew that any glitter of gold attracted white eyes. All he needed was that one instant of distraction.

Faster than the eye could follow, a two-shot derringer appeared in his hand. The first slug tore through Matt Parker's left eye, and he tottered to the floor, clutching at his face. His pistol dropped to the planking. An instant later, Will Keever took a bullet. It passed through the fleshy part of his arm and lodged deep within his lung.

Wise Thomas's large hands grappled for Malsum, caught him, and dragged him over the table top. The sorcerer was only seconds away from having his neck broken when Wenegawa, with a whoop, plunged his blade deep into Wise Thomas's shoulder. The powerful man fought to retain his grip, but the strength ebbed from his huge muscles like water being squeezed from a sponge. It was all he could do to remain seated and upright in his chair. Malsum stayed sprawled on the table, feebly trying to raise his will above the pain in his neck and spine.

Joe screamed in rage and jumped on Wenegawa's back, clawing for his eyes like a young bobcat. Tegagiche and Zebediah were facing each other with knives. Each man waited for the opening that would mean death for the other. The eldest son's attack had been so swift that Zeb had only had time to withdraw the hot knife from the stove to fend him off with. Soon he had the other knife from his belt to his left hand, and he parried with it, worrying the Indian.

Will Keever grabbed Malsum's younger son by the topknot and slit his throat while he was busy with Joe. He went to help Zeb, but he was coughing blood and weakening fast. He picked up Matt's pistol, trying to aim it, but his vision was blurred, and he was afraid to shoot, for fear of hitting Zeb. Zeb was bleeding from long slices across his chest and arms. Tegagiche was a skilled knife fighter, and Zeb was wearing thin.

The parson shook his head fearfully as Will tried to hand him the pistol. Young Joe grabbed it and cocked the hammer. He fired at Tegagiche, but the bullet went wide. The shot distracted the Lenape, and that was all Zebediah needed. With a swooping thrust he speared the man in the groin with the hot knife. Tegagiche shrieked, his eyes rolling back in his head. He dropped the knife and clutched at the weapon. He shrieked again as Zeb came up in a gutting motion that opened him up to the breastbone.

"Goddamn you!" Zeb wept. "Goddamn you all to Hell!" He stared at Tegagiche, gagging on rising vomit in his throat. He spewed it over the floor. He took the .45 from Joe's hand and leveled it at Malsum's head. The wizard raised slowly from the table.

"My God!" Nathan Banner exclaimed, as he watched Zeb place the pistol to Malsum's temple. "You'll burn in Eternal Damnation! You'll burn in the fiery flames of Hell! Heathens! Pagans! Disciples of Death!"

Cursing, Zeb slammed the butt down on Malsum's skull as the sorcerer began singing his death song. Malsum slumped, unconscious, onto the oaken top.

Will Keever sat on the floor, trying to keep from drowning on his own blood. Wise Thomas sat staring, clinging to his small son's hand. Matt Parker was dead on the floor, his mouth frozen open in a ghoulish display of tobacco-stained teeth. The entire matter had lasted a mere thirty seconds; there were three men dead in the house and two more very close to death.

Parson Banner mustered some of his wits and knelt beside Matt, beginning to pray for his soul.

"You hypocrite sonuvabitch!" Zeb choked, pointing the

pistol at the man. "Get out of here before I kill you! Take your stinking God with you! You're welcome to him!"

Sammy Parker gawked at the door as Nathan hurried from the cabin.

"Is . . . Is my pa dead, Mr. Simpson?" The boy stared at his father's corpse. Ezekiel Simpson and Will, Jr. pushed past him.

"Get your ma, son . . ." Zebediah said, covering Matt with his coat.

Sammy turned and ran off, sobbing. Seneca townspeople appeared at the door and the boy forced his way through them.

"Nathan! What's happened?" Nettie Parker appeared, running to the cabin with Mary. Her son stood before her, crying, unable to speak as she embraced him to her bosom.

The gaunt preacher took the horse's reins in his hands. His son, Luke, crowded next to him in the wagon, his eyes wide and shocked.

"The Devil has reared his ugly countenance among us!" the parson said. "Your man has died an unholy death among heathen savages, just as my girl child before him!"

"Pa's dead, Ma!" Sammy finally blubbered, as Nathan Banner and his son sped off furiously into the wintery night. "Malsum killed him!"

Young Will held his father's hand as Zebediah wrapped him in a blanket to transport to a hospital. The man controlled his breathing, knowing it would be a long time before he got help. His lung was collapsed, but he was strong and rugged. He'd see it through. He wouldn't die and leave a wife and four small children.

Wise Thomas died in his bed from his wound after struggling for life for nearly six hours. His wife Beautiful Mary and young Joe were at his side. Joe Hawk received the gold medallion from his dying father.

Joe felt the hatred directed at him as he and the boy turned their footsteps for home. He searched the woods with his eyes until he saw Shaman. The animal stood rigid like a grey ghost in the trees, his large eyes cruel and cunning. Joe cursed under his breath and raised his rifle to fire, but the stag was incredibly swift and gone from view before the Seneca chieftain could take aim.

"Grandpa . . ." Tommy tugged at the man's sleeve as he lowered his rifle unfired, both of them hearing Shaman as he beat an escape through the forest. "His eyes . . . they looked strange."

Joe Hawk nodded solemnly. "It begins anew," he said with resignation. He thought of the damnable precognition he had inherited from his mother and shook his head. He knew now that Malsum was truly a fearsome wizard, and that his power transcended death itself.

The Seneca village was a gathering of cabins and houses not unlike those the whites lived in. Some were unsightly and poorly tended, or merely plain and simple, as the Hawk home, while still others were quite elaborate, with whitewashed wood or aluminum siding and shingled roofs, such as the Goodman residence. All of the homes were built alongside one another around a main clearing in the center, but this was the only uniformity to be found. In the middle of the clearing were two wooden longhouses made of stout logs. Their design had not changed much in over 300 years and, in all likelihood, never would. These were communal buildings, used for meetings and religious services by the tribe; it was here that the settlement residents and Indians from the outlying farms gathered after learning of Malsum's presence among them once again.

Inside the larger longhouse, James Goodman and other Seneca men whom Joe Hawk had sent out to fetch the corpse of the Delaware shaman stood speaking in low voices with their chieftain and other sachems. Malsum's corpse was stuffed rudely into a burlap potato sack. Old men seated on wooden benches told exaggerated stories to children, correcting each other and waiting impatiently to butt in with different tales of Malsum's infamy to thrill their youthful audience. The old men had been youngsters the night Wise Thomas had been murdered. Tempers flared briefly with each tale of witchcraft and crimes. Leathery faces with bleary eyes shed emotional tears as the sad past was made known to the newest generation of Seneca. Wise Thomas was a great hero to them all. Young eyes repeatedly turned to the blood-stained sack by the doorway. Groups of women discussed and questioned reasons, wondering at the cause for the shaman's return. Some argued that a true witch could easily transcend the barriers of life and death. There would be nightmares for the foolish as well as the wise when next they all slept.

James Goodman, one of the few Indians who had a telephone, called the authorities and notified them, and then went back to the longhouse to stand vigil with the others.

Sam Parker followed the coroner's tire ruts over the snow-covered road leading to the settlement. The police car, a new blue and white 1952 Nash, bottomed out over the worst dips, jostling the Police Chief roughly.

It had been several months since he had last seen Joe Hawk, and it was with a genuine warmth that he clasped the Seneca's hand. Sam, like Joe Hawk, was in his mid-60's and grey-haired. The lawman, while over six feet in height, was several inches shorter than the giant Seneca, and overweight, but Sam had a way of carrying himself that made him look any man's equal.

"The call came through that he was killed by a deer," Sam said. "Was it Shaman?"

"That is how it appears," Joe said truthfully, leading the friend inside.

The coroner and his attendant, dressed in white trousers and blue coats, began cutting the potato sacking open. Sam and Joe watched as they lifted Malsum's remains onto a clean-sheeted gurney.

"He really got it good," the lawman said glumly as the driver attendant raised the Lenape's blanket to view his crushed chest.

They listened as the coronor diagnosed the probable cause of death while the attendant wrote shorthand into a notebook. When the man took hold of Malsum's wrist, saying, "Three fingers missing from the right hand," Sam Parker's face lit up with amazement. "Let me see that," he said.

Before he could say anything more, Joe led him to a distant corner where they could converse privately.

"What happened to his hand?" Sam asked. "No deer did that to him."

"No, I did," Joe said flatly, and before Sam could ask why, the chieftain added, "It was so our fathers' spirits would not forever feel cheated."

"Malsum?" Sam said incredulously. "That's Malsum?"

"Yes. The same coward who murdered your father." The Indian's dark eyes blazed for an instant.

"My God!" Sam was visibly shaken. "How did he manage to stay alive all these years?"

"A witch does not pass from life while he feels a debt is still owed him, or an enemy escapes his vengeance," Joe said solemnly.

Sam shook his head, not really hearing the old friend's words. "I thought he died in prison years ago," he said.

For a long while Sam was silent in contemplation. After a while he lit a cigar and offered one to Joe. They smoked, filling the corner with thick clouds and the odor of sweet tobacco. They watched as Malsum's body, surrounded with a throng of noisy children, was wheeled outside to the coroner's van. Joe Hawk turned to his friend.

"Your doctors will want to cut him open," he said. "When they do, they will find out that Shaman did not kill him."

"What do you mean?" A worried expression came over the lawman. "Joe, you didn't murder him?"

"No, but I would have, had I found him alive."

"Who did murder him?"

Joe said he didn't know, but he was a poor liar, and years of intimate friendship betrayed him. Sam's eyes told the Indian that he saw beyond the denial.

"Either you can tell me, Joe, or I'll have to start an investigation on my own."

"It is better if the matter is dropped," Joe said. "Why should you care who killed that scum?"

"We've known each other all our lives, trusted each other with many things," Sam said. "I'm asking you as a friend."

Joe hesitated, and then nodded. He finally said, "Zebediah."

Sam felt ill. He stared at his cigar accusingly and set it down on a window sill, watching the smoke rise and drift through the late afternoon shafts of sunlight. He unearthed long-buried memories from his childhood, of a boy with his face pressed against a mother's bosom. Beyond the smoke, through the window of the longhouse, he could see Joe Hawk's cabin. It changed before his eyes. It appeared as it had that night he saw his father lying dead on Mary Hawk's kitchen floor. The memory was still painful.

"Why did he do it?" he asked.

"Malsum wanted him to," Joe said firmly. "He made

himself appear as Shaman so Zebediah would shoot him. I found a deer head near his body. He had cut an ear off."

"He wanted to die?"

"He wanted to shed his body. Do not forget what he was."

"I don't see how Zeb could mistake a . . . yeah, I do," Sam nodded. "I imagine he was drinking. Accidental homicide under the influence of alcohol is manslaughter. It carries a mandatory prison sentence in this state."

"You would arrest an adopted son?" Joe's eyes flashed dark and angry. He took on a haughty look and held his hands out toward Sam, wrists together, waiting for handcuffs.

"I confess," he said. "I killed him! I have been in prison and survived, I will again."

"Goddamn you, Joe," Sam slapped the Seneca's hands down. "I was only thinking out loud."

"Sometimes a lawman thinks out loud when his duty is not clear. Perhaps you do not believe Malsum arranged for his own death, as I do. But it is true! Our son is not a murderer—although he thinks he is, and is afraid of capture. Would you do a son injustice?"

"Hell," a drawn-out sigh escaped Parker's lips. "I'll see if I can get the coroner to waive the autopsy," he said.

"You hear Jenny's voice, as I do," Joe placed a rough hand on his old friend's shoulder. "There is honor in your decision."

"That family's had enough grief," Sam agreed, a sad note in his voice at the mention of Jenny Simpson's name. He picked up his cigar as it rolled off the window sill onto the floor. "I've got to quit smoking these things," he said with disgust.

James Goodman looked at the corpse for a final moment in the coroner's van. His nephew, Tommy Hawk, the son of his dead sister, stood at his side. Although James was a college-educated man, for years he had believed that the violent deaths of his sister and brother-in-law were not due to unfortunate circumstance, but the workings of some powerful curse, as were many of the other misfortunes to his friends that he had witnessed in his short thirty-two years.

As a religious leader, a Faithkeeper, he believed this. Evil had always resided alongside good and would continue to do so until Tarachiawagon decreed otherwise. James dreamt many visions, and the old ones of the Seneca said that one day he would be a prophet when his hair turned white and his heart became entirely pure.

The coroner's driver recognized James as an official and handed him a clipboard with a form on it. He also offered him a fountain pen.

"Someone has to sign, so that funeral arrangements can be made," he said. The man protested as James read the form and handed it back unsigned.

"I care not what you do with this filth," James said. "Incinerate it, bury it in a septic tank, or throw it in a sewer. He is of no concern to me or my people!" James had seen the painted symbols on Malsum's chest and stomach—the many names of long-forgotten demons. And although little, if any, discussion of Malsum's evil schemes had passed between the Faithkeeper and his leader, he knew in his heart that soon there would be a great conflict and a visitation of death and tragedy. Still, as a spiritual leader of the Cattaraugus Seneca, he would take whatever precautions against Malsum that he could.

The attendant shrugged at James's refusal to sign the form. He walked inside the longhouse and came out a few minutes later with Sam Parker's signature and another form, also signed by Sam, requesting a waiver of autopsy for religious reasons.

The children pelted the van with snowballs and derisive taunts as the vehicle drove away with the corpse of the Delaware wizard.

James Goodman and other Seneca men doused Malsum's cabin with kerosene. They had examined the old structure and found signs of Malsum's recent presence. Pine boughs had been wedged into the window openings, and empty food cans littered the floor, along with a firebrand circle used for calling demons and spirits. Malsum had moved his bowels twice in a corner, proof that he had spent at least two days there—time enough to conjure whatever foul magic he had intended.

Sure that every artifact and personal possession belonging to the sorcerer was inside the cabin, James soaked the beaten leather satchel he had found with kerosene, and flung it through the open doorway. Torches followed. Flames erupted, eating their way through the roof and walls. The Indians sat in the snow with crossed legs while James prayed and performed rites of exorcism, his fingers touching sacred wampum beads of white and black. All through the afternoon and into the night the cabin burned under the watchful eyes of the Seneca. Each man offered special prayers of devotion to the Great Spirit and asked him to undo any evil that the sorcerer had in mind. They sang praises and passed the wampum belt back and forth with reverent care.

The wind increased with nightfall, and the structure took on a ghostly appearance. At times the wind shifted, forcing them to step back quickly into the woods to escape the heat. Shrub and nearby trees caught fire, and they had to work to keep the fire from spreading. A forest fire in the dead of winter with wet snow on the ground was unlikely, but the loss of even one Seneca tree for the wizard's cabin was one tree too many. Some men saw demons and evil spirits lingering in the flickering shadows caused by the fire, but they scorned such fears, hurling loud insults at the imaginary deities being driven from their unholy sanctuary. James was proud of them all and told them so.

"*Niio!* So be it!" James spoke as the walls collapsed into a heap of ashes.

"*Niio!*" they all said with one voice.

For a while longer they stayed, and then they doused the embers that remained with large quantities of snow, and departed for home, hopeful that they had successfully thwarted whatever evil schemes the witch-man had conjured.

Their chants and prayers could still be heard on the night winds as Shaman skulked out of the surrounding forest and walked amid the burnt destruction of Malsum's cabin. A crude wooden table with a tree stump base continued to smolder. The deer lashed out with his hind legs and struck it, sending a colony of fiery sparks shooting off into the tops of the pines. He snorted loudly and then walked away through the ashes into the dark woods.

Chapter III

Pete Simpson stepped from his office in the Gowanda Bank and locked the door behind him. As he walked through the bank, his heels clicking on the marble floor, Sharon Evans, an attractive girl with a full bustline and hair the color of winter wheat, came up to him.

"Mr. Simpson, I need you to sign an approval for these loans before you leave," she said, handing him a small packet of forms.

Pete nodded, leaned the contracts against a square pillar, and began signing them. The girl watched him interestedly. He was dark blond, good-looking, with finely chiseled features and hypnotic blue eyes, twenty-nine, and still single.

The girl fidgeted for a moment and then said, "Some of us are going over to the Wagon Wheel tonight for a few drinks and a little square dancing—"

"That's nice," Pete cut her off, handing her the signed papers. He said good night and began to walk away.

"Excuse me, but would you like to go with us?" The girl's face suddenly colored with embarrassment. "I mean . . . you don't have to date me—I just thought you might enjoy going."

"I'm sorry, Miss Evans," Pete said, "but I really don't have the time."

The girl nodded, said good night, and watched him leave, with a wistful hurt in her brown eyes.

Joyce Foster, a woman teller in her early thirties, walked over with a polite I-told-you-so smile on her lips and handed the eighteen-year-old her coat. The two of them had purposely lingered. Sharon now insisted that she had been sure Pete would go with her, that she had caught him staring at her a number of times during her three months at the bank.

"Not so much at you, honey," the older woman said. "I think you must remind him of someone from a long time ago. You're wasting your time with Pete Simpson. He's the type who only gives his heart once."

"What do you mean?"

The woman shrugged. "Come on, let's go," she said. "I'll tell you about it on the way to the Wagon Wheel. It's a sad story, but you must promise me that you will never mention it to him."

Zeb made sure he was alone in the kitchen. The vodka was hidden at the back of the refrigerator shelf, behind two half-empty bottles of ketchup and a quart jar of mayonnaise. He crouched behind the open door and chug-a-lugged away at his hidden supply.

"What are you doing in the icebox?" Pearl asked, entering the room. "We're going to be eating supper as soon as Pete gets home."

After a moment's silence, Zeb straightened up with a pitcher to his lips.

"My stomach was acting up a little," he said. "I just wanted a drink of milk."

Pearl looked at him distastefully. "I wish you'd stop drinking from the pitcher like that. It's bad manners."

"Hell, you know me, Pearl," Zeb said. "Just a regular slob, I guess." He put the pitcher back and closed the refrigerator door.

Pearl stopped him as he pushed past her to go into the living room where the theme music of "The Cisco Kid" could be heard blaring out of the television set.

"Make supper," he said. "I'll go watch TV with Charlie."

"You've been mean and irritable all day long—is something bothering you?"

"If you really have to know, Pearl," Zeb said, "I think I'm starting my period."

"Come on," she laughed. "Really—what's wrong, honey?"

"Nothing. Shit! Can't a man be depressed if he wants to be?"

Pearl searched his troubled face for a moment and then shrugged. She went to the oven and checked her meat loaf.

Zeb winced and headed for the living room when he saw her going toward the refrigerator.

"Zeb!" Pearl's tone stopped him in his tracks. "What's this?"

Zeb looked innocently at the bottle in her hand. A slight smile tugged crookedly at the left corner of his mouth.

"Damned if I know, Red."

"Good," Pearl chirped. She unscrewed the cap and poured the contents of the vodka bottle down the kitchen sink. "Then you won't mind if I pour it out."

Zeb's face tightened with disapproval, but he said nothing.

"Damn you!" Pearl said suddenly, a rush of tears looming in her eyes. "Do you want to die before you're forty, like your father?"

"My stomach's okay now."

"It is not! The V.A. doctors told us you've got the liver of a sixty-year-old man!"

"What do they know! Nothin' but a bunch of runny-nosed interns!"

Pearl's eyes blinked two tears down her cheeks, and she wiped them away quickly with her arm. "You promised me!" she accused. "You gave me your word!"

"You had no right asking me for it!"

"Well, just who the Hell does, then?"

"Nobody!" Zeb yanked his coat from a hook by the kitchen door and donned it hurriedly.

"The dispatcher called earlier," Pearl said, a worried look coming over her face. "You have to plow roads tonight . . . if you're going out to get drunk—"

"I'm going out to the barn to butcher a friggin' deer. May I?"

With a condescending look, Pearl walked over to him and leaned her forehead against his chest. It was an old con of hers, one that usually worked when she wanted to stop an argument in mid-stride. She waited for Zeb to embrace her. After a bit they both laughed when he finally did.

"Honey, I don't want to lose you," Pearl said. "You're poisoning yourself with this stuff. Can't you at least slow down some?"

"I have," her husband said half-convincingly. "I've practically quit altogether."

Pearl raised her face to kiss him, and Zeb accommodated her. He felt her hips pressing tensely, making tight little circles that started a warm tingle below his stomach.

"Horny?" he chided, grinning sideways.

Pearl smiled tauntingly and kissed him full on the mouth again.

This time there was a sudden hardening in response to her hips. Zeb's hands went to her buttocks, and she accelerated her motions. She giggled into his mouth and pushed him away as his ardour reached the bedroom stage.

"How come you're not wearing a bra?" Zeb said indignantly when he saw his wife's nipples taut beneath the thin printed fabric of her housedress. His hands moved gently to her bosom. He slowly pushed her away to arm's length, continuing to caress her breasts as casually as if he were milking one of their cows.

"What are you doing?" Pearl laughed, shoving his hands away.

"Where's your bra, Pearl Ann?"

"I took it off—the strap broke."

"Then find a goddamn pin and get it back on! I don't want you walking around in front of my brother with your big tits poking through your dress!"

"Zeb, what's wrong with you?" Pearl asked, trying to hide her pleasure at having such attention. "Pete's lived here for seven years now. He doesn't notice things like that."

"Yeah? He's a man, isn't he?"

"He's never even as much as hinted he'd like to make a pass at me."

The housewife's face was now wreathed in smiles, finding herself unable to keep a straight expression.

"Well, let's not give him any excuses then," Zeb said, irritated with her carefree manner.

Not able to help herself, the woman laughed enjoyably. "I love you when you're jealous," she said, her eyes sparkling with affection. She snuggled up against him and kissed him on the throat; her hand brushed over his pants until she felt him bulging. She raised soft lips to his mouth and kissed him, delicious with desire.

"Want to go to bed early tonight?" she said, her voice husky.

While Pete offered a prayer of thanks at the supper

table, Zeb leaned back into his chair with a wry grin. He looked at Pearl and Chucky with their eyelids lowered solemnly, heads bowed in humble respect. Normally the daily scene irritated him, and he generally came to the table after "Father Simpson" had finished his benediction. Tonight, however, he was in good spirits and feeling prankish. He made little tapping noises on the edge of the yellow table top, hoping his son would sneak a peek so he could try a funny face and make him laugh. But, as always, Chucky disappointed him and remained reverent throughout the ordeal—Pete had trained him well.

While they prayed, Zeb shoveled a large portion of meat loaf into his mouth and purposely smacked his lips. Pearl punched him on the arm as the grace ended.

"What's that for?" Zeb laughed.

"You know what it's for!" the auburn-tressed lady said, picking up her fork to eat.

Zeb put his fork down and arranged his hands in a gesture of prayer. He looked at the ceiling overhead.

"I sure do want to thank you for this food—Lord!" His lips pushed outwardly in mock-Negro fashion as he emphasized the Creator's name. "Some of it I grew. And some I worked my ass off to earn the money to buy it with," he said. "And some I killed and slaughtered; but I thank you anyways—Lord!"

Chucky laughed as his father struck his chest with clenched fists in mock humility, blinking his eyes rapidly like a Holy Roller in a rapture. Pearl cuffed the boy on the top of his head and told him to get back to his dinner.

"Never you mind him," she said peevishly. "I don't see anything funny about making jest of our Savior."

"I was laughing at his face! I wasn't laughing over . . ."

"Don't backtalk, son," Pete said firmly. "Eat your dinner, like your mom said."

Zeb watched his son's face as it reddened. The boy pouted over his plate, toying with his food.

"Hey, Charlie," Zeb shook his small shoulder to get his attention. "Ever hear the sound a canary with a harelip makes?"

The son refused to look at his father. His chin wrinkled, and he pressed his mouth into a frown.

"Come on, Charlie—did you ever hear it?" Zeb felt

67

responsible for the boy's scolding, and he wanted to make amends.

"Why don't you leave me alone, Pa?"

Zeb stiffened for a moment. Then he shrugged and concentrated on eating his supper.

Pearl noticed her husband's silent withdrawal. He and her son were so very much alike, even if they didn't realize their similarities. "I'd like to hear it," she said, wanting to keep the peace. "If it's respectable."

Zeb looked at her rudely. "Hell, you know me, Pearl," he said through a mouthful of mashed potatoes, "I can't tell any 'respectable' jokes."

Pearl matched his hard eyes. She had only been trying to help.

"Sis, this meat loaf is wonderful," Pete complimented, as he saw all the signs of an upcoming argument. "You're really a great cook."

"Thank you."

"Freep, freep," Zeb said under his breath.

Pearl turned to him as he stabbed green beans with a fork.

"What did you say, honey?"

"I said your meat loaf's dry, you overcooked it."

"I know. I forgot and left it in the oven too long . . . sorry."

The full rich aroma of perked coffee filled the kitchen as the meal ended. Pete rose from his seat as his sister-in-law began clearing away the dinner dishes.

"Sit down and drink your coffee," Zeb said. "Pearl can handle the housework."

The man began gathering plates, ignoring his older brother.

"No, she'll miss her program," he said, sniffling, his cheeks flushed with a cold. "It's my fault we're eating so late."

"Zeb's right." Pearl whisked the plates from the man's hands and pushed him back into his seat. "Sit down and relax," she ordered.

"Roads bad outside? You're home later than usual." Zeb eyed his son, who was still picking at the food on his plate.

"I stopped off for a drink."

The older Simpson's face filled with pleasant surprise. "You're kidding! I thought you never touched the sauce."

"I'm trying to shake a cold. I had a couple shots of whiskey."

"You've got another cold?" Pearl asked, suddenly worried. She dried her hands at the sink with a striped dish towel and hurried over to him. "I've never seen a body that loves flus and colds the way yours does!" She felt his forehead and pressed her knuckles to his cheeks and neck. "You're getting a fever!" she said.

"It's only a sniffle, Sis," Pete protested. "Really, it isn't any—"

"Don't tell me it isn't anything, Peter Simpson. You had pneumonia when you were fourteen. A cold can be serious to a body that has a lowered resistance."

She crossed the kitchen with a chair in her hands and stood on it, opening a cupboard door and stretching up for the medicine on the top shelf. Her heels lifted out of her slippers, and her trim legs took on a shapely definition. Zeb watched her bust jiggle heavily as she stepped down to the floor with a tin of aspirin and a bottle of cough syrup. A dark look came over his face as he glimpsed a shadowy areola through a wet spot on the thin dress where water had splashed while she had been washing dishes. He continued to glower nastily as his wife ran a glass of water at the sink, grabbed a clean spoon, and administered tender loving care to her brother.

Pete washed the aspirins down obediently, with a slightly embarrassed look on his face. Then he opened his mouth, as Pearl waited with a cupped hand to dump a tablespoon of medicine down his throat.

"Whoops!" she laughed, as a drop landed on his chin. She wiped it off. "Maybe we can nip this one in the bud. What do you think?"

Pete smiled and shook his head as his sister-in-law's eyes sparkled merrily, waiting for an answer.

"I think so, Nurse Simpson," he said, soft affection in his eyes.

Chucky's fork rattled as he dropped it on his plate. He sighed, "Can I be excused, Uncle Pete?"

"What about those green beans, there, fella?"

Chucky frowned and picked up his fork again.

"Leave 'em, Charlie," Zeb said tightly. "Go watch television."

"That's okay, Pa . . . I can eat them."

Zeb's mood suddenly ripened. "I said leave them!"

He stood up and went to the kitchen door for his coat. Pearl stared at him wonderingly, trying to grasp the reason behind his anger. A glance to Pete only brought a shrug from him.

"Aren't you going to have a second cup of coffee?" she asked.

"Piss on the coffee!" Zeb said, buttoning his coat. "I've got to get back to my butchering so I can earn enough money to buy you a . . ." As the words died in his throat he directed his gaze at his son, still pushing green beans into his mouth. He cooled some, and said to his brother, "If you're not too sick, I could use a little help."

"In a while," Pete agreed. "Let me finish my coffee and change into some old clothes."

"Yeah." Zeb opened the door and a gust of cold air entered the house. "I wouldn't want you to hurry or ruin your fancy outfit on my account."

Pearl began to understand some of the reasons behind his mood. She looked at him apologetically. "Don't stay out too late," she said, as though he weren't angry with her. "Or you'll miss your goodnight kiss."

"I'll manage to take the disappointment somehow."

Zeb went out and closed the door firmly behind him. Pearl watched him through the kitchen window as he walked from the porch into the snow-covered yard and headed for the barn. With a scolding look she yanked Chucky's supper plate from in front of him and scraped it clean into a garbage bag.

"Go run your bathwater and hop into the tub or no television tonight." Her words sounded as though she had fired them from a machine gun.

"I wasn't done eating, Ma!"

"Get out of here, Charles—right now!"

Pete jerked his thumb toward the parlor doorway as the boy hesitated, and the youngest Simpson trounced out of the room without another word.

"Wish he'd mind me like that," Pearl said, an expression of resentful envy in her eyes.

"Most boys his age give their mothers a lot of trouble. I did. I gave Jenny a peck at times."

"What'd Zeb give her?" Pearl laughed. "A bushel?"

Pete chuckled and began picking up the leftovers, carrying them to the refrigerator.

"I thought you wanted to finish your coffee."

"I don't like seeing you on your feet this late, Sis."

Pearl's resistance ebbed away as he smiled softly at her, rolling his shirt sleeves up to take over the chore of scrubbing the frying pans.

"What's wrong with him?" Pearl asked, as Pete nudged her away and handed her a dish towel. "It's getting harder and harder to keep him in a decent frame of mind lately."

"I don't know, Sis . . . it's just his way. I guess my taking a hand in Chucky's upbringing riles him."

"Well, if he took the time to display and teach him some . . ." Pearl stifled the aggravated words. "God, I wish he would stop drinking!" she said. "He's such a sweetheart when he isn't pickling himself in alcohol."

"You know—the meat loaf really was lousy," Pete said with a grin as Pearl began to get misty.

"You stinker!" she laughed, slapping him on the shoulder. "You aren't supposed to tell me that."

William Bendix's round comical face filled the giant seventeen-inch television screen.

"What a revoltin' development this is!" Bendix groaned.

Pearl and Chucky laughed as Bendix wrinkled his face, about to cry. They sat on the couch together in their bathrobes. Pete sat in the large armchair, having changed out of his suit into dungarees and a flannel shirt.

"That man is hilarious!" Pearl said, a smile still lingering as a commercial for the new 1953 Chevrolet came on, with Dinah Shore singing.

See the U.S.A. in your Chevrolet,
America is asking you to call . . .

Pete rose from the chair with a loud groan.

"I guess I'll go out and help Zeb for a while," he said.

Chucky jumped up from the sofa and started to take the new chess set down from a shelf below a mirrored shadow box where it resided alongside Monopoly and Chinese checkers.

"Put it back, mister!" Pearl said. "No chess tonight; your uncle doesn't have the time."

"Why don't you have him a game?" Pete asked. "Chucky could teach you."

The boy opened the box up on the coffee table before his mother and began setting the pieces on the board.

"This is a king," he pointed out, "and this is a queen, and this is a bishop, you have two of those, and this is—"

"Pete?" Pearl called as he started to leave the room. "Will you ask Zeb to wake me up when he comes in if I'm asleep? There's something I want to . . . talk to him about."

The brother-in-law nodded, pretending not to see the mischievous glint to her eyes, and walked off.

"Now pay attention, Ma! This is a knight, there's two—"

"Oh, look at the little elephants! How cute! What do those do?"

Outside, it had begun snowing. A strong wind drove wet sheets of snow through the moonless, starless night. Pete tripped and ended up hands down in the yard as he searched for the two hidden porch steps. He brushed himself off, huddled into his overcoat, and pushed through the piled drifts to the lighted barn fifty yards away.

"It's really coming down out there!" he said as he entered the workshop area and shut the barn door behind him. He opened the inner door to the stalls and looked in on the three cows, seeing that they were bedded down comfortably for the night.

"I don't think you're going to get your car out of the driveway to go to work," he said, taking his overcoat off and standing before the old pot-bellied stove in the middle of the room to shake his chill.

"Tom Heller's on swing shift," Zeb said. "He'll plow me out before he goes home."

Pete hung his coat on a nail and stepped over to the four milk cans that Chucky and Zeb had filled earlier. He took them by the handles, one at a time, and carried them over by the yard door. Luke Banner's hired hand, a friendly Negro named Mathias, would be by early in the morning with Luke's pickup truck to get the milk and leave four empty cans. Luke owned a Carnation dairy farm down the road, over a hundred cows altogether, and every morning a milk truck stopped by for their product. They would not stop by the Simpson farm for a measly four cans, though, so Zeb sold his milk to Luke for eighteen cents a gallon, and Luke sold it to the Carnation people for twenty-nine cents a gallon. Luke Banner was the closest thing to a rich man in the community. Some resented him for that, and said he was unfair and a chiseler besides; but Pete simply regarded him as a shrewd business man and respected him. A man becoming a success was the American way of life.

"The cans were fine where they were," Zeb said from his butcher block table where he was slicing venison.

"I just thought I'd save some strain on Mathias."

"Save some strain on . . . You ever see that man carry two full cans out at a time and swing them up over the side of a truck? That darky's got more muscle than the two of us together."

"You butchering that doe you shot yesterday?"

"Been so long since you went hunting that you forget an animal has to hang a while to get the woods taste out?" Zeb motioned to the doe in a far corner as she hung head down from a rafter.

The remark wasn't as bad as the belittling look. Pete felt himself growing belligerent. Once he had been a hunter. A better one than Zeb would ever be!

"I suppose not," Pete said drily. "You forget that a nice fine goes with killing deer out of season?"

"Shit!" Zeb exclaimed, a rude look on his face. "You work a city job, and right away you're one of them. There's no such thing as 'deer season' to country folks. Deer's meat, and people eat meat year 'round, not just for six weeks!"

"Yeah, I guess that's why O'Neil raises and slaughters hogs, and Bill Johnson ships a hundred head of Angus every fall."

"Meaning what?"

"Meaning that they leave the deer population in these parts to you and the Keevers, I suppose. I mean . . ."

Pete went to the two white freezer chests against a wall and threw the lids open, a disgusted look coming over his face as he saw the dozens of white waxed paper-wrapped packages of venison filling them.

". . . the county would really suffer from a meat shortage if you three suddenly gave up poaching, wouldn't it?"

"I don't need any goddamn lectures from you!" Zeb's eyes went wild with anger. "I bust my ass to provide for my family. Up all day, and I'll be up all night plowing roads. You've got no right telling me that I'm stealing anything. Taking a few friggin' deer don't hurt nobody!"

"I know you work hard," Pete said, gesturing with

opened palms for his brother to calm down, a half-apologetic look on his face. "I'm not saying that—"

"You see this meat?" Zeb went to the freezers and picked up two huge packages, flung them back inside, and slammed the lids down.

"That's hard come by—tracking, sitting, freezing my nuts off all day to get one shot—and then busting my goddamn back bringing it home! Spending my night time out here butchering it, when I ought to be in bed studding Pearl."

Zeb's anger receded, and he looked at his younger brother stiffly.

"As man of this house, I've got a lot of jobs to do," he said. "Which ones would you like to help with?"

Pete stepped over to the butcher table with his blue eyes narrowed.

"How do you want this marked?" he asked, as he quickly and expertly wrapped a chunk of venison in waxed paper.

Zeb stared at his back helplessly, drained of his anger and resentment by the pressure-relieving outburst. He had gone too far by insinuating that Pete and Pearl—

"We used to really like each other once . . ." Zeb said.

He shuffled over and stood at his brother's side, wanting desperately to be friends with the man, but not knowing how to go about it.

"I guess Ma's passing on put a stop to that, though, didn't it?"

He waited for a reply, a gesture, a hint that there was even the slightest chance of talking things over man-to-man, but Pete stood as if he had turned to stone, his eyes shut with an effort to block out the sight and sound of him.

Zeb pulled a flask from his back pocket and gulped down a stinging mouthful.

"Have a drink," he said politely, extending the bottle. "It'll help you shake that cold. You know, Pearl's right about colds being dangerous for you. That pneumonia back when you were a kid could really cause you a lot of trouble. You want a drink?"

"No!"

"Yeah. I guess we're a couple of Cains and Abels, us two. I'm . . . I'm sorry I got on your case just then.

It's just that I'm worried about something . . . need some-one to talk to . . ."

"How do you want this marked?" Pete repeated, a grease pen clutched tightly in his hand.

The huge buck remained frozen in the beam of the spot-light as Jimmy Keever brought the tank-like Hudson to a skidding halt on the unplowed highway.

"Get that big mother, Johnny!" he hollered. "You miss him, I'll shoot you!"

The brother hoisted the Browning 12 Pump to his shoulder and leaned into the butt rest. He poked the barrel out the open passenger window.

Blam! Blam! Blam!

The three shots rent the stormy darkness, and the animal reared and collapsed in the snow on the narrow roadside clearing.

"You got him!" Jimmy squealed. "I think it's Shaman!"

"Hot damn! It's got to be him—look at those fucking antlers!"

The two brothers threw themselves from the vehicle and pushed through the waist-deep snow.

"Didn't I tell you it'd be worth our while to come out! Didn't I?" Johnny said, as they floundered toward their prize. They had taken to the major highway with tire chains and confidence that the four-year-old Hudson Hornet would be the only automobile on the road until it was opened by Zeb. Two hours of searching, but they had finally shot one—Shaman, no less!

Or was it?

"Sonuvabitch!" Johnny cried out as he shone his flash-light on the trembling whitetail buck. The animal stared back at the light with frightened red reflector eyes. It twitched as it dripped thick blood from its nostrils and bearded chin.

Jimmy winced at the sight. "Give me the goddamn shotgun!" He snatched the weapon angrily away from his brother. "Three frigging"—*Blam!*—"shots at close range and you only cripple the poor bastard!"

"What's the difference?"

"A lot of difference! You aim for the front shoulder or head when you want to kill something so it doesn't have to suffer. You never had a bullet burning inside of you. But I have!"

"Oh, fuck you, don't go starting your shittin' war tales on me again!"

"What are you doing?"

"I'm going to bust his antlers off so we can get him in the trunk."

"With your foot propped there?"

"Sure, I do it all the time."

"You'd better watch out for those—"

"Oww! Goddamn! Goddamn! Goddamn!"

A sharp tine sliced through the sole of Johnny Keever's thermal boot.

"Stop hopping around now, you dumb shit," Jimmy said. "Take your boot off, and let's have a look. You sure are stupid!"

Like a colossal armored monster the snowplow passed over the highway, spiralling cascades of soft white crystals high into the air and piling a wall of heavy snow and ice onto the road shoulder.

Zeb drove the vehicle recklessly, enjoying the sense of danger that he felt. He was doing forty-five m.p.h., and the steering wheel fought constantly to break his grip from the resisting drag of tons of snow. Driven snow pelted the windshield and the endless stretches of forests and fields on both sides of the road. He was a king, five feet above the earth on a mobile throne.

Zeb stopped his snowplow alongside the Keevers' black Hudson and rolled his window down. An amused look came over him as he saw the heavy tire chains on the small tank's back wheels and the deep ruts behind on the closed interstate highway.

"Hey, Jimmy boy!" Zeb tooted the horn for a moment, expecting to be confronted with either one or both of the Keever brothers' faces from inside the dark car any instant. But no one appeared.

He slipped into his coat and stepped down to the road, leaving the plow's motor running and the yellow cab roof beacon revolving and flashing.

"You in there, Tree Climber?" Zeb chuckled, rapping the door glass with gloved knuckles. It was an old name that John Keever didn't appreciate. Tom Hawk had given it to him in grade school when one of Luke Banner's old grandfather bulls had chased the two of them across a meadow.

Tom had outrun the bull as he had claimed he could. But Johnny had lost his nerve and climbed a tree.

Zeb opened the door and inspected the interior with his flashlight. Empty shotgun casings were on the front seat and floorboards. The thick pungent odor of blood told him that the Keevers had a deer in the trunk. The passenger door was wide open, and he crawled through. A spotlight mounted on the fender was aligned on the wood's edge. He flicked it on.

The beam ended on the gray-furred body of a large doe lying dead in the clearing.

"Damn fools, jacking deer on a major highway," he mumbled as he trudged toward the doe's carcass, shining his flashlight in front of him.

As he reached the dead animal he peered into the darkened woods.

"All right!" he said loudly, cupping his hands to his mouth. "This is the State Police! Come out of those woods with your hands up!"

He chuckled as he waited, visualizing Jim and John Keever hiding in the trees with their hearts in their throats.

"Come on, you assholes!" he called.

He looked at the tracks and belly rubs in the snow; at least five deer had been with the doe. Jim might have shot another (he wouldn't leave a wounded animal to suffer) and gone back into the woods after it. It seemed like a logical enough explanation. Often a deer ran a hundred yards or better with a killing shot in it; fact was, it happened more frequently that way than not.

The yellow beacon on the snowplow cast strange shadows over the snow and woods as it revolved. The light and howling wind combined began to spook Zeb as he stood by the carcass.

"You boys don't get out here," he hollered, "I'm going to swipe your doe and take her home!"

At first Zeb thought it was his imagination—the wind playing tricks on his ears—but then he heard it again.

"Help me . . . help me . . ." the voice pleaded softly.

"Jimmy? Is that you, Jimmy?"

Zeb shone the hand light toward the woods, but the beam stopped at an impenetrable boundary of white cedar and hemlock. A shiver coursed through his stomach and up his spinal column, making the hair on his neck prickle. From battle experience and instinct he turned the flashlight off as he approached the woods. Again the faint voice drifted on the wind.

". . . oh God . . . oh God . . ."

If this was a prank—!

John Keever's new Browning Pump lay in the snow. Zeb picked it up. A man wouldn't leave his shotgun in the snow like that for a prank. His mouth felt dry. He thrust a finger inside the bottom magazine and felt around: one in the chamber, fresh; none in the loader. Damn! He didn't know why, but he was frightened, scared to go into the woods. It was like being back in the islands, forehead itchy, worried over Jap snipers. Two balls of fears, one in the throat and one in the guts, swelled inside of him. He'd be in trouble if they widened and met in the middle.

Once in the woods Zeb wanted to call out for the Keevers, but his instinct warned him to remain quiet and cautious. It had saved his life many times during the war, and he listened to it now, reconnoitering. The black forest was ominous and thick with shadows. Even the ground snow didn't relieve the darkness for more than three or four feet in front of him. The trees stood bunched together in frozen gray, some only inches apart. Tangled brush and blackberry thickets hindered sight and progress. The blindness added to his fear. He wanted to stop and empty his aching bladder as it worsened.

But no, he thought, only two times when a man is really helpless: when he has his pants down around his ankles taking a crap or when he's holding his pecker in his hand. He tried to rout his fear. He thought to himself wryly, if an owl or pheasant flies up in my face, I'm going to piss my pants for sure!

At first he thought it was water dripping down onto his uncovered head from the tree under which he stood. Then it struck him that the temperature had to be well below freezing. He bit down on the fingers of his left glove, holding Keever's shotgun at ready, pulled the glove off and felt his head. Before he brought his hand away, several drops splashed over his knuckles. Uneasily, he crept aside, peered up into the blackness. As he strained his eyes, he saw a bulky mass in the branches above. It didn't move and could well have been a squirrel's nest or a clump of broken branches resting on lower ones. And then he smelled his hand, tasted it, and his heart sank.

Blood! It was blood that he tasted!

His fear soared and engulfed him. He dug the metal flashlight from his coat pocket and pointed the beam into the cedar.

"Oh! Goddamn!"

Ten feet above the ground, John Keever crouched, face down, in the bough of a branch with his dead arms dangling grotesquely from his shoulders. His eyes bulged and stared, face bloodied and slashed, frozen into a gaping lifeless expression of horror.

Simultaneous with the first beam of light, Zeb heard a loud grunting and snorting sound close to his left side. Jimmy Keever's voice screamed gutturally.

"You bastard! You bastard!"

Zeb whirled and pointed the beam of light in the direction of the sound. There on the ground, his eyes glowing red from the flashlight, sat the biggest, ugliest stag in the world, with Jimmy Keever impaled on the antlers!

"Kill him! Kill him!" the crazed, tortured friend shrieked.

He screamed with horrible pain as Shaman struggled to rise from his knees, shaking his massive forked rack of curved hooks, trying to dislodge his victim.

"Oh, God! Oh, Jesus! He's tearing my guts out!" the man sobbed.

For an instant Zeb was too frightened to react. He brought the shotgun up to his shoulder with shaking hands and squeezed off a shot at what he hoped was the stag's lower chest and legs. The firing pin fell on an expired shell. Panicked, Zeb slid the pump and tried again. It was empty.

The stag was on his feet now, snorting and puffing, moving awkwardly towards Zeb. Will Keever's grandson screamed terribly as Zeb grabbed at him, trying to wrench him free. Shaman kicked at the cowering rescuer with sharp hoofs and tried to reach him with his teeth. The deer's strength was amazing. There was a loud cracking of bone as Jimmy's spine snapped, and the man lost consciousness and fell silent.

"Jimmy! Jimmy!" Zeb cried.

With a sudden swiftness the stag detoured into the woods, his head forced to the snow by Keever's weight. Zeb made a grab for the animal's back legs, to throw him, but hoofs punched into his groin and thighs. He dropped

79

with a loud groan. He knelt, fighting the pain, and urinated helplessly through his trousers.

John was dead; Zeb could see that with his flashlight.

Go after Jimmy, save him! Zeb's mind begged.

No! Get out! Get out fast—now! He's dead You can't help him, another voice seemed to say.

Blind fear conquered, and he ran headlong for the highway. His arm hit a tree, and the flashlight spun off into the darkness. The arm hurt terribly, his thighs and groin hurt, but he ignored the pain and fled on.

He broke from the woods in an accelerated gimp and tried to maintain the pace through the waist-deep snow. He floundered and went down into a closing coffin of soft powder. It froze his face and filled his mouth, choking him, as he struggled up and rubbed it out of his eyes.

Shaman would get him! He'd get antlers through his back like Jimmy had!

He spun and faced the woods, crouched, expecting to see the stag's immense bulk nearby. He was alone. The revolving beacon called: hurry!

A loud horrifying undulant screech whistled loud to his ears, and it felt as if his heart had stopped.

This can't be! his mind cried, as he fought his way toward the plow, hearing the stag's crashing pursuit in the woods at his back. He's a deer! This can't be!

A second time he fell, this time over the carcass of the doe. But adrenaline enabled him to get to his feet and bolt forward with hardly a moment's loss.

"A-a-a-ae-e-eeeee-eough!" Shaman's whistling shriek assaulted the fleeing man's ears.

Zeb saw him as he sprang from the woods into the clearing.

Whump! Whump! Whump!

He bounded through the deep snow, pancaking on his belly. He was four times as fast as Zeb!

Malsum's stag slammed against the plow door the instant Zeb pulled it closed behind him. With nothing but a window between them, the demon stag glowered at his elusive victim with two fiery eyes from Hell. Zeb shoved the clutch in, slammed the shift into compound low, and the mechanical dinosaur rumbled forward. Shaman reared and smashed through the door glass with unbelievable power and fury.

"I'll get you!" Zeb yelled, sloping away on the seat. "I'll get you!"

He shifted to first as the murderous beast rammed the solid door maniacally with an unbelievable frenzy.

Utko! Nyok'eh-Utko!

Terrible noises, shrieks, screams, bellows, blared. Zeb, overwrought, envisioned a pantheon of ghoulish monsters and demons lending voice to the stag as he continued to batter the door. For thirty nerve-wracking seconds, Shaman ran alongside the snowplow with poised antlers and baleful hate-filled eyes. As the machine reached forty m.p.h., the deer slipped behind. Zeb watched him for what seemed like minutes in the broken door mirror.

Each time the flashing beacon on the cab roof struck his eyes they would glow brightly. Finally, they were gone.

Zeb opened his lunch pail on the seat and fumbled with the large thermos of coffee that Pearl had made for him. It was hot and scalded the roof of his mouth as he drank, but he didn't care. He had emptied half of the brew before he left home and refilled it with Kentucky bourbon.

The liquor settled his nerves, but not enough. It was gone all too soon. As shame and anger took hold of him, he kicked the dash radio into silence and murdered Frank Sinatra.

The plow was half on the sidewalk, parked haphazardly in front of Sam Parker's office in Brant as the freshly awakened lawman pulled up in front, headlights glaring through the large plate glass window. The town was still dead to the world, the softened grey of dawn unannounced and hidden in the east.

"Kiss my ass!" Zeb cried.

"I'm telling you to slow down on that stuff or I'll take it away!"

"Don't try it, sonny! Don't even think of trying it!"

Dave Barnes, Sam's twenty-two-year-old deputy, a tall, lean, likable kid with sandy hair cropped short, shook his head as Zeb glowered and raised the bottle of Four Roses to his lips again.

Sam stood on the sidewalk and stared at the crumpled mailbox. The plow blade had jumped the curb and knocked it over, sheering its moorings. The office door opened and Zeb weaved drunkenly before his eyes.

"What'd you hit the mailbox for?"

"Screw the mailbox!" Zeb answered meanly.

Sam pushed him aside roughly and went inside to his desk. Barnes nodded a brief hello and frowned.

"He was shouting and carrying on real bad when he came in, so I gave him that bottle you had stashed. I guess I shouldn't have."

"It's all right, son," Sam said.

"Yeah, it's all right, if he doesn't kill himself!" the deputy answered. "He's drank damn near an entire fifth in fifteen or twenty minutes! I don't know how he stays on his—"

"Experience, sonny." Zeb smiled good-naturedly, shuffling over. "Plain ol' experience!" His words were slurred.

"The state police called in yet with any news?"

"Not yet. They must not have found anything."

"Tell it to me again, Zeb, this time"—Sam backed away as the man's whiskey-laden breath blasted his face—"you take after your pa more and more as you get older!" He squeezed his nose shut and grimaced.

"You drink, you old fart!" Zeb defended himself.

"Maybe so, but not at five in the morning like you— it'd kill me."

The telephone rang and Barnes picked it up. His face went blank as he listened.

"Troopers?" Sam asked as the man hung up.

Barnes nodded. "Both the Keevers are dead," he said. "They just brought the bodies in . . . They want us to notify their next of kin."

Zeb sank down into a chair and lowered his face. All three were visibly affected. Brant was a small community, and the Keevers would be missed by all. Dave had dated their younger sister, Kathleen, two years before and had almost married her. He had liked her two hard-fisted brothers. They had been men, especially Jim.

Sam thought about having to tell Donna and the kids, and he saddened. They would be overcome with grief. It wouldn't be so bad with Johnny's wife; they had separated months before, and she had moved into Buffalo and taken up with an old boyfriend.

"I figured yesterday that it was just a freak accident when that old Indian got killed," Barnes said. "I guess it wasn't."

Sam's eyes were on Zeb as his face sobered with fright.

"What old Indian?" Zeb asked.

"Forget it," Sam said quickly. "It doesn't concern you."

Zeb wondered, seeing the stern look on the older man's face, but, even drunk, he knew when to leave well enough alone.

Pete jumped from his seat as the phone rang. It was 6 A.M., and he had just finished milking the three cows. His coffee spilled on the table as he bumped the cup reaching for the wall phone. He picked it up before it could sound a second time, hoping it hadn't awakened Pearl upstairs. The 7 A.M. waking hour had been pushed by him on the woman. She had begun to look haggard lately, and he had argued her into a new schedule. Chucky didn't have to be outside for the school bus until 8:30, so there really was no need for her to be up and about any sooner.

Pete whispered into the phone, "Hello?"

"Pete? This is Sam. Can you come into my office before you go to work? I've got some bad news."

"Zeb? Has something happened to—"

"No, no—I guess I made a bad choice of words, there. Zeb's okay, he's just a little drunk, and I won't let him drive. Goddamn it! Get out of my ear!" Sam said.

Pete could hear his brother close by, claiming that he was perfectly capable of taking himself home.

"I'll be right there," Pete said, relieved at knowing Zeb was safe. "Has he been arrested for drunk driving?"

"No, nothing like that . . . look, it's bad news. I'll tell you about . . ." Sam broke off to yell at Zeb again.

"All right, I'm leaving now, Sam."

"Yeah, I heard you. Be careful, son. The roads are pretty bad."

Sam placed the receiver back in the cradle on his desk and spun around, clamping a tight hand on Zeb's shoulder and forcing him into the seat he had abandoned against orders.

"How the hell do you expect me to talk on the phone with you jabbering away in my ear?" the lawman told him. "You can't even stand without falling. Now sit there until Pete comes, will you?"

"I don' wan' that pisspot takin' me home." Zeb's eyelids drooped sleepily. "I can drive," he said, getting up.

One of the state troopers now standing in the office with several farmers and townsmen blocked Zeb's path.

"Do like Sam says," the black-leather-jacketed man

warned. "You set one foot in that snowplow, I'll arrest you for drunk driving."

Zeb sneered at the man, blew air through his lips, and walked over to another state policeman assigning areas to armed men who had volunteered to hunt Shaman. Each man had a rifle or shotgun leaning against the wall. They were filling their faces with coffee and donuts while they listened to his instructions.

"We'll start tracking at the point where we found the bodies," the trooper said. "From there we'll branch out through the woods."

Len Pfeister, a thin small man with an eagle beak for a nose and beady brown eyes, looked unfavorably at Zeb. They had grown up together but never had liked each other. other.

"You sure it was Shaman, Simpson? I mean, he had an ear missing and all?"

"Goddamn right it was Shaman!" Zeb was suddenly angered. "I know what that frigger looks like better'n you!"

The state trooper eyed Zeb disapprovingly.

"If you'll let us go back to our business," he said tightly, "we might get out of here faster and after that killer animal."

"Shit!" Zeb laughed. "You won't get him—you won't even see him!"

"Why?" Pfeister said. "You might be a good hunter, but I'm a better shot." He nodded, and Zeb wanted to laugh at him. "I'll bring him down," he said cockily. "You can bank on it."

The little man's solemn expression was too much for him, and Zeb burst out laughing. He was like a little banty rooster.

"You couldn't hit the bowl if your pecker dragged the rim," Zeb groaned.

"You wanna get Shaman? You wait'll I get some sleep," Zeb said. "Or go see Joe Hawk. Now there's a man can get Shaman if—"

The trooper wrinkled his nose as Zeb hovered close by. He turned away. "You stink," he said. "Go sit down before I knock you down!"

A malicious grin broke on Zeb's face. He began hiking his shirt sleeves up.

"You're going to get knocked on your ass, like the man says!" Sam called from the other end of the office.

The trooper stood waiting, with his arms folded across his chest.

"I didn't pick this fight, Sam. You heard him—"

"Sit down, Mister! I'm telling you for the last time."

Zeb threw an awkward right, slow and wide. The trooper blocked it easily and tapped him on the point of the chin. It was more than Zeb could take in his drunken state. His legs buckled and the trooper had to grab him before he hit the floor. Sam hurried over and helped the man carry Zeb to the desk chair.

"I guess that's what he needed more than anything else," Sam said.

"It was," the trooper agreed. "The man is suffering from shock. He should be out of it when he wakes up. He sure is an ornery customer."

Sam covered Zeb with a heavy coat, showing sad concern for a moment. He walked back to the state police sergeant to continue their conversation. Len Pfeister stood by drinking his coffee, looking at Zeb with a satisfied grin on his face. It slipped away when he saw Sam's critical eyes surveying him.

The trooper sergeant said to Sam, "That deer's been sticking people for years now, but he's never killed before. What do you make of him?"

"*Nyok'eh-Utko*," Sam said.

"Now what the hell does that mean?"

"It's Seneca for 'witch-deer'; that's how he came by the name Shaman."

"My guess is he's in rut, and mean because he can't get a doe."

Sam shook his head. "I doubt that. We get plenty of big-eared fawns around here every spring. No, I think there's something more to this."

The sergeant waited for an explanation. The men had been friends for many years, throughout their careers. Sam was a professional. If he had any theories that would explain the animal's strange behavior, and help them to find it, the sergeant was more than willing to listen.

"The Seneca say a . . ." Sam smiled. "No more Indian words. They say a curse is upon the community. A powerful witch has . . ." He tried to be more casual about it. ". . . taken possession of Shaman's spirit with his own."

The sergeant's serious face was wreathed in a smile, and he chuckled.

"For crying out loud," he said, "I thought that kind of superstition died out years ago! Joe Hawk will put a stop to that kind of nonsense."

Sam looked at the sergeant sternly. "Joe Hawk is the one that told me."

"He is? Are you kidding me?"

There was a crazy sort of logic at hand. Joe had said Malsum returned to exact vengeance. Will Keever had killed one of Malsum's sons. And now the deer had killed Will Keever's grandsons.

"No, I'm not," Sam said, aggravated by the man's smirk.

"Judas, you act like you believe it yourself!"

Sam weighed his reply. What did this man know about the Seneca? Who was he to set himself up as a peer on the question of what could or couldn't be? As a boy, Sam had believed the Delaware an evil wizard, just as the Seneca believed. It was certainly a foul demon that killed his father so cold-bloodedly! Malsum had made berserk threats at his trial.

"Have you any proof that Indian magic and witchcraft doesn't exist?"

"No, I guess I don't." The sergeant made an excuse about having to talk to his men and walked off.

Sam felt like a jackass. The damned horror of the Keevers getting killed must have unnerved him. In all likelihood the sergeant was being more realistic than he was. Still, Joe Hawk was no fool. He reached in his shirt pocket for a cigar and went to his desk when he found that he was out. As he slid the drawer open and took one, he heard the sound of soft sobbing nearby.

Zeb sat in the chair with his hands over his face.

"I'm sorry, Jimmy," he whispered hoarsely, "I'm sorry."

The Four Roses bottle on the desk was empty. Zeb glowered at it. Suddenly he grabbed the bottle and, with a strangled curse, threw it across the room at the wall. The brown missile shattered into shrapnel that made the occupants duck and cover their faces.

"You crazy bastard!" the trooper who had hit Zeb

before yelled. He stalked over menacingly, reaching for a set of handcuffs on his belt.

All of a sudden Sam Parker was in front of him, taking hold of the man's leather jacket and twisting it. The trooper was stunned to see the angry look on Sam's face.

"This is my office," Sam said. "Leave him alone."

Zeb didn't move a muscle when Sam draped a comforting arm over his shoulder. "Take it easy, son," the grey-haired lawman coaxed. "Don't blame yourself over something that couldn't have been helped."

"You remember that time Jimmy got a face full of skunk pee when we were kids?" Zeb laughed loudly, eliciting a smile from Pete. "He took my dare and yanked that tom skunk outta his hole by the tail!"

Pete chuckled softly. "His pa wouldn't let him in the house for three days," he said, remembering. "He made him sleep in the barn."

Zeb's eyes brimmed with tears for the third time since Pete had put him in the Chevrolet to drive him home.

"I'm gonna miss that old boy," Zeb said. "He was begging me to help him . . . and I ran . . . I left him there to die!"

"There wasn't anything you could have done," Pete offered.

Zeb's mood turned ugly. "He wouldn't of run if it'd been me!" he said. "Maybe you'd of run—but not Jimmy! He had more balls than you'll ever have. Don't tell me there wasn't anything I could do! Just because you know you'd of run!"

"Lay off me, Zeb!" Pete warned. He was forced to brake hard as Zeb opened the car door. "What are you doing?"

"I gotta . . . I gotta throw up . . ."

Pete watched him, sitting on the seat with his head out the opened door and heaving his whiskey-filled stomach onto the road, poor miserable wretch that he was! If he weren't his brother he'd have liked to plant his heel on his back and shove him out—drive off and leave him. He couldn't, though, because Zeb was his brother. Some times, like now, he hated him more than others. He hated him for Jenny. For Nora. For acting more like Zeke every day. He hated him for Pearl, for hurting her, for abusing her—for having her! But still he tolerated him, and why, he didn't know, or at least wouldn't admit.

"Shut up now," Pete said, as Zeb closed the door and leaned back into the seat, sickly and green. "Don't say another word to me!"

It wasn't long before Zeb started in all over again. They argued violently, and were still arguing when Pete wheeled into the yard in front of the house.

"We could get that deer together if you'd help," Zeb ranted. "You got a natural talent when it comes to hunting and guns—"

Pete turned the motor off, got out, slammed the door, and headed for the porch steps.

"You chicken-shit punk!" Zeb called after him, struggling out of the seat.

Pete stood on the porch and glared back. Zeb could see him shaking with anger. Something inside Zeb said this is it, go on, push him over the edge! Get him to fight you and everything will be good again!

"You know," Zeb smirked, "she really was a good piece."

Pete's eyes flashed hatred. He began walking towards his brother.

"What are you two doing?"

Pearl was suddenly at the door, her hair in bobby pins, a pink chenille bathrobe with red roses and green leaves tied around her waist and held closed at the neck. Chucky's freckled face could be seen pressed against the kitchen window.

"Come on, pisspot!" Zeb goaded, seeing Pete's anger diminish. "Be a man for once in your life—come on!"

"You leave him be, Zeb!" Pearl yelled. "You leave him alone, or I'll take a broomstick to you!"

Pete spun around and walked angrily toward the house again.

"Where you goin'? To get your rifle?" Zeb laughed sarcastically. "Go 'head, I'll wait for you!"

Pearl moved aside to let Pete enter the house. She stepped out onto the porch and closed the door behind her, her eyes flashing green daggers at her husband.

"You refuse to leave that man in peace!" she said. "I swear to Jesus, sometimes I think I married a maniac!" She went inside.

Pete was just slipping into his suit pants when Pearl barged into his bedroom without knocking.

"I'm getting dressed, Pearl," he said belligerently. "Do you mind?"

"It's going to take more than your hairy legs to make me leave this room," she said. "What's going on between you and Zeb? How come he's home an hour early, without his car, and you haven't even left for work yet?"

"Go ask him!"

"Peter Simpson!" The scolding tone stunned her. Her eyes started to burn, and she had to fight to keep her voice from cracking. "I've done everything I could to keep this family together," she said, "and . . ."

Pete's anger melted away with reproach as he saw the tears brimming in Pearl's eyes.

"Maybe I'm a meddling kind of woman, but I can't go through any more of this hatred between you two!"

"I think it would be better if I took an apartment in town," Pete said.

"Well that's a real solution! You do that now!"

Pearl opened the bedroom door and turned back on him. "You be sure to come visit Chucky and me in Gowanda at the Insane Asylum," she said.

Pete stopped her as she attempted to leave. Before he knew it he was holding her in his arms, and she was returning his embrace warmly.

He wanted to hold her forever—to make time stand still and spend the rest of his life there in that room with Pearl tight against him. Somehow he managed to push her back at arm's length; he smiled.

"What are we having for supper tonight, Red?"

Pearl laughed softly, seeing the humor in his blue eyes.

"I was gonna make pork chops with scalloped potatoes; okay?"

"Chocolate cake for dessert?"

"Triple layer if you like."

For a moment they smiled at each other, warm love radiating from their faces. Pete kissed her on the forehead and finished buckling his belt.

"I never could resist one of your bribes," he said. "Now go make that husband of yours yell uncle, and let me finish getting dressed."

"No more moving-out thoughts?"

"No, no more moving-out thoughts. You just don't want to lose a good dishwasher, that's all!"

Pete crunched through the snow in the yard. He had left Pearl and Zeb sitting at the table talking, with nothing more than a glance at his sister-in-law to bid her goodbye. His mind turned to the Keevers and Shaman as he reached his auto. He wouldn't get much work done today.

"Goodbye, Uncle Pete!" Chucky yelled from the road, where he waited to catch the school bus. The back of his coat was white with snow from sliding down the raised lawn bank. Brant was a few miles out of the way, but Pete needed the comfort of a friendly face.

He walked over to the edge of the yard and smiled down at the boy, eight or ten feet below. Their farm had been built on a gradual sloping hill, and Genessee Road had worn deep with erosion over the years it had remained unpaved.

"You want a ride to school?" Pete asked.

"You bet!"

Pete had to laugh, as Chucky tried in vain to climb back up the steep embankment. He spread his feet on the slope, planted them solidly, and stretched out a hand. After a few tries the boy made it up far enough to grab hold, and his uncle pulled him up the rest of the way.

"It's a lot easier getting down than it is getting up, isn't it?"

"You can say that again!" Chucky panted. "Do I get to steer?"

Zeb watched from the kitchen window as Chucky, seated in Pete's lap, turned the car around in the plowed yard. His small hands gripped the steering wheel as he maneuvered the vehicle expertly along the 200-yard-long driveway to the road. The close, warm relationship between his son and brother made him envious. Pete was the apple in that boy's eye, and he didn't mind letting it be known, either.

"Drink this," Pearl commanded, pushing another cup of black coffee in front of him.

"I don't want any more." Zeb pushed her hand aside, walked over to the cupboard, and took out a bottle of Wild Turkey. It had been a present from Sam the Christmas past and was covered with a fine coating of dust. It was the only bottle he didn't have to hide from his wife, being a gift and all. It was expensive and prized—but it was all he had at the moment, and he needed a drink.

"I thought that was for special occasions," Pearl said.

"Well, this is one, wouldn't you say?"

Pearl eyed him angrily, not knowing what he was talking about. He filled a water glass to the top with whiskey. His lips twisted into a sneer at the sight of her disapproving stare.

"Don't give me that God's-gonna-punish-you look!" he snarled. "I ain't never stopped drinking, and I never intend to—just let you think that so you wouldn't keep your ass in an uproar! I've been drinking friggin' vodka, so you wouldn't smell booze on my breath, for so long my teeth are aching—I don't like vodka!" Zeb tapped the opened bottle of Wild Turkey for emphasis. "I like whiskey! And this is real liver-loving stuff! So—tough shit, Pearl!"

"That's up to you, I guess, if you want to kill yourself," Pearl said calmly. "But just leave your brother alone when you drink. I'm fed up with your mean streaks. One of these days you're going to push Pete too far, and he's going to beat the living tar out of you!"

"Ha!" Zeb sneered, "that pantywaist couldn't fight his way out of your bloomers." He sneered meanly as he drank. "I'll bet he wouldn't have to fight his way *in*, though, would he?"

"You're not funny with that filthy mouth of yours! Why don't you drink your liquor and shut up!"

"Maybe you ought to stop mothering him so much and give him a little. It might make a man out of him."

"Maybe I ought to!" Pearl said. "It would serve you right. He's more of a husband and father in this house than you'll ever be capable of being!"

Zeb lowered his eyes from his wife's hot glare and felt the hurt rising inside. He drank his whiskey and began to pour more.

"You'd be a lot better off with Pete for a friend than that no-good Jimmy Keever and those other drunken bum friends of yours up at the Sportsman's Bar," said Pearl, knowing she had the edge now.

Zeb stopped pouring, looked at his wife unbelievingly. He was seeing a new woman—a cold, cruel woman! Jimmy Keever was dead and lying on a slab in the morgue this very minute and she was talking about him like that?

"Am I going to Hell, Pearl?" Zeb heard himself ask.

"Let's not get started on that today." Pearl started to leave the kitchen and Zeb clamped a strong grip on her wrist.

"I've got beds to make!" she snapped.

"Jenny Ma always told Zeke he'd go to Hell if he didn't mend his ways—tried to get the mean buzzard to take Communion before he died. He's in Hell, I guess—and she's in Heaven . . ." A grin broke out on Zeb's sad face. "What do you think? I wonder if that's grounds for divorce there?"

"Let me go!" Pearl said, prying his fingers away, "I haven't got time for your drunken nonsense!"

"Jimmy Keever going to Hell?" Zeb asked, as Pearl took her coffee and started upstairs. "Jimmy and Johnny Keever going to Hell?"

"As soon as their livers go! And you not far behind them!" Pearl yelled.

"Well, praise the Lord," Zeb said as a tear slid down his cheek and seeped into the corner of his mouth, warm and salty.

He shuffled over to the table as he heard Pearl reach their bedroom and slam the door. Alone, he sat down with his whiskey.

"Well, praise the Lord," he repeated, "Old Satan's got some more logs for his fire." He swallowed the smooth Wild Turkey, ignoring the growing pain in his stomach.

Pearl hung up the telephone and started to cry. All she could think of were those poor wives and children, and how they would never see their men again. She shuddered to think how close she had come to being one of them herself. Sam had called to check on Zeb and had told her what had happened. It was noon, and she was just now finding out. All morning she had remained fuming mad, working like an insane woman around the house. No radio on; no television on. Sam had asked her to try to understand how Zeb was feeling; to forgive Zeb his drinking and meanness this one time, as a favor to him if for no other reason. Men! Sam sounded like he had been drinking also. Maybe a little—he was on duty.

Zeb was sleeping on top of the covers when Pearl walked into the bedroom. She'd had a terrible time making him go upstairs earlier. He had thrown up all over the kitchen floor and himself. Pearl set the basin of warm water and towels down on the bureau and began unlacing her husband's leather hunting boots. His feet were sweaty inside double socks and smelled terrible. He was a factory of foul smells: whiskey, vomit, urine. Urine? Yes, she saw the dried stain on his jeans.

Zeb grumbled something in his sleep as she stripped him down naked and began sponge bathing him. She hoped he wasn't dreaming about the war again, or about Jimmy and Johnny Keever and last night. She hurried with the washing and toweled him down. She didn't want him to catch cold.

As she exerted her strength to get the covers out from under him, he woke up quietly. Pearl smiled and sat down on the bed, taking his hand.

"I scrubbed you down some. You feel better?"

Zeb nodded, seeing her eyes brimming with tears. Her eyelashes wet and stuck together as she blinked.

"Why didn't you tell me?" she asked politely.

"I give you enough grief as it is."

"I said such terrible things about those poor men."

"I don't think they'll mind . . . Jimmy looked right at me. I keep wondering if he knew it was me in the woods with him."

"Honey . . . I don't know what I'd do if I ever lost you. I feel sad for the Keevers. But I thank God in Heaven that He gave you the wisdom to run and save your life."

Zeb kissed the palm of her hand as she began smoothing his hair on his forehead. Pearl watched as he closed his eyes with pain, deep shame overwhelming him.

"They were going to cut me up in little pieces like they . . ." Zeb's voice broke. He choked hoarsely. "He fought the Japs and kept me from bleeding to death, Pearl," he said. "He didn't run! And look now how I've paid him back . . ."

Pearl slipped under the covers and held him as he wept. She pressed a tender cheek against his pinching whiskers and stayed brave for him.

"Go to sleep, sweetheart," she urged, "You'll feel better when you wake up."

Chapter IV

Shaman knew that the woods were full of men searching for him. The hunters had already killed a number of bucks and does. Even a yearling fawn, with the spots barely faded from his back, had been shot. It had taken Shaman the better part of the morning and afternoon to elude their trap, but now he was free of their tightening encirclement, resting in an apple orchard. Hungry, he pawed dried and rotten apples from beneath the snow and ate them.

From the edge of the orchard he looked out on the Simpson barn and farmhouse. He caught the scent of the cows and immediately knew whose home it was. His old adversary had often hung his coat in the barn to disguise his scent with that of the cows the night before he went hunting. And Shaman had known that familiar smell for many years now. As he felt the mysterious forces at play in his mind, he became the hunter instead of the hunted.

Bounding the distance of the cow pasture, the deer jumped over the wooden picket fence of the Simpson cemetery alongside the barn, and lay down to wait behind Jenny Simpson's headstone.

The orange school bus paused in front of the steep bank leading up to Chucky's yard and let the boy off. Some of the children in the half-empty bus waved goodbyes to him while they bounced around in their seats. Mark Banner stuck his tongue out and extended his index and little fingers.

The children on the bus laughed with glee when Chucky set his books down, made a snowball, and threw it at Mark's window. The snow crunched through the window before Mark could close it entirely and showered his face with wet, stinging slush.

"You stupid prick!" Mark was quick to open the window again and yell, closing it still quicker as another snowball almost caught him.

The bus pulled away with the children laughing and pointing their fingers at the beefy, yellow-haired youngster. Even the driver turned to young Tommy Hawk and winked his eye.

"One of these days that little Banner snot is going to get his block knocked off," he said, "and I wouldn't want to miss it for the world!" And then, hearing the Banner bully giving Mike Pfeister and Donny O'Neil a hard time for laughing at him, he added, "I hope the rich little bum gets his teeth knocked out."

"Charles! Don't slam that door, I have a cake in the—"

Pearl looked at her rosy-cheeked son disapprovingly as the kitchen door swung shut with a loud bang.

"Hey, Ma," the boy cried as he kicked his boots and shoes off together, his small freckled face excited. "Shaman killed the Keevers, and—"

"I know all about it, young man," Pearl said, opening the oven door with a pot holder and thankfully noting that her cakes were still rising.

"He chased Pa, too, and almost got him!"

"I said I know! Would you please keep your voice down? Your father's sleeping, he doesn't feel well."

Chucky looked at the empty bottle of Wild Turkey on the sink counter.

"You mean he's drunk, don't you?"

"Mind your tongue, you little snip." Pearl's eyes scolded him.

"Everybody in the county's out hunting Shaman now. Even Joe Hawk and the Seneca are looking for him." Chucky hurried out of his coat and greedily eyed the chocolate-frosted cupcakes on the kitchen table.

"That's good," Pearl said. "If the Seneca are hunting that terrible beast, then they'll get him."

"I don't think so, Ma. At least it won't be easy. Can I have a cupcake?"

"You can have one. Then you get out to the barn and see to those cows. . . . Why don't you think the Indians will get him?"

"Tommy says an evil wizard is inside Shaman, and he's going to try and kill all of us. That means he's as smart as a man now."

Pearl looked at her son munching casually on his cupcake as she placed a glass of milk in front of him.

"What in God's name are you talking about?"

"It's true." The boy nodded. "The wizard that Pa's grandpa sent to prison came back to get all of us because old Zebediah killed his son."

"That's ignorant talk, Charles—you don't really believe that."

"Why not?" Chucky shrugged. "I believe in the Devil, don't you?"

Pearl slapped his hand as he reached for another cupcake.

"Don't you ever let me hear you talking like a heathen again!" She pointed a stiff finger in his face, and added quickly in a hushed voice as she heard her husband coming down the stairs, "You mention one word of that foolishness to your father, I'll have blisters and welts on your little fanny before you even know what hit you!"

"Hello, Charlie." Zeb yawned, his bloodshot eyes blinking from the sunlight pouring into the room through the window. "Stopped snowing. Looks like we'll be done with storms for a while."

Pearl smiled at him nicely as he stood there in his striped boxer shorts, his chest hairy, the muscles on his arms and back rippling smoothly as he stretched and yawned.

"You have a nice sleep?" she asked, blushing a little as she noticed her son staring at his father's penis poking through the front slit in his shorts.

Without a word, she walked up to Zeb and, while kissing him hello, reached down, hidden from Chucky's view, and pushed him back inside, with a pinch for good measure.

"Shameless," she said as he winced and rubbed himself vigorously. "Go get your pants on before I go for my scissors."

"Be the best thing you ever lost," Zeb said, winking at her.

"Chucky, would you go get your father a pair of jeans from his drawer?"

"Yes, Ma'am."

Chucky went upstairs, embarrassed and glad to have an excuse to leave the room. He grinned to himself, knowing that his ma must have pinched him good to make his pa rub himself so hard!

"Get away from me, you nut!" Pearl laughed as Zeb tried to take her in his arms, a playful look on his face. "Stop it! Stop it!" she whispered as he laughed, and fondled her under her dress.

Chucky stood in his parents' bedroom at the top of the stairs and listened to his mother laughing and saying, "Ouch! Stop it, damn you!" and his father laughing along with her. Then they were silent, and he knew his pa was kissing his ma, and that she was letting him. Maybe even kissing him back and liking it. He took the dungarees from the bureau drawer and descended the stairs quietly, careful not to walk on the steps that creaked. Four steps down, where the kitchen ceiling met the stairway wall, there was a small crack where he could spy on them. It was as he figured, his pa had his ma pressed up against the kitchen counter, and he was kissing her hard on the mouth, rubbing and squeezing her full breasts with one of his strong hands.

Once he had peeped through the keyhole in the bathroom door when his mother was getting out of the tub, and he had seen her titties. They were big and creamy white with pretty pink rosebuds. He'd never seen anything so beautiful! Until that moment he'd always supposed they were no different than cow teats. Nora Cleary, his fifth grade school teacher, had a big bosom also, but he took pride in the fact that his ma's was bigger. All in all, Pearl Ann Simpson had to be the most beautiful woman in the world, he reasoned. When he grew up he'd marry a girl with big tits, but he'd make sure she had rosy pink nipples on them first! Not brown ones, like Tommy Hawk said his aunt had. He had seen her nursing his baby cousin once, and had scoffed at Chucky's vivid description, shaking his head and saying Chucky must be color-blind. The heck he was! Maybe Indians had brown titties, but white people didn't.

"That's enough," Pearl said huskily. "Your son's going to be coming down any second now, and I've got dinner to start. Now stop it!" she scolded, pushing him away and straightening her dress.

97

Zeb looked at her flushed face and grinned. "You think I can get my pants on over this?"

Pearl saw his condition and burst into laughter, heading for the stairs. She saw Chucky standing, with a guilty look on his face, halfway down.

"I . . . I was just coming down, Ma," Chucky squeaked.

"Well, okay," she said, her pretty face wreathed in smiles, "come on down then." Chucky walked toward her with his father's trousers in his hands.

"On second thought," Pearl said, "maybe you'd better throw me the jeans and hold up a minute." She could hear Zeb running the water in the sink and laughed until she thought she'd burst.

"What happened to this?" Zeb held up the empty Wild Turkey bottle and waited for an answer.

"I don't know," Pearl said innocently, as she frosted a triple-layer chocolate cake. A knowing smile betrayed her, "You must have drunk it all, honey."

"Drunk it all, hell! You pour my booze down the sink again? Do you have any idea what this one bottle cost?"

Pearl's eyes sparkled merrily. "Take another cupcake, Charles, and go see to the cows."

Chucky pulled his shoes out of his boots and untied them, knowing he'd get yelled at if he tried to slip into them. Pearl scolded him constantly for breaking the backs down. It was a careless habit with the child.

"Wait a minute, Charlie." Zeb began stacking cupcakes from a platter on the table into the boy's hands as he finished dressing for outside.

"You give those back!" Pearl tried to rescue the baked goods, but Zeb held her at bay.

"Hurry up, son!" Zeb laughed. "Run out before she gets you!"

As they fought, the plate of cupcakes was knocked from the table and several turned frosting side down and stuck to the linoleum.

"What you making your frosting with these days, Pearl Ann?" Zeb teased his wife as she had to tip them to break the suction. "Horseglue?"

Suddenly Pearl let him have it, and she and Chucky were the ones laughing. Zeb blinked at her peevishly through chocolate-covered eyes, scraping cake and frosting from his face with the edges of his hands.

"You bitch," he groaned.

"Watch your mouth!" Pearl laughed, and mashed another ruined cupcake against his hairy chest, grinding it in mercilessly.

She and Chucky doubled up.

"So you think it's funny," Zeb said. An irate Marx Brother, he snatched two cupcakes from his son's undamaged reserve.

Pearl backed up the bedroom stairs, laughing and screaming for him to stay away from her—that she didn't have another dress to put on.

"Guess where these are going, Red?" Zeb grinned.

"You wouldn't dare!"

"You'd better hope they don't fit!"

Pearl screamed and ran up the stairs with Zeb hot on her heels. Chucky heard the bedroom door slam and his mother's giggling shriek as his father forced it open before she could lock it.

"No! Be nice, honey—I'll clean it off you, okay?"

Chucky heard his father guffaw. Then came mingled laughter and a ruckus. Suddenly his ma shrieked again, and their laughter died to a silence.

"Oh, you lousy rat . . ." Pearl groaned. "Don't you try smooching me! Look what you've done to my . . ." Silence resumed.

They were probably kissing again.

Chucky walked into the living room and set his armload of treats down on the scarred mahogany coffee table. He strained to hear if any more sounds were coming from above the ceiling, but there weren't any. Sometimes grown-ups were worse than kids, he mused wryly, and bit into a cupcake.

The television had just warmed up with the images of Phineas T. Bluster, Dilly Dally and Clarabelle the clown when Chucky heard his mother's voice from the head of the stairs.

"Charles," she called, "I left the oven on. Would you turn it off for me, please?"

"Yes, Ma'am," Chucky answered.

"Thank you, honey. . . . Are you going out to do the milking now?"

"Will you hold still, Thelma!" Chucky scolded her, as the Guernsey fidgeted in her stall, almost stepping on his feet. "What's wrong with you gals?"

The three cows were skittish. Their black and white hides jiggled and twitched. Angela swished her tufted tail onto her back, as if shooing flies; only it was winter, and there were none of the bothersome insects around. Finally the young farmhand got four of the rubber connections on Thelma's teats, and the machine began sucking her milk out. The cow settled down some, feeling the welcome release of pressure in her udder. She wasn't showing yet, but Uncle Pete had matched her up with one of Luke Banner's prize bulls, and she was due to calf in the spring. His pa had said he could go to watch the screwing, but his ma had insisted she didn't want him seeing things like that yet. Uncle Pete had agreed with her and said there'd be time enough when he was older.

Chucky patted and rubbed Thelma's stomach affectionately, knowing there was a baby calf growing inside. At least he was going to be in on the birthing, his ma had promised—and that was probably a lot better than watching any old screwing!

A sudden gush of cold air entered the barn and Chucky stopped pitching hay into Margie's trough to see if his pa had come in to help him, as he usually did. Angela, the jittery three-year-old, kicked at her stall and began making a terrific ruckus, mooing for all she was worth. Chucky saw *him* as he walked warily toward the stalls. He was huge and ugly, with jagged scars on his coat, a black band around his muzzle, grey cheeks, and black skullcap. One of his eleven-inch ears was missing halfway down. Shaman saw him and stamped his feet loudly on the cement floor, snorting through his nose. As he lowered his massive antlers, Chucky inched his way into Margie's stall. Shaman's antlers were different from a whitetail's—they divided into two main beams, thrusting outward, terrifying in appearance. The boy's heart thumped loudly in his ears, and his mouth drained of saliva as the stag tried to squeeze into the stall after him. Margie retreated until her haunches were against the barn wall. She shook her head menacingly, with its sawed-off horns, and pawed the straw bedding, causing Shaman to stand and leer at her. With wicked yellowish eyes, the king deer steadied his murderous gaze on the boy.

"Pa!" Chucky screeched. "Pa!" But he knew it was no good—the house was too far away, and his father was upstairs in his bedroom, no doubt. "Get out of here," Chucky screamed at the deer. "Leave me alone!"

The stag lowered his tremendous rack close to the floor and bunched his powerful muscles to spring. Chucky held the triple-tined pitchfork in front of him to meet the charge. It was a pathetic weapon compared to the deer's head of sharp knives. The cows were going crazy, and the boy realized that it wasn't only Shaman he had to worry about. Margie, perhaps intending to protect him, began crushing him against the cinder block wall that separated her stall from Thelma's. Chucky had to drop the pitchfork and climb over the four foot wall before she mashed him with her bulk. The deer made a coughing-grunting noise in his blood-swollen throat and went after the boy.

All at once Thelma attacked the intruder and forced him away. The stainless steel milking canister tipped over and dragged behind. The connections ripped loose from her udder as she wrenched the extension cord apart. Chucky's blood froze as Shaman let out a barrage of horrible bellows and shrieks. The stag slashed and tore the old cow's throat and chest as she continued to back him away to the rear of the barn, trying to clamp her flat teeth on the scruff of the deer's neck. He punished her, but she took it bravely. Chucky jumped from the wall and ran, afraid for his life. Shaman, seeing the boy attempting to escape, suddenly outmaneuvered the cow and raced after him. Thelma stayed hot on his tail. She bawled with rage, as if the boy were her own baby.

"Pa! Pa!" Chucky screamed as he ran towards the front porch of the house.

Shaman caught up to him and tried to snare him with his antlers, but the boy dodged effectively. The lumbering cow moved between them, her spotted coat bristling over her shoulders. Each time the demon stag made a lunge at the boy, the old cow was there to intercept him.

The snow at the side of the porch was waist-deep and Chucky had to flounder through it, as the two battling animals had the steps blocked. He grasped the wooden railing and swung his body under, clambering to his feet on the swept boardwalk. Shaman tried to leap the railing but fell backwards as Thelma bit into his haunches. With an incredible surge of fury the deer spun and gored the cow, knocking her over on her side to wallow helplessly in the snow. She bawled loudly, expecting sharp antlers to pierce her soft underbelly at any moment. Amazingly, the stag ignored his advantage and leapt onto the porch, collapsing the wooden railing and pursuing the boy, who was just now slamming the kitchen door shut with a scream for his father.

Zeb tore down the stairs, pulling on his pants as he went.

"It's Shaman! He's going to kill me, Pa! Pa, he's going to kill me!"

"What's happening down there!" Pearl appeared at the head of the stairs in her bathrobe. As she reached the kitchen the deer burst through the kitchen window, shattering the glass pane, frame and all, as if it were made of eggshells and cardboard. The yellow formica-topped table beneath his forelegs hindered his progress, and he attempted to back out immediately, as Zeb crashed a heavy chrome-legged chair down on his bloodied antlers. Several pieces of antler broke away, but the immense rack protected the killer deer's head. With fear-crazed eyes on Zeb, the beast reached the porch again and bounded away toward the long open meadow.

The stag was just rounding the side of the barn when Zeb's first shot grazed his buttocks. The animal veered off and zigzagged as he raced for the distant orchard.

"You big bastard!" Zeb yelled, locking the bolt in place for another shot as he ran barefoot and barechested through the snow.

"I'll kill you, you dirty bastard!" He fired again.

The deer bellowed loudly as the second slug found its mark. He went down for an instant but then regained his feet and ran as though the hounds of Hell were on his heels.

Zeb stood and took careful aim, controlling his breathing as Shaman got further away. He led, hoping for a head shot. The distance was now better than a hundred yards, but he had made such shots before.

At thirty m.p.h., the stag wasn't an easy target. The bullet whined off through the air and into the forest. Two more rapid shots were fired, but it was futile. The stag reached the orchard and melted from view.

Pearl stood on the porch, holding her son in front of her, as Zeb hurried back to the house. She was frightened and guilty-looking as she watched her husband. Thelma bawled loudly from where she stood, shaking noticeably, blood dripping onto the snow from the wounds in her neck. She was ripped badly in places. Zeb went to her with concern, saw that the tears weren't terribly serious, and slapped her on the rump.

"Get in the barn, cow," he said, and Thelma lumbered off obediently.

It was dark, 7:30 P.M., by the time the last of the hunters arrived at the Simpson home. Some men waited by their vehicles in the yard, while some stood on the porch and drank coffee, smoked cigarettes, or shook their heads and discussed the boarded-up window. None of them had ever heard of a deer being so kill-crazy that it tried to get into a house. It was true that there was no braver, nor meaner, animal in the woods than a buck in rut when his testicles dropped and enlarged—but actually leaving the forest to try and kill people in their own home? Several of them believed the stag had hydrophobia; others recounted beliefs and suspicions similar to those voiced by the Indians. In any case, they all agreed that Shaman had to die. As an added impetus for their support, the county had increased the reward to $2,000.

Inside the kitchen, Sam Parker, Dave Barnes, two officers from the Fish and Game Department, and a half dozen New York State Troopers sat at or bent over the table, and studied the map Zeb drew. Pearl stood at the stove boiling coffee in a Pyrex coffee pot and three kettles. Straining the grounds through a wire mesh colander, she poured the brew into thermos bottles for Zeb, Sam, and the others.

After stitching and dressing Thelma's wounds, Pete came in from the barn holding a pan of sulphur paste. He began washing it clean in the sink. Pearl took it from his hands and did the chore herself.

Sam's eyes held a flicker of hope as he looked at the blond man. "I'd like to have you along, Pete," he said. "There's no better shot here."

"I haven't hunted in a long time," Pete said. "I don't think I'd be any good to you at this late date."

Zeb's face tightened at his younger brother's reply.

"Remember, he don't hold with guns any more," Zeb said to Sam. Sam found himself wishing he hadn't said anything as Zeb started on Pete. "You're just afraid you might have to shoot that bastard!"

103

"I asked Pete to stay home," Pearl said quickly, as the kitchen filled with wondering looks. "Chucky and I would be frightened out of our wits if we had to stay in this house alone tonight." Zeb saw Pearl's face pleading silently with him not to push the matter any further. He shrugged his anger off, capped his thermos bottle, and handed another one to Sam.

"You'd better take a shotgun too," one of the game wardens said as Zeb slung a rifle over his shoulder. "We're going to be in the woods and shooting at close range."

Pearl followed Zeb into the living room as he went to get Old Zeb's double-barrel twelve-gauge, and hugged him tightly.

"Honey, please be careful," she said. "That deer's so terribly mean. I wish you weren't going . . ."

Zeb felt her small and trembly against him and it made him feel good to know that she loved him so much.

"Don't worry," he said. "That old bastard had his chance last night and he blew it. He won't get another one."

With flashlights and Coleman lanterns the party of hunters started off across the cow pasture.

Alone now, Pearl watched her brother-in-law as he sat at the kitchen table and brooded over a cup of steaming coffee.

"You're feeling ashamed of yourself, aren't you?" she asked.

"I suppose I am."

"Well, don't! It's no shame to not hold with killing. There's always plenty of others in this world who are more than happy to do your share for you." She touched him gently on the cheek for an instant as she began gathering coffee cups and cake dishes from the table. "From what I hear, you take after your mom. I'd rather have Zeb more like you than you more like him."

Pete felt his blue mood lifting. With a warm smile he nodded his thanks to the considerate woman. "You want some help with those dishes?"

"You're too much!" Pearl laughed. "Get out of here before I boot you in the fanny! Go play some chess with your nephew and see if you can settle his nerves down."

Pete felt a surge of anger course through him as he thought of Shaman trying to kill Chucky. "Sis . . . you don't have to be afraid about anything tonight—"

"I know that."

"No, I mean it. It's true I don't hold with guns . . . but I'd never let anything happen to you or the boy. I swear that."

Pearl's green eyes danced with irritation. She put her hands on her hips and scrutinized him. "You don't have to convince me, Peter Simpson," she scolded lightly. "I know you're not a coward. I feel perfectly safe with you at home."

Pete smiled apologetically, wanting to thank her but knowing it wasn't necessary. He went to the sink and picked up a dish towel to help out.

Pearl stifled a rising protest as she saw the love in his eyes for her, the hurt and pain of his tormented mind over his many weaknesses. She began washing the cups and plates, standing next to him and liking his closeness. He had a way of gentleness to him that she had never seen displayed by any other man. He always looked nice and smelled so clean, even when he was perspiring in the heat of summer. The thought that one day some pretty little gal would sweep him off his feet and she would lose him made her sad.

"Is Thelma okay?" Chucky appeared in the doorway in his bathrobe with shiny scrubbed cheeks and a head of sopping wet hair.

"She's fine, son," Pete answered. "What's this, a new record? Two baths in two nights?"

Chucky grinned sheepishly. "I wet my pants when Shaman chased me," he said. "I thought I'd smell like pee to you guys, so I took another one."

Pearl watched as a pained look came onto Pete's face. The man sat down, taking the small boy on his lap, drying his hair with the dish towel. Then, unexpectedly, Pete hugged Chucky and kissed the boy on the side of the face as his emotions surfaced.

"Go on, you two," Pearl said, "get out of here and let me do my work."

Crybaby! she thought, as tears rolled down her cheeks into the soapy water.

Out on the pasture, Sam and Zeb walked abreast of each other. They were quiet for the most part, as was everyone else. It was a peaceful night with myriads of clustered stars casting a blue tinge onto the meadow.

There was no wind, and some of the men had their coats unbuttoned, sweating with the exertion of walking through the snow. Len Pfeister, thin and not weighing much, had the easiest time of it, only occasionally breaking through the hard crusted surface to the depth of an ankle or a knee. The dark orchard, set against a blue-black skyline ahead of them, was postcard perfect. The miles and miles of unbroken pine forests, surrounding the pasture on two sides and looming behind the shorter apple and maple trees in front, were impressively tranquil and beautiful. Their tall silhouettes reached up, it seemed, until they touched the stars themselves. A meteor whizzed high overhead in a streak of orange and then quickly snuffed itself like a blown-out candle on a birthday cake.

"Pretty," Sam said. "They say if you can wish on a falling star before it goes out, your wish will come true."

"That right," Zeb said. "I always heard it meant someone just died."

"I guess it depends on a man's outlook . . ." Sam slowed his pace and lengthened the distance between them and the nearest men. "You know, son," he said softly, "that Indian you shot and killed was the man who murdered my father."

Zeb stopped dead in his tracks.

"I don't know what you're talking about," he said.

"Don't you? True, folks say he was killed by Shaman. Even the coroner thinks so . . . but Joe Hawk smashed his chest in with a pair of deer antlers to protect you."

They began walking again.

"So what happens now?" Zeb asked.

"We leave it lie," Sam said. "We kill that murdering deer and we leave it lie."

"Sam, I want you to know it was an accident. I'd have sworn he was Shaman himself standing there!"

"That's the way Joe figured it. I thought maybe you found out he was Malsum and shot him for personal reasons."

"Come on, Sam. I remember hearing the story from Old Zeb when I was a tyke, but I've got no grievance over that. You're sure it was Malsum? I mean—he'd have to be eighty or ninety years old, wouldn't he?"

"More like a hundred and ten."

"You're shitting me! That Injun was a hundred and . . . what the hell was he doing back here?"

"He was released from prison just last week, dying of TB. Joe says he came back to kill us—to even the score for his sons."

"Then I guess I done everyone a favor. Is that what you're saying?"

"Not hardly. You did Malsum a favor. He wanted to die, according to Joe's theory."

"I kinda got that impression myself. Why, though?"

"Joe says his spirit is riding around inside Shaman."

"Shit, you trying to tell me that big frigger chased my kid today because some ghost is out for blood?"

"I'm not trying to tell you anything, except what Joe told me."

"Well, he's getting old and superstitious then. We got us a mean-ass killer deer on our hands, and nothing more. Come morning I'll be nailing his ugly head to my barn wall—ghosts or no ghosts!"

"I hope you're right."

"I know I'm right, old man. You keep up with me, and you'll see him go."

Sam stiffened at the remark. "I guess I am getting old, at that," he said. As they neared the orchard he saw Zeb slip two shells into the ancient shotgun. "But I'll tell you something in the way of an old man's advice—you take a shot at that deer tonight with your grandpa Zeb's shotgun, and it's liable to blow up in your face."

"Old wizard magic, huh?" Zeb smirked.

"No, just common sense. Those barrels were made for black powder. The metal's tired, getting old like Joe and me."

Zeb found Shaman's tracks leading off through the grove where the deer had lain down in the snow to pack his wounds. The hunting party spread out and followed the sign into the maple stand, where they came on a trail of fresh blood leading into the pine woods.

"Walk slow and stay in pairs. No loud talking, and, for Christ's sake, make sure of your target before you fire," one of the game wardens pleaded, adding, "We don't want any accidents or any more innocent deer being killed like they were today."

"He's bleeding some from Simpson," a trooper chimed in. "An animal has a tendency to lay up and lick his wounds when he's hurt. If we walk slow and stay quiet, we'll be on him before he knows it."

"Then let's cut the gab and get after him!" Zeb said, and walked ahead of them into the woods.

"Sounds like he's got the same bug up his ass he had this morning," the trooper sergeant remarked to Sam.

"Same one he had yesterday. Same one he'll have tomorrow, and the day after," Sam replied. He added with a shrug, as the sergeant waited for an explanation, "Forget it, it's just his way." He walked off after Zeb.

The hunters made the woods look as though someone had strung Chinese lanterns through them. Walking in twos, they spread out in a ragged line that extended 300 yards. If it hadn't been for the fact that their task was so grim, it would have been an enjoyable outing: nice weather, friendly companionship, hot coffee, and sandwiches. The forest was calm and beautiful, almost as if it wanted to lull them all into a sense of false security.

Dave Barnes, the youngest man on the hunt, had come on his own time, as some of the state troopers had. Seeing that Sam, his boss, had teamed up with Zeb Simpson, he paired himself with one of the Fish and Game men, a likable fellow named Kenny Green.

"How many deer in the state?" Dave asked.

"Somewhere around a half million, I guess," Green said.

"I multiply that times forty-eight, would I have the country's total?"

"I doubt that. Whitetail figures were about eight million, last I heard. Add another six or seven million mule deer and crossbreeds and I guess you'd have a fairly accurate total. Why?"

"I was just thinking," Dave shook his head, "what in the name of the Lord would we do if they all suddenly became like Shaman?"

Green laughed. "We'd pack up and give the country back to the Indians, I guess!" And then he frowned, saying, "You know, that isn't even one bit funny."

"Who was trying to be funny?" Barnes defended himself. "I'm serious—what could we possibly do against them?"

Green nodded. "There isn't any animal or man that can stand against a big deer or elk when he's in rut and hot about something. You know, everyone thinks deer are timid, shy little creatures, but that's only the way they are when they're not in breeding season. There's more people injured and killed by deer in one year in this country than have been injured or killed by wolves and wild felines in the last century."

"In one year? Are you bullshitting?"

"Hey! I've got the statistics available to show you. Ten thousand years ago, the meanest thing walking the earth was the deer. They tore sabre-toothed tigers up for breakfast, with a few cave bears thrown in for good measure."

"They were meat eaters?"

"No, but they might as well have been as far as Cro-Magnon man was concerned. That animal probably killed more of our ancestors on a hunt than all the predators combined. And those men were pretty stout fellows when it came to muscles and fighting! They went seven feet tall on the average."

Barnes shook his head with awe, judging by the man's serious manner that he wasn't ribbing him. "How big were the deer?"

Green chuckled, "Now that's the catch. They were six feet at the shoulder, and weighed better'n a ton, sometimes. Their antlers spread out for twelve feet and went 500 pounds—make a moose look like a runt next to them."

"Antlers weighing—Christ! That's probably more than Shaman weighs all together!"

"Just wanted to let you know," Ken Green said, "you're not the only one can tell spooky stories. You want to talk about girls or something?"

Together they laughed and went back to searching the thickets with their flashlights.

Len Pfeister was walking with one of the state troopers when they heard a loud rustling in a dense growth of ferns. The trooper raised his shotgun and nodded for Pfeister to shine his light into the foilage.

A young doe stared at the light, her eyes reflecting bright orange. She trembled and quivered, tried to raise up, but she was paralyzed with fear.

"Pretty little thing," the trooper said. "Take the light off her before she dies of fright."

No sooner had Len shifted the beam than the doe was off and running. The sound of her small carriage hurrying through the night woods was magnified, drawing all neighboring lights in her direction.

"Don't shoot," the trooper called out, in a slightly raised

voice that accomplished the job of warning the others. "It's only a doe."

As if all the hunters were one, their flashlights sought her out and stayed with her as she ran. Disappointed men could be heard griping and belly-aching up and down the line.

"She gave me quite a start!" Len Pfeister laughed. "I expected to see Ol' One-Ear come barreling down on us like an express train!"

"I know what you mean," the trooper said somberly. "I was the one found those poor bastards in the woods this morning. To tell you the truth, though, that buck's probably miles away from here. I doubt if we'll even see him tonight."

"In a way I hope you're right," Len said. "I've seen that ugly critter a time or two over the years in broad daylight, and he was scary to look at then. Old Clyde, my grandpa, says he'd scare the Devil himself out of these woods were he to meet up with that deer at night."

The trooper nodded in agreement and shone his light into the bushes where the doe had been a moment before. "Looks like she was bleeding," he said. Both men could see a large splotch of blood on the snow. "Probably one of them that got shot today during the deer slaughter," the trooper sighed with disgust.

"Yeah, probably so," Len said, wondering if the police officer knew that he had brought down two does himself under the excuse of thinking they were Shaman. It didn't do him any good—the game wardens confiscated the carcasses for the nursing homes. The only reason they let him come along tonight was because he had proven he had quick reflexes and a good aim—he'd killed each with one shot. Pfeister leaned his shotgun against a tree and crawled into the ferns for a better look.

There, mingled with the doe's tiny hoofprints, was a much larger set of tracks.

"Hey, look at—"

Shaman's immense rack suddenly burst into view. The stag bit Pfeister's throat, smashing his larynx and silencing him. The man's eyes bulged as he fought for his life, arms flailing and prying at the deer's clamped muzzle. Before the trooper could get over his shock and horror, the deer dragged Len Pfeister into the covering foliage, as if he were a small child.

"Fight him, man!" the trooper yelled. "I can't shoot!"

The law officer went into the ferns, yelling to the others, "He's here! He's here!"

Shaman could be heard making bestial snorting sounds. Len Pfeister gurgled and thrashed about wildly, trying to break the deer's stranglehold on his throat. As soon as the trooper's light found them, the stag released Len. Then with a shrill banshee-like call that stunned the officer, Shaman charged and hurled him into the air.

Suddenly they were all there, pinning Shaman in a dozen shafts of light as he ran in a circle, seeking a path out. Like fools they completely surrounded the demonic beast until *they* were just as trapped.

"Don't shoot!" Zeb yelled, seeing the dangerous confusion. "We're liable to hit each other!"

"Spread out!" one of the troopers yelled. "So I can get a shot at him!"

"Screw you, copper!" someone roared, "I ain't splittin' that reward with nobody!"

Shaman bolted as two shots were fired. A hole opened up as six men on the other side ran to the left and right, cursing the mad shooter. The eager marksman hadn't even scratched the deer!

This time came a terrible bestial scream as the deer ran for the opening without a second's loss. "A-a-a-ae-e-eeeee-eough! E-uh E-uh!"

Zeb filled the hole as the stag bounded toward him. He clamped the shotgun to his shoulder and held his finger over both triggers.

"Clear me a path," he shouted. "I aim to shoot.!"

Suddenly Sam Parker was standing next to him, also drawing a bead. Shaman was fifty feet in front of them, charging with his massive rack so low to the ground it was plowing a furrow of snow five feet into the air and falling over his scarred coat like a fine cloud of sifted flour.

"Now!" Zeb and Sam fired simultaneously. But the deer wasn't there any more! As if he had sprouted wings he leapt magnificently into the air and landed twenty feet behind Zeb and Sam. Both men hunched down instinctively to keep from having their brains knocked out by sharp hooves as the stag made the leap.

All at once a multitude of light beams zeroed in on the deer as he pressed for his escape.

"Get down!" Zeb yelled. He tackled Sam to the ground.

A fusillade of shotguns and rifles went off. The bullets whined and whirred their way into the night after Shaman's elusive, fleeing form.

"That's enough, you bastards!" Zeb roared, but they ignored him.

They were still firing fifteen seconds later, when the deer was either riddled like a sieve or was three hundred yards away with a wall of trees between him and the riflemen.

As the shooting stopped, Sam began to get to his feet, and Zeb pulled his legs out from under him. "Not yet!" he said, and he was right. Two more shots rang out, like the last firecrackers on a string with slow fuses.

"Help me!" the gored trooper cried loudly. "This man is dying!" He turned Len Pfeister onto his stomach and pounded hard on the man, trying to get his wind back for him. The trooper himself had a broken collarbone and two painful punctures in his chest, where Shaman's spiked antlers had torn through the heavy black leather of his coat, but he wasn't hurt critically, as Len was. The coat had saved his life.

Several men gathered around Pfeister as he thrashed on the snow-covered ground, struggling to get oxygen down his smashed throat into his aching lungs. His eyes bulged and rolled wildly as he pleaded mutely for help.

Zeb pushed his way through the onlookers, not knowing what was going on. As he saw Len's condition, he took out his hunting knife quickly and knelt down next to the suffering man.

"Oh, Christ, he's going to put him out of his misery!" a voice said.

"Maybe it's best," came a reply.

One of the troopers started for Zeb as he felt around with his knife on Len's neck for the soft spot.

"Leave him alone!" Sam Parker barked as he neared them. "He knows what he's doing!"

Len Pfeister was terrified, and fought Zeb to get the knife away from his throat, but then Zeb dug the blade in and twisted it, making a small hole as Len tried to rise.

With a loud rasping noise, Pfeister drew air into his struggling lungs from the opening at the base of his neck. His chest expanded like a balloon as Zeb hovered and massaged it with spread fingers.

"You take it easy now, Len," Zeb said quietly, laying the man down gently on the snow. "That big frigger ain't killed you. You're going to be all right, boy."

Len started to cry, his sobs coming through the hole in his neck like a worn phonograph record.

"Two of you men run back to my farm and call the fire house," Zeb ordered. "Tell 'em to be waiting with oxygen when he comes out."

Minutes later Pfeister was loaded onto a stretcher made from rifles and buttoned coats and carried toward the Simpson home.

"You can't go after that demon alone!" Sam protested as Zeb warned the men who remained behind that he wasn't taking any of them along.

"Shit I can't!" Zeb replied. "You mean I can't do it any other way, don't you?" He pointed accusingly at the farmers and state troopers. "You horses' asses can do all the shooting you want to, as long as I'm not around! But I'll be damned if I'll have anything else to do with you! If I hadn't let my missus talk me out of going after that demon bastard when I wanted to this afternoon, he'd probably be dead and skinned right now!"

"I think we ought to all call it a night," the trooper sergeant said. "Including you, Simpson."

"You're standing on my land," Zeb said, knowing full well his land ended at the maple grove. "Now it wouldn't be exactly nice for me to order you off my property. But on the other hand—" Zeb faced the stiff-necked sergeant boldly and looked him in the eye. "Don't be giving me no orders either!"

Sam went with him as he walked off to pick up Shaman's trail.

"I'm going to be moving fast and not taking too many rests," Zeb warned.

"You lead the way, son," Sam replied. "I'll keep up with you."

Shaman did himself proud that night. He was cagier than he had ever been before. His spoor dragged Zeb and Sam through, over, around, into, and out of every bramble, fallen log, and woodland obstacle that Mother Nature ever created.

By the time dawn broke, both men were exhausted, and they had only covered three miles of woods in nine hours. The last mile of the three Zeb had abandoned the trail completely, figuring he knew where Shaman was headed. Surer than Hell, he picked up the deer's spoor again on the other side of Red Jacket Hill where the Seneca Nation land ended and the rugged hills leading to the Alleghenies began.

Zeb knew the murdering beast was lost to him, but he didn't want to admit defeat. All night he had followed the trail of blood doggedly and with persistence, hoping that Shaman was wounded so badly that he would be forced to hole up. Now he cursed himself for not running ahead to lie in wait for the stag to cross Mohawk Meadow on his way into the hills. With the deer laying a false trail, there would have been plenty of time to cut him off.

Sam huddled over the campfire at the edge of the forest and looked forlornly at the steeply rising oak- and chestnut-covered ridge across the wide meadow. Spruce and pine trees capped the crest, and beyond that first ridge there were miles of other ridges; far behind those, the Allegheny Mountains themselves.

"We'll never find that smart bastard back there," Sam grumbled.

"Well, I aim to try, old man," Zeb said stubbornly.

They struggled through snow to their waist as they crossed the meadow. Sam suffered terribly, but he would not abandon the younger man.

Joe Hawk, James Goodman, and several other Seneca Indians, looking like they were all nearly frozen to death, came out of the oak forest in front of them. Although Joe was older than the others, none of them could match his pace. Each of the Indians was wearing snowshoes; Sam would have given half of his pension to have them at that moment. The two groups met halfway across.

"Any sign of him, Joe?" Sam asked.

"We sat and watched all night," Joe said. "We heard your shots and thought he would come." Joe glanced back at the hills with acute aggravation, turned to Sam and Zeb again. "He is a sly one. We never saw him."

"Maybe he didn't cross, then?" Zeb suggested hopefully.

Joe pointed with his finger towards a deep trough through the snow a hundred yards east. "He crossed there," Joe said tightly. "Before dawn, and on his belly, very slowly, so we would not see him."

"Sonuvabitch!" Zeb fumed. "Well, let's get after him, then."

"Go home to your family, Zebediah," Joe commanded. "We will not get another chance at him."

"He won't go far. He's wounded and he'll hole up."

"No. He will travel day and night now. He will go far into the mountains where we cannot follow him. He knows he cannot fight again before the wounds heal. If he tries, the stag will die on him, and he will have lost."

"What the hell kind of talk is that, Joe? 'The stag will die on him!' You saying that Malsum's ghost is in that frigger? I don't hold with that crock of shit!"

Joe nodded somberly. "You're much like your grandfather whose name you carry. You deny openly what your soul tells you is truth."

"We're wasting time! Let's get after him!"

"Only a fool would enter those hills!" Joe Hawk's face suddenly flared with anger and authority. "I have a greater need of vengeance than you," he said, "but my hatred does not rob me of my senses! Go into those mountains, and we will find only your bones when winter ends!"

Joe removed his snowshoes and handed them to Sam. Before the man could protest, he started off for home, potholing knee-deep in the crusted snow, and pushing through with high steps as if he were a tireless machine.

"I don't want your goddamned snowshoes, James!" Zeb snapped, as the boyhood friend began taking his own footwear off.

"You do if you're going back there," James said with a chiding grin. Then with a shrug of admonishing humor he added, "It's been real nice knowing you, Zeb."

Zeb watched the Seneca walking back to the Nation land. He was undecided, stubbornly trying to convince himself that Jimmy and Johnny Keever's killer might be a mere mile or two ahead. There were tracks to follow. Damn that old Indian! Didn't he know that Shaman had tried to murder Charlie?

"You know it's a bastard back there in the winter," Sam said. "The snow must be piled twenty feet deep in places. There's crevices—a man could fall through and suffocate without ever getting out."

"I've been back there before—I can do it okay."

Sam stopped the distraught man as he began to trudge off.

"There won't be much for him to eat once he's past the hills," he said. "He's shot up bad. Maybe he'll die."

Zeb nodded finally, sad resignation on his tired face. "He should," he half-whispered, "but I almost hope he doesn't. I want the satisfaction of killing that sonuvabitch myself!"

He hurled the snowshoes at James Goodman, as the Indian smiled charmingly, and then walked past him while he was putting them on. A moment later Zeb tripped, winded, and sat dejectedly in the snow. Sam and James helped him to his feet. He pushed them away with a curse and followed after Joe Hawk, one step at a time.

PART II

Misery

Chapter V

The doe watched the mice gnawing on the old antlers in the meadow. They were trying to gnaw through the discarded bones to the nourishing marrow inside, to claim whatever food the ants had left behind. The three-week-old spotted fawn at the doe's side seemed intrigued with the mice. He scampered up to them curiously, making them abandon their treasure and dart into hiding amid the brush.

As the doe began pulling at the new spring grass in the pasture, the young hart returned and nursed at her udder, forcefully tugging at the soft, warm bag. The sturdy tyke had large ears, indicating that he had been sired by Shaman or one of Shaman's offspring. The mother was a young whitetail who had mated for the first time the winter before. Until she dropped the fawn she had followed an older doe who had possessed a good instinct for survival. But now, on her own, the young mother's inability to sense danger was evident. The lure of the tender grass shoots on Len Pfeister's pasture had tempted her from the comparative safety of the woods, where the dense thickets were now budding.

The cows in the meadow ignored the doe and her fawn as the doe munched grass at their side. The wind was sweet with the scent of flowers and decomposing leaves, the grass delicious. The doe and fawn were the only deer on the meadow, although the sign of many others who had eaten their fill and bedded there the night before was all around them. The doe was content. Then the wind brought the scent of man. The cloying stench of human

119

sweat and clothing, saturated with swine blood, set her heart to pounding.

Her eyesight was poor, and she could not find the man. The wind was a drift of gentle breezes, without direction. She nudged her fawn flat down onto the ground and bounded away toward the woods. The frightful roar of a shotgun close at hand made the doe veer from her path, knowing now that she had been running into danger. She saw the man in the field as he fired a second time, grazing her neck. She ran headlong for the woods while the man frantically reloaded.

Just as she reached the protective foliage a slug tore through her stomach and brought her down. She crawled into a nearby thicket, quivering with fear and pain. The man did not bother to search for her. Ten minutes later the fawn was in the woods, bleating with the voice of a young lamb. She tried to rise up and go to him, but the mortal wound prevented her from doing so. She beat on the ground with her hooves, and the fawn crawled into the thicket, found her, and began licking at her wounds.

"I think the water's too muddy," Chucky complained, looking at the brown creek, still cold and swift from the melting snow in the mountains. Tommy Hawk and he were fishing with fiberglass poles and cheap baitcasting reels, using white grubs they had dug out of brown weed pods for bait. The ground was too cold to find red worms or nightcrawlers.

Fifty yards up the bank, where Genessee Road Bridge spanned the twenty or so feet of water, Mark Banner, Donny O'Neil, Mike Pfeister, and several other Brant boys sat fishing, their poles propped up on Y-shaped sticks stuck into the mud. Mark and Donny shared a filter-tipped cigarette, using the cement side of the bridge to shield them from any prying adult eyes. Luke Banner's sprawling farm was only a hundred yards away across the creek on the other side of the bridge and neither boy relished the thought of being caught.

"You're fishing for them wrong," Tommy said, as he reeled in a ten-inch speckled trout. "Take your sinker off and let your line drift with the current. You'll never catch any trout on the bottom."

Chucky watched his friend unhook the prize and slip it onto a string with wooden sticks tied to the ends. As he glumly began reeling in, his pole suddenly doubled over and he jerked it to set the hook. The fish pulled sluggishly on the line, its weight apparently immense.

"That's what you think!" he beamed, his face smiling as he reeled in with difficulty. "I got me a gran'daddy! You want to borrow a sinker?"

Mark Banner and the others ran over to watch Chucky land the fish. He dragged it up onto the bank. It lay there, gasping, two and a half feet of large silver scales and muddy pink fins.

"A sucker! A lousy, bony sucker!" Mark Banner laughed derisively.

"I told you, Chucky," Tommy said, baiting up and casting out into the current again, his line limp and weightless.

"You want him, Simpson?" Mark knelt down alongside Chucky as he unhooked the funnel-mouthed fish and prepared to throw it back.

"What do you want a nigger fish for, Mark?" Donny O'Neil asked.

"I've eaten sucker before," Chucky said. "They're good when the water's cold. Only they're real bony, and my ma don't like to fix 'em."

"Then let me have him," Banner said, a gleam in his azure eyes.

Chucky shrugged indifferently and handed the towheaded boy the squirming fish. "Watch out for the small bones," he offered.

Banner laughed and ran up to where the creek bank no longer sloped toward the water. "Who the hell wants to eat sucker?" he scoffed, then, turning to Mike Pfeister, said, "Watch the guts come squishing out of his ass!"

Mark slammed the fish to the ground and stomped on it, forcing out a sack of yellow roe. Another blow and the double air bags ruptured and popped. Mark ground the scavenger into a pulp. Some of the other boys laughed and joined in on the fun with him.

Chucky and Tommy watched the gruesome sport with contempt. Finally Mark picked up the mangled fish by the tail and began swinging it back and forth like a pendulum, spraying the clothes of his friends with blood and ignoring their gripes as they backed away.

"Hey, Simpson," he called, "How do you like your fish now?"

"If you didn't want to eat it," Chucky said, "why didn't you throw it back?"

Chucky ducked as the sucker whizzed by his head and splashed into the swift water, to be swept away by the current, trailing pink organs and white meat.

"There, I threw it back!" Mark scoffed, drawing more laughter from his friends.

"Let's get out of here and find another spot," Chucky said, as Tommy brushed blood and scales from Chucky's hair. "I don't like that creep, and there's gonna be trouble if I have to stay around here and look at his stupid face!"

Tommy nodded, reeled in his line, and took his trout out of the water. They started to walk off.

"What's the matter? Aren't we good enough for you, Charles?" Banner used the Simpson boy's formal name as a weapon against him, knowing he would take it as a dig.

"Lay off him, Mark," Mike Pfeister said, and then cowered beneath Mark's warning glare. Mike was much smaller than the freckle-faced tyrant and didn't want to chance a beating. The ruffian walked up behind Chucky and Tommy as they walked away. The others followed him.

'We're not good enough for Simpson," Mark taunted, directing his words to his friends. "You have to be a stinking Indian if you want to be friends with a Simpson!"

Tommy spun about and eyed the leering trouble maker.

Banner grinned at the young Seneca. "Who's that ugly old Indian with the big nose I see you with all the time?" he asked. "It looks like you're gonna be uglier in a few years, the way your nose is growing."

Tommy blinked under the barbed insult, his olive face tightening. He dropped his catch and fishing pole to the ground and clenched his fists.

"Get out of here, Banner!" Chucky suddenly pushed the larger boy away as he snickered at Tommy.

Mark slipped in the mud and arose quickly. "You shouldn't have done that, you dumb little twerp! Now you've got me mad!" He unsnapped his corduroy jacket and flung it to Donny O'Neil, taking up a very professional-looking boxer's stance.

"C'mon, Mark," Mike Pfeister pleaded, "You're bigger and almost a year older than Chucky. Leave'm alone!"

"Stay out of it," Mark warned.

Chucky bolstered his nerve and raised his fists into an awkward guarding position. Mark closed in to take a swing at the boy. Tommy Hawk pushed Chucky aside and stepped in front of him.

"This is my fight," Tommy said.

Mark's courage dwindled somewhat. "Okay, Indian," he chided, "take a swing at me—I dare you to! Mathias has been teaching me to box for two years."

"You're the one who wants to fight," Tommy said calmly.

"He's chicken!" Mark said to his friends, walking away to redeem his jacket. "I could kick his ass with one hand behind my back! C'mon, let's go back to our poles."

"He's not chicken," Donny O'Neil said, unwilling to miss out on a fight, or let the boastful Banner off the hook so easily. He wondered if Mark really was as tough as he said. "*Make* him fight you," he goaded, "*you* start it."

Mark sensed that he was trapped, but there was nothing else that he could do. He walked back and faced the stonelike Indian boy, assuming his favorite mean expression. He neither did nor said anything, however. After a moment Tommy smirked, seeing what he knew was fear on the boy's face.

"Come on, Chucky," he said, picking up their gear.

Mark saw the belittling looks on his friends' faces. Donny O'Neil snickered at him. They all knew that he, and not the Seneca boy, was the coward.

"I thought you wanted to fight?" Banner made one last attempt to save face before his friends. "Hey, Hawk-Nose, how come you don't have a mother and father?" he said. "Were they so ugly that your own tribe run 'em off?"

All of the boys laughed. They quieted as Tommy walked back to Mark, his black eyes smoldering. Mark sensed his dilemma and threw a punch, but Tommy ducked, slipped behind the boy, and grabbed him in a bear hug. He hoisted Mark from his feet and dropped him from a rise on the bank into the creek. The boy howled as he submerged in the icy water.

"You dirty Indian!" Mark hollered, as he struggled to get up the muddy embankment. "I'm going to kill you when I get up!"

Some of Mark's friends tried to help him as he continued to slide back to the water, but he warned them away with foul invectives, finally reaching the bank on his own. He twisted up his face and glared at Tommy as he stood by, ready to continue the matter should Mark so desire.

"You tried to drown me!" Mark said, and then he turned and ran for home. "You wait'll I tell my father, you red-skinned heathen!" he called, running for the bridge and yelling to get his father's attention.

Luke could be seen by the barn, unloading sacks of seed corn from a stake-bed truck with Mathias, his husky Negro hand.

"His pa is mean," Mike said. "You guys better get out of here fast!"

"I'm not afraid of his father," Tommy replied.

"Well, I am!" Chucky admitted, grabbing their gear quickly.

The two boys ran for better than a mile along the west bank and then crossed to the east side on a tottering log. They went into the woods where it angled to the creek beyond Luke Banner's cow pasture, and kept on until they were sure they were not being pursued.

The woods were heavy with the smell of musty leaves, and in many places they sank into the wet mulch up to their ankles, soaking their shoes and the cuffs of their trousers. They kicked apart toadstools as they walked, saying they were Mark's head. One particular tree harbored an entire colony of the fungus growth and they whipped the toadstools with their fishing poles until they tired of the game and found a dry log to sit on.

"Will your grandfather beat you when he finds out?" Chucky asked, imagining in his mind a wrathful Luke Banner demanding that Joe Hawk punish his grandson. The previous summer Luke had caught Chucky stealing frogs from his pond and on driving him home had insisted that his own father administer a "sound thrashing," as he had put it. His father had agreed, but then, after Luke left, he had dropped the matter with little more than an order for Chucky to stay away from the frogs.

"I don't think so," Tommy said. "It's not his way. But I know he'll be angry. Mark shouldn't have talked about my mother and father like he did!"

Chucky looked at his friend wonderingly. "Where are your mother and father?"

"They're dead," Tommy said. "A white man killed them."

"Why'd he do that?"

Tommy shrugged, looking a little sad. "I was just a baby when it happened. Joe says the white man lusted for my mother. She was very pretty. He killed my father in the woods and then he came to our home and forced dishonor on my mother."

"Did they send him to the electric chair?"

"No. Joe Hawk took him away from the police. He went to jail for a year for killing him."

They walked without speaking for a while. Then Chucky asked, "Did you know my Uncle Pete was in jail, too?"

"No, how come?"

"I don't know. He won't talk about it. It was before I was born. Maybe if you ask Joe, he'll tell you why, and we'll know then."

"He won't tell if it's a secret," Tommy confided.

"Well, whatever the reason, I'll bet it's a good one, like Joe's," Chucky said.

"I'm sure it is," Tommy replied. "Joe says your Uncle Pete is a man of honor. He was a close friend of my father's, like you and me are now."

Chucky nodded. "Hawks and Simpsons go back a long ways," he said. "You know, Tommy . . . I like your grandfather's big nose—and he's not ugly. You're not either. Mark Banner is the ugly one, with all those freckles on his face, and I'll bet your ma was pretty, too—as pretty as mine, even!"

"You're lucky to have a mother and father," the Seneca boy said, "I wish we were brothers, then your father would be my father also."

"You wouldn't want my pa for a father!" Chucky retorted. "He drinks and gets mean-mouthed, and he's always killing things and causing trouble at home."

Tommy's face filled with amazement. "You don't like your own father?"

"Heck, no!"

"But he's a famous war hero. He's brave and strong and he's got a lot of medals."

"Medals don't mean nothing," Chucky said. "All soldiers get medals for just doing anything, as long as they're in a war."

"Who told you that?"

"My pa, himself. At least he's truthful, I guess."

"Well, I like him. He's the only white Joe lets poach deer on Seneca land. Your father thinks he's sneaking them, but Joe lets him get away with it."

"You wouldn't like him if you had to live with him."

"Why? Because he drinks and kills animals? My grandfather drinks and kills animals. I like him okay."

"Joe drinks?"

"Sure. Drinking doesn't make a man bad. Joe drinks a lot when he's sad. He's gotten so drunk at times I've had to put him to bed myself. He has dreams about my mother and father . . . sometimes Malsum comes to him in visions, and he fights with him. I heard him and my Uncle James talking. They say Malsum is a demon, and that he is responsible for much of our grief."

"The only grief I'd have is if his deer caught me," Chucky said. "I hope he's dead, like Sam thinks."

Tommy's thoughts turned to the killer deer, to warnings voiced by his grandfather about entering the woods. He suddenly became aware of the dark shapes of trees and bushes, the hundreds of places where a big buck could hide. In another two hours it would be dark, and they still had better than an hour's walk to reach Chucky's home. It was another half hour to his home from there if he ran.

"Come on, we'd better get going," Tommy said.

There was a loud rustling noise in some nearby bushes as the boys walked past. Both froze with startled expressions on their faces. Suddenly the deer rushed them, butting them with his head and sniffing around Chucky's coat pocket with his little black nose.

Chucky smiled at the small creature. "I never saw a fawn do that before," he said. "He's not even afraid of us!"

The fawn pulled a chocolate Easter rabbit out of Chucky's pocket and bit off a large piece.

"His hunger is greater than his fear," Tommy said, looking at the thicket of bushes. "I wonder where his mother is?"

Chucky knelt and held the young hart while Tommy crawled into the bushes. The animal trembled and tried to break free, but Chucky held him tighter, and soothed him with gentle strokes.

"I found her," Tommy called. "She's dead!" He came

out on his hands and knees and brushed off his clothing. "She was shot in the stomach. She must've gone in there to die."

"I'll bet my pa shot her!" Chucky fumed.

"Too bad he didn't kill the fawn, too. He'll die on his own."

"No, he won't!" Chucky said. "I won't let him die! I'm going to take him home. Thelma's calf was born dead last week. My ma says she's grieving because she doesn't have a baby. Maybe she'll like him."

Tommy looked about the woods, listening as if he were entranced. Chucky asked him what he was doing and the Indian boy smiled and nodded. "Did you hear them?" he asked.

"Hear what?"

"The little *pukwudjinnies*—the forest people . . ."

"I didn't hear anything."

"They said, 'Yes, yes' in my ears just then. The fawn has good magic in him, Chucky. He was waiting for us to come. That is why he wasn't afraid of us."

Chucky raised his eyebrows skeptically, "How come I didn't hear them talking, then?"

"You have to listen very carefully."

The boys listened keenly. Chucky heard a low snorting sound, the sound of twigs cracking.

"I hear them!" he said, but Tommy only looked fearfully in the direction of the noise.

"That isn't them," Tommy said tensely. "Let's go. Hold some chocolate out to the little deer, so he'll follow us."

Shaman stood amid the dark trees, watching the boys and the fawn as they hurried away. His eyes were large and cold. A long jagged scar ran the length of his back where a bullet had sliced through the skin. The wound was still red and festering. Several other crimson patches of hide were furless where Zeb had shot into his flanks. He was sporting a new set of antlers. They were smaller and even more gnarled than last year's rack. A winter in the mountains with little food had left him gaunt, little more than skin and bones. But he was alive!

The buck followed at a distance, remaining motionless each time the boys stopped to look back. The deer knew they would not see him if he did not move. His newly-erupting antlers pained him. They were tender and covered with a fine coat of velvet. The right antler curved down low over one eye, malformed and stunted from the long starvation. It would be a deadlier weapon than the other, normal, antler when his rack hardened. Shaman's missing ear completed the grotesque appearance: the appearance of a nightmarishly disfigured monster, rather than that of a noble king stag.

Crack! The sharp noise froze the boys in their tracks. With hunched shoulders they slowly turned.

"You know you're not supposed to be in these woods!" Pete said. He held the pieces of a thick broken branch in each hand.

"I've been following you two for ten minutes, now. Can't either one of you hear?"

"We were too busy getting out of the woods, I guess," Chucky said. "It feels kind of spooky and all."

Pete's azure eyes scolded the boy. "Do you know you've got your mother worried sick?"

"How does she know we're in the woods?"

"Luke Banner was at the house a while back raising Cain about you two throwing Mark in the water." Pete knelt down and petted the fawn as it nosed around his legs.

"Mark had it coming. He started it, Uncle Pete!"

"I threw him in the creek," Tommy quickly confessed. "Chucky didn't have anything to do with it."

The fawn continued to nose around Pete's jacket pockets, inhaling the pungent odor of pipe tobacco. It made him sneeze, but the cherry smell kept him investigating curiously.

"I know that," Pete offered. "Luke's over at your house right this minute, no doubt, giving your grandfather an eyewitness account with Donny O'Neil and Mike Pfeister."

"You think Joe will whip Tommy?" Chucky's face filled with concern.

"That's up to him. I ought to whip you, mister, for being back in these woods and breaking a promise to your mother."

"Well, we couldn't very well walk home by Genessee Road with old Bible-spouting Luke shotgunning for us, could we?"

"You watch that mouth," Pete said. "You want me to take my belt off?"

"Don't waste your energy," Chucky groaned. "Ma'll see that it gets done right when I get home."

Pete smiled at the boy's sad resignation. Pearl should whip him, but he reasoned she would be too relieved to do little more than scold him severely.

"I hope she does, you deserve it," he said. "Where'd you get the fawn?"

"He adopted us," Chucky replied. "His ma was belly shot." An angry look came over his impish face. "I'll bet Pa did it!"

Pete disapproved of the accusation. "You don't know that," he said. "I've never known your pa to shoot a doe in the spring with unweaned young. Len Pfeister has been shooting every deer that crosses his path lately. I'd say he was a more likely candidate, wouldn't you?"

"I suppose . . ." Chucky conceded. "You think Pa'll let me keep the fawn and raise him?"

"I doubt it, but we'll ask him when he gets back from selling his venison in Buffalo." Pete picked the fawn up, letting it nurse on a finger. "It'll get kinda tiresome playing Mama to this little guy, you know."

"We've got a plan," Chucky said, winking at Tommy. The two of them smiled secretively, expecting Pete to question them. He merely nodded and walked off toward the Simpson apple orchard, cradling the fawn to his chest.

"Let me know how it works out," Tommy yelled, heading off in the direction of the Seneca Woods.

"Where do you think you're going?" Pete asked.

"Home." Tommy shrugged.

"Not through two miles of these woods you're not," Pete said. "You come with us and I'll drive you back after supper. James Goodman has a telephone, doesn't he?" Tommy nodded affirmatively. "Fine, I'll have Pearl call him and tell him to let your grandfather know you're safe."

"Joe doesn't worry about me," Tommy said defiantly. "He knows I can take care of myself in the woods—"

"Is that so? You're talking to the man who just got within five feet of your backside, son, and without you knowing it, either."

Tommy's face darkened. He clamped his mouth shut and fell in alongside Chucky.

As they walked out onto the pasture, two glaring eyes watched from the edge of the orchard. The stag whuffed and snorted, pawing up leaves and earth in a frenzy of hatred. Not until the sight and smell of his enemies disappeared did he turn back into the forest, where he would wait until darkness fell before joining other deer on the meadows to eat the new grass that would eventually strengthen his weakened body and nourish him back to health.

"I'll be a sonuvagun!" Pearl squealed, as she stood in the barn and watched Thelma allow the fawn to nurse. "Zeb's not going to believe this until he sees it with his own eyes!"

"It's hard enough to believe, seeing it," Pete laughed, affectionately scratching the cow behind her ears. "Thelma, you're some sweet old gal," he said. The cow nuzzled his neck as he scratched her.

After a moment she pulled away from Pete's hands to watch contentedly as the fawn yanked at an enormous teat. The four of them watched until the fawn drank his fill, went off to a corner of the stall, and lay down in the fresh straw to sleep.

"Looks like you guys won't have to play nursemaids after all," Pete said to the boys. He watched the cow settle down on her side next to the fawn. "You knew Thelma was going to adopt him, didn't you?"

"Sure did," Chucky said. He and Tommy grinned from ear to ear.

"How could you have known?" Pearl asked, and then she grimaced and tousled their heads playfully. "You little stinkers were just guessing and hoping, the same as Pete and me!"

"Were not!" Chucky said. "The *pukwudjinnies* told us Thelma would like him when we first found him."

"The puckwhuh—who are they?" Pearl laughed.

"They're like invisible little elves, who help Indians in the forest," Pete interjected. He surprised both boys with his knowledge. He turned to Chucky. "You heard their voices too, son?"

"Well . . . not really, I guess. But Tommy did. They told him our fawn has good magic in him." Chucky noticed the fawn as it woke up and studied him, big ears cocked straight. "Look at him!" he said excitedly. "See how he's listening to me tell you guys. He knows I'm talking about him!"

"You may have something there," Pearl conceded. The fawn's ears twitched at the sound of her laughter, and he stood on stiltlike legs, shaking his small button tail cutely.

"Aww, what a little darling," she cooed, and went into the stall to pet the animal. "You shut up," she scolded Thelma, as the cow mooed in discord, "he's not all yours, you know."

"So, he has magic in him, Tommy? What are you going to use it for?" Pete asked.

Tommy looked at Chucky secretively. Chucky hesitated, then gave his approval.

"To fight Malsum's stag," Tommy answered.

Pete nodded as if he had known all along. Pearl stopped loving the fawn and looked up at the boys.

"Indeed," she said. "I didn't know you had to fight dead bones."

Three miles away, as the sun set, the shaman stag walked out onto a meadow and began feeding on the new spring grass. The other bucks avoided him and acted skittish whenever he grazed close by. The does and fawns gave him an even wider berth.

Zeb was happy as he drove back from the city that night. He was pleased with the price he had bargained from Jake Strumwasser, the butcher who regularly bought his black-market venison. He had managed to squeeze another three cents a pound for his contraband from the shrewd businessman and also prevented Jake from cheating him out of almost $200. Strumwasser had weighed the meat on a jimmied scale and argued that there was only 1700 pounds gross weight. But Zeb had checked the load at a public scale beforehand and deducted the exact weight of the rental trailer. There was 2200 pounds—meat from four big bucks, two spikes, and seven does. Strumwasser had merely laughed and shrugged at the information, finally paying Zeb fairly. Butchered, packaged and wrapped, the venison had brought thirty-nine cents a pound; more than $850 for a winter's work. The folding money made a big bulge in his pants pocket.

The place that Zeb drove to on Route 62, the Sportsman's Bar and Grill, was an old favorite establishment of the farming community. Originally built in 1797 as a roadhouse, it was burned during the War of 1812 and then later rebuilt. Other generations had known it as Dougan's, but it had kept its current name and decor since the early 1900's.

The tavern was dominated by a rustic horseshoe-shaped bar with a black leather arm rail, and knotty pine walls that were covered like a taxidermist's workshop. The trophies included deer, bear, moose, and elk, and even a buffalo, no longer indigenous to the western New York area, was hanging in a corner. In the window a beer display lit up a beautiful brunette with a beauty mark on her cheek; her luscious hair was braided into a bun, reminiscent of the Gibson girls of the 1890's. She wore a white frilly blouse with a plunging neckline, and a cameo brooch which rested demurely above the cleavage of her swollen breasts. A round beer tray in her hands, with bottles of Genessee beer and ale, swayed back and forth, the contrivance of some mechanical marvel. The slogan read, "Ask for Jenny!" And many did. She was Zeb's favorite poster girl.

The light on the sign flickered with the closing of the door as Zeb walked into the tavern. Donna Keever, the tavern's chief attraction except for Jenny, was off playing shuffleboard with two of the local canning factory employees. She laughed joyfully at making a winning shot as a farmer, seated at one of the wooden tables in a captain's chair, called out, informing her that she had a customer. A wide grin broke out lopsidedly on Zeb's face as Donna turned, pleasantly surprised by the sight of him.

"Hello, sexy lady," he said.

The woman came over to Zeb and hugged him warmly. "You old bear rug hunter," she chided. "I haven't seen you since Jimmy's funeral. Where you been keeping yourself?"

Donna slipped out of his arms as he sat down on a stool at the bar. She poured a double shot of Wild Turkey for him and uncapped a bottle of "Jenny" ale, laughing at his reply. "Pearl wouldn't let me out. She went into heat and locked me up in her bedroom."

"Don't you wish!" Donna laughed. "Seems I know quite a few gals who still have sore backs from your single days. Probably the other way around!"

"Yeah, well, that was then." Zeb shrugged. "I'm over the hill now."

"Then so's Ferdinand the bull, huh?"

They chuckled, and Zeb downed his whiskey, washing the pleasant burn away with a long swig of ale. He laid a twenty-dollar bill on the counter and insisted that Donna have a Coke. It was a fact that the woman didn't care for strong drink. She agreed and filled his shot glass again but then refused to take his money.

"These are on me," she said.

"Go on," Zeb returned. "You work too hard for your dollars to be throwing them away on a drunk. Those kids of yours have to eat and have clothes on their backs. You keep it for them."

A little embarrassed, but knowing he was right, Donna took the money and rung up the sale on the cash register. Zeb looked at her warmly as she returned with his change and then suddenly took her palm and placed a wad of bills into it. "You take this," he said. "It's money owed Jimmy."

Donna started to tremble as she stared at her hand. The bills were crisp and new, all twenties.

"Zeb . . . there must be $500 here," she gasped.

"There's $700," Zeb replied. "That back two acres on your place is prime for potatoes, you know. I checked it this morning. Old man Murphy's boys will plant and harvest for a third share. What you don't spend on seed 'taters and tractor fixing should see you through until late summer, when you can sell the crop." Zeb patted her hands affectionately. "Hell, Donna, Jimmy wouldn't want you working in here. Quit this goddamn place and go back to farming."

Donna looked at him with tears in her eyes. Zeb touched her hair with a calloused hand. "Don't you cry none on me," he said. "I loved that man of yours. . . . He'd do the same for me or mine, and you know it."

"Does Pearl know what you're doing?"

"Hell, you know me, Donna." Zeb grinned. "She's the one that talked me into this."

"I'll pay you back, Zeb. I swear I will."

"I told you I owed Jimmy. I'm not looking to be paid back."

Donna picked up the whiskey glass in front of her and took a large swallow. She coughed and ran a glass of water at the bar sink, drinking it down. Zeb grinned at her and looked at his nearly empty shot glass.

"You owe me a drink, lady," he said.

Zeb listened to the heated argument between the boy and his girlfriend at a nearby table. He should have been

133

home and in bed hours ago, but the lively atmosphere of the tavern and the lure of good whiskey had delayed him. The two were just kids, eighteen or nineteen at the most.

"Well, I don't care if you think it's acting foolish," the young man said, "you shouldn't dance with other guys when you're engaged."

"I didn't do anything wrong! Stop making such a big scene, Jeff. Just because you don't like to dance doesn't mean I have to sit here like a bump on a log."

You're wrong, sweetheart, Zeb thought. If you're going to marry that boy and he doesn't want to dance, then you just put your jitterbug days behind you. He felt old beyond his years watching them. They reminded him of Pete and Nora Cleary, twelve years earlier when all the trouble had come. He wondered if the boy had an older brother and all at once hoped he didn't. The girl was too damn pretty.

"Why don't you two go home?" he said aloud.

"Why don't you mind your own business," the boy replied, and went back to arguing with his girlfriend.

"Well, shit. If you won't go, then I guess I'd better." Zeb got up and headed for the door, waving goodnight to Donna. She said something to him with a smile, but the sudden loud blare of a record on the juke box buried her words. Several couples stepped out onto the dance floor. As Zeb shuffled over to the bar to hear Donna, the fellow who had danced with Jeff's girlfriend a few minutes before left the stool. Zeb turned and watched disapprovingly as the girl deserted her betrothed and went off with the older man. Once on the floor she made a spectacle of herself, her shapely legs drawing hungry looks. Jeff evidently decided that he had taken enough and went after her.

"Get your hands off the lady, sonny," the man said, as Jeff began pulling his protesting girlfriend away. One thing led to another, and before it ended the boy found himself the unhappy owner of a bloody nose. He stamped out of the tavern, his fiancee running after him.

Zeb settled down on a stool at the bar, eyeing the roughneck who had punched the kid out as he returned to retrieve his drink. The man was still gloating over his easy victory.

"I thought you were going home, Zeb," Donna Keever

remarked with a worried tone as she caught his mood. Zeb ignored her, his green eyes locked tightly on the man as he began recounting other past exploits to several nearby drinkers. For a long while Zeb just listened, and then he walked over to the fellow.

"You know," he said, "I'm getting awful sick of listening to your big mouth. Why don't you go find another kid to beat up, and leave this side of the bar to the men." ·

The fellow's face tightened and he surveyed Zeb quietly. "I'll give you about ten seconds to back off, farmer," he said.

"I'm real scared," Zeb sneered.

"Don't fuck with him, John," a nearby patron warned. "That's Zeb Simpson."

"I don't recall having known you," Zeb said to the advisor.

"Hey, just leave me out of it! I don't want no part of you." The man walked away quickly.

"Zeb, please don't start a fight here," Donna said as she saw John's fingers fidgeting around his beer glass on the bar. Zeb took his eyes from the man for an instant to answer Donna, and John took it as his cue. In one sweeping motion he brought the glass down hard on Zeb's forehead. The glass shattered and Zeb reeled backwards, temporarily blinded from the impact. The dirty fighter charged, hitting Zeb over the eye with his fist. Miraculously, his hand was not cut.

"You don't look so tough to me," he bragged as Zeb shook his head and tried to clear his senses. Then he made the mistake of coming within Zeb's reach. Stiff fingers rammed into his throat below the Adam's apple and he suddenly found himself unable to breathe. Zeb drew back, deliberately taking his time, and shot a clenched fist at the man's gaping face. The heavy blow smashed the cartilage in John's nose, and he held the flats of his palms out as a sign that he no longer wanted to fight. His breath came back with a ragged asthmatic wheezing. "No more," he said, "I can't take any more."

"That's tough shit!" Zeb said and punched him again, knocking him down. "Get up." Zeb pulled a long shard of glass from his forehead, and the cut began bleeding. "You sonuvabitch! You'll think twice before you beat up another kid," he warned. "Now get up . . ."

The onlookers in the tavern watched as Donna Keever came over and took Zeb by the arm. "Come on," she said, "let him be. He's hurt pretty bad."

John picked himself up, holding his nose shut, as Zeb walked back to the bar with Donna.

"I told you not to fuck with him," a nearby voice said.

Chapter VI

Pete looked up as Zeb entered the barn. There was a gauze bandage taped to his forehead. Many small cuts above his eyebrows were scabbed over and daubed with iodine. He looked tired, his eyes bloodshot.

"You must have gotten in pretty late," Pete said. "Go on back to bed. I can handle the milking."

"I got other things to do," Zeb yawned. "Finish up and we'll go get Luke's tractor." He pointed to a dozen crates of young strawberry plants at the back of the barn. "Thinkin' of gettin' some of those in the ground today."

"Kind of a risky crop, isn't it? We might still have a bad frost."

"Maybe so," Zeb said. "But they bring good money and come early in the season."

Zeb explored his forehead, and he winced as he felt an embedded sliver of glass that Donna must have missed. He'd have to get Pearl to take it out later. No doubt he was in for a good scolding, but what the hell, he had it coming.

"How'd you get hurt?" Pete finally asked.

"I was in a fight. How the hell do you think I got hurt?"

Zeb took the coal shovel off the barn wall and began scooping cow manure from the stalls. He stopped, seeing the small fawn lying in Thelma's stall looking up at him curiously.

"Where in the hell did that come from?" he asked, leaning the shovel against a post and going in for a closer look.

The fawn trembled a bit as Zeb hoisted his rear end up to check his sex.

"Chucky and Tommy found him in the woods yesterday. Pfeister shot the mother, I think. You know how he hates deer now." Pete watched Zeb carefully, hoping he wouldn't object to the tyke. Thelma crowded Zeb and he pushed her away.

"Looks like he's gonna get big," he mused, feeling the hart's shoulders and back thighs. "He's got mulie in him, probably top four hundred when he's growed. More, if that no-good mother-humpin' Shaman is his papa."

"Might be," Pete said. "A mule deer'll seed five times as many does as a whitetail will."

"Yeah, well Shaman won't be doing any more seeding," Zeb said tightly. "I checked all his old haunts last week when the rain turned warm. He ain't never come back from the mountains. I think that frigger died up there."

Thelma's tail swished in Zeb's face as he knelt by the fawn. She backed up a little, raised her tail, and plopped a large pie to the straw on the cement floor. Zeb swore at the bovine and walked out, his dungarees spattered with brown manure.

"You leave that fawn in there, he'll either get trampled or shit on to death," he said, wiping his pants with the edge of his hand.

"Doubt that." Pete laughed. "That was just her way of getting you to leave. She's pretty attached to him." They both watched as the fawn went to Thelma and started nursing. The cow fidgeted a little and then settled. Zeb watched them, shaking his head with disbelief.

"Boys say he has magic in him," Pete said.

"Yeah . . . he's got sumptin'," Zeb agreed, still puzzled. "Never heard of anything like this before."

The fawn attacked the teat vigorously, making loud sucking noises. Soon he gagged on a mouthful of milk and had to stop to clear his throat. He went back for more.

Zeb grinned. "He sure is a greedy little bastard, isn't he?"

Half the cows in the world seemed to be housed in Luke Banner's barn. A thousand bales of hay in the lofts made them look empty. The structure was so gigantic that the roof was higher than a boy could throw a ball underhand. Double rows of 300-watt bulbs with large white reflector shields overhead lit the pre-dawn interior with the brightness of midday.

Mathias, Banner's herculean Negro foreman, looked up from a stall as Zeb walked by. He was disconnecting a milking machine from a cow with a saggy udder. His teenage son, Roosevelt, was busy with another milker, while his older boy, Wheeler, directed Puerto Rican farmhands whom Luke employed year-round and housed in shanty-type homes at the back of one of his fields.

"Good morning, there, Zebediah!" Mathias smiled joyously, flashing remarkably white teeth. As the Negro pumped Zeb's hand he said, "Looks like we had us another fight recently." He lowered his chin until it doubled, and peered at Zeb from under arched eyebrows, a twinkle in his eyes as he waited for the news.

"Yeah, we had us a little one." Zeb grinned lopsidedly, winking his less swollen eye. He liked Mathias, one of the few men he truly respected. Years ago the man had made it all the way to top contender for the middleweight crown, but a ruptured spleen had put him out of business.

"We won, I hope?"

"Hell, you know me, Mathias," Zeb gibed. "Hands down, boy!" Zeb punched him twice quickly on a bulging bicep, grabbed the muscle, and squeezed. The arm was like a cold knot of cement, smooth, firm, and unyielding.

"That's good! That's good, my man!" Mathias guffawed, his dark eyes sparkling. "Boy, you coulda been a cham'-peen for sure!" he said. "Yessir, but only because you wouldn'ta had to fight me, you understand," he added quickly.

For a few seconds they sparred, open-handed, until Mathias's laughter got the best of him and he had to back away. Zeb walked off to find Luke.

"What'cha doin' behind that cow there with your pecker out, Roosevelt?" he said to the teen-ager as he saw him unhooking a milker. The boy, at seventeen, was almost as heavily muscled as his father.

"You g'wan outta here, Mister Simpson," Roosevelt countered. "I ain't got no time for your razzmatazz this mornin'!"

"Where's your overseer at?" Zeb asked.

Roosevelt broke into laughter and pointed toward the far end of the barn. "That's what he is, all right," he said, motioning to two slight Puerto Ricans in the loft, struggling with a bale of hay.

The young man emptied the milk machine tank into

a can and tamped the lip on with a wooden mallet. He lowered his voice furtively. "He's probably readin' that Bible of his to the cows, tryin' to give 'em religion so they'll produce more milk," he said.

Luke looked up from his Bible as Zeb approached. His face tightened, and he rose up creakily from the scarred high-backed rocker. He was a tall man, lean of frame, with a leathery gaunt face and piercing ice-blue eyes. His black parson's suit and flat-brimmed hat reminded Zeb that this was Sunday morning. In another two hours Pearl would be pestering him to go to church. He never went, of course, and Pete took over the responsibility. But Pearl always goaded and pleaded, never willing to take no for an answer, just as she hounded him constantly over his drinking.

"Mornin', Luke," Zeb said, "I come to rent your tractor again."

Luke Banner stared at him with a look that made Zeb feel as though he should be struck with lightning for some unpardonable sin.

"You heard about my boy, Mark?" Luke's eyes continued to accuse.

"You mean about him gettin' thrown in the creek?" Zeb had to work to keep a smile from creeping onto his face. "Yeah, Pete told me a little while ago. Water's damn cold for baptizing this time of year." Zeb regretted the remark as soon as he voiced it, knowing it would rile the man, but he couldn't help himself. He disliked the pisspot Banner boy, with his rude ways, immensely.

"I see no humor in the deed, Zebediah," Luke said. "My son could have drowned! Your boy, Charles, stood by and let that young heathen throw Mark into a body of deep water. My Emily has a weak heart. She nearly suffered an attack when she saw Mark chilled to the bone and shivering."

Zeb frowned at the white-haired man, reached into his hip pocket, and withdrew a pint of whiskey, gulping down a mouthful. Luke eyed the action with bitter resentment.

"Yeah, well, I'm sorry to hear that, Luke," Zeb said, "but from what I hear, your boy started it. And it is sort of a well-known fact that he won the 4-H swimming meets last summer, now isn't it?"

Banner glared angrily and pushed Zeb's hand aside as Zeb proffered the whiskey bottle.

"Jenny Simpson must turn in her grave every time you walk by," the stern man said. "Look at you, standing here blaspheming the Sabbath with strong drink in your hand. The good Lord knows it was a God-fearing woman of decency who tried to raise you right. Zebediah, you're a grown man set in the ways of sin and not fit to raise a son of your own."

"You've said your piece, old man," Zeb said. "I come here to rent your tractor—not for a goddamned sermon. Now, if you don't want my money, you just say so and I'll go elsewhere."

Luke gripped his Bible more tightly and calmed himself, at the thought of losing the rental fee. "I spoke in anger," he said humbly. "The Lord knows I've always been neighborly with your family, and I still am. But you make it hard for me, son. Neighbors and friends of mine don't side with those murdering heathen devils. It isn't right that your boy plays with Indians and learns their ways like he does."

"Luke, you're not my father, so let's forget this 'son' crap. And since you want to talk about neighborly notions"—Zeb defiantly gulped down another swig of whiskey—"I sure as hell don't remember any Banners checking up the road to see us Simpsons going tattered and mouse-poor when my father died. But there sure as hell were a lot of 'heathen devils' with their arms full of groceries knockin' on the door!"

"Those were Depression years," Luke replied. "Times were hard. I was a man with three sons of my own to worry about." Luke's face filled with guilt at the mention of his now-grown children. He looked at the Bible in his hands searchingly. "I've tried to live my life according to the Good Book as much as any man. To be . . . to raise my boys the proper Christian way."

"Shit," Zeb groaned. "The book tell you to drive them kids off by cramming God and religion down their throats so hard they couldn't swallow? The book tell you to take 'em out to the woodshed every day over the simplest goddamned thing, and make 'em hate you so much that they haven't paid a visit in fifteen years?"

Zeb shook his head with disgust while Luke blinked distraughtly. "Tommy Hawk may be a heathen, his daddy before him, and his grampaw Joe as well," he said, "but I'd bet a bushel to a peck that young Tom keeps closer to the proper Christian way than that sass-mouthed little snot of yours. I'm sick of hearing how the Indians raped and murdered your sister Melissa. Sure as hell ain't the Christian way to hold a grudge for fifty years. For all you know it wasn't even an Indian who killed her. Might'a been a Catholic, or a Protestant, or even someone from your old man's church. No one ever solved the crime."

Luke grimaced and lowered his eyes, saying nothing. It was one of the few times in his life that he had ever been addressed in such fashion and taken it without wanting to return the hostility. Search as he did, however, he could offer no argument or defense when it came to the wound in his heart over his three estranged sons. He had always known deep down that he was at fault. His younger son, Mark, didn't even know his own brothers because of him.

"I've said my piece," Zeb said. "I'll be going home now."

Zeb was walking away when Luke called to him.

"Zebediah. Take the tractor with you," he said. "Keep it as long as you need it. Pay me whatever's fair and affordable to you."

Zeb didn't like the feeling of reproach coming over him as he watched the sad-eyed old farmer seated in his rocker, holding his Bible, and staring off into space. He shuffled back to the man and stood before him.

"Luke," he said, "I had a burr up my ass when I come in here, I guess. You're no worse than some, and a sight better than the loud-mouthed likes of me. I'll see to it that there's no more trouble between Tommy and Mark."

Luke Banner's expression smoothed, as a part of his torment ended. "I appreciate that, Zebediah. Mark is my last chance . . . the child of my old age, like Isaac to Abraham . . . I couldn't take losing him, too."

Over a thousand youngsters attended the brick elementary school in Brant. It was a modern three-story building, built two years earlier when the community was caught in the middle of a post-war baby boom.

The grades went from kindergarten to eighth. Each classroom, this day in mid-June, was filled with anxious girls and boys waiting for the 3:30 bell to ring and signal the beginning of summer vacation.

"Charles Simpson, promoted to sixth grade." The boys

and girls cheered as Chucky went to Nora Cleary's desk and received his report card.

"Congratulations," the attractive teacher said. "Thomas Hawk, promoted to sixth grade," Miss Cleary continued, and the kids cheered for the twenty-fourth time.

The Seneca boy walked over to his friend's desk and they compared report cards. It had been a wonderful day, this last day of school. They had arrived at nine A.M. and gone directly to the auditorium to watch an old Freddy Bartholomew and Spencer Tracy movie. The ending had been sad, and many of the girls had cried sentimentally. Mark Banner was caught crying, and threw a fit when some of the boys ribbed him. Then, when they returned to their classroom, Miss Cleary read aloud the last chapter of David Copperfield, after which they finished the day leisurely visiting with each other, as they were doing now. But the best part was yet to come, in another five minutes, when school ended for the year.

"How the heck did you get a ninety-four on the geography exam?" Chucky asked, discovering the gold star next to the mark on Tommy's report card.

They were both honor-roll students, about even all year long. Chucky had won in spelling with a sharp ninety-eight, but Tommy had rebutted with a ninety-five in arithmetic, winning by two points on the overall average.

Tommy looked at the eighty-nine written in under the June Exams column for geography on Chucky's report card. He grinned, seeing the envious expression on his friend's face.

"Not only are Seneca boys brave and strong," he said, "but we're also smarter than white boys!"

Chucky rained blows on him with a textbook and Tommy deftly captured the weapon and chased Simpson until a stern look from Miss Cleary put an end to their horseplay.

The bell rang, and everyone was up and running with smiling faces. The halls outside the classrooms on all three levels filled with noisy students anxious to start their vacations.

Miss Cleary stationed herself at the door and offered hugs to those students who wanted one. All of the girls embraced the pretty teacher, but most of the boys ran past her with red faces.

Miss Cleary took Chucky by the arm as he tried to

sneak from the room. Instead of a teasing smile, though, she gave him a stern look.

"Wait a minute, Chucky," she said. "I want to talk to you privately."

She bent down and kissed on the cheek a few girls who were saying goodbye, hugging them with her free arm.

Chucky urgently wanted to leave. Maybe, he thought worriedly, she had seen him staring at her bosom, and she was going to scold him. He'd die with embarrassment! She shouldn't have worn such a tight-fitting blouse.

"I've got to go, Miss Cleary," he said desperately. "I'll miss my bus." He felt her long fingernails dig warningly into his arm as he tried to pull from her grasp.

"The driver will wait for you," she said.

Now he knew she had caught him looking at her tits! His heart leaped into his throat.

The door closed, the last student departing. They were alone in the room. Chucky jumped the gun.

"I—I'm sorry I was staring, Miss Cleary," he apologized. She continued to hold him by the arm, the scent of her perfume, like lilacs, faint in his nostrils.

"What do you—" For a moment she wondered about his remark. Then the answer dawned on her, and her eyes twinkled with amused flattery.

"Chucky," she began, "at the start of the year I told you I thought you were the brightest student in the classroom, didn't I?" The boy nodded. "Well, I'm not so certain about that any more," she added, releasing him and walking over to the blackboard.

The soles of her feet lifted out of blue high-heeled shoes, exposing the dark cinnamon bottoms of her nylons as she began erasing the blackboard. Her bosom squashed slightly against the board, and her buttocks moved under her skirt as she stretched to erase the writing at the very top. Chucky quickly turned away, as he found himself wanting to stare.

While the teacher worked, she said, "It was ignorant and cruel, the way you and the other boys scolded Mark Banner this morning because he cried during the movie."

Chucky remained silent as Miss Cleary finished wiping the board. She went to her desk and sat down, the stern look still on her pretty face.

"I've always thought that one day you would be a

leader," she said, "but if all you feel is an urge to ridicule, then I guess I'm wrong."

Chucky wilted under her gaze.

"I thought it was very natural for the children to cry when Spencer Tracy died. Many men are intelligent and brave," she said, "but the most important assets to all men are kindness and compassion for their fellow man. Mark Banner rubbing his eyes this morning proved that I was wrong about him, also. He seems to have more compassion than you, Charles. And I'm going to work to bring that quality out in him next term."

Miss Cleary had explained earlier that she would teach a sixth grade class next September. Both Mark and Chucky were assigned to her.

Chucky felt a tingling starting at the back of his head. It spread and caused his eyes to burn. Miss Cleary was overly dramatic at times, but she knew how to reach the minds of her pupils.

"I'm sorry," he said.

"You should be sorry," Miss Cleary admonished. "I'm very disappointed in you. I don't like mean boys, and I won't have any in my class. Go start your vacation now. That's all I wanted to say."

Chucky glowered at the floor and clenched his teeth. "Goodbye," he said tightly. Tommy waited outside in the hall.

Before the boys could walk off, Miss Cleary opened the door, a guilty look in her eyes.

"Chucky, would you come back inside for a moment?" she requested. "Nice going on those exams, chief," she said to Tommy, giving him a wink.

"Thank you, Miss Cleary," Tommy replied, "and thanks for picking me for your class again next year."

Chucky went back into the classroom. The pretty teacher smiled at Tommy.

"Chucky . . ." Miss Cleary said, as the door swung shut and bumped the frame, "I don't want to send you on a vacation with a scolding." She lifted his chin, her eyes smiling, attempting to erase his frown.

The boy felt a hot flush on his face. Tears hovering in his eyes, he pulled away and rubbed them with embarrassment. The teacher bent and hugged him tightly, filling his nose with her fragrance. Her bosom crowded against his chest like it had against the blackboard, full and soft.

She held him, urging, "C'mon, give me a hug! We may not see each other for two whole months!"

Chucky put his arms around her, fearfully at first. He could feel his heart pounding wildly in his ears.

"Is that the best you can do?" she asked.

Chucky giggled as Miss Cleary playfully crushed him against her soft femininity. He tightened an embrace about her until his arms ached.

"Oh boy! Now that's what I call a hug!" the teacher exclaimed as the embrace ended. "Now let's say goodbye pleasantly. Master Simpson, I hope you have a fantastic, wonderful, scrumptious vacation!"

"Thank you," Chucky said, red-faced, his body aglow from her embrace still. "I hope you have a wonderful vacation too."

"I will," Nora said, winking at him. "And I'll let you in on a secret that none of the other children know. I'm getting married in two weeks."

"That's—that's nice," he said.

"Would you tell your Uncle Pete for me?"

"You know my uncle?"

"Yes. We went to high school together. Once we were very . . . very good friends."

As she bent forward to kiss Chucky on the cheek he saw her eyes well up with tears. She turned away quickly.

"My ma cries easily too," Chucky offered, embarrassed for her. "And sometimes for no reason at all." He offered this comment as a comfort, not able to comprehend her sudden emotion but feeling that he should say something.

Miss Cleary smiled and took a Kleenex from her purse on the desk and dabbed her eyes. "No way for a girl to act who's about to be happily married," she laughed nervously. "Go on, now," she said, "Tommy's waiting, and I don't want you to miss the bus. See you in September."

"How many quarts could I pick this week?" the town boy riding on the bus with Chucky asked. The bus was crowded. Even the aisle was filled to capacity with children riding out to Genessee Road to work the Banner and Simpson strawberry fields.

"About 300, maybe," Chucky answered. He was squeezed into a seat with Mike Pfeister and Tommy Hawk.

The town boy did some fast calculating and grinned. "That's enough to get the Pfleuger reel I want," he said.

Mark Banner leaned close from his seat across the aisle. "Which one?" he asked. "The one with the red stones?"

"No, they're green."

"That's the cheap one," Mark revealed, beaming proudly. "I've got the red one, myself. You come pick in my field, you'll have enough at the end of a week to buy the best. My pop's a better farmer than Zeb Simpson; our berries are always bigger."

"Does that make a difference?"

"It does when you can pick a hundred quarts a day!" Mark informed him. The town boy and several others nearby calculated with the new information.

"Your berries aren't any bigger!" Chucky stormed.

"Are so!" Mark retorted, sticking his tongue out and making a hateful face.

Chucky was going to push the issue, but then he thought of how Miss Cleary had gotten angry with him for teasing Mark in the auditorium. Many of Mark's friends had turned on him gradually, after Tommy had thrown him in the creek. Boys who had thought the Banner youngster was tough, and were afraid of him before, eventually began bullying Mark themselves, when they found out he was all talk and no action. In a way, Chucky felt sorry for him.

"Maybe his strawberries are bigger," Chucky said. "It's okay if you guys want to go with him."

Several of the town boys admitted that they did. Mark's eyes widened with amazement. He stared at Chucky's disarming smile skeptically.

"We'll be done picking our last patch in a few days," Chucky said. "It'll be another week before the green ones get big and ripe. I'll come over and pick for you in between if you want."

Mark could hardly believe his ears. "If you want," he said.

"Sure," Chucky agreed and held out his hand.

The Banner boy was dumbfounded. Other boys watched, wondering if there was a prank involved. Maybe Chucky was going to jerk his hand away at the last instant and pop his thumb out. It was always good for a few laughs. After a long watchful hesitation, Mark took Chucky's hand and pumped it, a wide grin breaking out on his freckled face.

"I'm sorry I teased you this morning," Chucky said. He

looked at his classmates a little worriedly and then admitted, "I cried, too, at the end of the movie, only nobody caught me."

Strangely enough, none of the other children laughed or ridiculed him.

"So did I," Mike Pfeister said sheepishly. "But I didn't cry when I broke my arm last year—and that's honest!"

All at once everyone was telling how they cried over the movie, wanted to cry, or caught this friend or that friend crying, or would cry themselves, if they ever saw the picture again.

Tommy stared out the bus window, feeling very much alone. Banner was a lifelong enemy, an Indian-hater. The world had suddenly betrayed the young Seneca. His own friend, Chucky Simpson, had caused all of the boy's hard-won friends to desert to the enemy's camp.

Mark shook Tommy's shoulder until he turned around and faced him. "You want to be friends with me?" he asked. He held out his hand.

"No, thanks," Tommy said.

Mark nudged him persistently. "I'm sorry about saying your mom and pop were ugly," he said. "I deserved to be thrown in the creek."

Tommy finally gave in, at the urging of the other boys, and shook Mark's hand.

"Your grandfather whip you?" Mark asked.

"No, but he took my .22 away from me. But I guess he'll give it back now, when he finds out we're friends."

Pearl handed crates of strawberries to Zeb as he stacked them in the rented stake-bed truck. A dozen kids kept coming, at regular intervals, with filled baskets from the field. Several girl classmates of Chucky's arranged the quarts in the crates and layered thin slats of wood between the three levels before hooking the tops on.

"Oh, I wish Pete would get home from work," Pearl groaned. "My arms feel like they're going to break off."

It was five P.M., and she had been working in the field since early morning. She leaned against the truck, exhausted, and wiped her brow. The June sun was fierce and she felt grimy and soaked with perspiration. She wished she could take her blouse and brassiere off and go naked, but there was no possibiltiy of that. She peered up at the truck bed. The remaining space hadn't seemed to lessen from the last time she had looked.

"Aren't you stacking them kind of high?" she moaned.

"Trucks cost money," Zeb replied, "and the more trips I take, the more I have to pay. Come on, we're almost done. I'm hot and want to get the hell out of here, too. You can rest later."

Pearl picked up another crate and hoisted it to him. "Oh, Lord, they feel like they have rocks in them."

"They better not have!" Zeb warned. "You got them little girls checking the baskets like I asked?"

"Yes, for crying out loud, Zeb, none of those children are cheating us. It was only an expression."

"Yeah, well you know me. I don't take nothing for granted. You keep checking those baskets." He took another crate from her arms effortlessly.

Pete hurried through the strawberry field to the truck at the end of the rows, having just arrived home from work. "Put that thing down, Pearl!" he snapped, as he saw her struggling with a crate. Pearl lowered the box and sighed thankfully at the sight of him.

"Thank God," she murmured.

Pete noted the sick redness on her face, her hands and dress stained with berry juice. He shot a contemptuous look at his brother. "What the hell's the matter with you?" he said angrily. "You trying to kill her?"

"I'm okay, hon," Pearl said, seeing the looks on their faces. She closed her eyes as Pete felt her forehead. He took his handkerchief out and wiped her face.

Zeb jumped down from the truck and began pushing crates onto the flat bed. It angered him that he had to feel like a tyrant. If Pearl was so goddamned tired, she should have just refused to do any more. He wasn't a frigging mind reader!

"Go in the house and relax for a while," Pete told his sister-in-law, loosening his tie and rolling up his shirt sleeves. "And don't go jumping into any cold tub water while you're still hot. That's the surest way in the world to get sick."

Pearl walked off stiffly, each step a burning punishment. She told the girls to take a break and to follow her to the house for soda pop for themselves and the other children, who were picking in the field.

Pete climbed onto the truck bed and stacked the crates Zeb was putting there. Neither of them spoke.

Chucky and Tommy carried a crate over and set it down at the abandoned check station. They watched Pearl walking off tiredly with the girls.

"Hi, Uncle Pete. What's wrong with Ma?"

"She's tired from me working her to death," Zeb said tightly. "You want to quit, too?"

Pete grimaced at Zeb, watching him work off his anger. He threw a crate up every ten seconds or so.

"You might as well slow down," Pete said, "because I don't intend to let you work me to death in this sun."

Zeb's lips parted in a sneer. "Gee, you're all worn out from a hard day at your desk, aren't you?"

Pete ignored his meanness and continued to stack the crates at a sane pace. Zeb ran out of room and had to stop. He vaulted onto the truck bed, in a hurry to finish loading. Chucky and his friend stood by watching them.

The boy drew a critical look from his father. "What are you standing around for, Charlie?" he asked. "You can't make any money that way."

"I gotta tell Uncle Pete something."

Pete looked at the boy. "What do you want to tell me, partner?"

"You know my teacher, Miss Cleary?"

Pete nodded. "What about her?"

"She told me to tell you she's getting married in a couple of weeks."

Zeb stopped working. It was hard to tell which brother had the most surprised look on his face. Zeb seemed to recover first. He met Pete's spiteful look with a taunt. "Well, there goes the best piece of ass in the county," he said maliciously.

The strawberry crate in Pete's hands suddenly sprouted wings. It soared off and smashed to the ground with a creaking groan. Berries mashed and scattered in every direction. Zeb eyed his younger brother coldly.

"Any time you want to finish settling our account," he said.

For a moment it appeared as if Pete was going to take him up on it. Then he left the truck and stalked off for the house, without saying a word. The boys followed after. Zeb went back to working by himself.

"You were right about your father," Tommy admitted. "I don't like him any more. What's a 'piece of ass'?"

"It means screwin'," Chucky answered. "And he was talking about Miss Cleary! I hope my Uncle Pete beats the hell out of him some day!"

Chapter VII

Joe Hawk walked slowly through the stand of oak trees, peering up into the August foliage. He pressed a finger to his lips and imitated the chattering bark of a red squirrel. It wasn't long before he drew a reply.

A squirrel appeared on a limb, fifty feet above, and looked down curiously. He saw the hunter, stopped his scolding, and began a hasty retreat back to his nest.

Joe raised the .22 and squeezed off a shot. The small animal fell from the branch and plummeted, crashing through the leaves. It struck the ground and was off, running instantly. A second later it keeled over and appeared to die.

Joe nudged the bushy-tailed rodent with his rifle. The squirrel reared up and seized the black pipe with sharp pointed teeth, then closed his eyes sorrowfully and died. Once, as a boy, the Seneca hunter had picked up a squirrel he had shot without first checking to make sure it was dead. He learned to never make the mistake again. The end of his small game rifle was scarred and nicked from many such encounters with Mr. Red and Mr. Grey over the years.

All morning the grandfather hunted, filling his pouch with red- and orange-furred squirrels. He was at peace with himself and with the world when he was in the forest. It was his element, his timeless heritage. Only once, during the First World War, had he left it for any length of time, and, of course, when they arrested him for slaying the murderer of his children, and sent him to prison.

The barren landscape of shell-pocked France would forever stay in his memory. He had killed men with less consideration there than he gave the squirrels in his bag. Prison had been a degrading experience. Some in there were like animals, with their perverted natures. It was not good for a man to leave his home and experience the filth of the world. The Great Spirit had never intended for the red man to become so cynical and distrusting.

Two more squirrels, and he would have enough for the hunter's stew that Tommy was so fond of. He searched the tree tops as he thought. He worried about the boy. It seemed he was becoming more and more like his white friends every day. Tommy had passed up hunting with him to go watch silly animation with Zebediah's son at the theater. Now the boy was only interested in doing what his white friends wanted to do. It bothered Joe that he might be losing touch with the boy at such an early age. But then, Tommy would not have him forever. Perhaps it was best that he found his way in the world now, and made alliances that would see him through when Joe was gone.

The reservations were growing smaller. Many Indians no longer lived on the Nation lands. They lived in cities where they worked at high-rise construction jobs, like the Mohawks, or in factories, like the Oneida and Cayuga. They were becoming diversified in their religious beliefs, as well. The followers of the *Gaiwiio* became fewer each year. One day, if not watchful, the Iroquois would be no different than those ethnic groups that had adopted America and were swallowed up by her complex fabric, forgetting their heritage and origins in order to fit into the overall Anglo plan. Inevitably, Tommy would not remain as close to the land or the ways as Joe Hawk had. He, and his generation, would become lawyers and doctors, bankers and aircraft pilots. Such realizations made Joe sad. Even now, the children preferred to speak English and many failed to learn their own native tongues.

When they reached adulthood, they would marry more frequently into the white race and the white part of them would eventually dominate altogether. How long would it be before there were no longer any Seneca?

His wife had deserted him for a rich white man when Tommy's father was only a baby. When Thomas and Virginia were murdered, years ago, she had called long distance from her big house with servants in California to ask if there was anything she could do.

"Yes," he had said. "Forget us, as we have forgotten you."

She had tried to take little Tommy to Los Angeles when Joe went to prison. But Virginia's brother, James, had gotten a paper from the courts that prevented her. He was a smart man, James Goodman, and a true asset to his people. By law he was Tommy's legal guardian, and when Joe returned home after a year James had asked to raise the boy among his own children. Joe had refused him.

His grandson was heir to a chieftainship, should he prove worthy, and no person would ever take him while Joe had breath in his body with which to care and provide for the boy.

Another hour's hunting brought two more squirrels and Joe started for home. As he walked, the woods grew strangely quiet. The *pukwudjinnies* whispered warningly. "Beware, beware!"

Joe remained still, melting into his surroundings, and tried to reason out what it was that was so disturbing. Hearing a slight sound behind him, he turned quickly.

The stag walked out from behind a tree and boldly confronted the Seneca. The fur around his throat was stiff and bristling. His eyes were a sickly yellow, as if mirroring the demonic possession of Malsum. Thick stunted antlers, with sharp narrowing points, had already hardened for fighting. One swooped low over an eye, twisted grotesquely, while the other reached upwards like the outstretched claw of an eagle searching for its prey.

The deer lowered his rack and pawed the ground, blustering and snorting like a Brahma bull.

"I did not think you were dead," Joe said.

Shaman continued to shake his rack menacingly. Suddenly he attacked a sapling, shredding its bark with his antlers in a display of tremendous power. The mangled tree was a graphic depiction of just what he could accomplish were the tree a man's flesh.

"Why do you wait, deer?" Joe said. "The rifle cannot stop you. It would be as a hornet's sting."

Joe heard a voice creep into his mind. Malsum cursed him from the Place of Shadows. The wizard gave him a vision of death beneath the cruel antlers of the deer.

With an angry cry of contempt, the Seneca flung his rifle aside and pulled his short-handled axe from its sheath.

"Come, Malsum!" he cried. "Let us see if you can kill me. It is your beast who will die, not I!"

The man knew no fear, because it had never been a part of his nature. He walked toward the stag unhesitantly, meaning to cleave its skull.

Shaman backed away and voiced a shrill, unearthly scream that startled the chieftain. It sounded more like the wild shriek of a banshee than that of a deer.

Joe could smell the animal's fear.

"Fight, Malsum!" he growled. "Let us finish this thing once and for all."

The deer suddenly spun around and raced off as the enraged Seneca rushed him. He crashed through the woods in wild flight, braying and rasping, quaking the peaceful silence of the woodland with an ungodly din.

Joe watched him go and then closed his eyes and listened, concentrating. If there were any warnings being offered by the little friends, he would not turn a deaf ear to them.

Then he heard them, very faint at first, and then their voices grew louder and he knew—he knew what it was that Malsum had planned!

The demon stag ran through the woods bawling loudly with rage. He attacked trees and slashed them with his sharp antlers, scraping bark and tearing off small branches.

His eyes kindled with a burning fire that seemed to consume his brain, transforming him into a beast of prey.

A whitetail buck in the woods bolted away, in fear for his life, when Shaman suddenly lunged at him. This was not rutting season and the whitetail was of no mind to fight the maniacal beast and allow himself to be crippled or killed. Fortunately he was fleet and soon outdistanced the pursuing wizard-stag.

Finally, when Shaman gave up the chase, he headed off in a frenzy for the Simpson farm.

Chucky and Tommy knelt by the fawn as it grazed in the meadow. He had grown considerably in the four months since they had found him in the woods, and the spots on his sleek back had all but entirely faded.

Chucky put his arms around the animal's neck, pulling him close, with aching worry on his young face.

"Last night I had a dream about Shaman," he confided to his friend. "I think he is going to try to kill Heart while he's still small."

Tommy's eyes widened. "It wasn't just a dream," he said, "it was a vision. The warrior god you have chosen forewarns you—you must prepare."

Chucky's worry increased. "How? What do I do?" he stammered.

The Seneca boy thought quietly for a moment with his eyes closed. When next he opened them he said, "We will have to make strong magic! Something to protect him with."

Thelma, the fawn's adopted mother, suddenly mooed discontentedly and swayed over, wanting charge of her baby. She seemed nervous.

"Don't pester us now, Thelma!" Chucky scolded. "We ain't got time for you!"

Several townspeople greeted Joe Hawk as he parked his old truck in front of Sam Parker's office in Brant. The Seneca chieftain returned their salutations politely but made it obvious that he had no time for idle banter.

Sam was at his desk filling out a routine report when the tall, broad Indian entered. He rose up with a smile and a handshake.

"You look worried," Sam said, seeing Joe's troubled face.

"Malsum's demon is back among us. I have just seen him."

"Shaman?" Sam's eyes lit up like sparklers. "He isn't dead?"

"He is not. He smells of hatred and wickedness. And he will kill soon, if we do not stop him."

"I'll get a hunt organized right away!" Sam reached for the telephone.

Joe rested his hand on the phone and shook his head. Sam looked at him wonderingly.

"This concerns only four families," the chieftain said. "Other hunters will never find him. They will only chase him far from us, so that he may come back and attack us when we least expect. Please believe me, old friend, only one who shares the curse can kill the shaman stag."

"I know you mean well," Sam apologized, "and I respect your judgment, but I can't take the chance. That animal's a killer. I have to put out a warning."

156

Joe Hawk nodded sadly and then brightened with hope. "Then tell them the deer was seen miles away from here, so the city bounty hunters do not converge on us like locusts. You and I will hunt Malsum's beast before tomorrow's dawn and kill him."

Sam pondered the offer and finally agreed. Joe picked up the telephone and handed it to the lawman.

"Warn the Keevers and Simpsons to protect their children."

"What about the Banners?"

Joe thought back to the night Malsum's sons were killed. "They are not involved," he said.

Sam looked at him wonderingly. Perhaps he was foolish, getting old—as Zeb often chided—but he was raised among the Seneca; he believed and trusted the childhood friend. Curses, demons, Indian witch-doctors—it all sounded like such fantastic tripe! Shaman had always been a dangerous menace but not a wanton killer, as he was now. Something had to have brought about the change, and the return of the centenarian Malsum was a better logic than most. The beast had killed the Keever brothers, attacked Zeb and Chucky. It had almost killed Len Pfeister, but didn't. And that was logical in its way, for the deer certainly could have, had he really wanted. Joe Hawk was no fool. If he said Simpsons, Keevers, Hawks, and Parkers were slated for murder, Sam wasn't going to argue with him.

Sam took the telephone from Joe's hand and dialed Luke Banner's number.

Pearl's patience was wearing thin with her son.

"I just wanna bring Heart in, Ma," Chucky whined. "Please?"

Heart?. It wasn't a real name for the fawn, for his real name was kept secret, but was a play on "hart," which denoted a strong buck. Pete had thought of it when the boys had informed him that they couldn't give the tyke a proper name, or reveal his identity, until he was full-grown.

"Please, Ma?"

"No! Go watch television. Sid Caesar's on, you like him. Stop pestering me or I'll thrash you good, Charles!"

Sam Parker had called two hours earlier, giving the news that Joe Hawk had seen Shaman in the woods.

Chucky was so worried over foolish heathen beliefs about Malsum plotting to send Shaman to kill his fawn, that he was making a mental wreck out of his mother. He wouldn't desist from trying to talk her into letting him go out to the meadow to get the tyke. But there was no way he was stepping one foot out of the house!

Damn Zeb, anyways! He had flown into a rage, grabbed his rifle and a handful of ammunition, and stormed off into the woods. Pete had been taking a shower at the time, and Pearl couldn't reason with Zeb or stop him by herself.

Chucky and Tommy had been kneeling next to Heart, chanting Indian prayers, when Zeb came up on them with his rifle. He asked what they were doing as he noticed a lump of clay hanging from a leather boot lace around the deer's neck. When the boys explained that the clay covered a charm to ward off evil spirits, Zeb scolded them angrily, and ordered them to get indoors before they felt the evil spirit of his palm on their backsides.

Minutes later at the house, when Pearl told the boys that Shaman was alive and had been seen by Joe Hawk, they wanted to run back to the pasture for the fawn. But she took them both by the ears and made them park their rumps on the living room sofa and watch the adventures of the Lone Ranger.

Now she was frightened. Pete had left to take Tommy home and wasn't back yet. She loaded grandfather Zeb's old shotgun and laid it on the sink counter, remembering the winter day when that horrible creature had burst through the kitchen window after her son.

"You gotta let me go, Ma," Chucky persisted. "Heart isn't big enough to fight Shaman."

"That animal's not interested in your fawn," Pearl scolded. "He's perfectly safe. Stop carrying on like a little pagan! Go make a voodoo doll and stick pins in it or something, but leave me alone!"

Pearl softened after the outburst. "Look, Chucky," she confided, "Thelma will bring them all in in a little while. You know that. I've agreed to let you keep the fawn in your bedroom at night until that awful deer is killed . . . but please don't push me any further."

Chucky wrinkled up his nose and stamped the kitchen linoleum.

Pearl took him by the shoulders, pointed him toward the living room, and swatted his bottom, shoving him off.

"Go watch Imogene Coca," she instructed.

Nightfall was approaching. Pearl opened the door and looked out furtively, hoping to see Pete pulling into the yard or Zeb coming home from his mad venture in the woods. She was worried sick over her man. That animal was cruel and unpredictable. The way he tore into Len Pfeister's throat proved that. She was worried about being home alone, also. Pete had suggested that they ride over to the Nation with him and Tommy, but Pearl was too anxious over her husband. She wished she had gone, now. She had no idea Zeb would stay out so long. Guns frightened her, and the old shotgun would be little comfort if that crazy deer appeared while her menfolk were away!

Pearl braved stepping out onto the porch. Thelma sauntered contentedly in the meadow, the bell around her neck clanking faintly over the distance. Angela and Margie were following her. The fawn was with them, scampering about playfully. Thank God! Thelma was leading them to the barn for evening milking. Pearl couldn't have withstood another moment of her tantrum-throwing son.

"Come here, Chucky," she called.

The boy swung the screen door open and stepped out onto the porch. The distraught woman draped an arm over her son's shoulder. "You see," she said, "Thelma's bringing them in now. I told you everything would—"

They both saw the small patch of tan step out of the apple trees at the far end of the meadow.

"Oh, my God . . ." Pearl whispered.

He was foul-tempered and snorting madly. Shaman eyed the cows in the pasture with murderous intent. A plaguing cloud of mosquitos hung over his face and antlers, trying to penetrate his eyelids and nose. One bug speared into a moist nostril slit and the animal snorted, shaking his menacing rack to momentarily drive the bloodthirsty insects away. Then he ran out onto the Simpson pasture toward the cows and fawn, blaring loudly like a bull elk.

The fawn pranced toward the oncoming stag innocently as the monster charged them. Thelma bawled at her baby, but he merely stood frozen, stiff-legged, and curiously trying to comprehend the rushing animal. Angela and Margie ran for the barn, their heavy bulks pounding over the sod.

Thelma charged headlong for Shaman, the short hairs

on her back and neck standing stiffly. The heavy bovine met the stag's advance head on.

Shaman went down under her immense weight and the cow rammed her head into his belly, instinctively trying to disembowel the beast. She could have killed him then, torn him to ribbons before he regained his footing, but Thelma's horns had been hacksawed off.

Shaman bolted to his feet and gored the cow, ripping a huge gash on her rib cage. The mother cow bawled in pain, but she still refused to give way while her adopted baby remained in danger. She bowled the deer over again, and he came up under her, slashing and tearing at her underbelly. The thin hide split open and the cow's intestines came through. She went into a frenzy, kicking and biting at the deer. Her hoofs smashed into Shaman's nose, causing the beast to lose courage and run. He headed for the protective woods and Thelma chased after him. Her intestines dropped out and unwound like a double chain of link sausages. She ran for more than a hundred yards before the pain of her injury stopped her. Teetering on shaky legs, the life blood gushing from her open stomach, she collapsed to the grass and rolled over on her side. The fawn came to her and sniffed the length of her body. He trembled, bleated miserably for her to get up, and butted her face with his nose and forehead, but all the cow could do was blink at him with pain-crazed eyes and wheeze heavily, frothing terribly at the mouth.

It seemed like hours to Pearl, standing at the bottom of the bedroom stairs with Chucky behind her. She held the shotgun, fearing that Shaman would come bursting through a window at any moment. At the first appearance of the stag, she had taken her protesting son and run back into the house, closing and bolting the door. At first they had watched the fight from the kitchen window, but when the combatants passed from their view she had maneuvered to the stairwell, not knowing where the beast might be. The narrow passage afforded sanctuary above and a vantage point on the living room and kitchen windows, should the stag come for them. She rattled off Hail Marys feverishly, praying that her husband wasn't lying dead somewhere in the woods. The beast had appeared in the very place where Zeb had gone into the apple orchard.

Pearl cried out with relief at the sight of Pete's car

pulling into the front yard. Her husband was with him and she quickly thanked her creator.

"He's here!" Chucky yelled, unbolting the door and racing out onto the porch.

"Where?" Zeb demanded.

"In the pasture, Pa! He's fighting Thelma!"

They stared sadly at the suffering animal. Thelma kept trying to raise her head off the ground to look at them, her immense bulk deluged under a swarm of mosquitos. Her brown eyes were full of fear and pain and she moaned low in her throat.

Pearl knelt beside the cow and stroked her, tears streaming down her cheeks as she felt her heart breaking. Chucky sat on the grass holding his fawn possessively, blinking back his own tears. Thelma had been part of their family as long as he could remember.

"It's hard to believe that a deer could . . ." The words died on Pete's lips.

Zeb turned to him with an angry glare. He had been searching the wood's edge with his eyes in the dwindling daylight, ready to snap his rifle to his shoulder in an instant.

"Yeah, well you better believe it," he said. "You want to stay here and cry with Pearl and Charlie? Or do you want to go get your rifle and come with me?"

"Don't you try it, Zebediah!" Pearl screamed, rising with her fists clenched. "Don't you even think you're going after that devil tonight!"

Zeb released the rifle from his grasp as Pearl wrenched it from his hands, standing angrily before him with her lips quivering, her eyes wet and sparkly with tears. Zeb put his arm around her, and Pearl leaned against his chest.

"You'd better shoot her," Pete said, as the cow bellowed with pain. "I can't fix her; nobody can . . ."

Chucky sobbed, hearing his uncle's words. The cow's loud mooing became a plea, begging them for help. She made great efforts to gain her feet. Pete sat on her shoulders and kept her down. Thelma gnashed at him feebly, her thick lips curling back over grass-stained molars, her mouth full of white sudsy spittle.

"Damn! Will you shoot her?" Pete demanded.

Zeb took the rifle from Pearl and walked over to the cow. He placed the barrel a few inches behind the back of her head, knowing that the shot would kill her instantly. Pete winced and turned away, unable to watch.

Zeb looked at his wife. She was horrified. She stood watching, with white knuckles to her mouth. But she did not turn away. Chucky sat on the grass, rubbing his eyes, and he watched also.

The thought of Pete's weakness angered Zeb. Jenny Ma's death was a long way back. Neither one of them could right the wrong of her dying. He knew how Pete felt. He himself had joined up for the war not really caring if he lived or died. But twelve years was long enough for a man to bury his grief, and Zeb was sick to his stomach of feeling to blame.

"You shoot her!" he said tightly, thrusting his rifle into Pete's hands.

The younger brother's face filled with revulsion. He tried to hand the rifle back, as if it were burning the skin from his hands.

"I can't—you know I can't!"

"Then that's tough shit, junior!" Zeb said, and began stalking off for the house.

Pearl watched Pete quake, trying to muster up enough nerve to shoot the cow. His hands trembled as if with palsy. The man's normally placid features became harsh, jaws clenched and grinding. The poor farm animal, blaring out deafeningly, trying to rise to her feet, no longer concerned Pearl as much as the sheer hell her brother-in-law was going through.

"Zeb!" she yelled, "you've got to do it!"

Zeb stood at a distance and looked at Pete with quiet concern. Pete's eyes pleaded with him.

"I—I—Jesus! I c-can't shoot her!" Pete stammered.

"Yes you can." Zeb's voice was strong and confident, like a father trying to give courage to his son. "Just put it to her head and squeeze the trigger," he said calmly. "You can do it. You have to."

"I can't! You bastard! You know I can't!"

"That's not your mother, you sniveling sonuvabitch!" Zeb said. "It's a sick cow!"

Pete's face contorted with frightful hate, his eyes bulged. No longer shaking, with a blurring swiftness, he raised the rifle and took aim on Zeb. Pearl's scream seemed to reach the man, and he spun around and fired a shot into the cow's head. The animal's incessant noise stopped abruptly.

Realization of the deed made Pete shake even more uncontrollably. He threw the rifle to the grass and backed away from it.

"Get away from him!" Zeb snapped, as Pearl went to the troubled man.

Pearl stood between the brothers. "Leave him alone. He wouldn't have shot you. He didn't know what he was doing," she pleaded. "You shouldn't have done that to him. It's your fault!"

Zeb shoved her aside roughly. He looked at his brother.

"You crazy lunatic!" he said, wrenching him from his feet and throwing him to the ground. "You ever point another rifle in my face, I'll kill you!"

"I—I'm sorry . . ." Pete stammered.

Zeb hauled the cringing man to his feet. "Sorry don't cut it, junior!" he said. "Not ever again, it don't!" He sunk his fist viciously into Pete's stomach, knocking the wind from him, and then caught him on the side of the face with a blow that hammered him back to the ground.

"Goddamn you!" Pearl cried suddenly, as Zeb started to drag his brother to his feet for further punishment. "Leave him alone!" she thundered. She wrapped her nails in her husband's hair and pulled with a savagery born of desperation.

Zeb's mouth opened mutely in pain and he struck out instinctively, backhanding the woman across the face. She slammed to the ground.

"Mama!" Chucky screamed and ran to her.

Zeb stopped now. He looked at his wife and son with horror. Blood welled from Pearl's mouth as she tried to find her voice and console the terrified boy.

Pete rose to his feet, his eyes cold and sober, watching Pearl wipe blood from her cheeks with her dress sleeve. She spat gracelessly each time blood overfilled in her mouth. Chucky hugged her, as she knelt on the grass, and sobbed miserably.

A thin wire that had been stretched taut in Pete Simpson's mind for twelve years suddenly snapped at the sight of Pearl stricken and bleeding.

With a loud curse he sprang forward and smashed his fist into Zeb's jaw. The blow catapulted the man into the air and knocked him down.

"Please . . . don't fight any more!" Pearl sobbed, attempting to get to her feet, fear etched on her blood-smeared face.

Pete made her sit back on the grass. Taking his handkerchief, he wiped at her mouth gently.

"You're one dumb bastard if you let me get full height," Zeb said tightly, shaking the cobwebs out of his head and rising to his knees.

The other Simpson walked over. "I'll take the chance," he said, standing before his brother, waiting with hate-filled eyes. He backed up a few steps to allow Zeb to gain his feet. A new strength he had never known was alive within him.

Zeb was up suddenly and heading in. Pete jabbed at his face with hard, short punches that connected, taking their toll on the older brother. He threw a powerful right, but Zeb blocked it expertly, landing a haymaker of his own.

Pete rocked back from the force of the blow, but he remained on his feet. With three stiff jabs he pelted Zeb's nose until it spewed blood, and he found his brother's weakness. Zeb couldn't effectively ward off a straight shot. He was such an easy mark, in fact, it was a wonder he ever survived the many fights he was in.

They circled each other warily, looking for an opening. While Zeb expected another roundhouse, the younger fighter continued with the jabs. Finally the older man went for broke, throwing a hard punch while he was still off-balance. Pete nailed him quickly without telegraphing the right cross he threw. Zeb sprawled on his back on the grassy pasture.

"You're better than I thought," he said, rubbing his jaw and sitting up.

Pete hovered, wanting to spend the hatred that had been held dormant for more than a decade.

"Yeah, you're pretty good," Zeb grinned lopsidedly, a glimmer of pride in his jade eyes. "Can you take it dirty?"

"Anyway you like, big brother!"

"Let's go for broke, then," Zeb said, "I like it dirty."

He pivoted on his arms and swung his legs under Pete, tripping him to the ground. All of a sudden he was on top of him, his hands flat, fingers extended stiffly. He poised for a chop to Pete's neck and then checked the blow at the last moment. He damned his murderous instincts. The all-important need to win—Pete was still his kid brother.

He pounded Pete with clenched fists angrily. "Goddamn you," he swore. "You shoulda said clean!"

Pete brought a knee up hard, catching Zeb under the chin and clacking his teeth together loudly, snapping his neck back with force. As Zeb reeled from the blow, Pete pinned him to the ground and arced a powerful punch to his face. His knuckles scraped over Zeb's dentures, cracking them and rupturing Zeb's lips, but the force of the blow against the sharp incisors crippled Pete's hand with pain. His fingers spread and straightened involuntarily, refusing to reshape into a fist again without difficulty. Blood trickled out over his fingers, and the middle knuckle bulged and glistened milky white under a torn flap of skin. Wincing from the injury, Pete rose to his feet and backed away, shaking his hand and trying to stop the intense throbbing.

Halfway to his feet, Pete slammed Zeb down with the side of his injured hand. He cried out as his fingers opened and quivered from the punishment of the added impact. His right hand was now useless.

"Have you had enough?" he asked, his breath hard and ragged. His neck ached from Zeb's chopping blow; he was sore all over.

"Go to Hell," Zeb said, getting to his feet.

Pete's lips curled back with disgust and his hatred reached greater heights. He wouldn't be satisfied until one of them was either dead or crippled for life. Zeb was no good. He was no different than the animals Pete had had to fight in prison, deserving of no more consideration.

"You bastard!" Pete swore. He coiled his useless arm around Zeb's neck and held him in a vice-like grip.

Zeb didn't have the strength to throw him off. Pete's left fist struck him in the face, high, around the forehead and eyes. He had learned to stay away from the sharp dentures. Zeb struggled to free himself, reaching for a handhold around Pete's legs to throw him, but Pete stood too solidly. The pain of Pete's flailing fist became terrible. From far off he heard Pearl screaming for his kid brother to stop. His head began spinning, and he was going to black out any second.

Instinctively his hand pried in between his persecutor's legs. His fingers closed tightly around soft bulging testicles. All he had to do now was squeeze hard and yank and it would be all over for Pete.

The thought repelled Zeb, and he gagged, cursing himself. His hand released and dangled limply at his side as Pete broke out into a frenzy of punishing blows to his face. And then Zeb blacked out.

Pearl began tearing at Pete's arm, sobbing for him to release her husband.

The ache in Pete's groin seeped up into his stomach. But still he raised his arm back with effort for another blow as Pearl did all she could to restrain him.

Then Chucky was crying, "Please don't hit him, Uncle Pete! Please don't hit my father again!"

Pearl kept prodding Pete to let Zeb go. He lifted his arm and let the woman lower her unconscious husband to the ground, then collapsed next to the boy, his eyes sad and rational as his mind cleared.

"I'm sorry, son," he said.

Chucky hugged him quickly, kissing him on the side of the face, bringing tears to the man's eyes. Then he slipped away to help his mother tend to his father.

Pete knelt next to them and saw Zeb's battered face. He breathed softly, "I didn't mean to let it go so far."

"I'm not blaming you," Pearl said with a scratchy voice, her mouth bleeding. "Only . . . please tell me he's not hurt too bad."

"I'm . . . not gonna die . . . if that's what you're worried about, Red," Zeb gasped, his eyes blinking open.

With a mixture of tears and laughter Pearl hugged the man to her bosom and tightened her trembling arms around him.

Zeb winced as he saw her split lip. It was pouting outward, and still bleeding where her teeth had bitten through the inside.

"I'll never strike you again," he said emotionally. "I'll cut my frigging hand off first!"

Pearl held him as he continued to apologize, telling her how sorry he was. She ran her fingers through his hair and massaged his scalp, wondering at how much it must hurt. She felt a warm wetness, then looked at her hands and knew. Her palms came up covered with blood, and hunks of skin were wedged beneath her nails.

Zeb washed the blood from his face in the kitchen sink. His eyes were puffed, one almost entirely shut. His nose and mouth were sore, but he came from hardy stock and wasn't hurt seriously. Two large knots swelled mountainously on his forehead, adding to his grotesque appearance.

Pearl watched him from the table, holding an ice cube to her mouth.

"You want to kiss me, fat lips?" Zeb asked, his eyes soft and apologetic.

"I wouldn't talk if I were you," Pearl countered. "Yours aren't looking very appealing, either."

They kissed each other softly, awkwardly, laughing with their puffed lips pressed together, numb and bulging. Pearl took a bottle of iodine and daubed his cuts and bruises. She painted a circle around his closed eye and giggled.

"What's so funny?" Zeb asked.

"Nothing. I warned you Pete would beat the tar out of you some day if you didn't leave him alone."

Zeb nodded sheepishly. "Well, you know me, Pearl."

Pearl's eyes filled with tears again, and she hugged the somber man. "Thank you," she whispered in his ear, "for not hurting him."

Zeb clung to her, soaking up her warmth and love. "Where's my brother? He come in the house yet?"

Pete stood outside the cemetery fence, looking at the headstones, as the August sun began setting in the west. Three generations of Simpsons were laid to rest in there. Chucky and Tommy had repaired the gate and had given the fence a fresh coating of white paint a week or so before. Pearl had everything looking clean and peaceful.

The names all seemed unfamiliar to the man. It had been many years since he had ventured this close—not since Jenny Ma had died, and he had been taken off to prison.

Sam was the one who had gotten him paroled, talked the president of the Arcade First National into hiring him on as a teller to impress the correction authorities. The only favor Sam had ever asked in return was that Pete enter the cemetery with him, the morning he arrived home, and kneel in prayer at his side before Jenny's headstone.

But he couldn't do it. And all the time that followed, all these years, he couldn't bring himself to pay his ma a visit.

True, he had bought flower bulbs and rose bushes for planting on occasion, but it was always Pearl who put them to earth for Jenny. Once in a while Zeb went in to pay his respects, usually for Christmas, Easter, or Jenny's birthday. Then they would argue, Zeb trying to talk him into visiting their ma's grave with him and Pearl shutting him up when his urging got out of hand.

As Pete stood there he thought back on that time twelve years before. It was still fresh in his mind, as if it had all taken place yesterday. The time in prison seemed vague and far away—a lifetime ago—but Jenny? How could he forget Jenny? Not even the barricades he had erected around the memory of her death and the circumstances leading up to it could protect him from the tragic sense of sorrow and misery that he now felt. Zeb's fists had done more than bruise and cut him; they had opened up old wounds, dormant infections beneath his skin. After many years, they were draining, wanting to heal, fighting for a cure.

Helpless to do otherwise, Pete allowed himself to remember.

The last two years of high school, Pete had gone steady with Nora Cleary. They were the ideal couple, a model to other teen-agers, their peers said.

Nora was beautiful, charming, and vivacious.

Pete was handsome, personable, athletic, and scholarly.

He went Ivy League, dressing the part, working hard for a scholarship to a good pre-med college. He was a startling contrast to his older brother.

Burly Zeb was a high school dropout. He was crude and dirty-mouthed, always drinking and brawling in the bars with Jimmy Keever. The two of them were inseparable. They worked the same jobs: canning factories, brick yards, driving trucks. If one quit or was fired, the other went with him. They'd even enlisted in the Marine Corps together, and gone through the war at each other's sides.

They pushed spending money into Pete and Johnny Keever's hands without their asking while the younger brothers were still in high school. Johnny thought it was great; he idolized both of them. But Pete was embarrassed and he resented it. He resented any favors from either of them, especially Zeb.

He resented being supported, being told to go off to college and become a doctor and not to worry about Jenny; Zeb would always see that they had enough money.

Johnny often bragged about Zeb's exploits and his brother Jimmy's exploits. He threw their names around whenever he was in a tight spot, liking their shadows hovering over him. But Pete would just as soon have forgotten that he knew either of them.

Zeb was something of a local celebrity to Pete's classmates, however, and they never let him forget that. Girls asked him to set up dates for them; guys offered money or undying gratitude if Pete would put a word in for them to have Zeb get some bully out of their way.

If all that wasn't enough, Nora Cleary thought Zeb was cute and witty and gallant.

Zeb called her Little Sis. Nora laughed at his jokes and encouraged his flirting. But Zeb was two-faced, and behind her back he checked up on her and made sure she was being faithful to his kid brother. He gave weekly, biweekly, and monthly progress reports to Pete. The first one went something like: "She went steady with Roger Bemis for six months, but all he ever got was titty squeezes through her blouse. No one's ever laid her yet, but watch out, that's a ripe and horny gal if I ever saw one!"

The bastard! He had had no right talking about her, investigating her like she was some common tramp! And when Pete told him so, Zeb simply replied, "Just looking out for my little brother's interests."

So Pete kept Nora away from him as much as he could and tried to keep an indifferent attitude. But he couldn't help it; he just didn't like Zeb.

High school graduation made Pete and Nora feel mature and grown up, but it meant another six years of waiting through college and medical school to get married. It meant long separations and doubts about fidelity.

For Pete, necking wasn't enough any more. He felt that going all the way would bind them closer together. That summer, he and Nora made love every chance they got.

By the time September came, Nora had missed her period twice and knew she was pregnant with Pete's child.

They tried to take the honest way out, and told their parents, starting with Jenny Ma. The tender-hearted woman had scolded them both, but afterwards she had cried and hugged them, smiling through her tears and agreeing to sign for Pete to get married. He was only seventeen. It meant giving up medical school, but that was acceptable as long as her son could face up to the responsibility of the hard work it took to have a good marriage and raise children.

Unfortunately, Al Cleary, Nora's father, wasn't quite as

receptive. He beat the living hell out of Pete, the night they told him, and locked Nora up in the house, calling her a whore.

That's when it all began.

Pete stood at the cemetery fence and forced himself to continue thinking about it.

Zeb wanted to get Al Cleary for the brutal beating he had given Pete. He wanted it so bad he had raved like a maniac, the night Sam Parker had brought Pete home in the back of his car with his face battered. Sam had been angry also and wanted Jenny to swear out a warrant to have Al taken into custody and made to stand trial. But Pete requested Jenny not to press charges, and she didn't. Zeb was fuming mad.

Al Cleary had the reputation of being one of the meanest barroom brawlers in the county. The only man who had ever beaten Al in a fight was Joe Hawk, and that had been years before. Joe warned Zeb not to start anything with the older man, advising that Al wasn't the average roughneck that Zeb was used to taking on, that the man might easily put Zeb in an early grave. The Seneca chief advised Zeb to forget the incident, saying that he would talk to Al himself and work out a suitable arrangement for Pete and Nora. But Zeb told him to butt out, that the drunken bastard had had no right beating up a scrawny kid for only doing what came naturally after dating a girl for two long years.

Hell, Zeb had hardly ever waited two days!

Not long after the beating, Zeb walked in on Al Cleary at the Sportman's Bar and picked a fight. Each man used every dirty trick he knew. They virtually destroyed the tavern, breaking every stick of furniture in the place. Zeb lost his front teeth and broke three knuckles on his right hand, but he was still on his feet when the brawl ended, and therefore the winner, according to his fan club. Al left on a fire department stretcher and spent three days in the hospital after getting sewn back together.

The Keevers and the entourage of local teen-agers that had followed Zeb to the Sportman's Bar that night offered themselves as witnesses to the fact that Al Cleary had started the fight. Zeb was just in there drinking, they said, and trying to be sociable, when Al started on him, they insisted. The state police released Zeb after questioning, and the tavern's insurance company slapped a bill of

$600.00 on Al Cleary for damages, before he was even out of the hospital.

Pete tried to visit the man to make amends, but Cleary wouldn't speak to him. He felt responsible for and enraged over what Zeb had done to Nora's father.

During the years when Pete had gone steady with Nora, Al had always treated him with warm humor and friendship. The man couldn't help it if he happened to love his own daughter. Pete figured he had deserved the beating the father had given him, regardless of the opinions of others. He should have forgotten college and married Nora, seeing that he was so anxious to have her.

When Al was released from the hospital, word had it he was going to kill Zeb on sight. He made the mistake of flashing a pistol one night, and Sam Parker arrested him and put him in the town jail. While he was incarcerated, Zeb went to his home and persuaded Nora's mother to allow Nora to elope with Pete. He then drove Nora out to the Simpson farm.

At first it had been wonderful, holding Nora in his arms again after a month of not being able to see her. But Zeb's scheme of eloping behind Al Cleary's back didn't seem honorable to Pete.

Zeb wanted to drive them out of state, where it was legal for a seventeen-year-old girl to get married. But Pete refused and told Zeb to mind his own business and stop interfering in their lives. Nora sobbed when he turned his anger on her, reprimanding her harshly for sneaking off behind Al's back and allowing the man who almost killed her father to escort her publicly from her home. Common decency should have prevented her from wanting to have anything to do with Zeb!

Zeb got angry and threatened Pete, yelling at him for making the girl cry. Jenny ended the argument before it could get out of hand, but she also agreed with her eldest son, and told Pete that he was still wet behind the ears. She called him a little pisspot, her favorite expression.

Pete thought back with the added wisdom of years and realized that everything else that happened that night was as much his fault as Zeb's—perhaps even more so.

After the argument, Nora pleaded for him to come out of his locked bedroom. But Pete ignored her, ignored them all. Through the door he could hear Jenny Ma and Zeb consoling Nora as they sat in the living room, hoping that he would change his mind. Jenny lifted the girl's spirits with women's talk about newborn babies and the joys of raising a family. Zeb was witty and made Nora laugh. For hours Pete sulked and listened to them, and then he came out of his bedroom only long enough to tell them off and to announce to Nora that, for all he cared, he hoped they never got married! Nora left the house crying on Zeb's arm.

Alone, Jenny Ma gave him a good talking to. The woman always made sound sense, and it wasn't long before she had him over his mad and more than willing to call Nora up and make amends—but Nora didn't get home for hours. It was 3 A.M. when she returned his call and finally admitted, under a ruthless interrogation, that she had allowed Zeb to make love to her.

Jenny was upstairs, asleep in her bed, and knew nothing of what had happened when Zeb finally came home. The noise of their fighting and of the back of Pete's head going through the living room window brought Jenny down the stairs in time to find her younger son lying on the floor amid a pile of torn curtains and splintered glass.

Pete ran into his bedroom and locked the door. He came back out with his loaded rifle pointed on Zeb.

Zeb warned him to put it down, or he would take it away from him. But Joe Hawk had trained Pete with the rifle since their father died. Pete was good with it, and no one was going to take it away from him. He put two bullets across Zeb's shoulders, making a pair of bloody epaulets, when Zeb started toward him. His third shot cut a path through the tattooed heart on Zeb's right bicep that said "Mother."

Jenny screamed and got between them, and Zeb charged Pete and wrestled with him for the rifle. They struggled, falling over furniture, rolling on the floor, cursing and shouting—and then the weapon fired, as if of its own volition.

The bullet smashed through Jenny's face.

Pete swung the cemetery gate open and walked past the well-kept graves to his mother's headstone.

It was a shiny grey slab of marble with white specks, engraved.

> Jennifer Ann Simpson
> Beloved Mother & Wife
> Born 1897 – Died 1941

Jenny had been eleven years younger than her husband, marrying Zeke at the age of eighteen. She was still young and pretty when she died.

Sam Parker had always been in love with her, and he had proposed twice a year after Zeke passed away. The night Pete and Nora told Jenny they wanted to get married and she gave her blessings, Sam came over, and she accepted his proposal. They were to have been married at Christmas time, when Sam could take a leave from the department. How very much he had been cheated of.

All these memories that had been buried for years in Pete's mind suddenly surfaced.

Jenny had still had a long life in front of her when he killed her. How could he ever expect to be forgiven?

Deep within, he felt Sam must really hate him for robbing him of his happiness. All his life Sam had been in love with Jenny. Pete remembered him crying like a child when he came to the house after—

Tears brimmed in Pete's eyes as he knelt down before his mother's headstone.

"Hello, Ma," he whispered. "I guess—I guess you know I've been home for some time now. I'm sorry I haven't come to talk to you sooner . . . but . . ."

The words choked in Pete's throat. He cried hoarsely. The sound was like a hushed laugh of misery to his startled ears. The overwhelming emotion was new to him. He couldn't remember the last time he had cried; he had thought himself immune. It felt terrible and he wanted to stop, to end the misery of it, but he felt if he did the shame and pain was going to build up inside until his heart burst. Helpless to do otherwise, he allowed the release to continue.

"I'm sorry, Ma," he sobbed. "I'm so very sorry . . ."

His mind flooded with the many pleasant images of the tender maternal love he had known through his childhood. Jenny's face and form appeared in his memory, a wisp of a ghost, unable to hold him and soothe away his heartache now that he needed her as he had never needed her before. His soul seemed to be washing itself clean with tears, tears that gushed forth unendingly, blurring his vision and stinging his battered face. He hadn't cried over Jenny Ma, even the night she died in his arms. Now God was paying him back for that.

He ached to be loved and forgiven, to be embraced

before his expanding consciousness leaked out so far it could never be gathered again and returned to him. He had committed the primal sin of matricide. How could he go on living with the guilt of knowing he had killed his own mother?

Suddenly Zeb was there behind him, pulling him up and holding him, his muscles taut and binding. Pete embraced him back, and they cried together. Half of Zeb was Jenny, and it was as if she herself were there. Zeb managed to speak, and his words fell like summer dew over a dry and thirsty land to Pete's ears. He said that Pete should stop blaming himself for their mother's death, that *he* was the one to blame, *he* was the one the courts should have held responsible and sent to prison.

Pearl stood on the meadow in the summer night and watched the two men she loved as they wept and embraced. All her problems seemed to vanish, unimportant, erased forever. Her heart filled to overflowing and she thought about the wonderful mother whom she had only known through the memories of others.

Jenny, in her wisdom, had made them forgive each other. She had reunited her sons, lured them into that peaceful place of death and lifted the curse of their lives from their shoulders.

And as Pearl turned and went back to the house, the old woman whispered in her ear that she would have gladly done so sooner, if only they had let her.

Chapter VIII

Mark sat on his bed pouting. He and his friends were going fishing for big cats in the morning, and big cats liked night crawlers best of all. But Luke had refused, at Emily's urging, to let Mark hunt the fat worms he could find in the pasture after dark. Sam's telephone call, warning them of Shaman's presence in the vicinity, had caused them to restrict the boy to the farmyard the entire afternoon, and the argument that all the Brant children were under similar parental duress was no comfort to the bait-hungry lad.

Still they were out there, prime for the taking! and the temptation was too much to bear, Shaman or no Shaman. He slipped back into his jeans and T-shirt and snuck off through the dark, sleeping house. He commandeered Luke's flashlight from the kitchen drawer and an empty tin can from the garbage bag and went outside into the warm midsummer night.

The stars twinkled above, a myriad of precious gems on dark velvet. The huge barn loomed dark against the bright sky, and the full moon seemed so close that it made the plum and cherry trees in the yard cast elongated shadows. A calf bawled for its mother in the pasture, sad and plaintive. Crickets chirped along the foundation of the barn as Mark rounded the mammoth structure.

Mark caught a half dozen of the plump little bugs and dropped them into the tin can. A fellow never knew when a big bass might come along, and everyone knew the only thing a bass liked better than crickets were crayfish, and Mark had caught plenty of those in the cow creek before Emily discovered his absence and scooted him back to the yard at supper time. Great! Now he had crickets to back them up with!

Some of the cows ran away from him as he approached them in the pasture; others just lay there, contentedly chewing their cuds and blinking at the beam as he aimed the flashlight in their faces.

He had to constantly shoo curious heifers and calves away as he searched for the night crawlers. The ground was too dry, and the only things he found were skinny, sickly-looking white worms. He had to go to the bathroom, and unzipped his jeans, spouting a stream of pee high into the air. A puzzled calf came within range and the boy delightedly peed in its face, laughing when it lapped greedily with its tongue at the jet of brackish liquid. He finished and put himself away, hopelessly directing his light back to the dry ground. The pickings were very slim indeed.

He thought of going to the frog pond, but he didn't want to leave the comfort and security of the bedded and grazing dairy animals, thinking that perhaps one might protect him if Shaman showed, as Thelma had protected Chucky the winter before. Then again, the wet muddy shore of the pond was the only solution if he wanted a chance at those cats in the morning.

Where he had cursed and ranted at the calves, shooing them away, he now attempted to coax them into following him. But they ignored him and refused to leave their mothers. So that was the end of that idea. He decided to return to the house and get back into bed. Sometimes Luke got up in the middle of the night with a full bladder, and he'd get a good chewing out and be kept home from fishing if Luke caught him out of doors contrary to orders. Lousy dry meadow! Mark went back to the house and snuck quietly inside.

Pearl listened to them as they drank at the kitchen table and swapped childhood reminiscences. She enjoyed seeing them like this. A side of Pete she had never dreamed existed revealed itself as he shared his brother's liquor. His laughter was full and spontaneous during the stories Zeb told. They both nearly split their sides every few seconds, it seemed. Pearl, herself, found the stories hilarious and didn't want them ever to end. Some of them had started getting a little raw, so she had put Chucky to bed an hour before, allowing Heart to sleep with him. But in a way she wished she had let him stay up and listen, his father and uncle seemed like such wonderful friends now. They were really going to be a family, for the first time ever!

"Remember that time Pa poured Joe Hawk a cup of apple jack? An' old Joe spit it out, saying' it tasted like pee?" Pete's eyes twinkled, his bruised face flushed and drunken.

"Yeah," Zeb chimed in, "Pa tasted some an' agreed with him. I was about fifteen—" An accusing eye fell on Pete. "Was that you peed in that jug?"

"Yep!" Pete said, patting Zeb's swollen cheek. "You an' Tom Hawk wouldn' let Johnny an' me go nightfishin' at the river with you, so we peed in Pa's fruit liquor, knowin' . . . knowin' . . ." Pete broke into laughter helplessly, unable to finish his story.

Zeb nodded his head with mock disgust, his bruised lips parted in a smile. He looked at his wife wryly, seeing her eyes aglow with enjoyment as she waited for the end of the story.

". . . Pa blamed Zeb an' made him . . . made him drink a cup of his own . . . of his own . . ."

"You dirty little bastard!" Zeb laughed, and attacked Pete's head, mussing his combed hair.

Pete wrestled away from him and backed away from his seat at the table, doubled over with hilarity.

"Ol' Zeke had me hang my wang out in the barn an' pee in a cup an' drink it, while he stood over me with a razor strap," Zeb informed his wife.

"Oh, how terrible! You're kidding!"

"Hell I am!" Zeb grinned, narrowing his eyes at Pete as he sat down in his chair again and poured himself another glass of Len Pfeister's corn liquor. "Our ol' man was one of those 'do unto others as they do unto you' believers."

" 'Do unto others as you would have them do unto you,' " Pearl corrected.

"Yeah, well, Pa never heard that version."

Pete poured the last few drops of corn from the jug. It was an effort for him to find the glass without spilling the liquor all over Pearl's new orange checkered tablecloth.

"How in God's name did you two drink all of that?" Pearl wrinkled her nose. Zeb had poured her half a glass of the firewater hours ago. She had tried one experimental sip and had had to drink three cups of coffee to wash the taste from her mouth.

"Heck, it's good stuff, Sis," Pete confided.

"Yeah, ol' Lenny makes ambrosia—pure Prohibition recipe ambrosia!" Zeb hoisted his glass and chased it with a swig from a green quart bottle of O'Keefe's Ale. " 'Member the time I used Ma's bloomers to clean cowshit off'n my new boots, an' she whupped you with a willow rod?"

Pete winced and rubbed his seat as if remembering the pain.

"Boy, she beat me worse than anything." He whistled. "I couldn't park my fanny on a wooden chair for a week!"

"Aha!" Zeb gloated. "Now there's one I did you on! I had shit on them bloomers from one end to the other, just hangin' on that clothesline flappin' in the breeze, pretty as you please!"

"I'd have killed you!" Pearl laughed.

"She darn near did—me!" Pete said.

" 'Member the time I caught you screwin' li'l Kathy O'Neil in the hay loft?"

Pearl's mouth opened and she stared with surprise at Pete. He blushed and shied under her look of amazement.

"C'mon, Zeb!" he protested. "Knock it off! That's personal. Kathy's a married woman now."

Zeb guffawed at his brother's embarrassment and stood up wobblily, graphically thrusting his hips back and forth. "Boy, I never saw anyone hump that fast in my life!" He roared with laughter.

Pete's red face reached a shade of purple. "Goddamn it, Zeb!" he exploded. "Will you shut up?" He looked at Pearl with embarrassment. "I didn't mean to cuss in front of you, Sis," he apologized.

Pearl waved him off, her green eyes smiling at him mischievously. "How old were you when you had your little love affair?"

"I don't know," Pete continued to blush, "maybe thirteen or fourteen. . . ."

"Thirteen!" Pearl gasped.

"Shit!" Zeb scoffed. "He wasn't much older or bigger than Charlie is now! Kathy might have been thirteen, she had boobs an' hair, but Pete—"

"How do you know she did?" Pearl shot at him quickly.

Zeb suddenly became confused. He grinned sheepishly.

"Go on—tell her how you know," Pete taunted, grinning broadly.

"What do you say we change the subject?" Zeb snickered.

Pearl scowled and punched him hard on the arm. He pulled her down onto his lap and slobbered on her neck, tickling her and making her hunch her shoulders squeamishly.

"You're the only gal for me now, Red," he promised.

"I'd better be!" Pearl warned, her eyes twinkling merrily but also inflamed with jealousy.

"Hell, you know me," Zeb said, "I ain't even looked at another woman since I met you. You're better'n any dozen of 'em put together."

"I heard those native girls in the Philippines were pretty obliging to American soldiers during the war," Pete taunted.

Pearl surveyed her husband's face carefully, ready to interpret the slightest wavering as an admission of guilt. If there was any, Zeb guarded himself expertly.

"Shit!" he answered with a sneer. "Those island broads were the ugliest bitches I ever saw in my life!" He looked squarely at his wife. "You didn't catch me comin' home with gonorrhea, did you?"

Pearl shrugged and gave in. She kissed him deliciously and got off his lap. "Just checking," she said.

Zeb looked at his brother smiling into his glass. "Thanks a lot, pisspot," he said.

"You started it, I didn't."

Pearl laughed at Pete with amusement. "I'd have never believed it of you, Peter Simpson," she teased, "fighting, drinking, carrying on with naive young girls, and sitting here getting liquored with Zeb!"

Pete didn't know how to answer her. A sad smile came on his face and his blue eyes took on a slightly haunted cast.

Pearl embraced him as he sat. Pete's eyes adored her. "I love you just the same though," she confessed and pecked a kiss on his cheek.

"You've always had a big ache in your heart over your mom, honey. I hope that it's gone now."

Pete gazed into her eyes. "Some . . . I guess it's gone some."

Zeb's drunken face twisted sorrowfully with rising emotion. He stood up and pounded the kitchen table hard with his fist. "It's gone and it's gonna stay gone!" he choked. "We been hatin' long enough for sumpthin' we can't do nothin' about! If we gotta hate, then let's hate that friggin' deer!"

Pearl felt her emotions trying to overwhelm her as Zeb shuffled over and took Pete in his arms for the fifth time since they had sat down to drink long hours before. This time it wasn't casual, a mere bond of friendship—they were reaching out to one another, applying balm to the wounds that had kept them apart their entire adult lives.

"I'm going to take my bath now . . ." she said in a wavering voice and left the kitchen.

She wiped her stinging eyes and walked through the living room to the back bedroom where Chucky was in bed. She looked in on him, finding him asleep; the bright stars cast soft light over him through the curtained window. Heart raised his head and stared at her with large sad eyes from where he was curled at the foot of the bed. She sat down next to the animal and petted him. He licked at her face and crawled closer. She fingered the lump of hardened clay hanging from the leather lace about the fawn's neck. Hidden beneath that clay was the image of Chucky's mysterious Seneca god. Tommy and Chucky had both insisted that Shaman would try to kill Heart. It had sounded foolish then, but now, after seeing what the beast had done to Thelma, she just didn't know what to believe any more.

True, male deer had a terribly nasty streak in them if they were bothered during rutting season, or were cornered or trapped, but they weren't deliberate, wanton killers by nature, the way Shaman was, stalking his prey like some wild carnivore. She could find no explanation short of the supernatural, and she was very frightened.

Tommy had gone to great lengths earlier, describing how Malsum wanted revenge for the deaths of his sons and had conjured up demon forces that had helped his soul to enter Shaman's body. Lord, how she wanted to see that animal destroyed! The threat of him hung over her family's head like a dark angel with an upraised sword. Heaven protect them when they hunted him in the morning. . . .

Zeb tried to draw a map of the Seneca Woods on a piece of tablet paper as he described to Pete how they were going to find Shaman. But he was so drunk he kept breaking the pencil point and sharpening it with his hunting knife, until there was only a worthless stub left.

"We need another pencil," he announced, as the point broke for the last time. He rummaged through the junk drawer in the kitchen cabinet for one.

"You find it an' I'll be right back," Pete said. "I've got to go to the barn and see a man about buying a horse." The walls and furniture kept bumping into him as he hurried through the house. His shoulders and knees smarted by the time he reached the bathroom door and opened it wide without knocking.

Pearl was standing in front of the medicine chest mirror putting her wet hair up in rollers, her bath water draining from the tub. She was as naked as the day she was born.

"I swear, Zeb, the way you barge in on——" Pearl turned from the mirror and saw that it was not her husband who had entered the room.

"Pete, what are you——" Panic-stricken, she grabbed a towel and covered herself.

"Jesus, I'm sorry, Sis," Pete stammered. "I didn't know you were in here; the door was unlocked."

"Go on out, and let me put my robe on," she said, red-faced, holding the towel in front of her as he stared at her, drunk and smiling.

"You know, you're very beautiful," Pete said softly. "I never imagined you could be so lovely."

His eyes became gentle, and he shut the door, remaining inside. Pearl knew that she should be alarmed and angry, but it all seemed so natural to her. After seven years of living with him it was as if he were her husband, as well as Zeb.

"Please go out, will you?" she coaxed.

Pete put his hands on her shoulders and bent down to kiss her. She turned her face for a moment, and then she felt drawn to him, her resistance breaking. She allowed him the kiss. The taste of strong liquor filled the inside of her mouth as he parted her teeth and pushed his tongue in. She caressed it with her own the way she did Zeb's when they were making love. Involuntarily, her body pressed against him, and as the kiss excited her she let go of the towel and embraced him. Her breathing became thick, and she shuddered as she felt his hands exploring her.

His touch, and the realization of what was happening, snapped her out of it. "Oh, my God!" she gasped, shoving him away roughly. "What are we doing!"

Pete stared at her nakedness, guilt seeping onto his face. A tremor coursed through Pearl. "Get out of here!" she cried. "Damn you, get out!"

Pete left the room, slipping out and closing the door quietly behind him. Pearl hooked the clasp and sat down on the commode, her brain screaming with accusations.

Pete was her brother! What had gotten into him? What had gotten into her? How could she have let him touch her like that? She had actually responded to his lovemaking!

A loud rattling and banging startled the woman as she sat thinking.

"Open the damn door, Pearl!"

Her heart pounded in her ears as she slipped into her bathrobe and tied it tightly about her waist. Cringing, she unlocked the door, and stepped back timidly as her husband came in, drunk and grimacing.

"What do you want?" Her voice was thin.

"Hell, you know me, Pearl." Zeb hastened, unbuttoning his fly. "When Mother Nature calls, us Simpsons just got to answer!"

Mark listened to the crickets clinking in the tin can. He had a book over the top, and occasionally an insect jumped high enough to make a sharp whack against the cloth cover. Sleep wouldn't come. All he could think about were the night crawlers stretched out on the muddy bank of the frog pond, a half mile from the house, at the end of the cow pasture.

He thought of the looks on everyone's faces when they heard how brave he was, to go to the pond at night all by himself. A small voice in his mind tugged, "Think of the respect and praise they'll shower on you. And you know you're not going to catch any catfish without night crawlers!"

Mark set the full can of worms down and swished his palms clean in the warm pond water. A bullfrog sprang from the bank and landed with a loud splash that startled him. Several other splashes followed from nearby. The pond was full of frogs. Luke raised them to sell to fancy restaurants in the city.

Mark toyed with the idea of capturing one, knowing that the boys would have to believe his daring nighttime mission then. But it was foolhardy to think he might catch one of his pa's yellow-bellied croakers bare-handed. They were too fast. And even if he did get lucky enough to palm one, it would be too slippery and too strong for him to hold on to. A frog gig or a fly rod, with a bug dangling in front of their noses, was about the only way, and since he had neither of those devices he gave up his scheme.

A small leopard frog hopped over next to the boy, and he grabbed it quickly. It was an invader to the pond, and an unwelcome one at that, for leopards rarely grew large enough for commercial purposes. Once having caught the runt, Mark discovered that he didn't really want it, but it didn't seem fair to have gone to the trouble of catching it only to turn it loose again. If he threw it into the middle of the pond, chances were it would be devoured before it could reach the shore. Bullfrogs were all appetite, and would eat most anything, even each other. But that wouldn't be any fun because he wouldn't be able to see when they caught him. The moon was nearly all the way down, and it was too dark. There was one thing, though, that was fun to do with frogs.

Mark broke a weed off and fashioned it into a slender blow pipe. He thrust one end up the frog's rectum and blew hard into the other end. The leopard frog's stomach swelled and puffed out like a rubber balloon and its kicking spasms slowed. Once Donny O'Neil had done the same thing to a small tree frog, and it had exploded. Try as he might, however, Mark couldn't make the leopard frog burst. He tired of the game and set it down in the water next to the bank. The frog tried to swim away but was helpless to do so. In a moment it turned over on its back and died, its little man-like hands outstretched in a gesture of pitiful supplication. Mark felt a twinge of conscience over the crime. Such cruelty was the very thing for which Miss Cleary had often scolded him.

"Sorry, froggie," Mark said, and threw it out to the middle of the pond, where it would be eaten and he wouldn't have to look at it.

A cloud drifted in front of the sinking moon and the meadow suddenly darkened. Mark peered at the obscure shadows of trees and bushes. Now that he had nothing to occupy his mind, he started to get a little afraid. He picked up his worm can and his flashlight and brushed off his knees, ready to sprint home.

A dark shadow snorted and walked towards him.

Mark breathed a sigh of relief as he saw the outline of the calf. He flicked his light on and shone the beam at the animal—but it wasn't a calf!

"Mama!" Mark cried with fright.

Shaman's hideous face and glowing eyes confronted the boy.

Out in the middle of the pond, a bullfrog splashed loudly as it found the bloated carcass of the leopard frog.

Zeb and Pete each took a fifty-pound pail of mixed lye from the barn as they walked off for the woods with their rifles. It was still dark, but they had no trouble finding Thelma's body. They poured the lye paste over the cow's remains and set the empty pails down.

"I hope the boy doesn't come out to see her before we can get her in the ground," Pete said.

"He's got to grow up sometime," Zeb answered. "Everything in the world isn't pretty. I just hope he doesn't ever have to fight in any wars."

"It was bad, huh?"

Zeb nodded. "They say Korea is worse. I'm glad you're exempt."

They walked off quietly toward the woods.

Joe Hawk glared at the boy as he appeared in the doorway of the cabin with his .22 rifle in hand. "I said you cannot go."

"Why not? I can shoot good, and I'd be safe with you by me."

"You will be safer at home. You are not going into the woods until the demon is killed. Go back inside."

Tommy stood in the doorway, trying to think of a more convincing argument. He had experienced another dream while he slept, and his mother had come to him. He wasn't sure, but he seemed to remember her telling him that he must find the stag and kill it.

"I have to go, Grandpa," he protested, "I had a vision and—"

"Must you shame me with your disobedience in front of my oldest friend?"

Tommy slipped back into the house and closed the door.

"He's a spirited little guy." Sam chuckled.

"Yes. And very stubborn and strong-willed!"

"Reminds me of another Seneca boy I knew once," Sam said.

"He reminds you of me?"

"Yes, very much so."

Joe nodded to himself and smiled. "But I was never disobedient."

"I remember a few times Wise Thomas lost his patience with you," Sam corrected, as they walked off through the predawn settlement.

Several of the neighbors' dogs trotted over with wagging tails for head pats from Joe. The old Seneca thought about his friend's counsel. He smiled and laughed a little, recalling some long-forgotten incidents.

"Yes, I remember, also, now," he said, "but you are wrong about it being a few times—it was many!"

Sam took cigars from his pocket as they chuckled, handed one to Joe, and lit them both.

"They'll top off that delicious stew you made for breakfast. You know, sleeping over last night was like being a kid again . . . I almost expected to see Mary cooking in the kitchen when we got up this morning . . ."

"Yes, sometimes I also feel her presence very strongly," Joe said. Then he frowned. "There will be no rest for the dead or the living until Malsum's evil spirit is cast from this world."

Pete bent down alongside Zeb and examined the tracks in the soft earth.

"That's him, all right," Zeb said in a hushed voice.

"You sure?"

"Should be—I've tracked and shot him more than anyone these past years."

"Looks like he came from Banner's pond."

"That's a good guess. A lot of deer bed down there at night, wade out for the lilies."

Pete felt the moist soil.

"I make 'em out as fresh tracks," Zeb said, "no more than two hours old at the most."

"Could be older; air got damp around three A.M. last night."

"I thought you turned in when we went to bed. What were you doing up so late?"

"I had trouble sleeping, so I got up and walked a spell."

"Pearl and me keep you awake with squeaky bedsprings or sumpthin'?"

Pete ignored the grin on Zeb's face and shrugged. "To tell the truth, I was sick to my stomach from all that drinking."

"You'll get used to it."

"I doubt that. I don't intend to make it a habit."

"Yeah, well, I didn't either. I guess the fact is I'm gonna try and quit. I promised Pearl last night. Man has a woman like her, I suppose he don't need anything else. You ain't the only one who was awake all night." Zeb grinned. "Thought that woman was gonna kill me!"

"We'd better cut the gab and get after Shaman." Pete walked off, abruptly ending the conversation.

For an hour they tracked the deer, and then his game became obvious. Shaman was a sly one, all right. He set false trails and ran in circles, leading his pursuers to believe he was just up ahead, when in reality he was behind them. They found fresh tracks that were only minutes old by turning around and heading back towards Luke Banner's pasture.

"See how he's running straight now?" Pete said. "He'll stay at the edge of the woods, thinking that anyone hunting him is deep in the middle."

"Sonuvabitch!" Zeb fumed. "I wonder how many times he's worked that trick on me before? Don't seem smart, though, to be near fields and farmhouses where dogs can pick up his scent."

"It is if he doesn't have a scent."

"What do you mean?"

Pete bent down and picked up several small chips of a dark greasy substance scattered around the tracks. He smelled them and handed them to Zeb.

"Recognize this?"

Zeb's eyes opened wide. "Manure? He's been rolling in cow shit?"

Pete nodded. "Learned that from Joe when I was a kid. A smart animal will always try to hide his smell when dogs are around, with whatever's strong and handy."

Pete started off at a fast trot. "My hunch is we've got

about two miles to go before he cuts back in again. I think I know where we can come out ahead of him."

Zeb followed, matching Pete's gait and rationing his breath for endurance. He felt admiration for his younger brother. After all the intervening years, Pete hadn't lost his touch. As a kid, he was one of the best at hunting and shooting. When he had pointed the rifle at Zeb the night before, and then spun around and shot Thelma without even a pause to aim, the shot had been as clean through the center of her brain as if he had held the rifle point-blank to her head. Pete had all his old talents again, and Zeb was damn happy to have him with him.

"You heading where I think you're heading? Red Jacket Hill?"

"Good guess. That's where we're going."

"Guess, hell!" Zeb protested. "We'd better pick up the pace. That bastard's headin' back into the mountains on us again!"

"Thought Joe said he wouldn't leave until he made a kill?"

"Yeah, well, that's a bunch of shit! There ain't no ghost in that frigger. He knows we're on him and he wants out."

"Maybe the cow was what he was after all along?" Pete offered.

"Could be. Too bad she wasn't in heat when he come on her."

"Why?"

"Saw a big buck trying to screw a cow once, when I was a kid. Only he couldn't reach her with his pecker. If Thelma'd been horny and a little friendly, chances are she'd be alive right now."

Pete stooped and looked at the tracks as they veered off into the woods. He motioned Zeb close.

"He'll cut in now and run the edge of Mohawk Meadow," he said, "making sure there's no trap before he crosses. We'll get on ahead and wait for him."

Zeb wrinkled his nose as Pete broke a crusted cow pie he had picked up a ways back and began rubbing the fresh manure over his pants and shirt. He rubbed his rifle with it as well.

"God damn!" Zeb pinched his nose shut. "Don't you think that gland smell we put on this morning is enough?"

"Seneca still keep cattle in Mohawk Meadow, don't

they? That's the only smell he won't be wary of. He's covered with manure himself. It'll be hard for him to find us unless he hears or sees us."

Zeb shook his head and dug out a handful of the greasy crud, smearing it over his clothing and rifle. Pete grinned at him. Every farmer was used to the smell of manure, even liked its pungent odor when it was a few days old—but rubbing it on your clothes was something else entirely.

They walked the pasture edge, peering into the woods in case Shaman should double back within sight. When the grassland ended they had to pass through a narrow stretch of pines. They moved like snails, making sure of every step, avoiding anything that could snap and give away their position. Suddenly Pete froze. Zeb wonderingly did likewise. The younger brother's face tightened, and he spun around.

Joe Hawk laughed low in his throat twenty feet behind them. He held up his hand, as if admitting he had been beaten. Sam Parker stepped out of the woods, a small twig crunching underfoot as he came, and Pete realized that it was Sam whom he had heard, not Joe.

"Keep your voice low," Joe admonished. "The deer is there." He pointed at the woods, motioning twice with a finger; his way of saying not very far, but still too far. "He thinks he is safe and is not trying to hide his trail. We will go to Sagoyewatha's Hill and wait for him to cross the big meadow."

Sam smirked at sight of the Simpson brothers' bruised faces.

"Looks like someone finally got tired of being pushed around," he said to Zeb.

"Yeah, well, you don't have to look so goddamn happy about it, old man," Zeb said, a touch of Sam's humor mirrored in his green eyes.

"You are brothers again?" Joe asked. As Pete nodded, the chieftain's eyes grew warm. "Jenny will be happy now," he said.

"Jesus, I wish I could have seen that fight!" Sam feigned disappointment. "Pete won, didn't he?"

"You old fart!" Zeb held out a piece of reeking manure to the grinning lawman. "If you're goin' with us, you gotta smear up in cow shit," he said.

"What for?" Sam asked. "You're wearing enough for the four of us by yourself."

"The odor is strong," Joe added. "There was no need for both of you to hide your smells when you walk so close together."

Zeb looked at Pete accusingly. "Did you know that? You dirty bastard," he groaned, as Pete cracked a smile.

The four men walked on then, heading for the narrowest part of the meadow, where Shaman was most likely to pass.

A twig snapped in a hedge of wild blackberry brambles. The intruder made rustling noises like those of a large animal. Four rifles butted against shoulders as the hunters waited. Often enough deer would forage for the wild ripe berries, impervious to the sharp thorns with their fur-covered hides. Shaman would have had to lose his senses entirely to be trapped and killed so ignobly, yet every man hoped beyond reason that it was Shaman.

"Ouch! Dammit!" The four quickly lowered their guns. A stiff look came on Joe's face as Tommy crawled out of the brambles at their feet with his .22. His scratched face blanched as he realized his dilemma.

"We could have shot you, son," Pete said sternly. "That's a pretty stupid shortcut to take. You must have more thorns in you than a porcupine has quills."

"I do." Tommy winced, climbing to his feet and lowering his eyes submissively from his grandfather's look.

"You three get the demon," Joe said. "I will take *Stupid* Thomas home where he belongs."

"Let me take him," Sam said. "All of you are better at this stalking business than I am. And besides, I make more noise than a cow would in here."

"I know a Seneca who makes noise like a herd of cows," Joe said sorely.

Tommy glanced furtively at his grandfather. He clenched his teeth tightly but held his tongue.

Joe then said to the boy, "Go with my brother and obey him. He has a strong hand, and my permission to use it on you!"

Tommy's eyes blinked with tears of shame. "Grandpa," he pleaded. "Let me go with you. . . . I can kill Shaman . . . I have had a dream . . ."

Joe looked at his grandson wonderingly. To hear the dream would force him to honor it. Malsum was clever and perhaps a sender of false visions. The boy was not fully aware of the great danger. "My eyes do not see as yours," he said, and then he turned his back on the boy and walked off.

"That little pisspot has spunk, hunting that big frigger with only a .22," Zeb said as he and Pete followed after the Seneca. "I wish some of it would rub off on Charlie."

"He does all right," Pete said.

"You think so? Every time I ask him if he wants to go hunting with me, he backs off. I don't think he likes me very much."

Pete looked at his brother's glum face. It was another one of those rare moments of confession that had been surfacing lately.

"That's as good a guess as any," he admitted. "A man has to earn a boy's friendship, even his own son's."

"Yeah, well, I suppose it's my own fault if he takes me with a grain of salt. You didn't like Pa very much, did you?"

"Not until after he died."

They walked out onto the meadow after the tall Seneca.

Luke stepped into the kitchen and washed his hands at the sink. He took one of Emily's dish towels and dried off, going behind her at the stove to see what she was cooking.

"That smells good, Mother," he said.

There was sow belly pork curling into rinds, hash browns and eggs in a separate frying pan, and a steaming pot of white gravy simmering on a back burner.

"Have you got biscuits or bread to go with that?"

"I sure do," Emily said, opening the oven for him to investigate two large tins of butter-glazed corn bread.

"My, my," Luke said, patting her affectionately on the shoulder, "you sure know how to spoil me." He sat down at the kitchen table in front of his setting and sighed tiredly. "Where's the boy?" he asked, seeing Mark's clean plate and silverware across the table.

Emily's face suddenly filled with apprehension. "Wasn't he in the barn helping you do the milking?"

Luke rose up, intending to check Mark's room.

"He's not in there," Emily informed him. She cringed and grabbed at her heart.

Luke hurried to her side. "You calm down now, Em,"

he said. "Maybe he snuck out early and has gone fishing with Donny already."

"Call the O'Neil's place and find out!" the silver-haired farm wife demanded.

Luke made her sit down at the table and poured her a cold glass of fresh orange juice. "Maybe you'd better take one of your heart pills," he coaxed.

"Please!" she cried.

Luke called Doug O'Neil's farm. Doug answered, saying that Donny was just now getting out of bed, and that as far as he knew, he was supposed to have driven over at 7:30 A.M. and pick Mark up. No, Mark wasn't at his place, and wasn't supposed to try walking the woods or fields, as they had agreed. Luke thanked the farmer for the information and hung up, trying to act calm and casual for his wife's benefit.

"Look, you hold the breakfast, Em," he said to the distraught woman. "The boy's probably out in back of the barn in the manure pile, looking for red worms. You know how upset he was because we wouldn't let him hunt night crawlers last night."

Em arose suddenly and hurried to her utility drawer. She pulled it open and looked inside. "Luke, where's your flashlight?"

"Now calm down, Mother," the lanky farmer said, quickly concocting a story. "I took it out to the barn with me this morning, so I wouldn't trip in a pothole on the way and break my neck. I must have left it in one of the stalls."

"Go find him for me," Em pleaded, "and if he's out in the pasture or at the creek I want him punished severely!" The woman sat down again, breathing heavily with a tightness in her chest. "My heart can't take this kind of aggravation!"

Luke checked the manure pile but found no sign of the boy having been there. Mathias joined him and they walked out onto the pasture. They searched the immediate vicinity and the nearby creek, all to no avail. Mathias suggested the frog pond at the end of the meadow when their loud shouts brought no response.

When they reached the pond each man went an opposite way around the perimeter, searching the bushes and reeds, intending to meet on the far side and search the nearby woods if they still hadn't found him.

191

Mathias looked at Mark's body floating face downwards in the water. At first he thought it was a dead swan. They used the pond at times. Then Mark's head bobbed, displaying his towheaded shock of hair.

"Oh, my Lord, child!" Mathias yelled, dragging the body onto the shore. He pried swollen leeches from the corpse. "Oh, sweet Jesus, have mercy!" he sobbed.

Luke heard the anguished man screaming with horror and ran towards him. He knew even before he reached the far side, he knew.

Mathias tore his shirt off and covered Mark's remains as Luke neared him. He jumped up and met the father before he could get close enough for a clear look.

"You don't want to see him, Luke." He blocked the grieving man's way, holding him firmly with his strong hands. "He's dead! You don't want to see him now!"

Tears streamed down the Negro's face as he held the father at bay.

"That's my boy," Luke said, his face twisted with grief. "Let me go to my boy, Mathias!"

"I got to tend to him first. You go back to the house and I'll bring him to you."

"No! That's my boy—he needs me! Let me go, nigger! Let me go!"

Mathias stood rigidly as Luke beat him furiously about the face and chest. He took the punishment without trying to ward off the blows.

"Please, sir," the man begged, refusing to relinquish his grip. "You've been a father and a brother to me. I can't let you see that child now, no matter how much you hit me. You'll have to kill me . . ."

Luke stared at his son's body covered beneath Mathias's buttonless work shirt. "You—you will bring him home?"

"Yessir, I just need a few minutes alone with him first."

The father saw a black leech inching across the bleached white toe of a sneaker, and he understood. He turned away and began crying.

"Be gentle with him," he managed to say.

"Yessir," Mathias said, his own voice broken. "I'll be very gentle with him."

He waited until the gaunt man walked off, his lanky frame shuddering with grief, before stripping the youngster down.

* * *

Shaman moved like a shadow along the edge of the meadow, seeking a safe place to cross. He tested what little breeze there was for any scent of pursuers, believing they were all far behind, following the false trail he had laid. He came to the narrowest part of the meadow and eyed the top of Red Jacket Hill, out toward the middle. The smell of cattle was heavy, and several grazed peacefully on the meadow grass. The deer stepped forward, intending to take the clearing at full stride. He would be exposed for thirty seconds or more before gaining the safety of the oak trees on the other side, at the base of the hills. Then something seemed to change his mind. Warily, he went back into the Seneca Woods.

"I've got to poop bad!"

"You wouldn't be trying to play a trick on an old trickster, would you?"

"I just have to poop real bad!" the boy insisted.

Sam stood by as the lad went into some bushes to do his business.

"Hurry up, Tommy," he ordered, after a few minutes passed. When no answer came, Sam went in to investigate.

He found the boy's toilet, but Tommy was gone. A feeling of dread raised a dry lump in his throat. Joe Hawk had trusted him with his grandson, and he had foolishly allowed the little fox to outsmart him.

Tommy crawled stealthily through the bushes and came out in a stand of closely knit pine trees. He stood up cautiously, searching for his guard, but Sam was not to be seen. He was still back on the other side of the bushes, waiting for him to finish relieving his bowels. The boy grinned mischievously.

So I move like a herd of cows, do I? he thought. Filled with elation, the eleven-year-old ran off through the woods.

He bolted out from behind a tree and snared the boy quickly as he ran past.

Tommy kicked and fought for all he was worth, but he was too strong for the young Indian. The boy's rifle was wrenched from his hands, and he continued to struggle valiantly, as his trousers were unbuttoned and unceremoniously yanked down to expose his brown bottom.

"Here's where you feel the heavy hand of the law!" Sam said with anger. He struck the boy's buttocks with several resounding blows, then released him and told him to pull up his pants.

Tommy did as he was told. Tears of anguish streamed down his cheeks, but he made no outcry. He was more humiliated for getting caught than he was hurt. It was the first spanking he had ever received in his life, and it shamed him terribly.

"You try running off on me again," Sam threatened, "I'll use my belt the next time!"

Tommy wiped his tears away and walked off for home, with the stern lawman directly behind him.

It was close to noon when they reached the Seneca village. Sam escorted his charge to the small store and purchased cold cuts and soda pop for the two of them. They settled on the front porch steps, and Sam put the sandwiches together, spreading gobs of mustard on the bread with his hunting knife.

"C'mon, eat!" he urged when the boy wouldn't touch his lunch.

Tommy sneered at him and turned his back to the man.

"Drink your Pepsi, then; you must be thirsty, anyway."

Contemptuously, the youngster knocked the soda over. The carbonated beverage fizzed out over the ground.

"It's Indians like you who give us whites a bad name," Sam chided.

The boy cracked an unwanted smile, then quickly masked it with juvenile stoicism.

"I guess it's your business if you want to go hungry and thirsty, sorehead."

James Goodman drove into the village in his little Henry J automobile. He halted in front of the store with an alarmed look as he spotted Sam on the steps next to his sullen nephew.

"You were hunting the deer with Joe, weren't you?"

"Yeah, Joe's still back in the woods with the Simpsons, trying to get him."

"Your deputy has been trying to get hold of you all morning. The deer killed Luke Banner's boy last night. His wife had a stroke and was taken to the hospital."

Sam threw the remainder of his sandwich down and climbed into James's car. He warned Tommy to stay out of the woods, entrusted him to the care of the store-keeper, and drove off with the Seneca Faithkeeper.

The boy thought about Mark Banner. He had been a

friend, and now Shaman had taken his life! Next it would be Chucky—if he wasn't stopped!

The storekeeper scolded Tommy as the boy clubbed the pop bottle angrily with the butt of his rifle, smashing it and spraying his clothes with soda. He tried to take the boy inside and had the rifle barrel whacked across his shins for his trouble.

Tommy ran off past his cabin at the edge of the village and went into the pines, where he could be alone with his thoughts.

The noon sun was hot and they sweltered as they lay flat on the hill, looking down on the meadow. Zeb had removed his shirt for comfort.

Less than a mile to the west, the Seneca lived in cabins and houses on small-acreage farms, with the village itself but another mile beyond. The meadow ended a hundred yards past the hill in that direction, tapering off into a narrow passage, but most deer wouldn't cross there for fear of men lurking in the woods. That end of the grasslands was where the cows usually bedded, and it was practically a back yard to the Seneca farms.

To the east, in all likelihood, was where Shaman would cross. At the base of the hill there was a large rift in the ground that made a gully spreading half the width of the meadow. The hunters felt this would be his route, and not the farthest eastern point, where it was immensely wide and the highway cut through the middle.

Their reasoning had eliminated such a possibility. A man hiding at that end who caught the deer halfway could get off a dozen shots before Shaman could reach the safety of the forest or the tree-covered hills on the south. Surely Shaman was aware of that fact.

At any moment they expected to see him running the ditch, and they waited, talking quietly to one another.

"When I spoke with you yesterday," Pete said to the Seneca, "you said the deer would stay in the woods until he made a kill. You counting our cow as that kill?"

"No. I don't know why he wants to leave now. Perhaps he intends only to hide for a while." Joe looked at Zeb with concern. "You are sure your family is safe?"

"Pearl's gone into the city with Charlie," Zeb said irritably, squashing a biting horsefly on his forearm. "Dammit anyway, Joe! Why do you have to keep insisting there's a ghost in that frigger? That deer's not out to kill anyone in particular, just whoever happens to get in his way."

"Is the belief of evil spirits so strange to your faith?" the chieftain asked.

"Now, what faith would that be, old timer?" Zeb asked.

"No disrespect, Joe," Pete said, "but a man's soul inside a deer is hard to swallow."

Joe smiled at them. "By your disbelief, is the story of the possessed swine in the Gospels therefore a lie? How many killer deer have you ever heard of? When life hunts death, it is only natural. But the deer is not natural; he is death that hunts life. For years I did not think of Malsum, but now I know he was forever thinking about us. The things of the past, the deaths of my children, of your mother, the misfortunes of our lives—blame Malsum for them. For it is true, whether you believe it or not, he is in the deer. The sorcerer spent his life cursing us, and now he devotes his death as well."

"I'd like to believe that, Joe," Pete said. "I'd like to believe it was your demon that killed Jenny."

"Inside, you must," Joe told them, "or you will spend your lives feeling shame. Do not forget, I have known you since you were children. I know you better than you know yourselves. You may believe that your hands fired the rifle, but it was Malsum's wizardry that guided the bullet."

Joe looked at Zeb's arm where Pete's shot from years ago had left a narrow line of scar tissue through the word "Mother" on the faded tattoo. He glanced at the scars on Zeb's shoulders. "Does brother kill brother?" he asked Pete. "Did you have enough hate in your heart to kill him?"

Zeb watched his younger brother's eyes sadden.

"No . . . I thought I did." Pete grimaced. "But I couldn't."

"And you?" Joe smiled at Zeb. "You knew he would not kill you when you charged his rifle."

"I knew," Zeb admitted. "Yeah, I guess you do know us pretty good."

"I'll tell you another thing I know." Joe's dark eyes burned with hatred. "Shaman is no longer the deer he was born to be. He is a demon—Malsum's demon!"

Shaman ran out onto the green meadow five hundred yards to the east toward the widest part. Pete saw him first.

He was little more than a tan eyestrain standing out against the darker grass.

"Sonuvabitch!" Zeb said between gritted teeth as Pete pointed him out. "Look at that brazen bastard!"

The deer stopped and faced the hill, purposely presenting himself as a target.

The three men fired simultaneously, but the buck remained unhurt amid the echoing volley. He reared on his hind legs like a stallion, and the distant sound of a haggish shriek carried to their ears.

"Waugh!" Joe bellowed, standing up and taking careful aim. "The demon laughs at us! He knows we cannot hit him!" He squeezed off another shot, kicking up grass near the beast.

"You frigging bastard!" Zeb fired six shots in rapid succession, emptying the magazine on his rifle.

"*A-a-a-ae-e-eeeee-eough! E-e-e-eee-uh! E-uh! E-uh!*" the deer answered Zeb's shots with a loud, taunting bray.

They watched the beast walk slowly toward the foothills, as carefree as if he had all the time in the world.

"Damn you!" Zeb rasped, quickly reloading his rifle.

Pete took a handful of dirt and threw it into the air, watching the dry soil swerve to the right before it dispersed. A grim look of determination came over him.

"Use my shoulder!" the Seneca commanded as the marksman stood and took aim.

Pete went behind Joe and rested his rifle on the chieftain's broad shoulder. He aimed, allowing for windage and elevation.

The stag looked back toward the hill as if he sensed danger. He broke into a fast gait and bounded for the hills. A bullet lodged in his flanks an instant after Pete fired, and he ran with a speed that was incredible.

"He fears you!" Joe shouted, as Pete levered out the empty casing and locked the bolt into place over a fresh shell. "You have the skill to make the shot!"

"Get him for me!" Zeb yelled, as Pete steadied again. "Get him for the Keevers!"

Joe stood perfectly still, the rifle balanced delicately on his shoulder. Tension grew as the deer neared the edge of the foothills, while Pete continued to take aim.

Crack! There was something final about the sound of the shot as it reverberated across the meadow.

Shaman stumbled and went down.

Pete crammed another round into the chamber and again took aim. But the tan carcass remained still.

"You got the mother!" Zeb rejoiced. "Goddamn, what a shot!" He raced off down the hill. Joe chuckled and affectionately put his arm around Pete. They followed Zeb.

The grass was stained with blood where Shaman had fallen, but he was not there. His trail went into the foothills a few yards to the south.

"He ran while the rise of ground hid him from our sight!" Joe said with anger.

"How the hell can any deer be so goddamn smart?" Zeb groaned.

Joe's eyes flashed. "Stop calling him a deer!" He stalked off, following Shaman's bloody spoor.

They climbed the first line of hills quickly, resting at the top, winded and sweating.

Shaman stood on the crest of the next ridge, willfully exposing himself to them. They snapped their rifles up but the deer dropped down the far side before they could take aim.

"Bastard! You frigging bastard!" Zeb shouted and ran down the hill at breakneck speed.

They topped the next ridge looking for Shaman, their chests heaving. Tiny needles stabbed their gasping lungs, and even Joe Hawk was winded and sweaty.

Again the crafty buck exposed himself, stepping out from behind a cluster of pines, and again he slipped from view an instant before they could take aim.

"Let's get him!" Zeb urged. "He's not much faster than us now—he's hurt!"

"Wait!" Pete said. "He's up to something, leading us on."

The Seneca nodded. "We will spread out this time. Watch carefully."

Joe went down the hill, veering to the left of Zeb. Pete went to the right. They formed an arc spanning three hundred yards as they crested the next hill. The last few feet to the top they took on their stomachs. They hid behind covering rocks and bushes and waited for the deer to flash on the southward ridge.

The minutes crept by, but Shaman did not appear.

They followed his bloody trail to the next series of hills. It headed on toward the mountains in the far distance.

"He's gone back in again," Zeb said. He got angry. "This time I'm not letting him go if I have to follow him to Pennsylvania!"

"He'd be hard put to outlast us while he's bleeding the way he is." Pete looked off to the southwest with a puzzled expression. He turned to the Seneca. "Remember what you told me about a wounded animal when I was a kid?"

"Yes; that they will always do the unexpected. You think he has turned?"

"It's worth a try. A loss of an hour can't make much difference. We'll have him by nightfall in any event."

They ran the top of the forested ridge, searching for any sign the deer might have made in cutting back. A mile to the west they came upon a mosquito-infested puddle of stagnant rainwater in a gully, shaded from the sun by an outcropping of rock.

There was a bloody wallow mark in the surrounding mud where the deer had lain and packed his wounds. He had turned back. His trail led toward the narrowest part of the meadow on the other side of Red Jacket Hill, where the cows grazed. Shaman had at least half an hour's lead on them, but they knew as they followed the deer that he was as good as dead. They would not allow him to cross over to the hills again, now that he was wounded and wearied from his loss of blood.

Demon or not, his legs would stiffen when he stopped to rest, and close pursuit would start him moving. They were all wise to his wide circling trails that ended up yards from where they began, and Shaman would not escape them with any such scheme.

By nightfall, Joe believed, the stag would be dead, and the wicked spirit of the Lenape sorcerer dispossessed and hurled from the world forever more. He would be found and destroyed if Joe had to search the forest with the combined might of all the Cattaraugus Seneca.

They climbed down the bordering ridge of the meadow, wondering if the deer was viewing them from the woods on the other side. It would make no difference. They had outfoxed him, and he was as good as dead. Nothing could save him this time.

Crack! Crack! Crack!

It sounded like a cap pistol from where they stood.

"Someone hunting squirrels with a .22?" Zeb wondered aloud.

And then the boy screamed, his death knell carrying across the meadow. A bestial bellow of triumph echoed through the hills.

Joe's face twisted with horror as the bellowing increased. He ran down the hill, discarding his rifle.

"*Haksot! Haksot!*" he cried in anguish. "My grandson! My grandson!"

PART III

Grief

Chapter IX

Nora checked the room, making sure she was not leaving anything behind, and stepped out into the hall. A few minutes earlier she had given the bellboy a dollar to take her bags down to the front desk.

In a way she was sad to be leaving Miami. It had been a wonderfully lazy two weeks lying around the beach, soaking up the sun until she was almost as brown as a coconut, but she was homesick now.

The unscheduled vacation had been prompted by sheer desperation, in order to escape her fiancé, Philip. She had broken off their engagement two months earlier, at the end of the school year, and he had continually badgered her, calling her on the telephone at all hours of the day or night, coming to her apartment and making a scene, crying and carrying on about how much he loved her, how much she was hurting him. She felt sorry for him, but she didn't love him, and marrying him would have been unfair to both of them. Nora didn't know what she was going to do with her life, but one thing was certain: she was not going to marry a man she did not love.

It was peculiar, she thought as she descended in the elevator, men were so very different from the appearances they presented. Phil had always presented a picture of inner strength and confidence. Yet, when the chips were down, his true character had shown through to reveal him as little more than a child, unable to cope with an emotional disappointment. She would never again make the mistake of being drawn to a man like Phil.

Her only other experience was with Peter Simpson; he was so quiet and gentle in his ways, so terribly easy to hurt, and yet never once had she heard a whimper from him. The morning the court had sentenced him to prison he had not broken down or asked for leniency, even after his lawyer pleaded with him. The truth was that real men like Peter were rare in a world filled with boastful male egos. Things could have been so different if only she had not let Zeb. . . .

The misery of it all saddened her, and she pushed the thoughts from her mind. All these years, and she was still hopelessly in love with a man who wouldn't even give her the time of day. It was too bad about Phil, but he would have to carry his cross, just as she had to carry hers.

The elevator doors opened on the lobby, and Nora went to the desk and paid her bill. The bell captain confirmed her 11:45 A.M. flight to Buffalo and put her luggage in the check room while she went off to have her breakfast.

She allowed herself two slices of toast, half a grapefruit and a soft-boiled egg. The admiring glances of her students would not diminish in September; her figure was in better shape than ever.

She thought of Chucky Simpson's awed fascination for bustlines, and it amused her. During the previous school year she had continually caught him gaping at her, more so than any of the other boys. She had never scolded him about it because she felt it was healthy. Pete had been a gawker also. Perhaps it was a genetic trait with Chucky. Or then again, maybe it was just a good proportion of the right hormones. In any event, she would have to say something to him about his staring sooner or later if he didn't correct the problem by himself. It wasn't exactly good manners for an eleven-year-old boy to go around mentally undressing women with an excited look on his face. He was a hearthrob in her life, just as another gawker, Mark Banner, was.

Earlier in the summer, Nora had called Emily Banner under one of the many pretexts she used with the stern woman to find out how Mark was getting along, and Emily had amazed her with the revelation that Mark and Chucky had become friends. The news had exhilarated her. Chucky and Mark becoming friends was more than she had ever hoped for. They had done nothing but bicker in her classroom all year. She recalled that the enmity went as far back as third grade, when Mark had failed and the Simpson boy had caught up to him. It would be nice if she could bring each of them a present from one of the souvenir shops, a reward, if nothing else. But she knew that it would not seem fair to the other children in her class. Still, she couldn't help having her favorites—for various reasons. They were the two brightest students she had ever taught, with the possible exception of Tommy Hawk, who was the hardest working and most sincere child she had ever known. He would make a wonderful leader of his people some day.

A waiter walked through the dining room pushing a cart with out-of-state newspapers, and Nora purchased the last night's edition of the Buffalo Evening News.

Her heart jumped as she saw the headline: TWO YOUTHS MURDERED BY KILLER DEER!

There was a picture of a body under a sheet being taken from the back of a Brant Fire Department ambulance by two volunteer firemen. She recognized Sam's deputy, Dave Barnes, standing sad-faced next to the gurney.

Nora read the columns telling the story. All she could think of was Chucky Simpson. The deer had tried to kill him last winter. She read the details, fearing that any moment she was going to run across his name. But all it said was that one child's corpse was found in a pond and the other in the woods. The authorities were withholding the names of the victims until the families notified their relations. Nora reread the article, looking for any clue that might identify the children. Her blood pounded in her ears, and her eyes could hardly focus on the small print.

The article described massive hunts being formed. There were hundreds of bounty hunters taking to the woods and game officials were arresting them as fast as they could. But they still expected a large number of innocent animals to be destroyed before the fever died down.

There were no names mentioned; no clues given.

Nora folded the paper and nervously lit a cigarette. She recalled the conversation with Chucky Simpson after his narrow escape with Shaman. Chucky had insisted that the spirit of some Indian sorcerer wanted to kill him because his great-grandfather Zebediah had killed the sorcerer's sons. At the time, the horror of the deer alone had been enough, and she had dismissed the tale of demonic possession as the fanciful imagining of a young boy. Now, seeing the front page of the newspaper filled with talk about an Indian named Malsum, and another story by a so-called spiritualist who claimed to be in contact with dissident Indian souls, warning that they plotted to inhabit every dangerous wild animal in the country and drive the white men from their stolen lands, she worriedly considered the possibility—but that was sheer insanity.

A man at the next table laughed for some reason, just as she finished reading the article, and the woman's intelligence told her that that should be her reaction. But all she could think of was Chucky.

Oh, God, two boys dead! She prayed that one of them was not Chucky Simpson!

She checked with the waiter for a morning edition of the Buffalo Courier-Express, but he had none, and none would arrive until after her departure. There was only one thing left that she could do.

Nora went to the phone booth in the lobby, closed the door, and dialed the long distance operator. The operator contacted western New York State information and obtained Zeb Simpson's telephone listing. The toll required a huge amount of change, and she had the operator charge the cost to her apartment telephone in Gowanda. Her heart raced wildly as she heard the Simpson telephone ringing, hundreds of miles to the north.

"Hello," a boyish voice said.

"Chucky? Chucky, is that you?"

"Yes . . . who's this?" The boy's voice sounded very weak and sad.

"This is Miss Cleary, honey," Nora answered with a faltering voice. She felt tears filling her eyes. "I'm calling long distance. May I speak to your mother?" Thank God he was safe!

"She and my pa are at Mr. Banner's house seeing Mark . . ."

"Have you and Mark been fighting again?"

Nora heard the boy say, "It's Miss Cleary calling long distance."

And then a familiar voice spoke in her ear. "Nora? This is Pete. May I help you?"

Pete! "Yes, thank you. I'm in Miami. I'll be flying home this afternoon. . . . I've just read about the deer killing two boys, but the papers didn't give any names. I was worried sick that one of them might have been Chucky. Do you know who they were?"

There was a long pause on the other end of the line.

"I'm afraid they were two of your . . . I know how . . . how easily you can go to pieces, Nora . . . What time will your flight arrive? I'll pick you up if you like."

He was going to see her!

"At—at—just a minute, please." Nora checked the information she had written on a piece of paper in her purse. "At 8:45 P.M. It's Capitol Airlines, flight 122."

"All right. I'll be there if you like."

"Thank you. But, please . . . You started to say it was two of my pupils, didn't you?"

A dreadful possibility she hadn't considered—the curse —if there was anything to it— Oh, God, no!

"I'm afraid so, Nora."

"Please tell me who. If you don't, I'll just call Sam Parker."

Again there was a long pause.

". . . It was Tommy and Mark . . ."

Nora felt her senses leaving her. He had said Mark!

"Mark—Mark Banner?" she whispered almost inaudibly.

"Yes. Were you very close to the boy?"

Nora dropped the telephone helplessly. She needed to scream, to get outside in the fresh air before she fainted. She opened the telephone booth door as the sobs rose in her throat.

After a moment she closed the door and went back to the telephone. She heard Pete's voice.

"Nora! Nora, answer me! Get hold of yourself!"

His words rang in her mind. "Were you very close to the boy?" he had asked.

She sobbed into the receiver. "Don't you know, Peter? Dear God, don't you know! He was our son!"

Neither of them spoke as Pete drove toward the Seneca Reservation where young Tommy Hawk was laid out in the longhouse. Pete had explained to Nora during the first few minutes of the drive that Mark could not be seen, that his coffin was closed, and Mathias had sent everyone out by late afternoon so that Luke could be consoled by his family. Mathias had evidently pleaded with, or threatened, the three grown sons, in order to bring them home; whatever method he used, it had brought results. Luke met his nine grandchildren for the first time. Their presence comforted him. Pete told Nora that he thought Luke was holding up well under the strain of Mark's death and Emily's stroke. Emily was in Buffalo at the Meyer Memorial Hospital, where they had the proper facilities to handle her condition. Unfortunately, she was not expected to recover.

Pete watched as Nora lit her third cigarette.

"When did you start smoking?" Disapproval flashed in his blue eyes.

His voice surprised her after driving in silence for so long.

"Oh, years ago, I guess," she said. She sighed discouragingly and threw the cigarette out the open passenger window. "I smoke too much. I'm thinking of quitting."

Pete nodded. "I gave it up when I came home. I smoke a pipe once in a while, but that's all."

"You always were good at giving things up," the teacher said.

Pete felt the implied meaning of her remark and lapsed back into silence. She had written him in prison, asking if there was any chance for them when he returned home. Al Cleary wanted her to give the child up for adoption. "I can get a job and move into an apartment away from my father. We'll wait for you, Peter." He never answered her.

She did the practical thing and gave the baby away.

Her father paid her way through the state teacher's college at Fredonia as a consolation.

"Do you have any questions you want to ask me?"

Pete looked at her guiltily. "I really don't feel that I have that right."

"You're very noble," Nora said. "I'll write you a long letter some day and explain everything. Who knows? You might even read it—but don't worry. I won't expect an answer."

The glow of a roadside cafe interrupted the darkness of the countryside. Pete slowed and wheeled onto the gravel driveway. Nora said no to a sandwich, and he went inside for two cups of coffee. Alone in the diner, as he waited for service, he had a chance to think clearly.

The news that Mark Banner was his son had shocked him. He had always known that he had a child somewhere, a little older than Chucky, but he had never given much thought to the matter. He had rehearsed tender things to say to Nora all day, but her stiff but polite greeting and dry-eyed composure when he met her at the airport cancelled those thoughts in a flash. Nora wasn't looking for any kind words from him and that was obvious.

They drove on toward the reservation, sipping at their coffee.

"Did Mark know you were his mother?"

Nora's eyes flashed angrily. "What do you think I did," she asked, "give him to the Banners and then ask for visiting privileges? I didn't even know I was his mother until last spring."

"You didn't give him to the Banners? How do you know he's your . . . our son, then?"

"Because he looks like you and he has the right birthdate."

Pete's manner toughened. "Then you're only guessing."

"I'm not guessing. Sam Parker checked for me."

Coffee spilled down the front of Pete's shirt as he took a sharp curve in the road too fast. He cursed quietly beneath his breath and looked for a flat spot on the dashboard to set the cup down. Nora took it from his hand.

"Let me do that," she said, taking his handkerchief as he attempted to wipe himself off. She opened the glove compartment and placed the two coffees there, balancing them carefully. She smelled a faint cologne on his freshly shaven face as she leaned close. It was a familiar scent, the same cologne he had worn at seventeen. He was consistent, to say the least. The soapy perfume odor touched off a sadness inside her and, after she finished drying his shirt, she scooted back over to the passenger side of the seat and withdrew from him altogether. She was unable to cope with the nearness and distance of him at the same time.

A white sign in the shape of an arrow appeared as they reached a four corner junction in the highway. It read "Cattaraugus Reservation—16 miles." Pete made the turn and drove on. A few miles further on, the pavement ended and a series of rutted dirt roads branched off into the forest. Pete continued over one of the roads toward the Seneca settlement. The way was dark and strange to Nora now, but as teenagers they had often walked these roads to go swimming in the creek, or to find a secret place where they could undress and leisurely lie around and make love. She wondered if Pete was recalling that time also.

The village was overcrowded with automobiles when they arrived. Hundreds of Indians and whites were gathered together in quiet discussion groups as Pete held Nora's hand and guided her through their ranks toward the longhouses. Some Indian faces Pete recognized from his childhood, and they him. At times he was forced to stop out of courtesy to nod hello or to ask after a fellow's family and well-being, but the amenities were never long or drawn out. Many of the Iroquois were dressed in ceremonial garb, as well as conventional wear, the former having taken part in the day's solemn funeral rites for Tommy. Although Joe Hawk had never been a great political achiever, and his chieftainship only extended over Cattaraugus, many important leaders from Tonawanda, Coughnawaga, Allegany, and reservations in Canada came to honor him and share his grief. Even delegates of the Seneca tribe as far away as Ottawa, Oklahoma, had attended.

The Tuscarora, Mohawk, Oneida, Onondaga, and Cayuga were present, and took part in the condolence ceremonies. Outfits were symbolic of their grief, all having parcels of blue or purple somewhere on their person, the colors for sorrow.

The *Lenni Lenape* Delaware themselves sent delegates, although they were not allowed to attend the rites and were made to wait with the white friends until the services neared completion. They listened to the grievances of the Seneca against Malsum, and together with the Iroquois Faithkeepers they conducted ancient exorcism rituals. They disowned Malsum as their forefathers had generations before. They heaped indignities and curses on his evil spirit, and swore friendship and brotherhood to the Seneca and the League, reaffirming that their differences and enmity was forever lost in the past. Other Algonquian tribes present also voiced their support and friendship. All Indians offered to help hunt Shaman, but the deer had escaped into the mountains and his trail had not been found yet.

Many shook hands with Nora and Pete, welcoming them. Total strangers embraced them with tear-filled eyes and thanked them for coming, as if they were important visiting dignitaries. Everywhere there was one white there were six Seneca trying to make him at home, conversing, explaining, interpreting the words of their various campfire discussions.

Inside the small longhouse where the rites had been held, an emotional eulogy was being delivered by James Goodman in his native tongue. Whites and Indians alike were present. Knowing their presence was not an invasion of privacy, Pete led Nora to the crowded doorway and listened. He recognized many of the words and phrases. They were strong words, descriptive words, like the resonant voice of the speaker himself. James was dressed in black, holding a string of pure white wampum beads in his hands. Pete interpreted for Nora whenever he could. The translation was often very poetic. They listened until the Faithkeeper lost his voice, clenching his fists and fighting to go on. Many inside and at the door broke down and wept. A Faithkeeper from Tonawanda took James's place, while relatives and tribesmen helped the grief-stricken uncle onto a wooden bench seat by the wall where the men sat. The speeches and discussions would last all night.

Pete saw the tears forming at the corners of Nora's eyes and he pried her away from the doorway. Her hand felt like ice when he took it, and there were goose bumps on her bare arms. He tried to drape his coat over her shoulders, but she softly refused, saying she wasn't cold.

The main longhouse, made of modern wood siding rather than rough-hewn logs, had a line of mourners waiting outside to file past the child. Joe Hawk had made many friends in his lifetime, and the turnout of whites, almost as great as the Indian attendance, had necessitated an additional wake in respect to their concern. Sam Parker was stationed at the door as Pete and Nora entered the line. He was wobbling drunk on his feet, quietly greeting the mourners and thanking them for attending. A Seneca man ahead of Pete said something kind about Tommy, and Sam answered him in unfaltering Seneca. Nora was moved, realizing that she had never known the true depth of Sam's friendship with the Indians until this moment.

Sam turned to welcome Nora, not seeing Pete behind her yet.

"Brother!" Pete said in Seneca. "We weep with pain and sorrow and cry . . ."—Pete tapped his chest gently three times—"my heart, my heart, my heart."

Sam looked at Pete blankly in a drunken stupor and then cracked a warm smile. "Awijah," he said. "That was very beautiful, Pete."

He clasped Pete's hand in a tight quivering grip and kissed Nora on the cheek. His eyes said something special and secret to her. "My heart is with you, child," he said. "I know what you must be going through." He looked at Pete wonderingly, and Pete nodded.

"Thank you," Nora said evenly.

Pete nudged her forward gently, to keep the procession moving. Sam greeted the next person in line, translating his English thoughts into Seneca.

The Simpson family walked over to them as they neared the front of the room where standing mourners blocked any view of Tommy's corpse. Chucky smiled vaguely at the teacher and took her hand as she reached out for him. Pete knelt down and straightened the boy's tie and tucked his shirt collar neatly inside the chocolate lapel of his summer suit coat.

"Ma, this is my teacher, Miss Cleary," Chucky introduced, as Pearl smiled at the unknown woman.

A startled expression came over Pearl for a fleeting instant. She recovered almost immediately.

"I'm very pleased to make your acquaintance," she said.

Nora returned her greeting cordially. The moment of surprise on Pearl's face revealed to Nora that her student's mother knew of the past drama involving her with the two Simpson brothers.

Zeb nodded politely to the pretty teacher, and she managed a smile for him, quickly diverting her eyes back to Pearl as the farmwife spoke softly about the beautiful rituals and services that the many attending tribes had conducted for Tommy. Zeb's nearness made Nora uncomfortable. A glance at Pete revealed nothing of his thoughts. She concentrated on the glowing woman before her. Pearl Simpson was very beautiful, she thought, even with her eyes bloodshot and red-rimmed as they were. Zeb Simpson always had gone after the prettiest ones.

He didn't deserve her! She was obviously a lady, a gentle lady.

"Oh, he's so handsome," Pearl said. "He's wearing beautiful white buckskins with beaded moccasins. He looks like he could just get up from that table and join us where we stand."

The procession moved forward, and Pearl released Nora's polite attentiveness. "You'll see for yourself," she said tearily biting her lip.

Chucky remained at the teacher's side as his parents went back to their seats. Pearl opened a missal. Taking a rosary from it, she began touching the beads and praying, her wet eyelashes lowered, her head bowed. Nora watched as the woman took her husband's hand and placed it on the rosary, moving his fingers up the beads. Zeb bowed his head from time to time, his eyes blinking. But for the most part he studied Pete and Nora while they inched closer to Tommy's corpse. Nora pretended not to notice his eyes on them.

Chucky crowded into line in front of Nora, and she draped her arms down the front of his suit coat, clenching his small hands. He returned her pressure as she caught her first glimpse of Tommy lying atop lush pelts in his princely Indian apparel. A tremor coursed through her as she thought of her own son only miles away, dead and locked inside a closed coffin awaiting burial. She felt Pete's fingers gentle on her shoulders as they stepped closer. Joe Hawk was speaking quietly in his native language to the Indians in front of her, intoning a prepared speech.

He stood stiffly alongside the body of his grandson, receiving condolences from mourners, rising like a stately mountain above the heads of the men in the longhouse. He wore a fringed suit of softened deer leather, and a bonnet of dyed eagle feathers that trailed and tapered down his back. When he moved or shifted, tiny bells attached to his headdress jingled, adding the depth of sound to his majestic appearance. The overhead lighting made the polished gold medallion he wore loosely about his neck sparkle and gleam brilliantly. He had always been an impressive man, with his giant height and breadth, and the ceremonial trappings he now wore seemed to transform him into one of Longfellow's ancient Iroquois gods. He and his grandson both looked magnificently regal.

"This is my grandson," Joe said in English, looking at Nora but not really seeing her. Nora could smell strong drink, but he appeared stoic and sober. Only his eyes reflected the hidden torment in his soul. They were shiny black—two ebony windows of wisdom numbed with sorrow.

"This is my grandson," he had said. "He was born to the Seneca Nation eleven years before. His people are heartbroken, for with his departing there will be no more of his father's blood among them. I am now the last living representative of that blood. I ask you to pray with me, that his spirit may be found by those who love and await him without the sorrow we all share, but with joy and much gladdening of his heart."

Joe bowed his head mechanically and murmured softly in Seneca.

Chucky stared blankly at his dead friend. Nora waited until Joe finished praying, and then lifted her own bowed head to address him.

"May I please touch him?" she asked, not knowing if it was forbidden.

"Thank you," the Seneca said. "Your prayers have not gone unheard."

God, Nora thought, he was in some sort of a trance! His mind wasn't even in this room!

"It would be all right," Pete whispered.

Nora touched the boy's hair. She bent down and kissed his cheek, looking at his handsome, sleeping face. He wasn't dead! He couldn't be! He was pretending! The entire thing was a terrible prank! She almost expected to see his lips part into a smile at any moment. A rush of tears came.

Joe's eyes blinked as he heard Nora crying softly.

"You are Tommy's teacher?" He stopped her as she went to move past him.

"I did not recognize you, daughter," he said when she nodded. "It has been many years." He smiled apologetically and said, "I know of your own sorrow. My brother, Sam Parker, and I share many secrets. Thank you for honoring me today with your presence."

Joe then placed her hand in Pete's hand meaningfully and held them together for a moment. The couple walked away.

Chucky remained glued to the floor in front of Tommy's corpse, refusing to leave. The Seneca chieftain stepped over to the lad and rested a huge rough hand on the back of his head.

"Tell me," he said solemnly, "what does Tommy say to you? Has he forgiven me . . . or does he hate his foolish old grandfather?"

The boy stood rigid as the old warrior embraced him. His arms crept out slowly and clung to the giant Seneca. He watched with startled eyes as Joe Hawk unclasped the gold medallion from around his neck and placed it in his small palm.

"This I now give to you," he said.

A hushed murmuring arose from the Seneca throughout the longhouse.

Joe folded the honored trappings carefully and stored them in the cedar chest at the foot of Tommy's bed. He dressed in clothes suitable for the mountains. Sam Parker slept on the boy's bed, snoring loudly from weariness and drink. The old Seneca gathered the supplies he wanted, rolled them into a blanket, and harnessed it to his back with strong leather straps. He took one last look at his lifelong friend, and left the cabin, stepping out into the darkness.

It was an hour before dawn, and the longhouses were filled to capacity with mourners. They were still arriving from distant places to pay their respects to his grandson. Their homage filled his heart with pride and made his grief easier to bear, but Joe could not withstand their tears and warm embraces any longer. He avoided them all, going through the bordering woods to the rear of James Goodman's home.

There was no need for him to be present when his grandson was returned to the mother earth. He had made his goodbyes to the boy hours before, and now his people could conduct the closing burial rites. He was going into the mountains to find the deer. The elders had warned him that he would perish if he stalked the demon alone, but he cared not, for he was already dead. Death seeking death, hatred seeking revenge.

As a small boy he had defeated Malsum, only to lose by a cheat. This time he vowed he would not be cheated. So the elders had warned that the deer would kill him, but he would also kill the deer. And afterwards! Afterwards, he would find Malsum's spirit if he had to descend to the very depths of the Land of Shadows and do combat with a thousand demons!

"I will go with you," James said, as he walked into the forest a short ways at his chieftain's request.

"No," Joe replied. "I would do this thing myself. It is my wish that none of you follow me. . . . It is my command."

James nodded. "I understand," he said sadly. "Many will ask for words."

"You are a counselor and a strong voice of our nation,"

the Oak of the Seneca answered. "I will give you words, and you will be my voice."

"*Niio!*"

Joe bowed his head in thought for a moment. When he next spoke his words were in the ancient tongue of his fathers, a language as old as the mightiest of trees in the forest.

"See that our children never forget who they are," he said, "for their strength is derived from the knowledge of their heritage, their history, their tradition.

"Protect our lands, for they still dwindle.

"There is love and friendship in all nations. Honor the friends I have made in my life, for they are your friends, your people, as they were mine.

"Do not make a legend of me, for I am not a god, and I am not a prophet. I am but a man. Say that I lived and then died. Anything more would be meaningless."

"We will meet again," James said, as the chieftain left for the long journey into the mountains.

A midsummer's breeze rustled through the pines, cool on Joe Hawk's face. It smelled of mint and resin, the warmth of home forever there.

A squirrel scolded and a crow cawed a warning.

"We will meet again," the Seneca chief answered, but his voice was thick and low and only the *pukwudjinnies* heard him.

Chapter X

The grease splattered and struck Pearl near the eye as she cracked the egg on the side of the skillet. She dropped shell and all into the pan, backing away from the stove and rubbing the eye with her apron bottom.

"Are you all right?" Zeb asked. He and Pete were packing knapsacks with canned goods and changes of clothing.

"What do you care?" Pearl retorted. She fished the shells out of the pan, cracked two more eggs open, and seasoned them. "All you care about is yourself!"

"Zeb, look," Pete said, "why don't you stay home? I can manage on my own."

"Why don't you, Zeb?" Pearl said tightly, glowering at her brother-in-law. "I guess one pile of bones back in the mountains is better than two piles!"

"I'll go with you, Uncle Pete," Chucky offered hopefully.

Pearl turned on the boy angrily with a spatula in her hand. She spun him around and raised it to strike his bottom, but didn't, changing her mind at the last moment.

"Go outside and play with your fawn. I warned you before to stop pestering them. You're not going anywhere, Charles!"

"Why can't I? Joe's my grandpa too, now; he adopted me."

Pearl shook her head, pulling her hair. She thought she would lose her mind.

"Get out of this kitchen, Charles, before I—" She waved the spatula.

"Jesus Christ!" Zeb took the utensil from her hand and

went to the frying pan. "Why don't you calm down? You're burning the eggs."

Pearl pushed him away from the stove and took back the spatula. She flipped the eggs over, breaking some of the yolks, but not caring.

Pete watched her scoop them onto plates, her face flushed. He pointed Chucky to the door and pushed him forward. The fawn was waiting for the boy on the porch as he went out, banging the wooden-framed screen door. Pearl turned and glared. She rattled the plates of eggs and bacon onto the table in front of her menfolk. Zeb mumbled something under his breath and went back to stocking his knapsack.

Pearl rapped on his arm, getting his attention.

"What if that—that *frigging* deer comes here while you're in the mountains? What will you do? Bury us, and then go back to hunting him?"

"There's no chance of that deer getting out of those mount—"

"Don't hand me that, Zeb. Why don't you just admit that killing that—that *thing* means more to you than your own family!"

"I'm going up there to find Joe Hawk, Pearl! You know he's been gone almost a month. Now I've let you put this off and put this off for so long I feel like one of your rags waiting for your period to start! I'm not putting it off any longer, so get used to the idea!"

"Your mouth is disgusting!"

"So's your tantrums. You say Charlie takes after me? Shit! You made him all shanty Irish!"

"Go on then! Only you're not taking my son into any mountains to commit suicide—and I'm not taking any trip to Elmira to visit my foster parents."

"Pearl." Zeb's manner softened. "There's a thousand hunters and game wardens between here and that deer. Now he's either dead or laid up with wounds. I think you are more worried about us than about yourself and Charlie."

Pearl ignored him. She took the frying pan from the burner, forgetting that the flame was still on, dropping it quickly when the hot metal burned the palm of her hand.

Pete was at her side in an instant. "That looks kinda nasty," he said. "You'd better let me put some butter on it for you."

"Why bother?" she said angrily, pulling free of him. "Maybe I just ought to let it burn! I'm getting used to pain. I ought to learn to like it, sooner or later."

"Sis, you know Zeb when he has his mind made. If you're really frightened, I'll stay home with you."

"It's okay with me," Zeb said. "In fact, consider it settled."

A look of reproach suddenly surfaced in the farmwife's eyes. She looked at Pete strangely as he spread butter on her hand. She could sense his strong aura of masculinity and she shrank away from his touch.

"No," she said, "I'd rather you went with my husband."

Pete's face filled with guilt. He nodded and went back to his knapsack.

Zeb began eating his breakfast, wondering over the two of them.

Two days after Joe Hawk had set out he reached the Seneca nation land in the Alleghenies. He had found no sign of the demon stag in the hills and forests, and had continued on, believing the killer to be still farther ahead. A day was lost skirting the farms and settlements of the Allegheny kinsmen, lest they try to stop him and persaude him to return home should he fall into their hands. He went farther into the mountains than he had ever gone before, but after almost two weeks of fruitless searching he had discovered no clue as to the whereabouts of Malsum's beast. During this time he grew thin from the meager fare he lived on, mushrooms, berries, an occasional trout or rabbit, but his hunger never gained an edge, such was his grief and his obsession for finding Shaman.

It was during one of his visits to a high meadow where the deer sign was plentiful that he came across Shaman's tracks. He distinguished these tracks from those of other deer who ranged the mountains by the wider space between the toes of his cloven hoofs. True, there were a few other mule deer mixed in with the indigenous whitetail, but Joe ignored the possibility that the animal he trailed might not be his quarry.

He caught up with the animal in a mountain forest of Pennsylvania, and shot him in the fading rust of twilight from a great distance. Charging in on the wounded beast with his knife and axe he became dismayed. The muledeer was not Shaman, but a younger buck of the same gigantic proportions. Disgusted, he put the animal out of it's misery and sat down to brood. Aggravated, disheartened by constant failure, he set up a permanent camp in the area; allowing the carcass to rot into the ground, food for the cats, and to see what evils the stench of death and decay would bring.

He ate none of the flesh, for he fasted in his grief, inflicting punishment on himself, blaming himself for the death of his grandson. He became weak and gaunt from the lack of nourishment. Bitterly, he sought a vision, sometimes cursing and taunting the gods. In defiance he sang sacred songs, adding to his self-degradation. The frigid mountain nights found him sleepless and without a campfire, more infliction that all but overcame him with arthritic pain. He withstood the cold huddled in his blanket, his back against a tree, his eyes opened and staring at the black nothingness of the woods. Soon the bitterness faded, only to be replaced with depression and melancholy. He felt that he must appear "evil and loathsome" in the eyes of the Creator. A man who had never known fear now suddenly became afraid that he would die before he found Malsum's stag. The guiding vision, he felt, was being withheld because of his arrogance and blasphemy. He repented sincerely, praying as he had never prayed before. He called on ancient gods until his mind rebelled with the anguish of his unheeded pleas. He reverted into a primeval Seneca, beseeching Haweniyu not to forsake his holy mission of retribution.

He spoke continually to the *pukwudjinnies*, hearing their faint whispery voices in his mind. He became wrathful, insulting the dark spirits, challenging them, taunting them to send their greatest against him.

It was recorded in legend of the Algonquins that the great demon Malsum, for whom the Lenape sorcerer had been named, was often cloven-hoofed, as a deer. The Christians said their Satan was cloven-hoofed also. Perhaps they were one and the same?

The old warrior took no chances; he dared them all to do battle. First, however, he bargained, they must send the foul Malsum demon, the former man, to him! As he ranted, he petitioned both good and evil forces, demanding his rights as a hereditary chieftain of the Seneca, fiercest fighters of the Iroquois, Keepers Of The Western Door, unequalled throughout the ages of the red man! His forefathers had conquered countless tribes and had been feared and coveted as the most powerful nation of all. White men had called them the Romans of the New World. In his veins flowed the blood of that warrior race! How could Haweniyu deny him this vision that he sought?

Finally, in a state of delirium, weak and feverish from his forced starvation, the vision came.

A cougar materialized from the shadowy depths of the night and settled on its haunches before the Seneca chieftain. His coat shone blue.

"I am Shetowalko," the cougar said. "What would you have of me?"

"I claim the right to do battle with he who has cursed my life, and the lives of those I love!" Joe Hawk answered.

"I do not know you. Which god do you serve?"

"The god of my strength! The god of my father's wisdom and the master of all demons such as yourself! By that god I demand you serve me! Reveal the demon, Malsum, who was once a man, to my eyes!"

The blue panther roared hideously and sprang onto the Seneca's chest. His fangs glistened as he snarled.

"Shetowalko!" a loud angry voice called.

A tall, naked Seneca warrior materialized from behind a pine. His hair was long and braided, muscles smooth and rippling over his body. The cougar sputtered and snarled, leaping for the warrior. The warrior caught the cat in midair and dashed him to the forest floor. The cat tried to flee and the warrior latched onto his tail. With a tremendous roar the blue panther turned on him, with gaping fang-filled jaws and sharp extended talons. They fought, rolling over the ground like a juggernaut. The gruff curses of the Seneca warrior mingled with the wild screaming of the cougar. Then the blue cat fell silent as strong hands clenched around his throat.

"Release me," the cougar begged. "Release me, and I will grant your son's demand!" But the warrior persisted, trying to wrench the cat's head from its neck.

As the warrior raised the panther above his head, muscles bulging to splinter the cat's backbone, the blue panther suddenly vanished and rematerialized in a cloud of vapor as a spotted serpent. The serpent hissed loudly and coiled in the warrior's hands. It bit the spirit on the face, sinking its poison-filled fangs with deadly swiftness. Still the warrior refused to release the snake, fighting for a lethal hold around its throat, behind the demon's blazing red eyes. The serpent hissed with pleasure as the spirit's arms grew weary.

Weak and dying from the venom in his body, the Seneca warrior sunk to his knees and released the spotted serpent. It crawled a distance away and coiled, its evil eyes gloating over its victory. The vanquished warrior then turned his sad eyes to Joe Hawk. His chest was ripped and torn to the bone by the panther, his face was puffed, and yellow venom oozed from the bites of the serpent.

"Would you fare better, Joseph?" the Seneca warrior asked. He then held up his right hand. The finger closest to the thumb was severed and bleeding.

"Father!" Joe cried out. He tried to go to the dying spirit, but his legs were now bound with heavy ropes. He held out his arms, stretching to touch. This was not a vision; this was real.

"Go home, Joseph . . ." the spirit of Wise Thomas said. "Our people need you. Go home, my son . . ."

As the Seneca warrior died, two black wolves materialized from the brush, slinking toward his body. They sniffed his corpse warily. Joe Hawk yelled hoarsely at them, trying to reach their throats with his bare hands. The pair snarled at him, snapping at his fingertips. Then they dragged the body off a few feet, where he presented no danger, while they gorged themselves.

They began to eat Wise Thomas's flesh, tearing off large mouthfuls.

"No!" the bound Seneca screamed at them. "Do not defile him so!" He sought his rifle, his knife, and axe, but his arms hung powerless at his sides. They, too, were now imprisoned with bindings.

The snake raised on its tail like a cobra and watched the wolves eating. It hissed loudly with pleasure.

"You have your vision," the serpent said. "Am I not all-powerful? Pay homage to me, and I will help you."

"No!" Joe Hawk said. "I will never humble myself before you! Release me, demon, and I will fight you myself!"

"It would be the same," the snake hissed. "You cannot beat me."

A feathered arrow shot out of the forest, piercing a wolf as he ate. Another arrow followed instantly, piercing the second wolf through an ear. They yelped loudly and ran in circles for a moment, trying to break the shafts. A barrage of arrows struck their black bodies, and they fell dead.

A number of young Seneca boys walked from the darkness. The spotted serpent coiled with fear and hissed at them in warning. But the children paid it no heed. They lifted the corpse of Wise Thomas in their small hands and carried him off into the shadowy forest.

"Come back!" Joe Hawk demanded. "Untie me so that I may fight!"

A single small boy returned from the darkness in answer to his anguished yell. The bound chieftain looked at him with wonder and awe. The Seneca boy was naked, and painted over his body were many magic signs and mysterious symbols of the Great Spirit. Around his throat he wore the gold medallion of the Hawks.

"Untie me! Untie me, Joseph!" the *future* cried out to the past.

"No, old man," the boy said stiffly. "See, and understand, if you possess any wisdom still."

Young Joe Hawk suddenly spun on the serpent. It uncoiled and struck at him, lashing out with dripping fangs. The boy dodged it agilely and laughed, a taunting pitch in his youthful voice. The snake's terrible fear filled the forest with a stench of sulphur. The boy circled it slowly, as a mongoose would a cobra.

When next the spotted serpent struck, the boy seized it by the throat and held it at bay. He thrust the gold medallion beneath its curved fangs and milked it dry of its deadly poison.

"Watch, old man!" the past spoke to the future. He pulled on the snake with strong young arms, until the spotted serpent ripped apart into two writhing lengths of reptilian flesh. He dashed the two segments to the forest floor and stepped back.

Two antlers sprang from the writhing flesh, and an evil stag grew quickly into existence. Its face and body was scarred hideously, an ear was torn off at the root. The beast's antlers were twisted and gnarled, deformed wickedly. It pawed at the ground, snorting and bellowing.

"Kill him, Joseph!" Joe yelled savagely. "Make him pay for his crimes against us!" Suddenly his heart was filled with horror and fear, for the boy was no longer Joseph, but he had transformed into his grandson, Thomas. The past was incapable of fighting the future.

"Tommy! Tommy, run!" the grandfather cried. "Run, or he will kill you!"

"I am stronger than he, Grandfather," Tommy said. "Why do you not put your faith in me? Did not your father believe in you as a boy? Believe in me, grandfather, and I will kill this evil stag for you! My heart is pure and without fear or shame, as yours once was, for I am a boy and not yet a man."

"No! Do not fight him," Joe choked. "Run away or he will kill you!"

Tears of shame and sadness formed in the boy's eyes.

"You have stolen my great magic with your greater doubt," the vision of Tommy said. "If only you had believed in me . . ."

Joe Hawk watched with horror and grief as the powerful stag charged his grandson and killed him.

"Malsum!" Joe raged as the beast transformed into the Lenape sorcerer. "I will kill you a thousand times for this!" He could not bear to look at the torn flesh of the boy.

The evil Indian faced him with glowering hate-filled eyes and cracked a gloating smile. "You cannot beat me either," Malsum taunted.

Once again the Indian took on the shape of the evil stag.

From where the boy's torn flesh lay, a young fawn suddenly grew. It emerged into a handsome hart with a white throat and large ears. Two horns, the horns of an innocent lamb, erupted from his head. The beautiful creature began to glow with a brilliant radiance that dispelled the darkness. The horns atop his crown grew into two sharply pointed knives. He faced the stag and pawed the earth, lowering his head for a charge.

Although twice the size of the hart, the monster stag shrieked with fear and fled for the shadows. The young hart bounded after in pursuit, dispelling the darkness wherever he went, forcing the night to depart, as if he were the dawning sun returned from night.

"Joseph," a sweet voice called from the light of day, "forget your vengeance and return home. Our people are filled with grief for you. Their hearts weep, and they pray constantly."

A beautiful Seneca woman in a white deerhide dress and white beads stepped forth and began untying his ropes.

"Joseph . . ." The radiant woman turned soft, loving

eyes on the old chieftain. "My poor son," she said, "go home now."

The form of Beautiful Mary turned translucent with the rays of the risen sun as the last rope faded away.

The vision ended with her consoling face and words.

Joe awoke with the noise of his rasping breath loud in his ears. He stared at the surrounding forest, trying to sort out the vision in his mind. With dawn the woods had come alive with the chirping of songbirds.

The Seneca rose to his feet on weak, aching legs. He looked at the vision's battlesite for a clue. The ground was undisturbed, and there were no telltale signs of any sort, only the many imprints of his own hunting boots.

"No," he murmured, "I will not go home." He looked off into the forest, suffering from his starved condition.

"I will not go home!" he yelled. "Do you hear me, Malsum! I will find your beast and kill him! I will not go home!" He looked above at the blue mountain sky and raised his fist, as if shaking it at the very face of Haweniyo. "It is my right!" he cried.

Intense hunger drew him to the bloated carcass of the buck he had shot days before. The decaying flesh was covered with maggots. He scraped off handfuls of the white larvae and ate them. The thought of eating such filth was repulsive, but his body craved nourishment, and the maggots were almost pure protein. He tottered to a nearby stream and drank deeply, washing their taste from his mouth.

There were small trout in the stream, but Joe Hawk was too weak to catch them by hand. After fashioning a spear, with his knife as a blade, he managed to skewer three of them. He ate one raw and took the other two back to his camp to roast over a fire. The food eased his suffering, but it would be many days before he regained even a portion of his former strength.

Wildlife, other than birds, was scarce in this part of the mountains, but he would not descend into the lower forests to go where disobedients of his tribe and white bounty hunters might be searching. There was no way that he would ever find the deer. The deer would have to find him, so it mattered not where he stayed.

For a week he ate anything that had food value: burdock, dandelions, grasshoppers, fish, even the broth of boiled bark. He found a beehive in a hollow tree and smoked it, gorging himself on the sweet honey. Later he stripped and covered his body with cool mud to draw out venom of the innumerable bee stings, allowing it to dry before he bathed himself in the stream. Gradually his strength returned.

He built a lean-to as shelter against the sudden rainstorms, and fell into a reguar routine of living. During the day he dried fish and set snares for the occasional opossums and raccoons that came to the stream at night. Sooner or later the Shaman stag's wounds would mend, and the beast would journey to Joe's campsite for their final fight. Of this he was certain, for he had more dreams, granting him his demands. He was asked to throw his rifle away, for the spirit of the sorcerer would offer battle only on his own conditions. Joe Hawk readily abandoned the weapon. He lived now only to kill the deer, and it was his nature to taunt death. His knife and axe would serve him well enough. He prayed that the deer would have enough courage to face these manly weapons of revenge.

The rifle had been useless to him. He had not used it to secure food, as the noise of a shot carried far through the mountains, and it might guide others to him. Outside intervention would destroy all chances of Malsum's eventual arrival. Also, the voices of rational men might persuade him to return to his people in disgrace and dishonor, a mere vessel for their kind words and sympathy. Better a warrior's death.

He believed the first vision, and felt the stag would kill him—but he might also kill the stag! He had to take the chance.

There was nothing else in life for him that could sway his thirst for vengeance. Killing the stag was an obsession. Death itself held no fear, only the threat of defeat.

The days and nights passed, and the Indian stayed in his camp, waiting with grim determination.

"Where the hell is he?" Zeb asked, wincing under Pete's knife as his brother dug a chigger out from beneath the skin on his back. "Damn his old hide! I'm fed up with these goddamn mountains! I'm fed up with trying to find him!"

"You want to give it up and go home?" Pete asked, pouring a small portion of whiskey over the opened incision. Luckily, the parasite had been discovered before it had burrowed too deeply.

Zeb eyed the bottle of whiskey passionately as Pete tucked it away in his knapsack. His fortitude against drink ebbed lower than ever. For three weeks he had not touched a drop, not even at Tommy's funeral. But the craving was always there. Sometimes, like a knotted fist in his belly, it would lash out and punish him. The strong spirits had been brought along to get Joe Hawk drunk when they found him, to make the Indian amenable to their intention of escorting him home. But the bottle in Pete's knapsack was now getting to be all that Zeb could think about.

"We can't leave him up here," Zeb answered. "Let's give it another few days anyways. And do me a favor?"

Pete frowned at his brother, scratching the two weeks growth of beard on his face. "You asking for a drink?"

Zeb's eyes frosted over with self-contempt. "No," he said, "I want you to break that sonuvabitch for me!"

Pete took the bottle out and poised it over a rock. He thought of taking one long swallow first but that wouldn't be fair. He smashed it, and the reek of whiskey filled the air around them.

"Let's try moving east for a while," Zeb said, his green eyes sick with discouragement.

Joe's stomach ached with fierce, stabbing pain. He sat up, awakening from his nightmarish slumber. He had to clench his teeth to keep from crying out. It felt as if a fire was raging through his insides.

On his bedding were the foodstuffs he had been eating. He looked at them accusingly. A dwindling pile of wild mushrooms in a corner of his makeshift shelter caught his attention, and he scooped up a handful of them and looked at their milky whiteness. The bottoms were a telltale white, showing that they were good to eat.

But in their midst was one with a black underside. The Seneca man smashed it in his hand and lay back, enraged with himself. He had eaten poison mushrooms! How many, he had no idea. If the number was great, the pain would increase until it eventually killed him.

"Old man!" Joe said of himself bitterly. "Foolish blind old man!"

He sat back up and thrust his fingers down his throat,

gagging on them. The pain in his retching stomach muscles threatened to punish him if he tried again. He fought the temptation to lie back and accept the lesser spasms of pain in hopes that he would survive. He blamed his bad selection of food onto Malsum's witchcraft, and it gave him strength. He would not die so easily. He thrust his fingers deeper down his throat.

Gall and vomit spewed from his mouth. Again and again he retched chunks of half-digested food. The pain became an all-consuming flame, and finally he fell back on his blanket, unconscious.

He awoke with a feverish brow and chills rippling through his body sometime during the night. It was raining hard outside and he was partially wet. His throat was closed with thirst and his stomach throbbed with a raw burning. He reached through the opening, cupped falling rain in his palms, and drank a mouthful. The water rewarded his throat but punished his stomach with a hollow aching. He had survived. Malsum would not cheat him. He caught more rain and drank until his thirst was quenched and the pain subsided. His blanket was mostly dry, and he stripped to the waist, rolling up in its warmth. Finally, he crawled back to a dry corner of the lean-to and fell asleep.

The *pukwudjinnies* burst in on Joe Hawk's sleep with loud callings and warnings.

"Who? Who calls Joe Hawk?" The Seneca opened his eyes and peered into the grey dawn.

Through the drizzling rain, the ghost-like shape of Malsum's stag appeared.

Another dream? he wondered.

And then the beast snorted and walked closer until the haggard chieftain made out his yellow hate-filled eyes. The deer thrust his muzzle upward, exposing his bulging verrucose throat, and bellowed a long drawn out challenge.

No, this was not a dream!

Joe threw off his blanket and sat up, reaching for his knife and axe.

"Come, beast!" he said in the tongue of his fathers. "Attack me so I might catch you by your horns and destroy you!"

Shaman ceased his noise and backed away, animal fear blazing in his crazed eyes.

"No!" Joe Hawk yelled. "Do not run from me. Fight me! Fight me, child killer!"

The deer spun about and raced back into the forest, bawling and braying with fright.

Joe staggered to his feet. The dizziness in his head and the pain in his belly washed through him and then disappeared as if by command. He followed the deer, yelling and cursing in Seneca.

"Coward! Cowardly killer of children!" he cried out in anguish, feeling cheated and forlorn. "I am but a man! Filthy demon! Fight me!"

The enraged Indian heard a crashing of brush close at his side, and as he turned the stag was already upon him, driving savagely spiked antlers into his flesh and smashing him to the rain-drenched ground.

As the deer whirled and charged, barbed head aimed low for the groin, the fearless warrior grappled for a handhold and succeeded. The stag reared back, lifting the stalwart giant from his feet, but Joe Hawk was a powerful man even weakened by his sickness, and the beast could not shake him loose.

"Now, deer!" Joe cried, as he held the animal tight with one huge arm about his rack. He maneuvered to Shaman's side as the beast shrieked in terror, aimed for a cleft between the deer's shoulder muscle and neck and plunged his blade downward. Shaman spurted forward, driven into a frenzy by the wound, and slammed his mighty adversary against a nearby tree. The Seneca chief lost his grip and the deer shook him loose and ran.

Joe regained his fallen axe, trying to stanch the blood flowing from his stomach wounds with his free hand. Shaman had suffered a perilous injury during the short encounter, for the knife was wedged in his shoulder, but it had also cost the Seneca dearly, and he would soon bleed to death if he did not bind his wounds.

The demon could be seen a short distance away, laboring against a low tree limb to pry the knife from his shoulder. Joe Hawk watched the animal use the branch as a fulcrum to pull the blade out by the hilt.

No mere animal possessed such deliberate intelligence.

It was as if Malsum was openly admitting to the old Seneca, in this final moment, that his spirit was harbored in the body of the deer. Two beings looked at Joe Hawk through Shaman's eyes: the pain-filled panic of a wild animal who wished to flee, and the glowering hatred of the evil Lenape wizard, who commanded that the deer stay and fight.

Joe limped toward the stag, a bold look of courage on his grim face. He wielded the axe in his right hand, holding his stomach with his left. The deer backed away and began circling him, favoring his wounded front leg. The beast snorted steamy puffs of breath into the morning coldness of the mountain air. And then he charged with incredible swiftness that caught the Seneca unprepared.

Joe's axe clacked uselessly against a bony antler, spinning out of his hand as he tried to cleave the deer's skull. The gnarled rack scooped him up, sinking deep into the soft flesh of his groin and thighs. The Indian was hurled effortlessly into the air.

As he fell to the forest floor, weaponless, his flesh torn, he lay still and feigned death. His fingers slowly closed around a smooth rock lying beneath his hand.

Malsum's devil deer strutted around his still form triumphantly, snorting hot air through his black nostril slits like a dragon breathing fire. The beast made little gurgling noises of satisfaction in his swollen throat. Joe Hawk lay on his side and watched through narrowed eyes.

The stag came up behind him, but the cool-headed Seneca made no attempt to move. His nerves were taut but under control.

As Shaman's antlers probed his back, the giant sprang to life and slammed the rock in his fist down hard on the stag's forehead. The beast collapsed, his legs buckling, his muscles jerking.

The force of the blow had caused an antler tine to dig deep into the man's forearm, severing an artery. The painful injuries twisted the Indian's face into a grimacing death mask. He dragged himself away from Shaman's carcass, leaving a wide path of red blood to mingle with the rain and soak into the earth. He regained his tomahawk and forced himself into a sitting position, folding his legs in front of him. His heart pushed blood from his opened arm and his many wounds. In a very short while he would be dead.

But it was well with him, and he was at peace with himself, for he had destroyed Malsum's stag, and he would die with a great victory in his hand. Shaman would rot into the ground, and Malsum would have him kill no other children. All that was left now was a desire to be laid to rest at the side of his grandson; otherwise the chief was vindicated and fulfilled.

"Tommy . . ," he whispered, as he finished commending his soul to the Great Spirit. "*Haksot*, come guide the spirit of a foolish old man . . . come to me . . . so that I do not despair on the journey. Come to me now . . . and wipe away the tears of this old man."

The great warrior's spirit departed his flesh. His noble corpse remained seated, the broad chin resting on his chest. Even death could not rob the son of Wise Thomas of his dignity.

Almost imperceptibly, the deer began to breathe.

They had to cover their faces with kerchiefs as they approached the corpse. It was covered with ants and maggots. Large black beetles had made nests in the putrefied flesh. The eyes had been picked clean by crows, and the ears pecked at until only the centers were left.

"Goddamn . . ." Zeb backed away and coughed from the stench. This was not a new sight for him. He had seen worse on the islands during the war; hundreds of enemy bodies, heaped into stinking piles by soldiers wearing gas masks, and bulldozed into mass burial pits.

Pete gagged and vomited, dropping to his knees and clenching his eyes to shut out the horror of it all.

"I'll be okay in a minute," he promised, as Zeb helped him to his feet. But he wasn't, and he threw up until his stomach was scraped empty and he felt as though his backbone pressed against his navel.

They covered the corpse with dry pine branches from the lean-to and burned it. Pete said a simple prayer in Seneca for Joe's soul. All night they kept the funeral pyre blazing and by morning there was nothing left of the beloved Seneca but his blackened bones.

With great respect and devotion, they wrapped the remains in the Seneca's blanket and took them home to give to his people for burial.

Chapter XI

Nora sipped at the steaming black coffee as she and Pete sat at the Woolworth counter in downtown Buffalo. It was only one week until Christmas, and the store was bustling with holiday shoppers.

At school, during the afternoon, Chucky had mentioned that his uncle and he were driving into the city to do some shopping. Nora's automobile had been in the garage for days, having a new engine installed. Her mechanic had not put enough anti-freeze in the radiator when he winterized the car earlier in the year, and sub-zero temperatures had frozen and expanded the water, cracking the block. The small-town mechanic was taking his time over replacing the engine, and had stalled for after Christmas, leaving Nora without transportation except for buses. Although Pete hadn't seen or called her since they attended the two funerals the summer before, she had taken the initiative and telephoned him at the bank, explaining her predicament. Pete had agreed to take her shopping with him and had picked her up at her apartment in Gowanda.

Chucky had decided to stay home at the last minute, Pete had said. And, even though it was not inhibited by the presence of a child, their conversation had stayed casual on the long drive into the city. Mark was constantly on Nora's mind, but she made sure not to initiate any talk regarding him. Once they had discussed Luke Banner's passing on, and his leaving half of all he and Emily owned to Mathias, but even then Mark was carefully avoided. Emily had died in the hospital in September and Luke, grief-stricken over the loss of his boy and wife, had steadily ebbed away, eating improperly and neglecting to take his insulin injections for the diabetes he had endured since middle age. Some said he had committed suicide, but others pointed out his strength of character and belief in God, and scoffed at such an interpretation.

"I hear you're dating a real cute girl from the bank," Nora said with a smile as they sat at the counter.

"Sharon Evans?" Pete shrugged. "She's just a youngster. I take her out dancing once in a while."

"I've seen her a few times," Nora said casually. "She's a beautiful girl."

"Yes, she is. She's very pretty."

Nora sipped her coffee. "Chucky tells me that you're dating a lot of girls now."

"A couple, I guess . . . Did you find some things for your students?" Pete motioned toward Nora's shopping bag on the floor.

"Just some pen and pencil sets. A few story books."

"It's very generous of you to buy for so many children."

Nora's lips parted in a full smile, revealing perfect, even, white teeth. "I enjoy playing Santa Claus once a year." She laughed. "Or is it Miss Santa Claus? I really do love buying for them though."

She took a cigarette from her purse and Pete took the matches from her, holding the flame away from her face until the flash died, and then lighting the cigarette for her.

"Thank you," she yawned, placing a red-nailed hand over her mouth, arching her back. Her full bosom thrust forward beneath a brown cardigan pullover that was a shade lighter than the tight-fitting skirt she wore.

Pete's eyes darted helplessly to her bustline, and she noticed and held the pose longer than she would have normally.

"Tired?"

"No, not really. My back aches once in a while. I think I'm overdoing my figure exercises."

"You should taper off. You don't really need them."

"You don't think so? I'm a little chubby around my waist." She patted her stomach and waited for his opinion.

"I can't imagine you ever becoming fat." Pete smiled. "Really, Nora, your figure is very nice."

"Well, thank you. We older women appreciate a compliment when we can get one." Nora laughed.

A teen-aged waitress began making her rounds at the counter with a coffee pot, offering refills. Pete placed a hand over his cup. "No more, thank you," he said. "We have to be going now."

The young girl smiled daringly at him, obviously wanting to let Pete know that she found him attractive.

"Come back again sometime—if you're interested in shopping," the girl said, blatantly pretending Nora did not exist. Pete winked at the waitress and smiled.

"I suppose we should get home," Nora agreed, with a slight edge to her voice. She stood and took her coat from the stool back as the waitress answered a call from another customer at the counter.

"I wasn't planning on going home just yet," Pete said, helping her into her coat. "There's a Danny Kaye movie playing at the Lafayette. He used to be your favorite. Would you like to go?"

"That would be nice," Nora said, after a startled pause.

Pete went to the cash register at the end of the counter to pay for their coffee, and the young waitress came back to Nora, appraising her critically.

"Your boyfriend's very handsome," she said. "You're a lucky girl."

"Yes, he is handsome. Only he's not just a boyfriend— we're engaged to be married."

"Oh. I didn't realize. You're not wearing a ring. How long have you been engaged?"

"Thirteen years."

"Thirteen—! Isn't that kind of long?"

"Not if you aren't oversexed, honey."

Pete came back for her and they left the store.

Main Street was lit with colorful Christmas decorations on every lamp post and store front. The grey winter afternoon had changed into evening while they had been inside, and the holiday settings were breathtaking.

Red and white buses lined the curb lanes, accommodating the shoppers and theater-goers.

The Buffalo Bank, a large domed building, almost an exact copy of the Capitol in Washington, D.C., was draped with brilliant lights from the fifth floor to the top of the dome. A glorious Christmas tree, it was topped with a lighted angel that smiled down on the crowds. Life-sized nativity scenes were housed in wooden mangers by many of the bus stops and were accompanied by short monologues on hidden tape recorders through speakers inside the chicken-wire fronts. Blue-coated policemen astride horses maneuvered through the congested street, waving to children and blowing silver whistles to direct traffic. The city, second largest in the state, had never looked more beautiful.

It was freezing cold, as it had been for two weeks, but as yet there had been no snow.

Pete and Nora walked along the gaily lit boulevard, caught in the bustle of the crowds. The theater they were going to was four blocks away, but Pete had suggested that they walk rather than fight the clogged traffic. He left the car in a downtown parking lot with the shopping bag of presents safely locked in the trunk.

Nora walked with Pete, feeling nervous and unsure of herself. Pete noticed that she was struggling through the crowd, having a hard time of it with her hands in her pockets.

"I'm sorry," he said, gently taking her shoulder and guiding her to the middle of the sidewalk. He held her arm and moved in close beside her, running interference. "You must think my manners are terrible."

"Now that you mention it," Nora agreed. She placed her hand in his. He wasn't wearing gloves, and his hand felt strong and large, more so than she had remembered. So many years had escaped them. He hardly resembled the skinny boy she had fallen in love with. She squeezed his hand on an impulse, and he tightened his grip. A very small gesture, perhaps, but one that made her happy and gave her hope.

Suited Santa Clauses stood in department store doorways ringing bells and thanking people who dropped donations into the little brass pots hanging from tripods. Nora took a roll of dimes from her purse and opened them up, holding the coins in her hands.

"What are you going to do with those?" Pete asked.

She smiled and poured him some dimes as they came up to the first Santa. "Watch," she whispered, a playful cast to her eyes, and dropped a dime in the pot.

"Merry Christmas, and God bless you, daughter," Santa said. "Thank you, son. Merry Christmas, and bless you."

Twenty-five feet further on they came to another Santa, and the scene was repeated.

Pete laughed openly as they reached the third Santa and a similar salutation was offered.

"What are you doing?" he asked. "You'll run out of

dimes before you run out of Santa Clauses. They're all from the Salvation Army; why don't you just drop all of the money into one pot?"

Nora smiled and winked at him. "This way we get more blessings," she said and went up to the next red-suited man. "Merry Christmas, Santa!"

In front of the Lafayette Theater was still another jolly St. Nicholas. He sat atop a glittering sleigh with a bag full of promotional coloring books from the movie, handing them out to children.

Eight live reindeer were harnessed to the sleigh, and parents lifted their sons and daughters onto the backs of the animals, some snapping pictures. One man had a throng of interested people waiting around him as he studied his watch, counting off the minutes before he took his photograph from the self-developing Polaroid camera he held. They all groaned with disappointment as the picture turned out to be nothing more than a black background with grey images.

"I told you." A white-haired man with three grandchildren hanging on his arm spoke up. "Thet thing ain't ever gonna work right—junk! You threw your money away, Johnny."

"It works," the camera holder said confidently. "I must have done something wrong." He examined the camera.

"Like color TV, if you ask me," the disgruntled grandfather said. "Experimental junk! They'll be off the market in two years!"

The camera owner, possibly a son of the older man, produced a crystal clear black and white photograph from his pocket and showed it smugly.

"Where's the color?" the grandfather asked.

"It's not supposed to be colored. They're still working on that."

"Hrmph! They'll never do it. Nothing but junk."

"They'll do it," the man answered confidently.

"Sure they will. And some day we'll walk on the moon, I suppose, like we saw in that other movie last week?"

"Well, I wouldn't go that far. I agree walking on the moon is a little far-fetched, but making a self-developing camera that takes colored pictures is only realistic."

The discussion carried on, with more pictures being staged with the grandchildren astride reindeer.

Pete felt guilty at not having brought Chucky along

with him. The movie, he realized now, was slanted more toward children than adults. The boy had wanted to go, but Pete was afraid that Nora would talk about old times and old heartaches, so he had left him at home. A sad mistake—the Christmas atmosphere would have been a tonic to him. He constantly brooded or erupted into anger, lately, and he was failing at school. The tragic losses of last summer had affected him deeply. It seemed all he wanted to do now was spend hours with his pet deer out in the barn.

"I wish I'd brought Chucky with me," Pete said aloud, then he noticed that Nora hadn't heard him.

She was watching the children sitting atop the reindeer, with a frightened look. For small deer, they had very huge antlers.

Pete nudged her to get her attention. "Those animals are gentle and well-trained," he said. "The children aren't in any danger."

"I know," she replied distantly. "I was just . . . thinking. Peter, how could a deer do what Shaman did? Do you really think he's dead now?"

"Yes, he is. Zeb and I found him back there. Joe Hawk killed him." He squeezed her hand tightly. "He won't ever hurt anyone again. It's best to forget about him."

"I'd like to believe he's dead, but Chucky says he isn't. He says he has dreams . . . visions."

An angry look surfaced on Pete. "He's a little boy with a big imagination, Nora. I can see I'm going to have to have another talk with him."

"I wish you wouldn't. He would feel that I betrayed his confidence."

Pete nodded. "I'll agree to that. But then you'll have to take the responsibility of setting him straight yourself."

A worried look came over the attractive woman. "I don't know that I can. I'm afraid I share many of the same delusions, if that's what you feel they are. I have my own . . . nightmares."

Pete shrugged. There was really nothing else for him to say. People seemed to enjoy frightening themselves with myths, arguing to keep them alive. It was a shame that Nora had that trait. Joe Hawk had said he would kill the deer, and he had. There was really nothing else for him to say. It would be like talking to Sam, or James Goodman, or Chucky himself. They had their beliefs; Zeb, the county authorities, and Pete had theirs, backed with proof. Shaman had been a killer animal, for whatever reason, a statistical freak, but now he was dead. Joe Hawk had lost his life seeing to that. And there was no doubt. The hoofs on the decayed carcass matched Shaman's tracks perfectly.

Evidently the deer had attacked Joe and injured him badly before Joe managed to put a shot into the beast and kill it. There was no way of telling for sure, but Shaman's remains must have been at least a week older than Joe's. It was grim to think that the rugged old Seneca had hung on to life for days afterwards, suffering without anyone there to help him, but that was what appeared to have happened.

The admission booth opened, and Pete went over to purchase their tickets.

The movie was good, filled with songs and laughter. Danny Kaye played the part of Hans Christian Andersen, and towards the end of the feature it got quite sad, when Hans found out that his lovely ballerina didn't return his love. Nora leaned her head on Pete's shoulder and suffered through it rapturously.

The show let out around eleven P.M., and they walked down Main Street to the lot where Pete had parked his car. They held hands and talked about the movie, being careful not to slip and fall in the fresh layer of powdery snow. While they were in the theater it had begun falling, and, even though they were pleased by this, they were both a little worried about driving the thirty miles home before the roads became impassable. When it snowed in western New York State, it generally didn't know when to stop.

They listened to soft music on the car radio as Pete drove from the downtown shopping strip, now just a ghost of itself, all of the stores closed and darkened, only a few buses and autos on the street. Nora felt more at ease with Pete now, and she kicked off her shoes and stuck her nyloned toes onto the heater to thaw out, soaking up the blessed heat. As they left the lighted city and reached the dark suburbs she moved over nearer to him and rested her head on his shoulder, as she had in the theater. He wasn't talkative, and she fell asleep before they had covered ten miles.

Nora awakened as the forward motion of the auto ceased.

"Oh, are we home already?" she asked with mild disbelief, seeing that Pete had parked in her driveway. "I'm afraid I wasn't much company for you."

The neighborhood was covered in a blanket of virgin white. Large snowflakes drifted down onto the windshield.

"Were the roads slippery?"

"A little bit. They'll get worse before they'll get better."

"Yes, I would imagine they will. Do you have time to come in for coffee? Are you hungry?"

"I think I ought to get home while I can," Pete said.

"They keep the highways open pretty good around—" Nora laughed. "I'm telling you? Your brother drives a snowplow. Are you sure you wouldn't like to come in for a while?"

"Some other time, Nora. It is rather late, and, even though tomorrow is Saturday, I have to get up early."

"Okay. Will you call me?"

"Yes. I had a nice time tonight. We'll have to get together again soon."

Nora saw the phony smile on his face. He was speaking to her as if she were one of his lousy bank clients applying for a loan!

"Should we wish each other Merry Christmas now, then?"

"If you'd like to."

Damn him! Christmas was a week away. He obviously didn't have any intention of calling her again.

She smiled at him, hiding her anger, and let her coat slip back onto the seat, no longer interested in leaving the warm automobile just yet. She reached across Pete and pushed the headlight knob in, darkening the car.

Pete turned to her as she twined an arm around his neck. She intended to give him a good night kiss, and he decided to make it short and emotionless, so that even a kiss couldn't be misinterpreted as chance for an involvement of any sort.

A light scent of perfume lingered as Nora pressed her lips to his. They were soft, and tasted sweet. He found himself unable to pull away when he tried; the woman was holding him. The tip of her tongue pried gently at his closed lips, and he felt a quick involuntary hardening as her tongue slid in, warm, and wildly caressed the inside of his mouth.

She retracted, leaving her lips parted, occasionally biting at him. She drew his tongue into her mouth and held it tightly, sending shivers through him. His hardness swelled, torturing him wonderfully.

Nora smiled like a temptress as the kiss ended.

"Can't you come in for a while?"

"Nora, this isn't right. I don't want to hurt you, but I don't think we should try to pick up the pieces of something that's been lost to us for years."

Nora's eyes flashed with an anger that even the darkness couldn't conceal. "I'm not going to make you sign any contracts. I simply want you to make love to me. If you try to say you don't want to . . ."

Pete stiffened and hissed through his teeth as she suddenly clasped his hardness through his slacks.

" . . . then you're a damned liar."

He pried her fingers loose as she began rubbing and squeezing him.

"Get your coat on," he said. "I'll see you to your door."

"Are you coming in?"

"Thank you, but no thank you."

Pete struggled at first as she kissed him again, but soon her pressing lips subdued his protests. After a deliriously heated moment, he responded to the tugging at his belt and zipper and helped her to undo his pants. He fondled her through her sweater, going under it and unclasping the brassiere, all the while clinging to her mouth with his own.

She dragged her fingernails over him and touched him in ways that soon had him aching for her. She whimpered audibly as his hand went under her dress. The insides of her thighs were on fire. Her panties were silky and soaked through with her own wanting. He had never known her to be so exciting—had never known any woman to be so exciting.

Her fingernails dug into his back as she embraced him with a trembling urgency. He positioned himself on his knees over her and tried to take her. But the narrow confinement of the seat hindered him.

She waited, anxious, with heavy breathing. But the delay gave Pete a chance to think.

"This isn't right," he whispered. "We'd better stop."

"No, please, Peter . . ." Like a contortionist, she raised herself up, took him tightly in her hands, and forced him deep inside of her. He gasped as she thrust herself at him. Suddenly he exploded. As he slipped away she held him tightly in her arms. The smell of sex was thick in the car.

"What's wrong?" he asked, as he felt her trembling. "Are you cold?"

Nora pushed him away and sat up, reaching for her coat and packages. For long seconds she sat with clenched eyes.

"Goodbye," she said finally, her voice quivering, "and Merry Christmas!"

Pete stared at her speechlessly as she hurried from the auto and watched as she unlocked her apartment door and went inside without a backward glance.

He sat in the car for long minutes trying to sort things out. It wasn't his fault! Goddamn her! She had gotten just what she wanted.

Just so they had the record straight—

Pete went to the apartment door and knocked, expecting Nora to open it immediately and invite him inside. She was going to get an earful! He didn't like feeling the way he did. She had no right, opening up old wounds. He should have told her to go to hell earlier, when she called him at the bank. Christ! Tears! He actually had tears in his eyes

He knocked again when she didn't answer. The snow drifted down, covering his clothing, melting on his face and neck. Where the hell was she?

The door swung inward as he turned the knob. He stepped into the living room. A small fir tree stood in the corner, decorated with glowing bulbs and silver tinsel. It cast colored light patterns onto the ceiling. She wasn't in the room.

He closed the door quietly and walked through to where he imagined her bedroom would be.

As he stood silently in the darkened hall he could hear her crying softly. His eyes became accustomed to the dark, and he made out the silhouette of her form lying across the bed. He walked into the room.

"I'm sorry, Nora," he said. "We acted like a couple of kids."

Damn! he thought, that wasn't what he wanted to say!

The woman tensed and stopped sobbing as she heard his voice. She continued to lie on the bed, keeping her face buried in her arms.

"I don't want to talk about it," she said. "You'd better go before the roads get any worse."

Pete's anger suddenly drained, leaving him empty.

"I am sorry . . . Please believe that."

"Just go, damn you!"

Pete sat down on the bed and touched her hair. It was long and wavy, with a wonderful texture. He tried to think of appropriate words. But she had bared his soul to him, exposed his terrible bitterness.

"All my life I've been hurting people," he said finally. "Throwing them aside because they're not as perfect as I think I am." He knew now why he had never liked little Mark Banner. Nora had probably recognized himself in the child. His sarcasm had shown the boy to be a Simpson, a little Pete Simpson!

"I'm really not worth crying over, Nora. Do yourself a favor and forget me."

Nora sat up and trapped his hand as he began to leave. She leaned her forehead against his chest and embraced him as she felt his arms encircling her back.

"I still love you," she said. "I've never stopped loving you."

"Nora, it was a long time ago. I have to be honest. I'm not in love with you any more."

She began unbuttoning his coat, kissing him softly on the face.

"I'll make you love me again, Peter," she whispered. "I'll make you forgive me . . ."

She felt calloused fingers gliding over her stomach and opened her eyes as they entwined in her pubic hair.

"Darn you, Zeb!" Pearl cried, seeing him sitting up in bed reading a folded True Adventures magazine. "Turn the light off and let me get some sleep!" she groaned, pushing his hand away.

"Hell, you know me," Zeb replied, replacing his hand as he continued to read. "I'm at the good part. The cannibal's daughter is screwin' the shipwrecked sailor. Gotta keep goin' until I find out who eats who."

Pearl pushed his hand away again and shook her head ruefully.

"I've got to get some sleep!" she said. "If you want to do it, then turn off the light—right now!"

Zeb paused for a moment and then shrugged. He clicked off the lamp and crawled over on top of her, hiking up her nightgown.

"Don't kiss me," Pearl protested as he groped for her

mouth in the dark. "I don't know which of us has the worst breath."

Zeb sighed and concentrated on business.

The bed springs started to squeak rhythmically and Pearl stiffened, stopping his motion.

"Don't make so much noise!" she scolded. "I don't want Pete hearing us."

"You don't have to worry about that. He's not even home yet."

There was no response as Zeb resumed his lovemaking.

"What time is it?"

"I don't know, around three A.M. C'mon, will you? I've got to go in early."

"Do you think he might have gotten stuck in Buffalo or on the way home?"

"Stuck in Nora Cleary's bed is probably more like it."

Pearl moved under him, hurrying him, and he finished prematurely.

"Thanks a lot!"

"You're welcome. Now let me go to sleep."

Zeb waited for a few minutes and then turned the night-stand lamp on to finish reading his story. He read for another half hour and then got up to get dressed.

It wasn't any fun going out at four A.M. to plow roads, but he supposed he should be thankful for the opportunity to make the additional money right before Christmas. There was a ball bearing shooting arcade for $18 that he had been eyeing for Charlie at Sears, Roebuck, and a new automatic washing machine for Pearl. Pete had offered to pay half the cost, but now Zeb would be able to pay for it entirely, if the snow held up and he could log enough hours. He looked forward to seeing their faces come Christmas morning.

Pearl muttered something as Zeb finished getting into dungarees and a warm long-sleeved flannel shirt. He leaned over the bed and kissed her softly on the lips. He shouldn't have disturbed her sleep earlier. She had been sitting up until one or two A.M. every night for the past two weeks crocheting afghans, filling orders for Christmas shopping money. Zeb looked at her haggard face and smoothed her hair back from her forehead. His love welled inside and he bent down and kissed her again.

"Get out of here, Pete!" she mumbled.

"What?"

"Oh, my God! What are we doing?" she said loudly.

Zeb felt his heart pounding in his ears. He stood by the bed and looked at his wife as she drifted back into quiet slumber. For five minutes he stood like a statue, trying to sort things out in his mind. Then he blackened the room and walked downstairs quietly.

Dave Barnes looked up from his desk as a snowplow with an amber beacon revolving on the roof parked outside in the night.

"Hey, Zeb!" he said elatedly, as the somber man stalked into the office. "How is it out there, pretty bad?"

"I've seen worse. Not much wind right now."

Dave poured a cup of steaming coffee from an electric percolator on a wall shelf. "Seen Sam lately?" he asked as he handed Zeb the hot brew.

"Not for a month or so, anyways. How's he doing?"

"Fine. His drinking's way down. If you talked to him now, I think you could get him to go on the wagon this time."

A sad expression crossed Zeb's green eyes. He took a sip of the coffee and set the cup down. "Yeah, well, I think you better appoint someone else for that job, Davy boy."

The deputy watched as Zeb opened Sam's bottom desk drawer and pulled out a pint of Old Crow. He laid two dollars on the desk and walked out, untwisting the cap and breaking the seal.

Chapter XII

The school bus pushed through the frozen slush on Genessee Road, its clanking chain-covered wheels crunching ruts into the ice.

It was the middle of February, still winter, but it gave signs that it would leave early. Frequent thaws with rain, interspersed with snow and sudden freezes, brought more than one catastrophe to the Simpsons. They lost over a third of the apple trees in their orchard, trunks split open like hot rocks thrown onto a fire, limbs cracked off from the weight of rain suddenly turned to ice. A section of their barn roof had collapsed, as numerous other roofs had across four counties. Traffic accidents were up to an all-time high. It would be a short winter, perhaps, but certainly not a good one.

The bus driver parked alongside the Simpson yard and levered the door open. He eyed Chucky critically as the boy stepped down to the road.

"You really aim to ride that deer?" the driver asked.

"Sure do," the boy said confidently. "I'll show all of you."

"Well, you show me and I'll believe," the driver replied.

He watched from the open window, as the children did. Chucky stood in his yard and whistled shrilly, with his fingers wedged between his teeth.

The deer raced from the barn and sped toward the boy. Moments later the animal was at his young master's side, nudging him playfully like a friendy billy goat.

"What's that thing hanging around his neck?" a boy on the bus called out loudly.

"It's his magic. His secret identity," Chucky said, fingering the clay-covered object.

His face reddened as the children laughed and jeered.

"I thought Clark Kent wore glasses!" The derisive laughter of the children rose. "Let's see you ride Superdeer like you said you could."

Chucky steadied the animal, praying that he wouldn't buck him off, as he had on other occasions. He stroked the pet's fur, swung a leg over his back, and climbed on, holding onto his neck. The deer remained motionless, as if awaiting a command.

"Now you'll see!" Chucky yelled triumphantly. "Let's go, Heart!"

The young buck bolted away with the boy on his back, leaving the children and driver with their mouths agape. In an instant he reached the front of the house and Chucky jumped down.

"Now you gotta believe me!" he yelled across the distance.

The driver tooted his horn in reply and the bus pulled away.

"I guess we showed them jerks, boy!" Chucky said, feeling the bony nubs rising out of the hart's head. In a short while he would have two sharp spikes.

Pearl opened the kitchen door and stepped out onto the porch with a disapproving look.

"Charles, you know what your father said about getting up on that deer's back! Why did you do it again?"

"I had to show 'em, Ma. They were teasing me, saying I was a liar, all the way home from school."

"Well, maybe if you weren't such a braggart you wouldn't get teased," Pearl admonished. "You'd have looked pretty silly if you'd have gotten bucked off just then."

"Heart wouldn't throw me. He loves me."

The sugary smell of boiling maple sap drifted from the kitchen. The deer sniffed at it greedily and wagged his white patch of a tail.

Pearl looked at the creature and grimaced. "I would, too," she said, "if you hand-fed me sugar and candy every day. It's a wonder his teeth haven't rotted out of his head. I don't want to see you up on him again, young man. He's a wild animal, after all."

"He is not wild! He's gentle."

"He won't be for long, according to what your father tells me. If you want to argue you can come in the house. I'm not going to stand out here on this porch listening to your sass and freezing to the bone."

They went inside and Pearl shut the door.

"Undo the clips!" Pearl scolded as Chucky stood in the kitchen, kicking the floor with his boots to loosen his feet from his shoes. "Winter's almost over, and I don't intend to buy you a new pair at this late date. You must think your father and I are made of money!"

"When are you gonna stop yellin' at me! That's all you do all the time!"

Pearl's stern look left as she saw his consternation.

"I guess I'm becoming an awful nag," she said, smiling at him. She bent down and helped him undo the boots. "You still love me?"

Chucky grinned sideways at her polite expectant look. "Yes, Ma'am," he replied. "Can I have some maple candy?"

"How's school going for you?" she asked, handing him a piece of the boiled-down sugar in the shape of a rooster.

Chucky crunched on the candy without answering.

"Honey, I asked you how you're doing in school?"

"Okay, I guess . . ."

"That's not what Nora tells me. I understand you flunked most of your January exams."

"Jeez, Ma! Are you going to start on me again?"

"I don't know what to do with you any more," the mother complained sadly.

She went back to stirring the sap in the large kettle with a wooden spoon. She would boil the sap until it became thick and gooey, then scoop it into animal- and flower-shaped molds to harden. The product brought in a good deal of money from the confectionery shops. And they needed it badly, now that Zeb had resumed drinking and was squandering a considerable amount on whiskey. He was enough of a heartache and worry, without Chucky adding to her misery.

"You're a bright boy, with a good mind if you'd just use it," Pearl continued. "It's your future you're throwing away. I'm not trying to scold you, honey."

Chucky took his coat down from the wall hook and fished around inside the torn lining for the large valentine Nora Cleary had given him. It was an expensive card with a young buck and doe on the front cover. The romantically drawn doe was saying "Won't you be my deer, Dear Valentine?" On the inside it displayed the two cartooned animals with hearts gathered around their heads like haloes.

Chucky erased the schoolteacher's penciled sentiments and addressed the card to his mother.

"Who's the pretty valentine for?" Pearl asked. "Are you sweet on some girl?"

"Heck, no!" Chucky said. "It's for you."

The mother accepted the card with a warm smile, her sad mood lifting as Chucky wished her a happy Valentine's Day and kissed her on the cheek. She discerned the erased pencilings, and that it represented the wrong gender, but she pretended not to notice.

"Thank you, sweetheart," she said, genuinely touched. "But I'm afraid I don't have one for you."

"That's okay, Ma. Can I have a piece of candy for Heart?"

Pearl laughed and shook her head. "You little charmer," she said, picking up two pieces from the table, "you're both going to lose your teeth before the sap stops running!"

Chucky cleaned out Angela's stall while he waited for the milking machine to finish with Margie. His father had been called out to salt the roads, so the entire chore had fallen upon the boy. Heart pestered after him as he laid fresh straw, nudging a bulging pocket.

"Charles!" Pearl stalked into the barn angrily. "You little snitch!" she fumed, as she saw the deer greedily crunching up a piece of candy and zeroing in again on the coat pocket. "Hand them over!"

The boy emptied a vast quantity of maple sugar into his mother's hands, with a sheepish look on his face.

"You thief," Pearl said, "I'll burn your sticky fingers off if I catch you snitching any more!"

The hart pranced around her and shook his fanny, begging to be rewarded with a treat as she walked from the barn. "No!" she said, "You get enough." At the door, away from Chucky's view, she pushed a candy into the deer's muzzle and smiled at him. "You're a little heathen, like your master," she whispered, "but I guess I love you, too."

The deer went back to Chucky as Pearl closed the door, preventing him from following her. He sniffed at the lad's empty coat pocket as his master disconnected the milking machine from Margie.

"Not there!" Chucky said, hiking up his coat. Both front pockets of his jeans bulged. "There!"

"It killed how many children?" Pete asked incredulously.

"Over two hundred," Nora repeated, rising up from his lap, where she had been reading, lying on the couch while he sat watching a boxing match on television.

"Let me see that." Pete took the book from her hand and skimmed through it, a frown growing on his face. "How do you know this is true?"

"Some museum in France has the entire story documented. It happened in a farming region called Le Gevaudin."

"I don't know why you bother to read this stuff," Pete said critically.

"I'm trying to understand about Mark and Tommy. Pete, we've got to stop ignoring Chucky's warnings. This Beast of Le Gevaudin is a precedent of what Chucky says about Shaman. Some sorcerer in that region from 1765 to 1767 either dressed up like a strange animal or *became* a strange animal, and attacked children. He killed over two hundred children. It's awful. My God, what would we ever do?"

"Nora, why do you torture yourself like this?" Pete shook his head. "The deer is dead. There's no doubt about that." He tapped the book cover. "Two hundred years is a long time to invent, exaggerate, or misconstrue facts, you know."

"It hasn't been exaggerated," Nora said stubbornly, taking the book from his hands and opening it up. She thumbed through the pages, finally finding what she wanted.

"Here, read this," she said.

Pete shrugged and took the book, reading:

Although believed to have been killed many times during the two years of his murderous reign, the monster did not die and successfully avoided hundreds of the King's dragoons scouring the fields and woods, whereas over a hundred wolves and wild dogs were destroyed, their population decimated. The Beast's cunning ways and long absences often led the villagers to falsely believe they were no longer in peril—

"And look at this." Nora pointed further on in the text.

In almost every instance the Beast tore out the hearts of its victims and drank their blood, leaving the bodies otherwise untouched. It walked on its hind legs like a bear, and peered through the windows of the homes its attacks had bereaved.

"Don't you see?" Nora said, "It wasn't afraid of going into the village. Just like Shaman wasn't afraid to go to your home. Peter, there is a definite similarity—so much that it makes me shudder."

Pete stared at her blankly for a moment and went back to reading:

A fourteen year-old boy, Jean Chateauneuf, was murdered on January 15, 1765. As the boy's father sat mourning his child in his darkened home on the following evening, the Beast placed its forepaws on the window sill and glared in at him with a demonic expression. The father shouted for help, but in the deepening winter dusk the creature easily made off, mocking with antic gestures its frightened and half-hearted pursuers.

Nora grabbed the book and flipped rapidly to the last page, seeing that she had Pete's attention. She pointed to the bottom paragraph and sat back watching him as he read:

The last-named possibility, however, seems most consistent with the known facts, particularly when it is remembered that the Auvergne area was noted during the Middle Ages for its sorcerers, some of whom allegedly turned themselves into wolves at will. The strange Beast may have been a last crazed inheritor of this tradition, slaking his sadistic bloodlust with the ripped-out hearts of hundreds of Gevaudanois children.

"You see?" Nora said as Pete closed the book. "Could

that creature possibly have been anything other than a—than a sorcerer? Peter, I'm worried about Chucky. I'm worried about all of you. If Malsum was a true sorcerer, as Joe Hawk believed—"

"Nora!" Pete raised his voice to stop her as she began to get excited. "You're not being rational about this," he said. "Look, even if this Beast in France was a sorcerer, it says nothing about possessed animals, and certainly nothing about a possessed deer!"

Nora arose from the sofa and went to a record cabinet alongside the television set. She slid open the cabinet door and displayed two large stacks of cloth-bound books.

A ring referee on the screen held up a fighter's arm and said into a microphone, "The winner-r-r, by a unanimous decision . . ."

"Which one would you like to read first?" she asked.

In December the bucks had shed their horns, leaving them docile and defenseless. For the remainder of the winter months, they had followed after old does who would lead them to food and water and guide them through times of danger.

Zeb watched the buck warily lagging behind the three does as they stepped out of the pines to cross the clearing. He was a big fellow, weighing maybe four hundred pounds or better, and it was easy to imagine him as Shaman.

He squeezed the trigger and the rifle recoiled hard into his shoulder. The high-velocity slug ripped through the deer's face, bursting his eyes from their sockets as he crumpled in his tracks, dead before he hit the ground. The does scattered and ran off in different directions. Zeb took aim on the largest female. She was an easy shot, but his finger froze on the trigger, and he let her go. He couldn't kill her. She was meat, and meat meant money, but Zeb barely had the heart to shoot a buck any more.

The buck's antlers were new, and covered with a grey velvety flesh permeated with blood vessels. If the timid bastard had relied on his own instincts instead of the does', Zeb reasoned, chances are he would never have gotten a shot at him. He grimaced and took a drink from a near-empty whiskey pint. That's what he got for trusting a female!

He sat down on the buck's carcass and stroked his warm fur, feeling sad and wishing he hadn't shot him.

"Hell, I guess you were too goddamn stupid to last much longer on your own anyways," he said, unsheathing his cutting knife.

He drank the remainder of his whiskey and threw the bottle away. Foggy from a full day of drinking, he stared at the stag's beautifully furred antlers, and a contrast suddenly occurred to him.

Why didn't his boy's deer have velvet on his antlers still, as the buck that he had just killed did?

Heart had only had two horny nubs on his head six weeks before, at the beginning of maple sugaring time. The velvet had dried and scraped off a few days ago. The little bastard was wearing out a post in the barn sharpening his spikes on it. For Christ's sake, they were ten inches long already! It wasn't normal for a deer to go into rut so early in the year. August, perhaps even as early as July—but April?

What the hell was going on? Some yearlings didn't even get spikes their first season out. Something had accelerated the fawn's rate of growth. Maple sugar candy? He sure as hell got enough of that.

Maybe the little bastard was magical, like Charlie claimed. If Joe Hawk was still alive that's probably what his explanation would be. Zeb had looked at the hunk of clay around the hart's neck a number of times, wondering what the boy had hidden beneath. He knew most of the Iroquois and Algonquin gods of war from a lifetime's association with the Indians. There were Menabozho, Goweh, Hinu. Tawiskaron and Tarachiawagon were the strongest. And he had intrigued his son to tell him the supposed source of his magic, but the boy couldn't be had, saying that he couldn't tell anyone until the deer was big enough to fight Shaman. And that was going to be damn hard to do, since Shaman was dead. There was no doubt about that—Joe Hawk had killed him. They had found the rotting carcass up there not more than fifty yards away from his body.

Still, in a way, Zeb was proud of his son for having enough strength to hold on to what he believed in. If he wanted to believe that Shaman was still alive, fine. What a man believed in wasn't as important as having something to believe in.

He had had something to believe in, once.

The buck was too heavy to hoist onto his shoulders after

he had gutted it, and he removed its head and legs to lessen the load. After that he managed, and started off for home.

As he reached the barbed-wire fence at the edge of the Seneca Woods with his venison, James Goodman suddenly stepped out from behind a tree.

A tight disapproving look appeared on the new Seneca chief's face.

Shit! Zeb thought disgustedly, as if he didn't have enough problems.

"Kinda looks like you caught me this time," he said. "But it took you eight goddamn years to do it! What's the fine gonna run?"

"I'm not going to fine you," James said. "Why should you think that? I was on my way to your house to speak with you when I"—the Seneca looked sadly at the half-drunken farmer—"heard your stomach growling. You drink too much, Zeb."

Zeb dropped the carcass to the ground. He stretched and rubbed the soreness out of his shoulders.

"Yeah, well, you know me," he said. "What's on your mind, James?"

The Indian's eyes gleamed like black agates, old and wise with deep crow's feet at the sides. "Shaman is not dead," he said.

"Bullshit!" Zeb exclaimed. "We found his bones up there."

"They weren't his. You and Pete were wrong. He is alive, and he is going to be coming back again soon," James said.

Zeb stared at him irritably. "How do you know that?" he finally asked.

"What is your opinion of our beliefs on the demon animal?" James countered.

"You mean do I believe he's possessed by Malsum?" Zeb thought for a moment. "Hell, I don't know. My boy says he is. I guess anything's possible. Why?"

"Because it's true," the college-educated Indian said. "Zeb, I want to tell you some things, but I don't think you're going to believe me."

"Well, why don't you just try me and we'll see," Zeb said.

James looked at him searchingly, almost as if he were in pain, and then he began.

"In the Bible," he said, "there is a story about angels who fought with each other. The scribe writes that the wicked ones were cast into hell after a battle. These angels became demons. Both our peoples believe that. I believe that. Malsum must have known how to call on those demons, and he enlisted their help when he died."

"That's very interesting, James," Zeb said, interrupting. "But that crap don't tell me how you know Shaman's alive and coming back here again."

James shrugged and nodded. "First I have to tell you some things that Joe wants you to know."

"Well, you've sure as hell waited long enough, now haven't you?" Zeb remarked. "He's been dead going on nine months."

"He didn't tell me nine months ago, Zeb, or I would have told you then."

Zeb wanted to pry at the riddle, but the confident gleam in the Seneca's eyes held him at bay. James' face seemed to glow with an inner radiance.

"Malsum has started another . . ."—James groped for the right wording—". . . another war between angels, let's call it. The demons are bolder now, because of him. And both sides are waiting to see what the final outcome will be. If Shaman wins, Malsum will become a prince of demons. . . . There are many other deer in these woods."

"Oh, shit," Zeb groaned. He looked at James and shook his head. The Seneca watched as he bent to hoist the deer carcass back onto his shoulders.

"You ought to be ashamed of yourself, James; a grown man with schooling, and you sound like my kid. Shit! You're ten times worse! Do me a favor—don't talk any of that garbage to Charlie. He's got enough problems."

"He's going to have more," the Seneca said solemnly as Zeb positioned the deer. "He's the one Shaman wants to kill most."

An intense anger came over Zeb. "You friggin' witchman," he said, starting to shake. "Don't involve my kid in this angel-demon shit if you know what's good for you!"

"Don't be an ass," James said. "I'm trying everything in my power to get him out of this, but there's nothing I can do. There's nothing any of us can do! Charles took it upon himself to challenge Malsum and—"

Zeb threw the carcass down and struck the Seneca hard in the face, knocking him to the ground. He pinned him with a knee on his chest and grabbed him by the throat roughly.

"I've got enough problems," he said between clenched teeth. "I want this crap to stop right now. You're making all of this up, and you can't tell me otherwise. Shaman's dead!"

"What I've told you is true," James said. "He's not dead."

"Fine! Then I'll track his ass down and kill him myself! Where is he? Who saw him?"

A rivulet of blood trickled down from the corner of the Indian's mouth. "I saw him," he said, "in a dream."

"You sick bastard," Zeb moaned. He released James and backed away, shaking from his jittery nerves, wishing he had a drink. "Those dreams don't mean anything."

James rose to his feet. His left cheek was skinned on the inside from Zeb's punch, and he spat blood. Deliberately, he removed his hat and waited for the rugged farmer to look his way.

Zeb's eyes opened wide as he saw the younger man's black hair interlaced with white streaks.

"Tell me, Zeb," James demanded, "does this happen overnight from a dream that doesn't mean anything?"

He turned and walked away.

Chapter XIII

A grey sky and a drizzling rain so light that it seemed more like dew confronted Pearl as she left the house and headed for the barn. A severe storm was on its way north from the south and was expected to arrive by late afternoon. The Weather Bureau had warned that there would be high winds and driving rain throughout the week.

The buckets in the maple grove needed emptying, as Pearl still had the trunks tapped, trying to squeeze every last drop of the precious sap from the trees. Other farmers had stopped harvesting a full week before, when the sap slowed to a trickle and watered down. But Pearl had kept on to earn the few extra dollars that could still be gleaned. So far her candies and syrups had brought a badly needed $400 into the house. Today, however, would definitely be the last harvest of the year, with the start of heavy rain, and she was relieved that it was finally over. The back-breaking work and sweet, sickening smell of sap thickening in kettles on the kitchen stove every day for seven weeks had left her exhausted and nauseated. If she never saw another piece of maple sugar again it would be fine with her.

Normally Pearl would have let the Seneca women tap the trees and do the work for a share of the profits, but the poor apple crop last fall, and Zeb's return to drinking, had left them shorter than ever. Zeb had gone back to poaching deer to bring in money, but he very rarely shot one and it was really just an excuse of his to go off on his own during the day where he could drink without being scolded. Pearl didn't know what to do about him. She

256

couldn't reach him. He seemed so terribly depressed but about what she had no idea. Hard work kept her out of arguments with him, but it did little to relieve her worry. Life had become a tedious struggle, and with Pete leaving the household in June to get married, Zeb seeking their fortune in the bottoms of brown bottles . . . ? But they would manage somehow; they would have to.

And there was another problem. A few days earlier, when Zeb had killed the big buck, he had come home nervous about something. He warned Pearl to stay out of the maple grove and when she pressed him for a reason he fairly shouted, "Just do what I tell you! And keep Charlie close to home!"

Pearl's first fear was that Zeb had found out that Shaman was still alive, as their son insisted. But Zeb denied that. And, when she continued to harass him for an explanation, he finally admitted that he had shot a rabid skunk (or what he thought was a rabid skunk) and he wanted them out of the woods until the matter was settled. Pete took the next two days off from work and went hunting with Zeb. It was all very strange. Early this morning Zeb had gone off again, this time by himself.

Pete had fallen far behind in his work at the bank and he couldn't afford to miss any more time. He had caught a cold, traipsing around in the woods for two days, and he had left for work this morning looking as though he would die by noon. It was his own fault for not taking care of himself, Pearl thought turbulently as she entered the barn. She had warned him the day before to see a doctor and get some prescription medicine, but he had ignored her. She had enough things troubling her, she thought, without the added burden of her brother-in-law's health. He was Nora Cleary's man, so by rights Nora should be the one to worry about him! Pearl wouldn't admit it to herself, but she was unhappy over their engagement.

The sight of the dead buck hanging upside down from a rafter, with his stomach gutted and his head missing, made the woman feel queasy as she went into the workshop for the wagon that she used to bring in the sap. Her period had begun and that, along with her nausea from the maple sugaring, had her insides in an upheaval of cramps. She had to divert her eyes and turn away from the gruesome corpse. God, it was such a terrible way to bring money into the house!

Chucky's hart pushed into the workshop from the inside door of the stables, where he lived with Angela and Margie. He was a welcome relief in the grim surroundings.

"Hello, honey," Pearl cooed, as the animal walked up to her, waggling his rump. She petted him, and he began sniffing around her coat pockets for a treat. There was none, but by this time the farm wife smelled like a walking maple sugar factory to the tyke.

"I don't have any candy," Pearl admonished. "You get enough from Chucky. It'll be a wonder if you're not loaded with pinworms!"

Heart's big brown eyes saddened as Pearl pushed him back inside the barn and closed the door on him, bolting it shut. He was so precious. A gentle animal, just as Chucky said he was, but he was becoming fierce-looking with his long horns, and getting jittery and temperamental around Zeb. Last night while she was helping Zeb do the milking, their conversation had turned to a discussion over Chucky's heathen beliefs, and Zeb had wonderingly taken hold of the charm around the deer's neck. The animal had pawed the ground, grumbling in his throat, and had broken Zeb's hold on the piece of clay and backed away, menacing Zeb with his horns.

"Sonuvabitch!" Zeb had sworn and slapped him hard on the nose with the back of his hand. Heart had then slunk away to a corner, lain down, and glowered at Zeb for as long as he remained in the barn. Zeb's presence always seemed to bring out the worst in the animal. It would break Chucky's heart, but any day now the deer would have to be led off into the woods and turned loose. It was a shame, but Heart was big enough now to pose a real danger, and it had to be done.

Pearl headed for the maple grove, pulling the wagon behind her. Zeb was in the woods somewhere, hunting deer, or trying to find rabid skunks, and if he caught her there would be trouble. But Pearl wasn't going to let the sap spoil in the buckets over fear of a rabies danger that was highly improbable. The coming storm could be upon them any hour, and heavy rain would dilute whatever sap there was in the buckets and render it worthless, if she didn't gather it beforehand.

Inside the barn, the hart suddenly pricked his ears and stood rigid. He went to the back wall of the structure and peered out through a crack at Pearl walking through the meadow. The wooden-sided wagon with the two upright milk cans in the box squeaked noisily. The deer pressed his eyes tighter to the crack. He became nervous and excited as he watched, snorting and pawing at the straw-covered cement floor.

Pearl turned around as she heard him butting and kicking at the wall, attempting to get out. Normally she let him go with her to romp through the woods. On the last trip, however, he had buried his muzzle in a bucket of sap and had made a pig of himself.

"Heart! You stop that, Heart!" Pearl scolded. She could see the deer's face through the space in the boards where he was looking at her impatiently. "You go lie down, you little stinker!"

The deer's face disappeared from view. Pearl waited for a moment; hearing nothing, she continued on.

The young hart raced back and forth through the barn, looking for a way out. Pearl had closed the outer doors, which were usually opened a crack, and boarded them to keep the animal confined. Running again to the rear of the structure, the yearling proceeded to prance about frantically.

"How mean!" Pearl said. "Oh, how mean!"

She stood at the front of the grove with dismay and looked at the havoc and cruel wreckage of three days' work. The buckets on every tree had been knocked off, their contents spilled and soaked into the ground, the buckets themselves dented and banged in. There was no telling how much money someone's spite had cost.

At first Pearl harbored suspicions that the Seneca had done it because she had not offered them the usual partnership arrangement. But the more she thought about that the more the idea shamed her. None of them would do this. The Seneca and the Simpsons had always been the best of friends, and they knew what a hard time she and Zeb were having trying to make ends meet. They had even offered the $2,000 bounty for Shaman to Zeb and Pete, for bringing Joe Hawk's remains home last summer, when the county accepted the hoofs as evidence and issued a check. It didn't make sense that any of them would do this over a loss of wages, when they had argued for days trying to make her husband accept the reward money. Then who did?

A rustling in some bushes at the far end of the grove caught Pearl's attention. The greyish tan of a deer's form momentarily flashed and then disappeared from sight.

"You come out of there, Heart!" she yelled. "You're the one that did this! You wait until . . ." It dawned on Pearl that she had locked the hart in the barn. She stared at the bushes, shaking from the hidden visitor. What if it wasn't Heart? Her fear began to rise.

Chucky insisted that Shaman was still alive, guided by Malsum and intent on killing all of them.

Zeb and Pete had hunted something for two days together, and not necessarily rabid skunks.

The woman's fright edged towards panic as a series of muffled groans and snorts issued from the brush. She imagined malevolent eyes studying her with a murderous hatred. Trembling, she pulled the wagon over and stepped into it, reaching up for a limb to pull herself into the safety of the branches above.

There came a loud noise, as if the deer had burst from the brush, the sound of hoofs beating across the ground.

The farmwife struggled desperately to gain the sanctuary of the limb, but the maple bark was wet from the fine drizzle and slippery. She lost her grip and fell backwards into the wagon, banging her head as the thing tipped with a clattering of empty milk cans.

She cried out as she saw the tan legs of a deer with black dewclaws standing over her.

Zeb was in the pines searching for any telltale sign of Shaman when he heard Pearl scream. His wife! Horrified, he pictured her beneath the antlers of the demonic stag. He ran for the maple grove, hurdling debris in his path, bursting through thorny thickets, taking the shortest route possible. The terrible fear in his mind drove him at reckless speed. His mouth twisted into an expression of horror as he remembered Joe Hawk the day Tommy—

"No!" he said aloud. "God, please no!"

Pearl looked at the hart nudging her coat pockets with a moist black nose.

"Damn you!" she wailed. "Damn you, anyway!"

She pushed the animal's muzzle away roughly and stood up, still trembling from the frightful experience. Her coat was caked with mud from the fall, and her knees were scratched. The back of her head throbbed.

"You did this," she cried, kicking a dented bucket. "I don't want you around me another minute! Get out of here!"

Heart bolted as she made to strike him with her hand. He eyed her nervously from a safe distance. Suddenly, he riveted his attention on the bushes where Pearl had seen him lurking moments before. He sniffed the air and snorted, pawing at the ground and lowering his spikes as if he were going to charge.

Pearl's anger subsided as she watched him, wondering what had changed his behavior so quickly.

"There's nothing in there," she said, and then wrinkled her brow as she thought she heard something sneaking away.

From the other end of the grove, Zeb came running toward her like a madman. When he saw her startled face looking at him, he stopped, his fright melting away, transformed into thankful relief. He leaned against a tree, holding his stomach and trying to catch his wind.

"You screamed," he gasped. "What the hell did you scream for?"

Pearl went to him and put her hand on his heaving chest.

"I'm sorry," she said, seeing his anguish. "Chucky's deer was poking around in the bushes, and he frightened me. Are you okay?"

"No, I'm not okay! Jesus Christ! You scared the living hell out of me!"

Pearl leaned against him, putting her arms around his back.

"I'm sorry," she repeated. "I know you didn't want me out here, but I had to come and get the sap before the storm moves in this afternoon."

Zeb's breathing began to settle. He looked at the strewn wreckage of buckets lying on the ground, and the pet deer, who was still busily peering off into the woods with his nose pointed into the wind.

"He do this?"

"I don't know. But I think he must have . . ."

"That settles his hash!" Zeb said with a tight glare. He took Pearl by the hand and led her through the maple grove and apple orchard to the pasture.

"What are you going to do?"

"Go on to the house." Zeb removed his belt and made it into a leash about the hart's neck.

"What are you going to do to him?"

"Make sure he doesn't bother us any more. Now go on home."

Pearl walked off apprehensively. "Please, honey . . . He's only a baby. Don't hurt him."

As Zeb saw his wife safely reach the house porch, he went back into the orchard with the deer.

Pearl watched until the white apple blossoms hid them from view.

She was in the kitchen coating her scratches with stinging iodine when she heard a rifle shot from afar. A moment later, as she stood on the porch watching anxiously, Zeb walked out onto the pasture. He was alone.

The Indian youth squinted at Chucky.

"My father says Joe Hawk gave you his gold medallion because he was drunk and out of his mind with grief. Any magic it had would be gone now. You're not a Seneca—you're not even an Iroquois."

"He wasn't drunk!" the youngest Simpson replied. "And Joe liked me a lot, so it is too magical. My ma keeps it in her jewelry box, but when I take it out at night and hold it, it gets as bright as the sun and gives off heat."

"You swear that on your honor?" the Indian asked.

"Well," Chucky frowned, suddenly lost for words. "Maybe it doesn't get bright—but it does give off heat when I hold it! It's loaded with powerful magic."

"Everything's magical to you, Simpson," an eighth grader remarked. "You ride that deer around your yard and say he's magical too, just because he lets you climb up on his back. You're a fool!"

Chucky tightened his jaw and turned away, staring out the bus window. He had dreamt about the gold medallion last night, and was overheard by the Mohawk boy during lunch hour when he told Donny O'Neil. The Indian had blabbed the news all over the cafeteria. Stupid Mohawk!

Mohawk meant 'man-eaters'. They had been ferocious cannibals once—probably still were!

In another minute or two the bus would stop at his home. He would be all right if he could only outlast the goading sarcasm of the eighth graders. The school principal had held him and Donny in detention for fighting, and they had been forced to ride on the junior high bus. Chucky had called the Mohawk troublemaker an obscene name. Luckily, Donny had pulled his fat from the fire when things got out of hand, and the two of them had given the older boy a good lesson in the art of rough-housing. Donny helped to stand off the bigger boys, but he had gotten off the bus at the last stop, and now Chucky was alone and exposed even more to their barbs. He wished he had gotten off with Donny and walked the last half mile up Genessee Road, but that would only have made him appear a coward and he didn't want any eighth graders thinking that!

The driver suddenly stopped the bus and walked back to where the eighth graders were teasing Chucky. "That's enough!" he said hotly. "You shut your mealy-mouthed traps, or you can get off and walk! Simpson, you come up front with me before they get you so mad you have to kick the tar out of them," he urged.

"Oh sure!" the Mohawk youth said. "I'd like to see him try it alone!"

"If he can't, I've got a boy in high school who would be more than happy to do it for him," the driver added.

"I'm not afraid of these creeps," Chucky said, "and I don't need anyone to fight my battles for me."

The driver nodded and smiled at his tight pout, remembering the Corps, when he had served under his father, Zeb Simpson. "Suit yourself, son," he said with a chuckle, and went back to his seat. Real moxie, he thought, just like the old man.

As they drove on, the older boys continued to harass Chucky, but he ignored them.

"See you tomorrow, Charlie Hawk!" one of the boys yelled as Chucky stepped off the bus in front of his home. They all laughed.

Thunder rumbled in the sky far to the south and west as the lad clambered up the steep bank to the yard. The wind was cold on his face. Miss Cleary had warned that they were going to be in for a really bad storm. It had already caused floods and taken a heavy toll of lives and property in the southern states. Nora had asked the children to stay indoors when they arrived home.

Topping the embankment, Chucky whistled for Heart, expecting the deer to race from the barn and greet him as he did every day. The barn doors were ajar, but the pet did not appear. A worried feeling came over the boy. He had had a dream the night before, but he couldn't remember what it was about. Why could he never remember the ones that seemed so important? He walked off toward the barn.

Pearl opened the kitchen door and looked sadly at her son as he whistled again.

"It's liable to start raining hard any minute, honey," she said. "Come on inside and have a piece of chocolate cake. I made it just for you."

The boy sensed that something was wrong, and suddenly he remembered a part of his dream. Heart had died in that dream—his father had killed him!

He set his school books down on the edge of the porch and ran past her without a word.

It was dark inside the barn as he entered. The intruding wind stirred up the pungent smells of straw and cow manure. He walked to the rear, where Angela and Margie were lying in their stalls chewing their cuds, patiently awaiting the evening milking. Margie mooed a greeting to him, and he petted her bony forehead absentmindedly as he searched the shadows for his deer.

On the back wall of the barn the boards had been busted away and then patched over with plywood and tar paper. Something had happened—but what? Heart wasn't in the barn.

Zeb peered up from his butchering, his hands drenched in blood, as his son stepped into the workshop through the inside door. The man was sad-eyed and seemed worried.

"Hello, Charlie," Zeb said, "How was your day?"

"Okay, Pa . . . Where's my deer?"

The boy watched with mounting fear as his father expertly sliced a hindquarter of venison into pot roasts.

Zeb said quietly, after a difficult pause, "I had to run him off today, son. He's too big and horny now for you

264

to keep. He frightened your Ma pretty bad and busted outta the barn. He spilled the sugar buckets over in the grove and kicked them all to hell."

"Heart wouldn't do those things!" Chucky cried. "He loves Ma! He's always loved Ma!"

"Not today, he didn't. The little bastard tried to gore me in the apple orchard. Charged right for me!"

"Is that when you run him off?" The boy had to blink to hold back his tears.

"Yeah, that's when I run him off."

Chucky turned to hurry away.

"Where you going?" Zeb asked.

"I've got to find him! There's a storm coming, with lightning and thunder. He'll be cold and afraid, out in the woods all alone."

Zeb took the boy's arm in a tight grip. "You go in the house and never mind that animal," he said. "You're not running off into any woods!"

"He won't be far away, Pa. It won't take me long."

"I said no, Charlie. That deer's gone, and he's going to stay gone. You won't find him around here."

Chucky looked at his father with accusing eyes. The boy sensed a lie on his father's face.

"You killed him, Pa," he said suddenly, tears streaming down his cheeks. "You killed my deer!"

"I didn't, son. I just run him off. Try to understand. I had to."

"You're a liar!" the boy screamed, looking at the red butchered venison, dripping with blood, on the butcher's block. "Heart wouldn't run off, no matter what! You killed him! You killed him, and you're cutting him up now!"

"I'm not. That isn't him up there. I shot this deer last week."

The eleven-year-old pulled away from his father's grasp and began crying.

"I hate you, Pa," he sobbed. "You killed my deer on me! You're mean and wicked!"

Zeb's eyes filled with misery as he took hold of the withdrawing boy again. "Charlie, stop crying. You won't find him around here because I grazed his fanny with a rifle slug to make him scared and keep running."

"You're a liar! I hate your guts—you stinking drunk!"

Zeb backhanded him across the face in a flash of anger, before he could stop himself. "Don't you talk to me like . . ."

Chucky spun around and struck out at him with madly flailing fists. His nose spurted blood over his mouth and chin as he struggled.

"Let me go!" he screamed. "I hate you! I hate you!"

A wave of shame washed through Zeb. He hugged the boy to him with a taut trembling. He had never hit his son like that before. He winced, dreading that he had broken the boy's nose.

"I'm sorry, Charlie," he said hoarsely. "Goddamn, I'm sorry."

The boy pushed away from the embrace and clawed at his father's cheeks, pinching the flesh until the man released him. He backed away, and, with a burst of speed, ran crying from the workshop.

Pearl was at the kitchen door as her son squeezed past her, his blood-smeared nose cupped in his hands.

"Oh, my God!" the mother said. She attempted to take hold of the boy, but he ran off for his bedroom, locking the door behind him.

"Chucky, let me in!" the distraught mother pleaded, pounding on the door. "Dear God, what's happened?"

"Go away!" Chucky cried. "I hate you, too!"

Zeb appeared in the hallway, his cheeks scratched and beaded with blood. Pearl stared speechlessly at her husband's gouged face.

The jamb splintered and the bolt broke away as Zeb put his shoulder to the door. He winced with pain as he saw his son sitting on the bed, sopping away the blood from his profusely bleeding nose with a corner of the white chenille bedspread beneath him.

"I hit him pretty hard," the grieving father said. "You'd better take a look at his nose. I think I broke it."

Pearl saw his scratched face, but there was no time for questions now. She hurried to her injured son and tried to calm him. Zeb walked out of the room and left them alone.

"He'll hurt some for a while," Pearl said as she found Zeb in the kitchen drinking whiskey from a full fifth bottle. "But I don't think his nose is broken." She lowered her eyes from her husband, remembering the shot she had heard. "I tried to tell him that you wouldn't kill his deer, but he wouldn't believe me . . ." She herself didn't know what to believe.

"What did he say to make you strike him?"

Zeb bit into his lip and wiped his eyes with his shirt sleeve.

"It don't matter none," he said. "I shouldn't have lost my temper like that . . . I've tried to make the boy love me, or at least understand me. Tell him I'm sorry if he ever has a mind to listen."

Pearl followed him into the living room as he took his rifle down from the wall pegs and put on his coat.

"Honey, where are you going?" she asked. "It's going to be dark in another hour. There's a storm brewing outside."

"I need to get away and think."

"Why are you so upset? You haven't hurt him that bad. He only has a bloody nose."

"Never try to reason with a drunk," Zeb said. "Charlie's had my number all along. I knew he didn't like me . . . but I didn't think he hated me."

"Is that what he said to you?" Pearl's eyes widened. "I don't care how he feels about that deer! I'm glad you hit him. He's a little pisspot! I've watched him snub your friendship from the moment your brother entered this home. I've let Pete spoil him with presents and playing until he pushed you right out of the picture—but not any more!"

"It's not Pete's fault that the boy loves him and not me." Zeb said, ". . . I don't blame you either for . . ." He grimaced and fell silent.

A startled look tinged with guilt appeared on the pretty farmwife's face. "You don't blame me for *what?*"

A lightning flash lit the darkened sky as Zeb opened the door and walked from the house. Thunder pealed loud and ominous, and the first few drops of rain fell. Pearl hurried after him.

"Honey, it's you we love," she said. "You're the one we love!"

The rain came fast and furious suddenly as they stood in the yard facing each other. Neither seemed to mind, how-

267

ever, oblivious to all except for the terrible moment of truth that was upon them.

"I don't blame you for anything, Red," Zeb said. "Pete's a good man. I guess something was bound to happen sooner or later . . ."

"I don't know what you're talking about!" Pearl's eyes filled with tears. "I swear I love you. I haven't done anything . . ." She choked.

"Forget it," Zeb said. "You and the boy would both be better off without me." He left her in the yard, standing in the rain, and walked out onto the meadow.

Helplessly, Pearl watched him go.

Pete sat at his desk, sniffling, with a runny nose, and suffering from a headache. He didn't know how he had gotten through the day.

Chasing after ghosts for two days in the woods, he thought. He and Zeb both needed to have their heads examined!

It was going to feel good to get home and into bed. Nora wouldn't appreciate his not coming over, but he was in no mood to lie around her apartment and let her mother him. She would just have to understand that when a man was sick the best medicine for the ailment was home, especially in lousy weather like this.

The telephone rang as he walked through the empty bank. He was the last one to leave, having stayed overtime to catch up on his work.

He noticed his extension button lit up on his secretary's phone, and he picked up the receiver, thinking that it might be Nora.

"I was just leaving to come home, Pearl," he said, as he recognized his sister-in-law's voice.

"Good," Pearl replied, her voice strained but under control. "You can come home and collect your belongings."

The words stunned the man, and he sat down in the nearest chair.

"Goddamn you!" Pearl suddenly sobbed. "What did you say to my husband about me?"

Immediately Pete had the meaning of her accusation. "I didn't say anything," he answered. "I swear I didn't."

"He knows about that night," Pearl said. "I don't believe

you! I want you out of our home forever!" She slammed the phone in his ear.

The rain and wind weren't so severe beneath the tall pines as Zeb walked into the Seneca Woods. In another few minutes it would be nighttime, and he would have the sanctuary he sought. These woods were a good place for him. They held memories, precious memories, memories of hunting with his father, memories of Joe Hawk teaching him and his son Tom how to track, memories of another day and time when he was young like Charlie, and eager for life, enriched with the thrill of it all, and looking forward to every experience. So long ago—it was all so terribly long ago . . . men raised their families, fought wars, ran here and there, lived their lives, and died, but the goddamned pines just stood still in one spot and seemed to live forever!

He looked at the half-empty bottle of whiskey in his hand. If he drank it fast, he thought, it might finally burst his aching liver and put an end to his miserable existence. Then again, it might not, and he would find himself alone and without consolation. He nursed the remainder of the whiskey, drinking it slowly until darkness settled around him.

He was drenched to the skin, and the rain was cold, but the liquor kept him warm inside. As long as he didn't move around too much, his stomach wouldn't spoil the pleasure of the drink.

It was wrong of him to let Pearl know that he had found out about her and his brother, and he regretted it now. But he couldn't help himself at the time. Charlie had made him hurt too bad.

"I hate your guts—you stinking drunk!"

The boy had his mother's smarts; he was correct on both counts: a man couldn't be drunk without stinking.

He thought of his wife. She was a good woman. She was probably sitting at home, worried about him, right now. It gave him comfort of a sort. At least she would pity him, even if she had stopped loving him. She had loved him, once. That was one thing that was decent and good about his life. No man had ever known the love of a finer woman than Pearl.

From high above came a cracking noise as the wind tore a large branch away from the trunk of the pine under

269

which Zeb stood. It crashed to the ground and leaned against the tree, making a sheltered wigwam of sorts.

Zeb crawled beneath it and sat down, grinning drunkenly over the windfall. The rain no longer bothered him. All over the tall Seneca Woods, tree limbs were splintering, reverberating like rifle shots, and falling to the ground with loud crashes. He liked it, revelling in nature's fury.

The elements—thunder, lightning, falling branches—it was the Judgment Day, Armageddon, the end of the world! Old Jenny Ma had taught him the Bible well when he was a boy. He could spout verse with the best of them.

"For as the lightning cometh out of the east, and shineth even unto the west; so shall also the coming of the Son of Man be."

Great! Just so he didn't come before the whiskey ran out!

A tree not too far away creaked loudly and splintered at the top. The tall section fell to the ground with a painful crash.

Storm, hell! This was a hurricane! Another goddamn Indian god! Hura'kane making his big scene.

It suddenly dawned on the drunken man that the wind might be wreaking havoc at home. He would never forgive himself if Pearl or the boy needed him and he wasn't around. He decided to sneak back in the darkness and lay up in the barn. That way he could keep an eye on things without having to display his stinking drunkenness.

"I hate your guts—you stinking drunk!"

"Oh, my God! What are we doing?"

Only what horny people have been doing ever since Adam and Eve—that's what you're doing, Pearl Ann.

The man's emotions surfaced as he drank, and he wept with despair. He imagined his wife, fevered and thrusting beneath his brother as Nora Cleary had thrust beneath him. The old shrapnel wound in his groin ached sympathetically. He had come home from the war half a man. Unable to father more children, he had been impotent for almost a year, until Pearl's beautiful body and tender lovemaking had cured him. She could never cure him now—nothing could. Even his son's love was lost to him.

The wind was hard to walk in, coming out of the south at Zeb's back the way it did. It pushed him into trees and whipped small branches and debris at him. Eventually his

270

whiskey ran out, and he was alone with his despair. He smashed the worthless bottle against a rock, the wind so loud in his ears that he didn't even hear it shatter. In another instant he tripped and fell, rising to his feet slowly, like a drunkard trying to gain his balance on a merry-go-round.

Lightning flashed, white hot and blue in front of him. Deafening thunder came simultaneously. He laughed and sat down. The Iroquois gods were angry. They were trying to give him a heart attack! A pine tree burst into flames at the top, as if it had been struck by an exploding meteor.

Sam Parker had once seen a meteor fall to the ground right in front of him. He said it had looked like the moon falling but was no bigger than a walnut when he dug it out. Good old Sam! He was another stinking drunk!

Zeb watched the rain pelt out the lightning fire in the treetop in a matter of seconds. He looked at the rifle in his hands. It was dangerous to hold metal during a thunderstorm.

Zeb held the rifle up high, grasping it by the butt and wobbling drunkenly as visions of shy Gary Cooper portraying Sergeant York, and his rifle being struck by lightning, crept into his mind. This caused him to laugh hilariously.

"Hey, Lord," he yelled. "You wanta give me religion? I'm a war hero too, you know! Got medals and a battlefield commission to prove it! I wouldn't shit you, now!" he taunted.

When the next blinding flash of lightning came, however, it didn't strike Zeb's rifle. But it may just as well have, for the jolt it gave him.

Malsum! There in the woods, not twenty feet in front of him, stood the old white-haired Delaware Zeb had accidentally killed.

The flash ended. The thunder died. The forest darkened. Zeb stood and pressed against the bole of the pine at his back, struggling to clear his inebriated mind.

"Malsum . . ." he said aloud.

Could he rely on what he had just seen? He thought perhaps he was having the d.t.'s, finally, after his long career of drinking. During the war, he and many others had seen strange things at night that didn't make sense; robed figures standing in front of them like specters, bearded men, harbingers of death, usually before a big battle where a great many men would die.

The next flash of lightning came and Zeb stepped out from the tree with his rifle pointed, expecting to find Malsum standing there.

Shaman!

The stag charged him with a loud, shuddering, banshee-like howl that forced the wind to dwindle in its wake.

Zeb had time for one shot before the beast was upon him, tearing into his legs and stomach with sharp-tined antlers, slamming him back to the ground. The man tried to push the demon away in the darkness as it slashed at his belly, trying to rip through the wet heavy fabric of his coat. He could feel the monster's hot breath.

Jesus, the stag was going to kill him! Zeb cried out as he felt the antlers dig into his stomach, tearing him to ribbons. He tried to roll away, but the powerful bastard held him too tightly, rooting after him like a boar, with pig-like grunting.

The antlers pierced deep. Zeb felt his insides ready to tear loose. For a moment he controlled his panic and placed his thumbs on the demon's eyes. He felt the softness of a bulbous orb beneath his right thumb and pushed in hard. The eyeball gave way and popped from the socket, bursting apart and covering Zeb's hand with a pulpy wetness. Shaman shrieked hideously and backed away before Zeb could claim the other organ.

As quickly as the witch-deer had come, he was gone. The wind and rain and darkness swallowed him.

Zeb tried to stand, but the pain in his stomach seared him with hot flames. He reached down to touch himself with shaking hands, afraid at what he knew he was going to find.

"Oh, God," he cried. His stomach was nothing but a gaping hole.

He pushed himself along the wet ground with his heels until the top of his head struck the bole of a nearby pine. Withstanding the pain, he forced himself into a sitting position.

The next lightning flash showed him his stomach in all its horror. He leaned back and began to sob, waiting for the death that he knew would claim him. He remembered the Delaware cackling with laughter and spitting in his face moments before he had died. Malsum had sent the wizard stag, and now Zeb himself would die. His mind flashed to the recent meeting in the woods with James Goodman.

"He will have to face Shaman when he comes for him."

A greater terror filled the man, and he cried out with anguish.

"No!" he screamed.

He spied his rifle on the ground and crawled over to it, using it as a crutch to pull himself up.

"I'll get him for you, Charlie," he sobbed. "Don't you worry, son, I won't let that frigger get you!"

And then he fell over with a muffled groan, and lost consciousness.

Pete shone the hand light on his brother, cringing at what he saw.

"Who's there?" Zeb murmured, blinking his eyes.

"It's me, Zeb . . ."

Pete bent and cradled the man in his arms.

"Watch out for him," Zeb cried out fearfully. "He's out there! He wants to kill us! Malsum's inside of him, like Joe said!"

"Take it easy," Pete said.

He scanned the forest, sweeping the trees with his light. The dark woods confronted him with a thousand hiding places, but the stag did not appear. He held his rifle at ready.

"He's gone now," he said, unbuttoning his coat and removing his shirt.

"Take me home, Pete," Zeb pleaded. "I don't want to die out here!"

"You hold on," the younger brother said, "I'll get you home. You're not going to die, Zeb. Lie still and let me bind you."

He tore his shirt into strips and wrapped bandages around Zeb's stomach and back, tying the ends tightly. Zeb lost consciousness during the ordeal, but his pulse and heartbeat remained strong. Pete shivered with the cold rain and wind on his bare skin, as he dressed Zeb in his warm, fur-lined raincoat and hoisted the man to his shoulders, fireman style.

Zeb cried out loudly with pain from the sudden shift of weight, but Pete steeled through, knowing it was the only way. Zeb might bleed to death if he left him to go for help. Or the damned deer might come back to finish murdering him. He slung his rifle over his left shoulder, unable to abandon it for fear of Shaman. The guiding flashlight in his hand kept him from tripping in the lightning-interrupted darkness.

Zeb slipped in and out of consciousness while Pete made the two-mile journey. At one point the man cried out his wife's name, and Pete said quietly, "Zeb, I've got to . . . I've got to talk to you about something."

Pearl came out onto the porch as Pete staggered into the yard, hunched over double from Zeb's weight on his shoulders, barely able to take another step. A lightning flash revealed Pete's bare chest smeared with watery blood.

"Call an ambulance," he gasped, as he maneuvered up the porch steps.

Zeb was unconscious as Pete carried him through the living room to the downstairs bedroom. He could hear Pearl in the kitchen shouting into a dead telephone for the operator. Chucky was nowhere to be seen, evidently still in his room.

Pete struggled into his bedroom. Pearl had packed his clothes and had his suit coats laid out on the bed. He clawed them off onto the floor and lowered his brother to the bed as gently as he could manage. He wanted to collapse but only allowed himself a brief straightening to ease his cramped back muscles. A violent cough racked his frozen lungs as he labored over Zeb. His nose was a mass of running mucus, and chills raced through his body.

Pearl cringed in the doorway, frightened out of her wits.

"The telephone's dead," she said. "What are we going to do?"

The lines always went out during a storm with high winds.

"Get me some clean towels," Pete ordered, stripping Zeb out of his raincoat. The smooth fabric was smeared with blood.

Zeb stirred a little, grimacing in pain. Pearl remained motionless, staring at her husband.

"Get me the towels!" Pete snapped. "We've got to stop this bleeding and get him to the hospital."

Pearl ran from the room then, reappearing an instant

later with an armful of towels and linens. She dropped them onto the bed, now entirely in control of herself.

"Let me do that," she said, deftly untying the knots in the blood-drenched bandages.

Pete unlaced Zeb's boots and pulled them free. His jeans were soaked and more difficult to remove.

"Don't try to unwind any bandages that are stuck to him," Pete instructed. "Get a pair of scissors and cut them off."

Again Pearl raced from the room and was back in a moment. Her hand went to her mouth as Pete ripped Zeb's shorts apart at the seams, revealing dark punctures on his thighs and lower abdomen.

"Sweet Jesus," she whispered.

"Cut the bandages," Pete said calmly.

The woman trembled as she exposed the horrible wound, but she found the strength to help Pete bind her husband.

Zeb slept as they wrapped him in warm blankets, infant style, until he looked like an Egyptian mummy.

Pete slipped hurriedly into an overcoat lying on the floor.

"I'll pull the car up close to the porch and come back for him," he said. He left the house at a run.

Zeb opened his eyes as Pearl hovered over him, drying his wet hair gently with a towel. He pulled his arms out from under the blankets and reached up for her. She pressed her face to his cheek and embraced him.

"I love you, honey," she said. "I love only you."

"I love you," Zeb whispered. He smiled at her and touched her lips.

Pearl held him tightly as he began to convulse.

"Don't die," she choked. "Please Zeb—please don't die!"

Chucky woke in the darkness. He listened to the rumble of thunder off in the distance. The lightning was now further away, and not nearly as bright through the back window as when he had fallen asleep. As he lay in his bed the sound of his mother's crying reached his ears. She had been crying earlier over something, and the thought of her still crying after all this time saddened the boy. Undoubtedly, his Pa was off somewhere getting drunk and his Ma was worried for him.

His teeth clenched as he thought of his father killing

Heart and making his mother so unhappy. His Pa was no good, and he hoped that someday . . .

The door suddenly opened and the dark shadows dispersed, a subdued light entering the room. His Uncle Pete stepped in and sat down on the bed. Chucky could hear his mother more plainly now as she wept heartbrokenly.

"Are you awake, son?" the uncle asked.

"Yes, sir," the boy replied. "Is my Ma going to be okay?"

"She needs you, Chucky," the man said with a cracked voice. "Your Pa . . . Your Pa . . ." and then the boy understood as his uncle nudged him from the warm bed and walked him out to his mother's arms.

Chapter XIV

James Goodman called out to the party of Seneca men as they walked through the rain with shotguns and rifles, heading into the pine forest. They paused and waited for him as he left his home and joined them.

"We will not find him. I must tell you that again," the young chieftain said.

"Still, we must try," a Seneca man replied solemnly. "When the storm ends, the white city hunters will fill our woods and chase the stag back into the mountains. You say the deer lusts for the blood of Zebediah's family. Let him lust for our blood also, then, for we considered the man a brother."

James Goodman merely nodded and led them off into the Seneca Woods as they all echoed their spokesman's sentiments.

If only they could kill Shaman—but James knew they could not. The stag could only be destroyed by one of those chosen for revenge by the sorcerer.

Somehow, however, they must triumph. The good and faithful could not go on living forever in a world beseiged by evil and death.

The casket was made of mahogany, with brass hand-rails, and surrounded with many bouquets of flowers.

Zeb looked especially handsome, and had a peaceful smile on his lips. Pearl had instructed the mortician to lay him out in his Marine Corps dress uniform, and the undertaker had gone to great lengths perfecting a hard spit-shine on the shoes and the bill of the cap until they shone, mirror-like. The hat rested on the white satin lining of the open casket, beneath Zeb's arm, as he would have carried it in life. It was even whiter than the satin lining, a tribute to his meritorious conduct in service to his country.

His medals were displayed in a glass box on a pedestal at the head of the coffin. Master sergeant's chevrons had been stripped from the old uniform, and gold lieutenant's bars and a chestful of ribbons pinned on.

A letter of gratitude and commendation from President Franklin D. Roosevelt was framed and displayed on the casket lid. Just below, an award that had been presented only 431 times during World War II—the Medal of Honor.

Pearl had wanted it this way. Zeb would have objected. He had never discussed the war years in any detail with her and had always ignored the medals and shrugged off the valor that had won them, but Pearl wanted their son to know, and to be proud of him. She wanted him to know what a wonderful man his father had been. She wanted everyone in the overcrowded home to know what a wonderful man her husband had been.

The wake was not held in a funeral parlor, but at the Simpson home. Donna Keever and Nora Cleary helped Pearl reopen the formal front parlor off the kitchen that had been closed since Jenny's funeral there.

By the time the mortuary brought Zeb home, the room had been prepared and filled with flowers. Jenny's over-stuffed mohair furniture, maroon and blue, was freshly vacuumed and had white lace doilies pinned to the arms. Folding chairs, loaned by the mortuary, were spaced about. A prayer chapel was placed in a corner of the room, with a stand of commemorative candles blessed by Father Ryan from the nearby parish.

Zeb's friends spared no expense, sending floral arrangements and gifts of money to help Pearl meet the expense of burial. Many even offered to cover the costs for a funeral to be held in town, but Pearl explained that Zeb was at home because he would have wanted to be. His parents and grandparents had all received their final rites in this home. Also, an all night vigil could be maintained, where it would be much more difficult and trying for Pearl to do so in a mortuary.

The wake was only for one night, as a day had been lost

with the undertakers. In the morning, Zeb would be conducted to the Brant parish for a Requiem Mass, then brought home once more to be laid to rest in the Simpson cemetery, next to his mother.

The neighbor women sat in the parlor all day with Pearl, comforting her as best they could and praying with her at the chapel. They complimented Zeb's manhood, his military distinction, his kindheartedness. They touched Pearl deeply at times with their warm stories of how Zeb had helped them, loaned or given them money, as Donna Keever recounted in a burst of emotion. They all admitted that a heart of gold had beat beneath Zeb Simpson's gruff exterior. Zeb had probably made love to over half of them before their married lives began, but the thought didn't trouble Pearl. She knew Zeb had been a rogue when she married him. He had always been a faithful husband to her, though, and that was the only thing that truly mattered.

She had always been a faithful wife, she told herself over and over. Pete had assured her that while bringing Zeb home, he had told him all there was to tell about their brief moment of passion. Her husband had understood.

Once Pete revealed that he had explained to Zeb, and Pearl learned that she herself had exposed the guiltily kept secret in her sleep, she apologized to Pete and tearfully agreed to his suggestion that they now forget the matter.

In a few months Pete would marry Nora Cleary and be gone from the Simpson household, but they would never stray far—he and Nora had promised.

Nora fretted constantly over the deer but was careful not to speak of the animal to Pearl. She knew the creature was out there in the stormy woods, waiting to murder again—but then, so did Pearl, and Pete, and all those present.

Every man at the wake gathered at the kitchen table, gulping down hot coffee laced with strong drink and offering their services in finding and killing Shaman.

Sam Parker felt deep remorse and suffered from flashes of anger as often as the monster was discussed. From time to time he would get up silently during a conversation and walk into the parlor to stand before Zeb's corpse. He would stand red-eyed for long minutes, touching Zeb's face, patting his bloodless hands. As soon as the funeral ended, Sam had stated, he was going into the woods to find the deer and kill it, or die in the attempt.

The radio and television stations informed the community that militia and trained, professional hunters were waiting for a break in the weather to hunt down the killer and destroy him. The newspapers played up and recapped the occult angle, until they caused a pandemonium of superstition that had even the most conservative tongues wagging with excitement over the possibility of dead Indians, wronged by whites, returning as killer deer.

The telephone, when functioning amid the storms, would ring incessantly with reporters and curiosity-seekers wanting to know about Malsum and his infamous curse. Sam Parker wrathfully handled any who attempted to disturb the privacy of the Simpson home in person. And there were many, especially reporters from the cheap sensational tabloids, who were always looking for gory or gruesome murder cases to exploit. They hovered like vultures. "Thank you for seeing me, Mrs. Simpson. I'm authorized to offer you $200.00 for exclusive photographs of your husband's wounds."

Finally, after a busy day and evening of crowded activity, the well-meaning mourners left the Simpsons in peace and quiet, to face alone their grief. The prayers and tears of friends had kept them occupied, but now they were left alone with the desolate realization that Zeb was gone—completely, utterly gone. They were never going to see him again in this life. The only one who didn't seem to have a hard time staying dry eyed was Chucky.

Pearl made her bed on Jenny's sofa in the parlor where she could spend the night close to her husband. Nora Cleary came into the room with coffee and a piece of apple strudel. She was dressed warmly in pajamas and a robe, as Pearl was, having been invited to spend the night with the family.

"I made a fresh pot of coffee," Nora said. She nodded at the plate of pastry in her hand with a hopeful smile. "These are delicious. Please, you must eat something, Pearl," she urged.

"I'm sorry, honey," the wife replied, "but I'm really not hungry."

There was only a year's difference in their ages, but Pearl felt much older than the pretty schoolteacher. Nora seemed like a young girl, a little sister. She was vibrant, full of life. Pete was lucky to have her—they were both lucky.

Pearl's heart sank as she secretly admired Nora. She felt so alone, so completely abandoned. For the first time since Zeb's death she thought about herself and her future, and with a gnawing, aching emptiness she despairingly gave the feeling a name . . . widow.

"Your coffee is wonderful," Pearl said, sipping at the brew.

Nora sat down in a chair and smiled at her warmly.

"Thank you. Pete told me how you like it." She cast a furtive glance toward Zeb in his opened casket. "Are you going to be able to sleep tonight?"

"I think so, honey," Pearl answered. She had hardly slept for two days. Her forehead floated with a fuzzy sensation from exhaustion.

Pete and Chucky came into the parlor, both dressed for bed. They wore the bathrobes Pearl had bought them for Christmas. Her son's was red and white checked cotton, like the one she had selected for Zeb. A sort of father-son arrangement.

Pete's was blue and white checked cotton; an uncle arrangement.

The colors had been selected to convey a certain message to Pete, and, it was hoped, to Chucky.

Pearl stood up with alarm at the sight of her brother-in-law. His cheeks were scarlet, as if sunburned. That he was suffering with a high fever was obvious.

"My God, look at you!" Pearl said.

"I'm okay, Sis." Pete felt her cool hands on his face. They were gentle. "Nora gave me some aspirin," he said.

"He's awfully sick," Nora said worriedly. "I don't know what else to do for him."

"I'll go make some honey and lemon mixed with cloves and whiskey," Pearl said, leaving the room. "It should sweat the fever out."

"I can do that," Nora said with concern, following her. "You should stay off your feet and try to rest."

"I'm fine," Pearl insisted. "Let me do it. I have a special recipe."

Nora agreed and let the woman go about her business.

She colored a little, feeling the part of a stranger, an intruder on a closely-knit family. For years Pearl had taken care of her husband's brother. Apparently she was still quite capable of doing so.

"Why don't you go to bed, dear?" Nora said, as she saw Pete standing by the casket, looking solemnly at Zeb. Chucky stood in front of him, staring at the medals, as he had been doing all day.

Pete didn't seem to hear her. She watched him as he closed his eyes and gripped his brother's fingers. She wanted to comfort him, but she felt so strangely out of place.

Chucky stood by rigidly, his eyes staring and blinking.

Pete bent over and kissed his brother's forehead.

"Say goodnight to your father," he said to the boy.

"Good night, Pa," Chucky said morosely.

Pearl returned, explaining that the honey was cooking on the stove. Her words died on her lips as she saw her son turning away from his father with a tight frown.

"It's past your staying-up time, Charles," she said sternly.

"Can I sleep here with you, Ma?"

"No," Pearl replied. "Your father doesn't like you crawling into bed with me. He says it will make a . . ." A pained expression came on the woman's face. "He *said* it will make a sissy out of you. Your uncle will be getting married and moving out soon—" A furtive look toward Pete betrayed the sadness in Pearl's eyes, a resigned austerity. It was barely noticeable, but Nora saw the sister-in-law's dismay.

"You're the man of the house now," she instructed. "So you might just as well get used to not hanging onto my apron strings."

"Yes, Ma'am," Chucky said.

Nora's heart went out to the boy. She wanted to hold him in her arms, to tell Pearl how cruel she was being. He was only a little boy! But common sense prevented Nora from speaking up. Again she felt alienated from the family.

"Give your Ma a goodnight kiss and go to bed," Pete said.

His voice seemed heartlessly severe. Nora couldn't believe his callousness. She felt anger rising inside.

Pearl's eyes glistened with tears as her son hugged her briefly and made to leave. She took him by the shoulders.

"You really didn't love him, did you?" she accused, her voice quavering.

The boy stared at his mother, hopelessly lost for words. The smell of honey and whiskey cooking on the kitchen stove became thick in the room. Nora couldn't take any more.

"I'll go see to the remedy" she said, and left.

"That man loved you so much," Pearl said to her son. "And . . . and all you could do was break his heart. I never once saw you hug or kiss him, unless you were put up to it! You really did hate him, you heartless little snot!"

Tears filled the boy's eyes.

"Good! I'm glad you're crying," Pearl snapped. "I'm sick of smiling at people when they tell me what a brave little boy I have! You can cry over that lousy deer your father shot, but you can't . . . you can't cry over . . ."

Chucky ran from the room as his mother sagged against the wall and gave way to the sobs rising in her throat. Pete took her in his arms as she appeared ready to collapse. He held her tightly, trying to calm her.

"I must be out of my mind to have said such terrible things to him!" Pearl sobbed. "My God. My God. You've poured the grief of the world into my heart . . ."

Nora caught the boy as he hurried through the kitchen, heading for his room. She intended to console him, but he pulled away and stamped off without a word.

After he left she gazed out the window at the rain. Lightning flickered in the distance. An even greater storm was on its way in from the west. It was night, but the blackness beyond seemed almost comforting, compared to the dark shadow of grief that now hung over this home. What evil face pressed to the window pane, she wondered, gloating and leering over a family's misfortune? Was it the face of a deer? Or another Beast of Le Gevaudin?

Nora went into the parlor, hearing Pearl crying, and thinking to be of help. She stood by as Pete embraced his sister-in-law, holding her tightly, his flushed face filled with devotion. For long seconds she watched them, studying them and learning of their closeness. Finally she returned to the kitchen, turned the honey off on the stove, and went into the living room to sit in the darkness with her thoughts.

The boy awoke to the sound of the wind howling outside. Blowing rain beat against the window pane, rattling it with a thousand tiny fingers. For a while he listened in the darkness, straining to hear the gentle voices of the little forest folk. But the *pukwudjinnies* no longer whispered their secrets to his ears. Even Joe Hawk and the many warriors from ages past had abandoned his dreams. The gold medallion of the Seneca now seemed like any coin of cold metal in his hands, its magic dissipated by his broken faith and troubled mind. Heart was dead, rotting away in the barn on his father's workbench. His father was dead. Such a *weak* god he had chosen to champion his cause, he thought. Malsum had won after all! One day the wizard's deer would come for him, and then he would come for his uncle, and his mother.

Even now as the boy thought thus, he could imagine the Old Demon laughing and nodding his head in agreement.

His father's friends, carrying on at the kitchen table earlier, pledging that they would find the stag and kill him, would be unable to do so. Shaman would elude them, guided by Malsum as he was. Nothing would ever stop him.

Suddenly he didn't care. A great emptiness filled the youngster's heart, and he walked out into the hall.

His Uncle Pete was asleep. The sound of his congested breathing could be heard throughout the downstairs. The minty smell of a gurgling vaporizer cleared the boy's sinuses as he stood in the open doorway.

Miss Cleary, soon to be his Aunt Nora, was asleep on the couch in the living room. For a moment the boy contemplated waking her. She would hold him to her soft, warm bosom. She would love him, even if everyone else had turned against him. But he left her side anyway, still not knowing what he sought. The dark house seemed strange and unfriendly, lonely. If only his father hadn't died . . .

He wandered through the house to his grandmother's parlor. It was hard to get used to there being another room off the kitchen, after so many years of just seeing a bolted door that had been painted shut, a door that had taken his uncle considerable time and effort to get open.

Soft candlelight, diffused by cranberry votive jars, wavered on the ceiling, relieving the darkness that permeated the rest of the home. He entered the death room warily.

His mother was asleep on his Grandma's sofa. She snored the way Uncle Pete did some nights, when he was especially tired—the way his father had. The rasping noise troubled him. His Ma had never snored before. She was older-looking now, her pretty face haggard and etched with harsh shadows and lines. A frown pulled at the corners of her dry lips. The boy wanted to lie down with her, but she didn't want him—she didn't love him any more.

There was Pa in the fancy box. Handsome, smiling, not a care or worry. He was with Grandma and Grandpa in Heaven. Jenny Ma had come and taken him. The boy's eyes smarted. It was mean of his Pa to die!

He went to the coffin and looked at the medals. His Pa had been a famous war hero. All day men had told him stories of how his father had saved lives during the war. How he had killed enemy soldiers who would have slaughtered his wounded men if he had turned and fled with the others. Sam Parker had told him to be proud. The man had hugged him privately in his bedroom and wept, his breath foul and stinking of whiskey like his Pa's had been at times. The old lawman told him to model himself after the good things about his father, and not the bad; to love his father and respect him for the good things, and forget the bad.

Why hadn't Pa told him about the war? Why hadn't Pa told him what a good man he really was? He'd always thought he was so bad!

Pa had said he wasn't a hero. He had said all soldiers got medals for just being in the war, and that wasn't true! Everyone said he was a hero. Why did he have to lie?

The son reached out hesitantly, taking hold of his father's clasped hands. They were ghastly white, the fingertips shrivelled, the fingernails shiny and cleaner than he'd ever recalled seeing them before.

"Pa, I'm sorry for saying I hate you."

The stinging in the boy's eyes suddenly became unbearable. He wasn't ever going to see his father again! His father was dead!

Zeb's face felt cold as he touched it with the palm of his hand. The mortician had covered the scratches on his face with make-up. His father's flesh was rigid and unyielding.

"Don't be dead, Pa!" Chucky suddenly cried. "Please don't be dead, Pa!"

He began to weep, finally feeling his loss.

His father was dead. His father was dead, and he had wished him dead—had hated him dead!

"I'm sorry, Pa! I don't care about no stupid deer, Pa! Please come back. I love you! Honest, I love you, Pa!"

Nora woke as she heard Pearl crying. She thought for a moment of waking Pete, knowing that he would be a comfort. But Pearl's crying seemed urgent, and she felt there wasn't enough time to wake him.

"Pearl, dear . . ." Nora began as she saw the woman standing in the parlor looking at her deceased husband. And then she saw Chucky, as Pearl moved aside, and she herself was overwhelmed.

A small boy, lonely, possibly afraid in the night had crawled up on his father's chest and fallen asleep.

The Beast no longer leered at the window.

Over two hundred mourners gathered on the Simpson pasture, braving the morning rain as they waited for the funeral procession to return to the family cemetery from the Catholic church in town. Television crews shot footage, and reporters interviewed as many of the local residents as were willing to speak. The Seneca who attended refused to comment about Malsum and his "supposed" curse, as the newsmen referred to the affair. Still, there seemed to be an abundance of authoritative sources on the matter. One fellow from the city, parked on Genessee Road selling hot coffee and doughnuts out of his panel truck, proved to be a leading expert—or at the least a colorful story-teller.

A company of Marines, waiting in the back of a tarpaulin-covered troop transport, jumped out and lined the cemetery fence as the Cadillac hearse arrived and drove out onto the meadow. The Marines snapped to attention at the command of their officer, as the casket, draped with an American flag, was carried solemnly by the pallbearers to the open plot.

Pearl, dressed in black, with a black veil and hat, held

286

her son's hand. Pete stayed at her side and shielded her from the rain with a black satin umbrella.

The field was a veritable crop of black umbrellas this morning.

Once the casket was settled onto the straps, the American Legion band from Gowanda assembled beneath the erected canvas awning in the tiny cemetery and played the national anthem. Everyone stood at attention.

Pearl wept quietly when a Marine began playing taps. The tearful notes of the bugle tugged at her broken heart, and she was not the only one that the beautiful call had touched.

After the taps, Zeb was honored with a three-volley salute, and Father Ryan ended the services with a short eulogy. The young officer commanding the Marines presented the widow with the folded flag from the casket, while his men remained at attention along the cemetery fence. The hero's funeral reached its finale.

The Simpson family sprinkled dirt onto Zeb's casket and walked away to the house. The mourners, whites and Indians alike, then filed past and paid their last respects. As the procession ended, Sam Parker, Mathias Brown, James Goodman, and Len Pfeister lowered the coffin into the cement-lined grave and then, with a heavy thud, they sealed the hole with a slab.

As the mourners left the soggy meadow Chucky appeared at the cemetery fence. He watched the men shovelling dirt and mud into his father's grave. Huge scoops of gummy soil left their shovel blades all too fast, their loud thumps horrifying to the boy's ears.

"You're not supposed to be out here, son," Sam Parker said. "Go on back in the house. You're getting drenched."

Chucky opened the fence gate and walked up to the grave site.

"Child, get out of here," Mathias scolded as he saw the lad's face twisting with grief.

"Stop!" the boy blubbered, as he looked down and saw that the hole was nearly filled. "Stop burying him so fast!" He wrenched the shovel from Mathias' hands and held it raised like a weapon, tears running down his cheeks. "You get out!" he ordered. "I don't want any of you burying my Pa! I'll bury him myself!"

James Goodman turned to the others. "A son has the

right," he said. "Zebediah would be proud. We should all be proud."

The friends stepped back from the plot and watched as the boy shovelled small quantities from the mound and gently slid them into the hole.

Pearl remained downstairs only long enough to thank the many guests and then went up to her room, leaving Pete and Nora to see to the amenities. Thankful for the solitude, she undressed and slipped wearily into bed, her mind still tormented with grief.

She was beginning to doze off when the bedroom door opened and Chucky stepped inside. For a moment the mother smiled tenderly at the boy. But then, as she saw him sopping wet and his new suit trousers caked with mud, she reprimanded him. "Look at you! What have you been—"

The tears in her son's eyes stopped the scolding. Pearl left the warm bed and stripped the youngster down to his underwear.

"I didn't hate him, Ma," Chucky sobbed.

"I know, honey. Come under the covers and lie down with me."

"But you said—"

"Never mind what I said. A girl can change her mind if she wants to."

Chapter XV

Shaman left his hiding place in the hills south of Mohawk Meadow where he had been driven by the Seneca. While the Seneca had searched for him in the woods, a few even venturing into the hills, it was as James Goodman had predicted, and they had not discovered his whereabouts. An hour before, they had abandoned the hunt temporarily, and the stag now moved, knowing that they would be after him again in earnest when the storm ended the next morning. Neither the vastness of the Alleghenies nor the admonitions of their leaders would deter the bitter tribesmen. Regardless of the witchcraft involved, the Seneca vowed that they would kill the deer before he could claim another kinsman.

The state authorities, embarrassed at having closed the case wrongfully the summer before, now promised the public an official hunt that would not terminate, regardless of expense, until the killer animal was conclusively destroyed. A healthy reward, already many times larger than the bounty returned by the Seneca, continued to mount hourly, as private sportsmen's clubs and an outraged citizenry attempted to influence the participation of professional big game hunters.

Those "prophets" who alleged contact with the spirit world maintained the premise that Shaman would emerge victorious. Supposedly, hundreds, or even thousands, of woodland animals would be possessed by dissident spirits upon the successful completion of Malsum's curse.

As night came, the demon stag crossed Mohawk Meadow at the narrowest end and ran as if guided, never once breaking his stride until he reached the forest. Lightning coursed overhead through the dark downpour. Thunder pealed almost simultaneously with each flash, assaulting the animal's sensitive hearing. Still he kept on.

Handicapped by his missing eye, the deer dangled in the barbed wire that separated the Seneca Woods from the privately-owned farm lands. The steel barbs ripped his chest, and he challenged the barrier with an irate braying, the thick fur on his throat bristling. He stepped back a few yards and leapt over the fence effortlessly, leaving the pines.

He passed through the Simpson maple grove, stopping at the edge of the apple orchard to glare evilly at the distant farm buildings. With the driving wind at his back, the rain matting his scarred coat, he snorted and walked out onto the meadow.

"He's out there, Charlie! You make that sonuvabitch pay!"

The boy's eyes popped open and he scanned the darkened room. His mother slept beside him in the bed, toasting him comfortably with her warmth.

"Pa?" Chucky called.

Pearl mumbled something in her sleep and was quiet. It had been a dream.

The boy worked his way out of the bed carefully, so as not to awaken his mother. The braided rag rug beneath his feet felt hard and waffled. He crept to his father's chest of drawers silently, still ill at ease from the dream, and slid the bottom drawer open. His fingers closed around Joe Hawk's short-handled axe. It was heavy in his hands. Armed with such a deadly weapon, a boy had little to fear of the dark.

As an added fortification, he redeemed the gold medallion from his mother's jewelry box. He looked at the heirloom wonderingly, unable to see it clearly. He needn't have looked, for he knew its stamped detail well. On one side was a cross, and the reverse depicted an Indian chieftain being knighted by King George III. Bigger than a silver dollar, it filled the palm of his small hand. He clenched the medallion tightly and prayed. A shiver left his stomach and coursed up his spine, spreading with a radiant warmth throughout his chest. The boy felt an overwhelming sense of forgiveness as his faith and courage returned. Involuntarily, his eyes began to burn and a wide smile seeped onto his lips.

A pantheon of Seneca faces, stalwart warriors, flashed through his mind. The *pukwudjinnies* fairly screamed a welcome to his ears. A voice even further away than the whispers of the little forest folk called forth, *"Niio!"*

The boy found himself caught up in his new strength. His dream no longer troubled him and he understood his magic.

"Niio!" he whispered, rubbing the last tears of childhood from his eyes. *"Niio Dekanawidah!"*

The boy went to the window as the *pukwudjinnies* spoke to him. He rubbed the condensation from the glass with his pajama sleeve and pressed his face to the pane. Directly in front and below, at the back of the house, an old field that was occasionally seeded with clover or alfalfa ran on towards the creek and Luke Banner's farm. To the right lay Genessee Road; to the left, the edge and side wall of the barn. The little cemetery was beyond, a way out onto the meadow.

It was there that Chucky knowingly turned his attention, waiting for the next flash of lightning. It came, and with it came a vision of horror.

Shaman! The stag stood over his Pa's grave, eerily illumined by the storm. As if he knew the boy was viewing, the king of devils raised his gnarled rack and looked toward the house. His one malevolent eye reflected red in the lightning and then winked out as the flash ended.

The initial shock passed. The boy's mind filled with anger. Shaman was gloating over having killed his father! He was out there, taunting, daring the boy to challenge him.

"Goddamn you!" Chucky whispered. The words felt strong and manly on his tongue. "Goddamn you all to Hell, Malsum!" he rasped vehemently. "You frigging bastard!"

"Wake up, Uncle Pete!"

The feverish man opened his eyes and shielded them from the harsh light flooding the room from the ceiling lamp.

"What's wrong?" he croaked, clearing his throat and coughing with painful congestion. He noticed the room vaporizer, boiled dry and unattended. It was all he could manage just to breathe.

"Did Nora come back?" he asked.

"She dropped your medicine off and went home," Chucky said irritably, anxiously shaking his uncle awake. "Never mind Miss Cleary. Shaman's here! He's standing on top of Pa's grave!"

Pete's grimacing face went blank. "You're sure of that?"

"Yes! Come see!"

Together they went upstairs into Pearl's bedroom, the only room in the house with a window clearly overlooking the cemetery.

"Do you see him now?" Chucky asked, as a lightning flash lit up the sky.

The boy felt a startled jolt in his uncle as he pressed against him.

"Don't worry," he said confidently, squeezing the medallion in his hand. "We can win. I know we can."

Pete held a pillow stuffed with goose feathers over his chest and stomach and had his nephew strap it to him with leather belts. The man burned with fever as he fitted his coat over the downy armor. Knowing that his faculties were impaired by his condition, he had thought of the pillow as an added safeguard should Shaman catch him unawares.

Chucky left the room and came back in, fully dressed, by the time Pete had finished lacing his boots.

"I'm going with you," he said.

"No, you're not!" the uncle said sternly. "You park your fanny upstairs on your Ma's bed, and you don't move it until I get back."

"Please, Uncle Pete? I've got magic again. You've gotta let me go," the boy pleaded. "I can back you up with Grandpa's double-barrel."

Pete looked at him indecisively.

"Get it and bring it here," he said.

Pete opened the breech on the old shotgun and checked the chambers carefully. Zeb had kept them clean and well-oiled. The weapon showed its great age, but it appeared functional and in good shape. He then selected a box of home loads his brother had hand packed with ball bearings. At close range they would devastate anything they struck. If he was fortunate enough to catch the bastard off guard, he could cut him in half with just one shot.

"The line's dead," Chucky said as his uncle walked into the kitchen with the shotgun and rifle.

Pete frowned. "It figures," he said, holding the receiver to his ear for a moment. He had thought to call Sam for help. Still, even alone, he decided, he would play the hand dealt to him. He hung up the phone and gave the loaded rifle to his nephew.

"I'm taking the shotgun," he said. "Be careful with this. Go on upstairs by your Ma now."

"You said I could—"

"I didn't say any such thing! I mumbled something about needing help, that's all. Look, son, when this shotgun goes off, it's going to scare the hell out of your Ma. I want you there to calm her."

"He might sneak up behind you! I can watch your back."

"Uh huh, and who's going to watch yours?"

"You don't understand. I've got my magic again."

"Dammit!" Pete snarled, his patience at an end. "Get up there right now!"

He pointed the boy to the stairwell.

"I'm sorry," he said stiffly, "but if anything goes wrong, I'd feel better knowing you're in here able to protect your Ma. You know how to use that rifle?"

"Yes, sir."

"No matter what—don't come out!"

"Yes, sir. Good luck, Uncle Pete."

"Don't need it," Pete said, patting the heavy bed pillow beneath his coat. "I miss and he gets me—he'll have his throat slit with nothing more than feathers to show for his trouble." He pointed to the long hunting knife in a scabbard on his belt, winked at the boy, and went outside. He closed the door quietly but firmly behind him.

A gust of wind sent a cold tremor through the man as he walked slowly across the front porch. The ground between the house and barn was all mud puddles. Heavy rain pelted the water like beavers with slapping tails. He skirted the puddles, taking the left side of the barn, where he could approach the cemetery from the front and survey it from a safe distance. The lightning was consistent on the southward horizon and gave him enough light to see by as he inched forward. His mouth was dry with fright, but what he was doing had to be done. The deer had to be stopped!

Shaman was no longer inside the white picket-fenced cemetery as Pete stepped out from the end of the barn to confront him.

While the hunter searched carefully, a slight splashing noise, different from that of the rain or the runoff pouring down from the barn eaves, alerted him. He spun around, crouched low, his weapon level and ready.

The giant stag halted, glaring at Pete with thirty feet still between them. There was no way the monster could escape! Pete's fingers held steady against the dual triggers. The ball bearings packed in the shell casings would make hash out of the deer before he could take one step.

Shaman remained perfectly still as Pete held the twelve-gauge on him. He trembled noticeably.

"Look at you!" Pete said. "I'm supposed to believe that you're some kind of a goddamned demon? You murdering—"

"Let me live and I will go away forever. Does not your God teach mercy?"

"W-what?"

Pete stared incredulously at the animal as the image of a pathetic old Indian formed in his mind. Words, other than his own thoughts, came to him. His arms began to feel like lead, and the shotgun sagged as he felt his senses being numbed.

"Goddamn you!" he yelled, shaking off the unholy intrusion. "Goddamn you, Malsum!"

The stag suddenly bolted towards him, and Pete squeezed the triggers. The deer stumbled with a shattered front leg as a blinding flash exploded in Pete's face. With a startled cry, the man fell to the ground, his ears ringing and his face feeling as if it no longer existed.

"A-a-a-ae-e-eeeee-eough! E-e-e-eee-uh! E-uh! E-uh!"

The demon hobbled forward and impaled the defenseless man on his antlers. He snared Pete's stomach and pressed him to the ground, tearing through the outer garments until every powerful slash brought a cloud of erupting feathers. Pete felt himself sinking into unconsciousness. He groped for the knife on his belt, but his right hand was broken at the wrist from the exploded breech. He cried out in fear as he realized his helplessness; in another moment he would be dead—the deer was going to kill him also!

"Shaman!" a shrill voice screamed.

The beast spun around, presenting his one fiery eye to the boy.

Chucky faced the animal, drawing a bead on him with the heavy, tottering rifle to his shoulder. He pulled the trigger with all of his strength, but nothing happened.

"The safety! Take off the safety!" a voice in his mind shouted.

Blam!

The hellish fiend hobbled away as the shot grazed his back.

The youngster tried to find the animal in the rifle sights again, but the black night closed around the deer and swallowed him. Chucky worked the bolt and fired after him blindly, increasing the circle of pain on his shoulder from the recoil. The stag bellowed, and the marksman caught a glimpse of him limping away for the orchard as a lightning flash lit up the meadow. Then he was gone.

The porch light suddenly came on, and Pearl opened the door.

"Mama!" Chucky called. "Uncle Pete's hurt bad!"

Pete was delirious as they helped him into the house.

Chucky steadied the injured man as he sat in the kitchen chair, while Pearl dressed his face with ointment. Pete's eyebrows and eyelashes were burnt off, and most of the skin on his right cheek was blackened with powder burns. Luckily, none of the shrapnel had struck him. Had it done so he would have been killed.

"Try the telephone again!" Pearl said worriedly.

"It's no use, Ma," Chucky replied, listening to the useless instrument for the second time since bringing his uncle into the house.

"Then we'll have to do for him ourselves," Pearl said firmly.

Damn! She wished Nora hadn't gone home after getting Pete's medicine. Nora knew how to drive and would have been able to get Pete to a hospital. It was the middle of the night, and although Nora would be back in a few hours, the man desperately needed medical attention now.

"Chucky . . . did you get him?" Pete's mind returned as Pearl wrapped a wet compress over his burns.

"I got him good. He's out there in the pasture, dead as bones."

Pearl looked at her son hopefully. "You're sure he's dead?"

"Yes, ma'am. You don't have to worry any more. He's dead," the boy assured. A gentle smile of confidence tugged at the left corner of his mouth. The father seemed resurrected in the son.

Pearl's eyes filled with tears and she wiped them away.

"Good," she said, "I'm proud of you."

"We'd better get Uncle Pete to bed," the boy urged, as the man began shaking. "Be careful of his hand, Ma, it's turning purple. I think it's broken."

Pete's teeth chattered as they undressed him. "C-cold," he said deliriously, "very c-cold."

"We'll have you under the covers in a moment, honey." Pearl hurried, unbuckling Pete's wet trousers and zipping them off.

"He's shaking something terrible, Ma! Do you think he has pneumonia? Miss Cleary had a fight with him while you were asleep. She wanted him to go to the hospital, but he wouldn't go."

Pearl didn't answer the boy, not wanting to alarm him more than he already was, but in all likelihood Pete did have pneumonia or was very close to it. She knew she had to get him warm somehow, and quickly.

She undressed him down to his skin and piled the bedclothes high over his shuddering frame as he continued to shiver.

Zeb had contracted malaria during the war, and from time to time it had come back on him suddenly, punishing him with intense chills for hours. Blankets alone had never kept him warm.

"Aren't we going to put his pajamas on him?" Chucky protested. "How come you left him bare-naked?"

The mother looked at the boy helplessly. "Sweetheart," she said, "bad chills can drive a body to death faster than a fever. We have to get him warm as soon as we can. Get undressed and crawl into bed behind him. Press him tight if you love him, honey. This is no time for being bashful."

Pearl snapped off the light, plunging the room into darkness as Pete shivered and moaned. For a moment she paused with second thoughts, but she knew there was no other way.

As Chucky undressed quickly, he could hear the soft swishing of his mother's nightgown as she pulled the garment over her head. He knew she was disrobing also. His eyes grew accustomed to the darkness, and he made out the silhouette of her beautiful form as she slipped into the bed and embraced his uncle, pressing the entire length of her body against him.

Pete protested feebly as Pearl took him in her arms. "There's no other way," she cut him off. "My God, you feel like an icicle. Lie still now and try to go to sleep."

"Uncle Pete, it's okay," Chucky said. "You gotta get warm or you could . . ." The lad couldn't say the word, didn't want to even think the word: die. He hugged his uncle's back, feeling his cold rump. And then, because the boy had been forced to grow up in just a few short days, and seemed to be getting pretty good at reading minds, he added innocently, "My Pa would want my Ma to hug you. Honest, he would!"

Chucky listened to the oppressive rattle of his uncle's breathing. It had seemed to lessen somewhat in the past hour and he hoped it was a good sign, but he didn't know for sure. His mother had prayed in a whispery voice for a long time, her words barely reaching his ears, and then she also had drifted off.

"Ma?" the boy probed. "Ma, are you awake?"

When she didn't answer, he left the bed quietly and gathered his clothes from the floor, careful not to make any sound. He bundled the garments in his arms and sneaked away through the darkness.

The night wind blew fiercely as the boy stepped out into the drizzling rain. After the warm bed and his uncle's sweaty backside, he was cold, and he shivered.

As he stood for a moment listening to the thunder from the receding storm in the distance, he was struck with a sense of unreality. He had expected to be afraid, but strangely enough he was not, and he walked boldly, somehow knowing that the deer was a long way off.

He went into the cemetery, respectfully careful not to

step on any of the grassy mounds that belonged to his grandparents. He knelt in the wet mud of his father's grave and prayed solemnly for a while.

The northern horizon flashed lightning like an artillery barrage. He thought of the war, and the amazing courage that his father must have displayed in order to have won the nation's highest honor. That knowledge now swelled his chest with pride.

"I love you, Pa," he said as he rose to his feet. "And don't you worry none about me. I'll get him for you. Come daylight, you're gonna see me nail that frigger's head to the barn wall, just like you said you were gonna do!"

The young hero then left the cemetery and trudged off across the meadow. His father's chrome six-battery flashlight revealed Shaman's tracks as he went. His uncle's freshly-loaded rifle felt heavy in his hands, and he carried the man's long hunting knife in its sheath on his belt. As an additional comfort, Joe Hawk's short-handled axe was tucked into his waistband.

The gold medallion hung around his neck on a chain, warm and pulsing with a life of its own over his heart. His dungaree pockets bulged, crammed full of his father's precious war medals. The boy was taking no chances. His magic felt real and substantial. As he advanced unhesitantly toward the dark foreboding orchard, he chanted a Seneca hymn petitioning his great warrior god to stand by him and grant him a chief's victory.

When he neared the end of the meadow, he halted suddenly, feeling eyes on him from behind. He whirled and flashed the light over the path he had come. The beam easily stretched the distance to the cemetery and barn, exposing the bald nakedness of the flat meadow in between. His rifle at ready, he swept the light back and forth knowingly, hoping to catch a reflecting eye. Search as he did, however, he could find nothing to justify his alarm. Mystified, he walked on into the orchard. At times he stopped and looked back, the hair prickling on the nape of his neck. He was sure that he was being followed.

The high wind blowing through the apple trees brought the tiny voices of the *pukwudjinnies.*

"*Not there. Not there,*" they whispered. "*Ahead of you. Ahead of you.*"

Shaman's trail passed through the orchard and into the

maple grove. The boy saw his mother's sap buckets strewn over the ground, their metal sides dented and kicked in. The wooden harvest wagon, which he and his uncle had built the year before, lay on its side, with the wide boards caved in and splintered. The grove smelled evil, as if permeated with an odor of rotting corpses.

It took the lad several minutes before he realized that the wizard stag's tracks had led him around in a circle. Confused, he looked to the tops of the trees and asked aloud, "Where is he?"

"In the pines," the little friends responded. *"He's in the pines!"*

The night was darkest among the sweetly-scented woods. The tall pines, closely set and brooding over narrowed paths with rain-enshrouded limbs, loomed over the lad and made him feel small and insignificant.

His heart beat loudly in his ears, and he pressed tight against a thick tree and shielded his back, nervously fingering the safety catch on the rifle and making sure it was in the off position. Malsum's demons invaded his impressionable young mind, trying to panic him and make him flee for home.

"Hakosothowah, Hakosothowah," Chucky murmured, calling on the noble grandfathers of the Iroquois for strength.

In answer, the gold medallion on his chest grew hot and tingled. An unfastened pin on the back of a medal in his pants pocket pricked into his thigh as he shifted his weight from one foot to the other. The gnawing fear left him, and the demons fled in the face of such wonderful magic.

"Thank you, Dekanawidah," the honorary Seneca grandson said.

A wet branch of soft needles, stirred by the wind, brushed lightly across his cheek, feeling like a kiss from his mother. Another branch reached out and caressed his face as he started off again, prying beneath his collar and making him hunch his shoulders.

"Stop it, Tommy!" the hunter said, as prankish laughter reached his ears. "I don't feel like fooling around now."

He passed through the pines and came to a thicket of chokecherry brush, the bitter berries green and unripened. They formed an impenetrable hedge that blocked the beam of the powerful flashlight. He noticed Shaman's tracks going into the coverage. He avoided the brush as the *pukwudjinnies* warned him to keep away. He made a wide detour and surveyed the opposite side from a safe distance, scanning the hedge carefully with his light.

Blood! There were patches of bright red blood smeared all over the leaves!

"I know you're in there!" Chucky yelled out angrily. He raised the high-powered rifle, holding the flashlight in his left hand under the stock, using the beam like a scope.

A loud rustling shook the bushes.

Blam!

The stag grunted loudly as the boy fired. The noise of the detonation was brief and made a sharp punching sound.

His Pa had said that was a sure sign of having hit something—he had called it plugging the echo.

Chucky levered the bolt quickly, ejecting the spent cartridge and loaded a fresh round into the chamber. His shoulder throbbed from the recoil as he took aim and waited. He sensed the hidden beast moving toward him from within the bushes.

Blam! He fired again.

"A-a-a-ae-e-eeeee-eough! E-uh! E-uh!"

With a hideous bellow the demonic monster sprang from the hedge. Even wounded and crippled, with his right foreleg hanging by a shred, he was incredibly swift.

The small marksman barely had time to fire before the nightmare was on him. The shot was futile, a miss, and the stag rushed on like a juggernaut.

The first charge was ungainly and clumsily executed, and Chucky sidestepped the terror and ran, simultaneously attempting to reload his rifle. The empty brass casing from the last shot jammed in the ejecting mechanism. Half out, it wedged tight and blocked the return of the bolt.

The crippled stag chased after the dodging boy as he sprinted into the pines. Each time his elusive prey escaped him, the beast turned the dark forest into a theater of hideous shrieking.

Finally the animal stopped, winded and unable to catch the lad. Chucky turned and faced him defiantly. He dropped the useless rifle and lifted the short-handled axe from his waistband.

A cackling laughter arose in his mind as the deer lowered his antlers and twisted his head from side to side, glowering at him with his one remaining eye. He hobbled forward, slowly at first, and then, a few feet away, he bellowed angrily and charged.

The boy struck out with the axe, splitting the hide over Shaman's narrow skull, but the blow had little effect on the monster. A massive steam shovel, the sorcerer's stag scooped for the boy with the gnarled rack atop his head.

Chucky clung to the deer's rack tenaciously as it stood and tried to shake the boy loose. Hot fetid breath blew through his trousers as his weight dragged the beast's face close to the ground. Aware that Shaman was standing on only one front leg, he tried to kick it out from under him.

The stag twisted his muzzle and clamped down on the inside of a fleshy thigh. The boy cried out and released his grip as he felt the first crush of painful pressure. The axe spun out of his hand as he fell to the ground.

Suddenly *he* was there like an avenging angel on a howling wind!

A tan streak with tapered sabers flashed through the black forest, thrusting twin horns into the stag's side as he hovered, a menacing death, over the boy's precious life. The monstrosity emitted a surprised shriek as the little animal bowled him over.

"Heart!" Chucky cried with disbelief as he saw the pet.

The giant beast stayed down, while the young spiked buck stood over him with poised knives, pawing the forest floor and snorting meanly.

It was Heart! The boy could see the lump of clay dangling from a thong about the buck's neck. His Pa hadn't killed him! He should have believed! Heart was the one who had been following him all along!

He rose to his feet, almost overcome with emotion. The fur on the young deer's back bristled as he continued to stand over Shaman.

"Have mercy on me!" a voice in the boy's mind begged. *"Does not your God teach mercy?"*

The little buck backed away from the cowering demon, taking a protective stance in front of his small master. He groaned angrily and fidgeted, as if waiting for a command as Shaman rose up awkwardly.

"Thank you, my son." That voice again. *"Thank you for letting me go."* The wounded animal began to limp away.

"Go to hell!" Chucky shouted. "Get him, Heart! He killed my Pa!"

Shaman tried to dodge the avenger as he charged. Strong tapered spears pierced his flanks, but the wounded monster was not as helpless as he appeared. Twisting around like a snake, he ripped open a flap of skin on the smaller combatant's ribs. The young buck ignored the gash and this time plunged his horns deep into the stag's front shoulder. With a shriek the beast collapsed, his other front leg mangled now, as well.

A violent wind lashed through the pines, howling with the fury of a tempest. The boy sought the sanctuary of a thick tree and held on as the squall drove his buck away from the wizard's stag.

Suddenly the heavens unleashed a downpour of rain, and the wind abated, as if subdued by a greater power.

Once again, tainted shadows and the demonic army of Malsum's forces crowded into the boy's head and tried to rob him of his courage. He clenched Joe Hawk's gold medallion in his fist.

"I'm not afraid of you!" he yelled. "I'm not afraid of any of you!"

He unsnapped the long hunting knife from his belt sheath and held it for stabbing as he approached the crippled stag. The beast glowered at him with a yellow-orange eye.

"Stay, Heart," Chucky ordered, as the deer moved to intercept him. He could see that his friend was injured badly and would need sewing. "You done your job," the young master said. "Now, I'll do—"

The noble hart was having none of it, however. He reared on his hind legs and protected the boy as Shaman suddenly lunged forward. Instead of the boy's face, the wicked antlers found Heart's stomach and ripped it open. Maniacally powerful, the monster tossed the little deer onto his side and slashed for his vitals.

"No!" Chucky screamed.

He sprang onto Shaman's back, straddling him, and sunk the hunting knife deep into his flesh. The pinned hart clamped his muzzle on the demon's throat and held him fast, biting as Shaman tried to reach the boy with his antlers. The stag's blood bubbled through his nose slits as the knife plunged repeatedly, taking its toll. Finally the demon shuddered with a loud laboring of breath and collapsed.

Heart crawled out from under the stag, his innocent eyes glazed with pain. He hemorrhaged from his mouth and lay staring at his young master atop the defeated beast.

Chucky pressed the knife point against Shaman's throat. The beast stared helplessly at him through his one eye, too weak now even to raise his head. The boy could sense the spirit of the Delaware sorcerer screaming with fright, knowing he was about to be driven from the world. He also sensed other spirits waiting nearby to take the blackened demon where he could never again bring harm to mankind. The brooding forest seemed to be filled with spirits, warrior gods waiting for the moment of expulsion.

"Go to Hell, Malsum!" Chucky answered a final plea in his mind. His young muscles tensed and drove the blade down, and the tormented animal died, his hideously disfigured face skewered to the forest floor.

A cleansing breeze swept through the woods, taking with it the stench of decay and evil. Rain pattered through the regal forest, the applause of angels. Yet, like the youth in the Ode of the Oak Trees, his victory had cost dearly, and he had little cause for joy.

The small warrior went to his life-saving friend and embraced him. The spike buck looked at him sadly, suffering from his fatal injuries. Chucky knew the wounds were too severe to heal. Having been raised on a farm, he knew what had to be done.

Now that he was not being pursued by the stag, it took the boy only a moment to loosen the jammed cartridge from his rifle.

"I love you, Heart," he said, "but you know I gotta . . . you know I gotta."

The tyke looked at his young master with large trusting eyes, as the boy placed the rifle behind his ear and squeezed the trigger.

The whispery voices of the *pukwudjinnies* called out and tried to console the boy as he dropped to his knees and pressed his face against the hart's wet fur, allowing the sobs to ease his grief, but he wouldn't listen to them.

The gold medallion tingled against his breast, but the sensation went unheeded.

He hugged his little friend's body, thinking of the powerful warrior god within who had helped him, and his tears lessened.

And then a voice reached into his thoughts from a faraway place that only children can glimpse and comforted him.

"Come on, Charlie. Stop your crying; we just won!"

Epilogue

Pearl awoke and sat up in the bed, startled with the realization that she had somehow fallen asleep. The first golden rays of dawn poured through the bedroom window, accompanied by the twittering of a treeful of sparrows in the yard. The lingering illusion of a beautiful dream ebbed from her consciousness, and she clutched for it unsuccessfully as it drifted away.

Pete was asleep in the bed next to her, his blond head resting on a pillow, the right side of his face swathed with a compress. She lifted the covering gently and viewed his burns. Black specks of gunpowder were embedded in his cheek and would have to be removed surgically. The burns were puffy, but at least there was no sign of inflammation. His forehead felt cool; there were tiny beads of damp sweat in his hair. The fearful symptoms of pneumonia were gone. She was puzzled, but relieved and thankful that her diagnosis had been wrong.

Chucky was not in his bedroom, nor was he anywhere in the house. She called out the kitchen window for him as she tried the wall phone, finding that it was still out of order. That the boy could be so casual, to be attending to chores in the barn after—of course! He had gone into the meadow to look at that terrible deer he had killed. The thought of the beast made her lips come together in a sneer.

From the porch she could see the meadow clearly. There was no deer carcass or boy to be seen on the flat grassland. Fear rose inside of her as she guessed the truth.

She ran back into the house and rushed upstairs to get dressed.

A dozen glorious beams of sunlight filtered down through the forest canopy onto the boy as he slept with his cheek pressed to the little deer's fur. Several grey does and a princely buck watched over him curiously as they munched on tender pine needles a short distance away. The buck stepped forward gingerly to examine Shaman's carcass, sneezing on the scent in his nostrils, and walked back to the does.

Suddenly a doe cocked her ears and stood rigid. She thumped the ground loudly with her front hooves and bolted away timidly, her tail held high like a flag, with the white underside displayed as a warning of danger. The other does chased after her, and the buck galloped casually into the forest. He stopped, standing motionless, waiting to see what it was that had frightened the doe.

Pearl made a loud outcry as she saw her son lying next to the dead hart. Shaman's gruesome corpse, pinned to the ground with a hunting knife through his throat, sent a shiver of revulsion through her. She threw down the pitchfork in her hands and ran to her son.

The boy awoke as he felt his mother's trembling embrace.

"Are you all right? Chucky, are you all right?"

He stared blankly for a moment at his mother's pretty face, her lower lip quivering with emotion.

"Don't go cryin', Ma," he said. "We don't have to cry no more." His freckled cheeks dimpled with a proud smile, only a tinge of sadness in his clear green eyes. "We won!" he said exuberantly.

Pearl hugged him tightly.

"Heart and me killed him," the son said. "We had to, Ma. Nobody else could do it."

Pearl watched as her son recovered Joe Hawk's short-handled axe from the forest floor and knelt down alongside the shaman stag's carcass. His young eyes sparkled with pride and a sideways grin tugged at the left corner of his mouth.

"He don't look like such a mean frigger now, does he, ma'am?"

Pearl watched as the boy hacked away at the deer's neck with the axe.

"We got a reward coming for this sonuvabitch, and no—"

"You watch your language, Charles Simpson!" the mother scolded.

The boy's face reddened with embarrassment.

"Yes, ma'am," he said sheepishly. "Excuse me, please."

The mother turned her attention to the wonderful pet who had given his life for his master. Her eyes filled with love and she stroked the tyke's fur, feeling his stiff, cold body beneath her palm.

She wondered over the lump of clay around the buck's neck and fingered it curiously.

"You can look at it now if you want to," Chucky said, interrupting his labors.

She laughed and addressed shiny, smiling eyes at the boy as she peeled the hard brittle substance away to discover what pagan warrior god of the Seneca the boy had chosen as his champion. She laughed, because she had never expected to recognize the hidden charm, not being a person who was up on her Indian fetishes. But then, Jenny Ma's missing rosary crucifix was not exactly an Indian fetish.

". . . One day the god Dekanawidah, who had been born of a virgin and who had come across the lakes in a white stone canoe, found Hiawatha's cabin in the forest and revealed himself and his mission to Hiawatha . . ."

an Iroquois creation myth, ca. 1552 A.D.

By The Author of
COLD MOON OVER BABYLON
and **THE AMULET**

GILDED NEEDLES

MICHAEL McDOWELL

In the 1880's Lena is queen of The Black Triangle, Manhattan's decadent empire of opium dens, gambling casinos, drunken sailors and gaudy hookers. With her daughters and grandchildren, she leads a ring of female criminals—women skilled in the arts of cruelty.

Only a few blocks away, amidst the elegant mansions and lily-white reputations of Gramercy Park and Washington Square lives Judge James Stallworth. He is determined to crush Lena's evil crew, and with icy indifference he orders three deaths in her family. Then one Sunday, all the Stallworths receive individual invitations— invitations to their own funerals.

When you cross some people you may wind up dead. When you cross Lena you will end up wishing you were...and wishing you were...and wishing...

"Readers of weak constitution should beware!"
Publishers Weekly

"RIVETING, TERRIFYING, AND JUST ABSOLUTELY GREAT."
Stephen King, author of THE SHINING

AVON Paperback   73698/$2.50